LECIA CORNWALL

Secret
Life
OF
Lady Julia

A V O N

An Imprint of HarperCollinsPublishers

AVON BOOKS
An Imprint of HarperCollins*Publishers*
10 East 53rd Street
New York, New York 10022-5299

Copyright © 2013 by Lecia Cotton Cornwall
ISBN 978-0-06-220245-1
www.avonromance.com

First Avon Books mass market printing: June 2013

Avon Trademark Reg. U.S. Pat. Off. and in Other Countries, Marca Registrada, Hecho en U.S.A.
HarperCollins® is a registered trademark of HarperCollins Publishers.

Printed in the U.S.A.

10 9 8 7 6 5 4 3 2 1

To Olivia, who reads every word before anyone else. Your advice is precious.

THE
Secret
Life
OF
Lady Julia

Chapter 1

~~~~~~ 🙰 ~~~~~~

London, October 1813

When she looked back on the events of her betrothal ball, Lady Julia Leighton blamed it on the champagne.

Or perhaps it was the heady scent of the roses.

Or it was the fact that Thomas Merritt was not her fiancé, and he was handsome, and he'd been kind, and called her beautiful as he waltzed her out through the French doors and sealed her fate.

Most of all she blamed herself. It had been the perfect night to begin with, every detail flawlessly executed, every eventuality planned for.

Except one.

She had waited twelve years for her betrothal ball to take place, and it certainly turned out to be an evening she would never, ever forget.

She had been engaged to marry David Hartley, the Duke of Temberlay, since she was eight and he was sixteen, and as she smoothed the blue silk gown over her grown-up curves, she had hoped that David would, at long last, see her as a woman, his bride-to-be, and not just the child who lived next door.

She *was* grown up, and pretty too—a chance flirtation in Hyde Park had proven that, and she'd barely been able to think of anything or anyone else since. She wondered now what Thomas Merritt might think of this dress, as she preened before the mirror. Mr. Merritt treated her like a woman, while everyone else—David, her father, her brother—all saw her as little Julia, even if her pigtails were long since gone.

She pushed him out of her mind and practiced a co-quette's smile in the mirror—the smile she meant to give David when his eyes widened with pleasure at sight of her tonight. She planned to sparkle every bit as brightly as the diamond clips her maid twined into an artful coiffure of dark curls, or the magnificent Leighton diamonds glittering at her neck, wrist, and ears. She slid her betrothal ring—a sapphire surrounded by pearls the size of quails' eggs—over her glove and stared at herself in the glass. She had been raised to be the perfect duchess, and she certainly looked the part.

"Let me see."

Julia turned, waited for her mother's nod of approval. If the Countess of Carrindale thought her daughter looked pretty, she kept it to herself.

"We'd better go down," was all she said, and "Decorum, Julia," when Julia tried to descend the stairs a little too eagerly, anxious to see the appreciation in her fiancé's eyes.

But David wasn't waiting at the foot of the stairs.

He wasn't even at the door to the ballroom, or in the salon with her father.

She felt her heart sink.

"You look well tonight, Julia," her father said, casting

his eyes over the jewels, as if assessing their value against her own worth, before turning away to take her mother's arm.

She glanced up at the portrait of her bother James that graced the wall of the salon. He smiled down at her in his scarlet regimentals. If he were here, he would have bussed her cheek, teased her, told her she looked very pretty, and made her laugh, but James had been killed in battle in Spain a year ago.

She felt the familiar pang of grief as she met his painted eyes. She missed his friendship, his easy company, and his advice. Her childhood had ended with the heart-wrenching sorrow of his death. "Courage," he might have whispered now, squeezing her hand. She let her fingers curl around his imaginary ones. James had been her protector, her friend, and her confidant. She hadn't felt as safe as she did with James until—Thomas Merritt's smiling face passed through her brain. She looked down at her satin gloves. He'd squeezed her hand as well, but it hadn't felt the way it did when James touched her, or even David. It felt, well, intimate, admiring, the kind of caress a man gives a desirable woman.

She felt her cheeks heat at the memory of the encounter in the park, and gave the painting a pleading look. Would James have been horrified at her behavior? No, he would have done the same thing himself, had he been there.

Thomas Merritt was a complete stranger to her. She had never seen him at the balls and parties she attended, and she really should not have even deigned to speak to him without a proper introduction. If he'd been a proper gentleman, he would have walked right past her, ignored the fact that she was standing alone in the middle of Hyde Park with tears stinging her eyes, but he'd stopped, and pressed his handkerchief into her hand, and just in time to rescue her from the curious eyes and prying questions of Lady Fiona Barry, the *ton*'s worst gossip.

She'd been prattling too much, perhaps, about the details of the wedding, and David was looking bored, which made her try all the harder to amuse him. He'd seen some people he knew across the park and stopped walking, taking her hand off his arm and stepping away. "Wait here, Jules. There's someone I wish to speak to," David had said. She'd caught his sleeve.

"I'll come too, and you can introduce me," she said, but he'd shot her a look of irritation. "Surely I should know your friends, David. They might be guests in our home some day and—"

"It's business, Julia," he replied sharply, plucking his arm out of her grip. "Be good and wait here, and I'll buy you an ice at Gunter's on the way home."

Stunned, she'd watched him walk away, leaving her behind as if she were an annoying child.

"I would have promised you diamonds," a voice said, and she'd turned and regarded the stranger by her side. He was watching David's retreating back.

"I beg your pardon?" she said, though she didn't know him, and knew she should not speak to him at all. He could be anyone, or anything. But he smiled at her, his eyes warm, and her breath stopped.

"To wait, I mean. I would have promised you diamonds, or something infinitely better than a Gunter's ice, unless of course you prefer those to jewels. Even then I wouldn't have left you alone in the first place, not with every man in the park watching you with such obvious admiration."

She held her tongue and glanced around. The park was indeed filled with curious eyes, and all of them no doubt wondering why she, Lady Julia Leighton, was without an escort.

"It's quite all right," he said. "Think of me as your protector until your brother returns."

"Fiancé," she murmured.

His brows shot upward toward the brim of his hat, rakishly tipped on dark curls. "I see."

Embarrassed anger filled her. "Do you? And just what do you imagine you see, my lord—"

"'Mister' will do. Thomas Merritt," he said, giving his name and bowing. "And you are?"

"The Duke of Temberlay's bride-to-be!" she snapped, rising to her full height. She still barely reached his nose, even in the tall, lavishly feathered bonnet she wore. There was amusement in his eyes, which was not the impression she'd hoped for.

"Forgive me, Duchess. At first glance I thought perhaps you were a younger sister he finds annoying, or a cousin he'd been instructed to squire about for a bit of fresh air, against his own choice. He treats you as if—"

"It's none of your affair how he treats me!"

He put a hand under her elbow. "Ah, but it is, as your temporary protector. I cannot leave the most beautiful lady in the park all alone, especially when she is on the verge of tears."

It was exactly what James might have said, and that only added to her desire to cry. She blinked back tears. "I never cry!"

He pressed his handkerchief into her hand. "Of course not. Shall we stroll along the path a little way? Lady Fiona Barry is heading this way, and I hear she can smell tears from a hundred yards." He took her arm.

Julia's stomach froze. *Fiona Barry?* This was disaster! She would report everything to her mother, then to everyone else in the *ton*—David's absence from her side, the lack of a proper escort, and of course the presence of the handsome stranger by her side.

"Laugh, my lady," he murmured, leaning under the edge of the feathered bonnet.

"I don't think I can," she admitted.

"Then I shall make you smile. I will promise you diamonds and pearls," he said.

"I prefer emeralds," she murmured.

He looked down at her, his eyes moving over her face and her elegant new moss green walking gown. "Yes, I can see that they'd suit you very well indeed," he said, his voice low, seductive, something in his gaze suggesting he was imagining her draped entirely in emeralds and nothing else at all. She felt heat surge through her body, and she couldn't help but smile.

"There now, that's better," he said, but his eyes remained on hers. He had gray eyes, glittering and dangerous, filled with the kind of male admiration she'd never seen directed at her before this moment. She'd been wrong. *This* was where childhood ended, with the first look of male appreciation a girl received. She liked it very well indeed. Her spine turned soft for a moment, and she had the oddest desire to lean into his strong shoulder.

"Good morning, Julia," Fiona Barry said as she approached. Julia's spine stiffened to attention at once, and she tore her gaze from Thomas Merritt's handsome face. Fiona was examining the gentleman as if he were a cream cake and she was starving. "And who is this? Do introduce me, my dear."

"This is Mr. Thomas Merritt," Julia said. Even her voice sounded more adult, husky and soft. "Mr. Merritt, this is Lady Fiona Barry, a dear friend of my mother's."

He bowed over Fiona's hand. "Good morning, Lady Barry. A pleasant morning for a walk in the park, is it not?"

"Indeed," Fiona said. "But where is Temberlay, my

dear?" she asked Julia. "I was sure I heard your mama say you'd gone walking with him this morning when I called."

Julia felt her face heat. Fiona could also sniff out lies. "He's just—"

"He's been called away for a moment, and he asked me to escort Julia," Thomas Merritt said smoothly.

"I see. And will you be attending the betrothal ball on Thursday?" Fiona asked, accepting the explanation, lost in Thomas Merritt's dazzling smile.

"No," Julia said hurriedly.

"I wouldn't dream of missing it," he countered, and smiled down at her, turning her knees to water again, squeezing her hand ever so slightly.

Fiona grinned, baring her teeth like an aging hound scenting prey. "It is an event not to be missed. The Countess of Carrindale gives the most marvelous parties, and her dear daughter's betrothal ball will surely be the event of the Little Season, surpassed only by her wedding." She sighed like a bellows. "I remember you in leading strings, Julia. It is hard for me to imagine you all grown up and about to become a duchess, my dear."

Julia felt Thomas Merritt's eyes on her once more, warm and appraising. He squeezed her hand yet again. "Forgive me, but I've remembered an appointment I cannot break, Julia." Even her name sounded honey-sweet from his lips. "I'll leave you to chat with Lady Barry."

He kissed her hand, and she felt the warmth of his mouth through the lace of her glove. It flowed through her limbs like whisky. "It was a pleasure," he said, looking into her eyes, and she could see that he meant it, that he was stepping away with regret. Her tongue wound itself around her tonsils, making speech impossible. And then he was gone, walking away without looking back, his long legs eating up the cinder path until the trees swallowed the sight of him. She suppressed a sigh of regret, just as Fiona heaved one of her own.

She let Fiona tell her the latest gossip without even hearing it. She felt like a woman. Not a lady, or a bride, or the daughter of an earl. A woman.

It felt like stepping into the heat of the sun on a cold day, and she wanted more.

"Julia! Did you hear me? It's time to go in. We all miss James," her mother said, and Julia realized that she was standing in the salon, staring up at her brother's portrait, and seeing not his face, but Thomas Merritt's. "You are the future now, Julia. Your son will not only be Duke of Temberlay, but also the next Earl of Carrindale." She didn't want to think of the fact that she was simply the conduit for the next generation of the peerage.

"Temberlay has waited long enough," her father added gruffly, barely glancing at his late heir.

He hadn't spoken James's name since the news of his death came, and he was no doubt pleased the wedding would take place at last. The nuptials had been delayed while her family mourned, but men without heirs to succeed them were ever anxious about the future, though David hadn't objected to the delay. How could he when his own brother, Nicholas, was a captain in the same regiment as James? Every man in the regiment had escaped certain death thanks to her brother's heroic self-sacrifice. She was proud, of course, but she wished—just a little— that he had found another way to save the others, so she might still have her brother with her now, tonight, when she needed his reassuring arm to lean on.

Julia drew herself up straight. She was a woman now, a lady, and a duchess-to-be. She could and would stand on her own two feet. She cast one last glance at James, and pushed the image of Thomas Merritt's appreciative smile out of her mind. She would soon see the same look on David's face.

"I'm ready."

She followed her parents into the ballroom, brilliantly lit with a thousand candles. Jewels glittered, regimental badges gleamed, champagne sparkled, and her betrothal ring shone brightest of all.

David didn't even notice her entrance. He was deep in conversation with a group of gentlemen as Julia approached, just a trifle irritated by his inattention tonight, of all nights.

"Good evening," she purred, and dipped a curtsy. The gentlemen bowed.

"Oh, hello, Jules," David said with a vague smile. He dropped an absent kiss on her forehead—the kind of kiss her brother might have bestowed on her. David didn't tell her she looked pretty. Nor did his eyes light with pleasure, or anything else. In fact, he looked away from her, swept the ballroom with a bored glance, and took a glass of champagne from a passing footman without offering one to her. She reached for her own glass, and David's eyebrows quirked in surprise, as if he thought her still too young for wine. She gave him her practiced coquette's grin and sipped.

Her mother beckoned them to the receiving line, and David took her glass and set it down with his own before he offered his arm. "Shall we?" He led her to her mother's side and stood with his hands clasped behind his back as they waited for their guests to arrive. Julia watched the cream of the *ton* descending the stairs like an invading horde, drew a shaky breath and pasted on a welcoming smile.

Lady Dallen swept in like an ill wind, examined Julia's

necklace through her lorgnette, and wished her happy in a dry tone before going to stir things up in other corners of the room.

Lord Dallen slapped David on the back and said he looked forward to playing cards tonight, once "this betrothal business" was concluded, as if Julia was an interruption to the evening, and not the reason for it. David, damn his eyes—she borrowed one of her late grandmother's favorite and most forbidden phrases—looked extremely pleased by his lordship's invitation. In fact, he gazed at Dallen with the kind of appreciation *she* had hoped for. If that was the way to his heart, she would have to learn how to play cards before the wedding. Her mother would hardly approve, but what else was a bride to do?

David didn't enjoy poetry, or music. He didn't read or hunt. They would have to spend their evenings at Temberlay castle doing *something*. She felt a blush rise at the other idea that came to mind, but she was an innocent, and he had never so much as hinted at the physical aspects of marriage that would transpire between them after the vows were said. Why, she'd learned more about that from a single glance into Thomas Merritt's glittering gray eyes.

"David, my mother has agreed to allow me to waltz this evening," she said, leaning into his shoulder, brushing against him in the most unsisterly way she could manage in her parents' ballroom.

He patted her hand and smiled vacantly at her. "I don't know how to waltz, Jules."

Her heart sank to her ankles.

"Then perhaps—" But she didn't have a suggestion. She folded her tongue behind her teeth and turned to smile at the next guest. Her heart stopped dead in her chest.

"Thomas Merritt," he said in a dark voice, as if they'd never met. He bowed over her hand, his grip warm through her glove, his eyes never leaving hers, filled with a mischievous, knowing, intimate stare. The heat in that look set her heart beating again, very fast. He smiled, a slow, dangerous grin, and his gaze roamed over her. *His* appreciation was perfectly obvious. Her heart climbed higher still, and lodged in her throat, making speech impossible. A lock of dark hair fell over his brow, and she clenched her fist against the urge to brush it back. He did so himself in a polished gesture as he stepped away.

He was the handsomest man she'd ever seen. Her imagination hadn't played her false. He was just as she remembered him from their brief encounter. She let her eyes linger on the lean length of his legs, the breadth of his shoulders under the black wool of his evening coat as he walked away. She dared to guess that *he* waltzed . . . among other things.

He glanced back and caught her looking. She felt heat rise over her cheeks, and she made a small sound of dismay as he grinned at her again.

"Pardon?" David asked, glancing down at her.

"Nothing," she managed. She snatched another glass of champagne from a passing footman and took a long restorative sip. The bubbles were almost as thrilling as Mr. Merritt's wicked smile.

She watched him out of the corner of her eye. He did not go into the card room or join the other guests. Instead, he leaned against the wall insouciantly, in her line of sight, and watched her. She felt her composure slip. Suddenly her gown felt too tight, too low-cut, and the room too warm.

She sent him a scathing glance, meant to discourage such behavior, squelch it utterly, but he had the audacity to wink at her. It made her stomach wobble and her knees weak. She plied her fan, hid behind it.

Had he come to reclaim his handkerchief? It was upstairs, hidden in her drawer.

"Stand up straight," her mother whispered. Julia stiffened, but with more annoyance than grace as the waltz began and David disappeared into the card room, arm in arm with Lord Dallen.

"D'you suppose they'll take a house together by the sea for the summer?" he quipped, and she turned to find Thomas Merritt beside her, watching David and Dallen go. He was so tall she had to look up to meet his eyes. "May I have this dance?" He extended his hand as if he was already sure of her acquiescence.

A thrill rushed through her. There was something about this man that warned her to say no, to run for the safety of her mother's side, but she was a grown woman. Surely the tingle low in her belly at the look in his eyes proved that well enough.

"Thank you." She took his hand and let him lead her out.

He waltzed smoothly. "You look beautiful, by the way," he said, as if he knew she'd craved the compliment, exactly the way she'd needed a protector in the park. Did he intend to make a habit of rescuing her?

"Thank you," she said again. She was acutely aware of the heat of his hand on her waist, searing through the layers of silk and lace. He made a perfectly proper touch feel intimate, as if they were alone. She felt a tingle of something unexpected course through her as his eyes dropped to the slopes of her breasts and lingered before he met her eyes again.

She *felt* beautiful.

"Does His Grace realize just how lucky he is? I wondered that the other day when we met."

"Of course he does," she said tartly, and felt her skin heat. How bold that sounded.

"You're blushing, but you shouldn't. A woman should be aware of her worth." His gaze flicked over her jewels. "Beyond the value of her jewelry, of course. I'd be willing to wager you've been betrothed for a very long time, or it's an arranged match, perhaps, since he already behaves like you are an old married couple, bored by familiarity."

"We have known each other since—forever," she said breathlessly. Why did every word out of her mouth make her sound like a ninny?

He quirked an eyebrow upward. "Forever is a long time. I suppose when someone looks constantly at a familiar object, no matter how lovely it is, they cease to see its beauty."

Exactly so. David would always see her as the child he'd grown up with. She imagined their wedding night, how awkward that was going to be. She stumbled.

Mr. Merritt caught her, lifted her, twirled her through the air and took the next step before he set her back on her feet. For an instant her breasts were pressed to his chest, her heart pounding against the hard muscles under his shirt. His hand spread wide on her waist, supporting her, and his thumb brushed the underside of her breast. Another rescue.

She swallowed a gulp of heady surprise.

"You look flushed, my lady. Perhaps some air?" he asked, glancing toward the French doors that led to the terrace.

She looked out into the velvet darkness of the late spring evening. She should refuse. It was against all the rules she'd been taught. But she was an adult, almost a married woman, and she nodded and let him waltz her out onto the terrace.

"Would you care for some champagne?" he asked, and stepped inside to beckon to a passing footman. He took two glasses and brought one to her.

She watched the bubbles dance in the light that spilled from the ballroom.

"Shall we drink to your happiness?"

"I am happy."

"Oh, I didn't doubt it for a moment," he drawled in a tone that suggested he doubted it very much indeed.

"David is simply—" She hesitated. What? Kind, titled, stiff? Her grandmother's nickname for him came to mind. Dull Duke David.

"Oh, I know. He is handsome, rich, and safe."

"Safe?" She met the mischievous glitter of his eyes in the shadows. He laughed.

"Interesting you chose that word out of the three."

"Well, of course he's the other two things as well—and more. I suppose he's safe, too. Who would harm him?"

He tilted his head. "I meant he's a safe choice of husband. Not likely to do anything unexpected or in the least shocking." He sipped his champagne. She watched his throat work above the edge of his cravat, his skin dark against the white linen.

Dull Duke David, she thought again, and pushed the idea away. "Such as?" she said, made bold by the wine.

He studied her for a moment, reached to caress her cheek, then ran his thumb over her lower lip. "Such as waltzing you away into the garden to steal a kiss, which I have wanted to do since I met you in Hyde Park. But then, I'd bet that even his kisses are safe. Do they set you on fire?"

"I—" She began a tart response that it was none of his affair how David kissed her, but she had no idea. He had only ever offered dry pecks on her cheek or forehead.

His lips were always cool. She stared at Thomas Merritt's well-shaped mouth. She'd wondered what it might be like to kiss him too. In fact, the idea had occupied her thoughts far more than it should have over the past two days.

He held up his champagne and stared into the amber depths. "A woman should feel like there are stars coursing through her blood when a man kisses her properly. Even if it is the simplest brush of his lips on hers, she should feel it in every inch of her body." He stepped closer, leaned in. "Is that how His Grace's kisses make you feel? Breathless, hot, desired?"

Could a kiss really feel like that? Suddenly she wanted to kiss a man who could never, ever resemble a brother.

Or her fiancé.

She lifted her face to his, stood on tiptoe, her mouth watering. "Show me," she said.

He didn't need a second invitation. He took her glass, set it on the edge of the balcony, cupped her face in his hands and lowered his mouth to hers. His lips were warm. She could taste the champagne on his breath, smell the soap he used, the scent of his own skin. A thrill of pure excitement ran through her, curling her toes. She tightened her fingers on his arms.

He didn't pull back. His lips shaped to fit hers, moved over her mouth expertly.

Oh my.

Her hands crept up to touch his face, to draw him closer. With a sigh, she kissed him back.

He licked the seam of her lips, and she drew back in surprise. He merely shifted his attention, laid a dozen kisses along her jaw, down her throat, blazing a trail of fire. She tipped her head, gave him access, permission. Above her the stars did indeed glitter.

He put his hands on her waist, spanning it, and drew her closer. She slid her arms around his neck, pressed against the warm length of his body. He nibbled a particularly delicate spot under her ear. "Oh," she sighed, shivering. Her eyes drifted shut but she could still see the stars.

He captured her mouth again, nipped at her lips until she drew a breath and opened. He tangled his tongue with hers. He tasted of champagne. She moved closer still, marveling at the way her hips fitted to his, how her curves perfectly accommodated his angles. His heat radiated through her clothes. More. She wanted more. She pressed her tongue against his, experimenting. He gave a soft groan, and his hands slid up her back to cup her neck and tilt her backward, deepening the kiss.

Oh, she did indeed feel breathless, hot, and desired!

Something tickled at her brain, the tiny part that could still think. She should step back, move away, go inside, but she could not stop kissing him. How had she ever lived without kisses? She hadn't even known such sensations existed. It was like the first sip of champagne, the heady tang of summer berries purloined from the garden, the sweetness of honey and wine and cake all in one. Surely this was what her grandmother had meant when she told her romantic stories, whispered them in her ear so her mother couldn't hear, of kisses such as this, bestowed on a princess in a tower by a lover who dared to climb the vines to her bower.

He pulled away, and cool evening air rushed in like sanity. Julia opened her eyes and stared at him. He was staring back, just out of reach, his face in shadow, breathing hard as if he'd been running.

"I think we'd better stop." His voice was an octave lower than it had been. It vibrated over every aroused inch of her flesh. Good sense returned like a dash of cold water. She should be ashamed—scarcely a dozen feet away, her guests were dancing, drinking, celebrating her betrothal to another man.

Dull Duke David.

She didn't know what to say. Her lips still tingled, and despite the chill of the spring evening, her body burned.

"I'll go back inside. You'd better slip in later," he murmured, looking over his shoulder now, scanning the crowd for curious eyes, worrying far too late if anyone might have seen them. David could call him out and shoot him for the liberties he'd taken. Would he shoot her too?

He was far too busy playing cards.

Mr. Merritt bowed, backed away. The light hit him, illuminated the copper lights in his dark hair, the silhouette of his lean body—the body that only moments earlier had been pressed against hers—then he stepped inside with a single regretful glance at her and was gone.

She put a hand to her lips, swollen and soft.

She needed a mirror.

She needed a cold bath.

Julia picked up her skirts and hurried along the terrace to the French doors that led into the library. She slipped inside and leaned on the cool glass for a moment. The room was dark and empty. Light from the street spilled through the windows, painting long golden rectangles on the floor.

Her heart slowed. The library was a place of sobriety and decorum. Somewhere beyond the double oak doors the party continued. She could hear laughter, voices, and music. She crossed to the mirror but could not see anything in the darkness. Was she different now? Disheveled? Did she look wanton? She smoothed a careful hand over her hair, checked for loose curls, touched her swollen lips, felt the tingle on her cheeks where his rougher skin had grazed her.

Of course she was different. She'd been different the moment she met Thomas Merritt, and now—

She perched on the edge of one of the armchairs that smelled of cigars and her father's hair oil. With nervous fingers, she tucked back a strand of hair. In a moment she would have to walk back into the ballroom, and act as if nothing had happened, but her heart was beating against her ribs like a caged bird.

She jumped to her feet when the door opened.

The light from the hall raced across the room, blinded her for a moment. Was it her mother, looking for her, or David, perhaps? Would they be able to tell what she'd been doing in the dark garden with the handsome stranger? Guilt tightened her gut even as resolve stiffened her spine. She had received many lectures in this particular room, standing on the carpet before her father's desk. She clasped her hands behind her back, as she always did, ready to face the consequences, whatever they might be.

Thomas Merritt stepped into the silence of Lord Carrindale's library and waited for his eyes to adjust to the dark. He had come to the lavish betrothal ball for one reason, and it wasn't to wish the couple happy.

He had no idea when he met Julia Leighton in the park that she was Carrindale's daughter. She'd been a lovely, distraught lady in need. He should have walked away, but he couldn't. Not when he saw the tears in her eyes. When Fiona Barry had said Julia's name, mentioned the betrothal ball, the very ball he had every intention of attending anonymously, he should have taken it as a warning.

From that moment, things had gone awry. For one thing, the countess was not wearing the magnificent tiara he'd come to steal, which meant it was most likely still in the safe. And for another thing . . . He glanced up at the shadowed portrait of the grim-faced Earl of Carrindale and grinned.

I've been kissing your daughter.

That was the other problem—the luscious lips of Lady Julia, the bride-to-be, Carrindale's unexpectedly lovely daughter. He'd noticed the stunning necklace she wore, of course, and the matching earrings, and then he saw the woman behind them, and the jewels had paled by comparison. She was even more beautiful than he remembered from their brief encounter.

Fool! He wasn't a natural thief, didn't find it easy, and the distraction didn't help.

Thomas wasn't the kind of man who lost himself in a simple kiss. He wondered how far he would have let it go if sanity hadn't saved him. And what if he'd been caught with Julia in his arms? Would Carrindale have called the watch, or simply had him spirited away to a watery grave in the stinking Thames? The earl would certainly not insist that she marry a rogue like him when she had a duke in hand.

His pedigree was good enough, though not as high as the Duke of Temberlay's, or would have been had his brother not disowned him for his sins. He was plain Mr. Merritt now, a man who made his own way in the world without family ties to help or hinder him. This adventure would gain him only a memorable kiss, perhaps a stolen tiara—and one of Julia's diamond earrings, a souvenir of the encounter. It rested in his breast pocket now.

He licked his lips to refrain from taking it out and looking at it, and tasted champagne. He'd never kissed anyone like Julia Leighton. None of the rich widows, the bored *ton* wives, the milkmaids or whores he'd known compared. He marveled at Temberlay's stupidity in not knowing how lucky he was. What kind of man could resist the delectable charms of a woman like Julia? They had been betrothed for years. Surely by now Temberlay had claimed his right to touch her, bed her.

He shook his head, freeing his mind from that image, so he could find the damn safe and get the hell out—

The rustle of silk caught him by surprise.

She stepped out of the shadows. A mixture of fear and unexpected pleasure kept him rooted to the floor.

"How did you know I was here?" she asked him. "I thought—"

He knew what she thought, that he'd left the ball—which he would have if he'd had any sense at all—and she'd never see him again. She would have wondered about her lost earring longer than she'd remember him. Suddenly the diamond bob weighed heavy in his pocket, and he could feel it against his breast like biblical guilt.

Though shalt not steal. Not kisses, or jewels.

But a man had to eat.

He caught another hint of her perfume—it was on his clothes, would stay with him for days. Violets. It was a sophisticated, unusual scent for such a young woman. It spoke of hidden depths, secrets. Most debutantes wore lavender or rosewater.

"I—" He was lost for words. He glanced at the small landscape painting on the wall behind her, which probably hid the safe. For some reason, men like Carrindale always chose to hide their treasures behind nondescript art that wouldn't otherwise have a place in their elegant homes. He could hardly stride to the picture, take it down, and ask Julia for the combination to the safe.

He supposed in other circumstances a gentleman—or even a rogue like him, if he had any sense—would bow, make a joke of his inexplicable presence in this dark room, say he mistook the door for the way to the jakes, and take his leave before there was trouble.

But he was already in trouble. He couldn't take his eyes off her, the way the faint light outlined the shape of her neck and shoulders, the shadowed vee between her breasts, the ghostlike shimmer of her gown. The glitter of her jewels paled before the gleam of her eyes. His mouth watered.

"I—" He tried again, but she gave a desperate little sigh and rushed toward him. He opened his arms, caught her. Her lips landed on his, and it began all over again.

He was powerless to resist. He wanted this woman. He couldn't recall a time when he hadn't been in complete control with a lover. He never lost himself to passion. Women were a means to an end, for physical gratification or gain. He offered them pleasure, took what he wanted, and left before they could beg him to stay.

But it was different with Julia, and he couldn't begin to say why. Perhaps because she was forbidden to him, belonged to another man. Was it the thrill of stealing something he otherwise couldn't have? No, it was the lady herself—beautiful, trusting, half innocent, unconsciously seductive. She'd set his blood on fire with a simple stolen kiss in a dark garden, and now—

He knew exactly what she wanted.

Him.

It wasn't rescue this time. It was plunder. She was making soft sounds as she sought his mouth, pressed her lips and her hips to his. He lifted her into his arms, carrying her the few steps to the deep leather settee, laying her down, his body on hers, as desperate as she. Her arms tightened, pulled him nearer. He was wrapped in her perfume, mesmerized by her eager kisses. She let him raise her skirts, slide his fingers up the silk of her calves, thighs, hips.

Her hands fumbled with the buttons of his shirt, then fell away as he found the wet center of her.

"Oh," she sighed, and his fingers played over her, bringing her pleasure before he took his own. She gripped his lapels, pulled him down against her as she cried out, her body bucking against his fingers. He caught the sweet whimpers in his mouth.

He reached for his flies, opened them expertly with one hand as he kissed her, unable to get enough of her mouth.

She gasped as he entered her, and tensed beneath him. She was tight, almost too tight.

Nervous, no doubt. He should have locked the door, but it was too late for that. He was beyond reason, beyond stopping, but she didn't ask him to. She gripped his shoulders, her nails digging into his flesh, right through his shirt, a sweet, sharp, sensual pain.

He didn't last long. One last, long thrust, and he filled her, felt the hot rush of release.

He fell against her, stunned. He stroked her face, kissed her gently, still buried inside her. He couldn't read her expression in the low light.

What the hell had he done?

He moved off of her, turned away and used his handkerchief to clean himself before he fastened his clothes.

She sat on the settee, arranging her own clothing, trying to fix her hopelessly disheveled hair.

"Oh no, my earring! Well, my mother's, actually. I've lost it! She'll lecture me for an hour on carelessness, heedless behavior, and—" She began to laugh.

"What's so funny?" he asked.

"Heedless behavior!" she said. Her laughter faded. "I should not have—"

Nor should he. Not here, not now. The stakes were too high. He sighed. He wished he could afford to leave here empty-handed, with nothing but the memory of a lover that finally made him feel something, even if only for a moment. The diamond in his pocket would feed him for a week, the Carrindale tiara for a month, and Julia's necklace for half a year.

She was searching the floor for it, and he almost relented. Taking her hands in his, he pulled her close for a moment, distracting her. Desire surged again. What the devil was the matter with him? He did *not* allow his feelings to get in the way of his survival. He hadn't even realized he *had* feelings until now. He kissed her gently, making it farewell. She pulled away.

He braced himself for tears, accusations, but she simply said, "You should go. The French doors lead to the garden, and there's a gate that leads to the mews and the street."

"Yes," he agreed.

"I shall go upstairs. I'll send my maid down to mama to say I have a headache."

There was no mention of Temberlay. Had the duke even noticed she was gone, that she'd been absent from the ballroom for nearly an hour? Thomas glanced at the ormolu clock on the mantel.

Less than an hour.

He straightened his rumpled cravat as best he could and bowed over her hand. Her fingers coiled around his for a moment, as if she could not bear to let him go. He pulled free gently and let himself out.

It wasn't until he'd reached his lodgings that he saw the blood on his handkerchief. How could he have been so stupid?

Lady Julia Leighton had been a virgin.

Chapter 2

Thomas waited outside Carrindale House in the rain until he saw Julia get in the coach and drive away. He followed her to Bond Street, watched her alight and go into an exclusive modiste's shop. He watched through the window as she tried on a gown of sapphire blue silk. The shop assistant spread a lace veil over her dark hair, and a bitter taste filled his mouth. Her wedding gown. He clenched his fists and stepped away to wait for her to emerge.

"Why Lady Julia, how pleasant to meet you here so unexpectedly," he said brightly, as if he had merely chanced upon her in the street. He watched her pale cheeks bloom like roses, saw fear war with curiosity in her eyes.

She dipped a curtsy and turned to her maid. "Wait in the coach. I'll be along in a moment." After the girl complied, she whispered to him, "What are you doing here?"

"I found your earring," he said, and taking her gloved hand in his dropped it into her palm. It was the only excuse he had come up with to see her again, returning what he'd stolen. Well, half of what he'd stolen. "It must have gotten tangled in my clothing when we—" She shot him a wide-eyed look of horror, and he fell silent. "Are you—well, my lady?" he asked stiffly, resisting the urge to touch her flaming cheek.

She glanced at the earring and closed her hand on it. "You've rescued me yet again."

There were a million things he wanted to say—apologies, offers of marriage, confessions of feelings he had no right to, everything from concern to—affection. He'd call it that.

"Someday I shall have to return the favor," she said.

"I came to see if—" But she tilted her head, and even if her blush betrayed her embarrassment at what had passed between them in the darkness of her father's library, she schooled her expression into the same polite look of interest she'd given Fiona Barry in the park. She did not need him, after all. She was stronger than she looked. He felt admiration for her. She would make a magnificent duchess.

He took her arm and escorted her the few steps to her coach. "So when is the wedding to be?" he asked.

"January. At Temberlay Castle."

They reached the vehicle, and he let her go and bowed. "Then I shall wish you well," he said. "And happy."

She lowered her gaze. "I am . . ." She paused, and he watched her throat bob as she swallowed the lie. "Thank you," she managed.

He kissed her hand, felt her fingers tighten on his for an instant. He let her go and walked away, resisting the urge to look back. Whatever the future held for him, it did not include Julia Leighton.

Chapter 3

〜

August 1814, London to Brussels

It wasn't home anymore—merely England now, Julia told herself as she stood at the ship's rail, watching the chalk cliffs disappearing behind the fog that blanketed the coast, white on white, a body disappearing into a shroud.

Appropriate, she thought, since a ruined lady was indeed dead to almost everyone who had known her in better times. Her father had told friends she was dead after he'd discovered her sin, and disowned her on the spot. He had insisted she leave the country, not just his house, since it wouldn't do for "decent" folk to see her ghost walking the streets of Mayfair, and feel the need to ask awkward questions.

No, it was better this way, a fresh start, a new life all her own.

In her arms, Jamie squirmed, waved chubby arms at the seabirds that wheeled overhead. She kissed her infant son and passed him to his nurse, and watched as they hurried belowdecks out of the wind. It would be hours before they reached Antwerp, and Julia knew she should go below too, but she stayed where she was and let the salt wind buffet her, wanting one last glimpse of the coast.

Her parents had never even asked about the child, named after her brother James, the family hero. In better circumstances, Jamie would have been his grandfather's heir, the next Earl of Carrindale, but he faced an unknowable future, like she did.

It could be far worse, Julia thought, tightening her hands on the rail. Her fate was not so terrible as David's. He'd died in a duel, scant days after she broke their engagement and confessed she was with child by another man. She did not fully understand the circumstances of the duel. The details had been buried along with David, yet another family secret. It wasn't Thomas Merritt who killed him. She had refused to name her lover, and besides, Mr. Merritt had taken ship and gone from England soon after her encounter with him, mere days after she'd seen him on Bond Street, and long before she knew she was pregnant. She'd made discreet inquiries about him. It had turned out his name was well known, and he was a most popular topic for gossip. He was a rogue, a charmer, disowned by his family too, for his own ruinous behavior. Not at all the kind of man who rescued ladies in distress. Yet she could not entirely blame him. She shut her eyes. So much sorrow and misery had been caused by her foolish desire for a kiss—a kiss that had ruined so many lives. As much as she wished to banish Tom Merritt from her thoughts, forget him forever, she could not.

"Good afternoon."

Julia turned to find Major Lord Stephen Ives standing behind her, his cloak open to reveal his scarlet military tunic, bright as blood against the silver fog.

She felt a pang in her heart. It was the same tunic her brother had worn, from the same regiment, the Royal Dragoons. James had died a hero in that tunic, and it was due to James's bravery that it turned out she wasn't entirely without friends after all.

Nicholas Hartley, David's brother, had stood by her. He'd given up his commission in the Royal Dragoons when David died and he inherited the title. He'd come to see her when he returned to England, as bewildered by the circumstances of David's duel as she was. Nicholas never once blamed her for the way things had turned out. A friend from her childhood, he was as close to her as her own brother had been. He had arranged for a house, a midwife, and a nurse, and when her father insisted yet again that she leave the country, Nicholas had arranged an introduction to Major Lord Ives, and a chance for honorable employment.

She was now the paid companion to Lord Ives's sister, Dorothea Hallam, hired to accompany the brother and sister out of England. Stephen Ives was a diplomat, on his way to the peace talks in Vienna, and his sister was a recent widow, alone in the world. Neither had asked for details of her scandal fortunately, since she had used up all the favors. It was time to stand on her own two feet, rescue herself and her son from the consequences of the past.

"Have you been out of England before?" Major Lord Ives asked now, coming to stand by the railing, yet keeping his distance from her. Was this how it would be from now on, respectable folk refraining from touching her or coming too close for fear that scandal was catching? Stephen Ives's face was carefully blank, correct, but not unkind.

"No, I've not traveled, but I've heard many stories," she replied.

"From your brother, no doubt," he said with a polite smile.

"Actually, it was my grandmother." She swallowed. "And you, my lord—have you been far afield, aside from Spain? War seems a hard way to see the world." Someday she would work up the courage to ask him how James died, but she barely knew Lord Ives yet, was still learning the boundaries between a servant and employer from this side of the coin. Once, she had been his social superior—an earl's daughter, the fiancée of a duke—but she was no longer even his equal.

He studied her face for a moment, gauging her interest, perhaps, and she held his eyes.

"Yes, war is the hard way to travel. I saw Portugal, Spain, and France through a soldier's eyes, in ruins, mostly, after battles." He forced a dry smile. "Now I'll see Paris and Vienna as a diplomatic aide. I trust it will be much more pleasant, if, of course, the other envoys all agree to behave themselves at the peace negotiations."

"A least there will be no guns or swords," Julia said.

"No, we're not enemies anymore, nor yet are we friends. A war of words can do as much harm as a battle."

She knew that. Her maternal grandmother had once been married to a diplomat, had traveled with him, learned protocol, foreign manners, and how to tread cautiously in the presence of courtiers and kings. Julia's toes curled in her shoes. She was secretly thrilled to be walking in Arabella's footsteps. Would she meet pirates or pashas or kings? Kings at the very least, she supposed, since every one of the crowned heads of Europe were expected to take part in the peace conference.

A maid came on deck and dipped a curtsy to Major Lord Ives before turning to Julia. "Lady Dorothea wants you, Miss Leighton. The sea is making her feel poorly."

She pulled her woolen shawl tight around her throat against the wind.

"Then I'll not keep you from your duties," Lord Stephen said, dismissing her.

Julia followed the maid below. Would she ever get used to being addressed as plain Miss Leighton? She was not Lady Julia any longer. She was Lady Dorothea Hallam's paid companion.

It wasn't an unpleasant post. She had known Dorothea slightly in happier times, like regimental sisters, since Dorothea's husband Matthew had also been a Royal Dragoon. They attended some of the same parties, danced at the same balls. But Dorothea lost her husband and newborn son to fever, and had barely recovered herself. Her grief had made her a recluse, and Lord Stephen could not leave her behind when he accepted his posting, so Julia was hired to keep her company.

Julia knew he hoped the trip to Vienna would improve his sister's health and lift her spirits.

She opened the door to Dorothea's cabin, and a second maid looked up gratefully, then thrust a clean basin into Julia's hands before taking her leave to empty the full one. Dorothea was as pale as the fog outside, still retching.

Julia put a cool cloth on her forehead.

"Will the boat sink?" Dorothea moaned, clutching Julia's hand. "Death surely couldn't be more horrid than *mal de mer*."

Julia rubbed Dorothea's hands. "It won't be long until we land in Antwerp."

Dorothea sank into the pillow and stared at the low ceiling. "D'you remember the last ball you attended?" she asked dully.

"Yes," Julia said carefully. She would never, ever, forget that night.

Dorothea sighed. "I can't. I know I must have danced with my husband. I must have been happy, but I don't remember anything specific about the evening. I'm afraid I will forget the details, the little things, about our life together."

"The room was filled with flowers, and everyone was drinking champagne," Julia said. There were flowers and champagne at every ball.

Dorothea smiled wanly. "Oh yes, of course. I remember dancing with Matthew, laughing at something he said." Her brow furrowed. "What could he have said? I should have committed every word to memory, just in case—"

"He told you how beautiful you looked," Julia said.

"Yes. I was probably wearing that blue silk gown he liked."

"The night was warm, and he brought you champagne on the terrace," Julia went on, seeing another party, another face, in her mind.

"Did he?" Dorothea asked.

Julia fixed her eyes on Dorothea. "Of course."

"I suppose he must have," Dorothea sighed. "One ball is so like the others, but I would have liked just one memory I was sure of, our last waltz, our final supper together. It happened so fast, at the end. Matthew said he had a headache, and the baby was fractious, and then I was trying to keep both of them alive, but I couldn't. I remember very little about that day either, or any day since."

"You will," Julia soothed. Dorothea would remember everything when she was ready, but right now her stricken face showed Julia that she couldn't manage it. Lord Stephen had told her how fragile his sister's health was. She had resorted to laudanum to sleep away her grief, and the drug left her a shell of herself. Julia held the basin as Dorothea called out her husband's name and was sick again.

Hours later, Dorothea was still green and queasy as Lord Stephen carried her ashore and put her in the waiting coach.

"A few more hours, Doe," he said, trying to sound jaunty. "We'll be stopping for the night in Brussels." His sister lay back against the squabs and shut her eyes.

He handed Julia into the coach. "I trust you were not affected by seasickness on the voyage, Miss Leighton?"

She wrapped a rug around Dorothea's knees. "Not at all." He shut the door and the coach lurched forward.

"Where's the baby?" Dorothea murmured.

Julia glanced at her. Did she mean her own child or Jamie? "Jamie is with his nurse in another carriage," she said. Her son, and Thomas Merritt's too. She pushed the thought of him away. Whatever else she regretted about that night and its consequences, she could not regret Jamie. He was the love of her life.

Dorothea shut her eyes against the jolting of the coach. She clutched at the watch she wore pinned to her dress, which held painted miniatures of her husband and her son, and sighed deeply. She opened it and a lullaby played.

"We'll be in Paris within the week," Julia said, to distract her from the discomfort of the trip. "I believe I shall buy a new bonnet."

Dorothea pursed her lips. "I won't go out. I am still in mourning, but I'm certain Stephen will escort you wherever you wish to go."

Surely Stephen Ives would have official duties to attend to, and far better company than his sister's companion to squire about the city, Julia thought. What if someone had heard of her disgrace? She must remember that her new place in the world was in the shadows. She didn't want

Lord Stephen's kindness in hiring her used against him. Society's good opinion turned like a rabid fox, and once bitten, it was fatal. He had his career, his own reputation to consider.

"It's the Fête de St. Louis in Paris. The whole city will be celebrating—there will be receptions, parties, even fireworks to honor our arrival," Julia coaxed. "Surely Lord Stephen will take you to—"

"No one will be looking for *our* arrival. They will be awaiting the Duke of Wellington. We will scarcely be noticed," Dorothea said tartly. "I don't think I could endure such a crush. I would prefer to stay in, rest my nerves. Stephen says there will be weeks of travel before we reach Vienna."

"But think of the adventures we'll have!" Julia said.

"Bad roads, worse food, lumpy beds, vermin," Dorothea countered. "I shan't go out until we've reached Vienna, and even then . . ." Her voice trailed off.

Julia settled back as Dorothea fell asleep. It was for the best. A companion—or a ruined woman—did not go to parties, and surely she, of all people, should know adventures could be dangerous things.

Chapter 4

Paris

Thomas Merritt stared down at his dance partner, the wife of an English baron. She was chatty and flirtatious, ready for an adventure on her little junket to Paris. The city was full of English ladies now that the war was over. The newest French fashions called them across the Channel, and they were arriving daily, in droves.

He glanced at the open doors that led to the terrace. Gauzy white curtains swayed in the wind, beckoning him to waltz the lady outside.

The shadowed terrace was perfect for seduction. Under the guise of stealing a kiss, he could take much more. A caress of the cheek, a distracting, drugging kiss, and she wouldn't even notice her jewelry was gone until she returned to her lodgings. And she would never know it was him. He was careful never to take too much . . . just a single earring, or a bracelet, perhaps—something that might be easily lost on an evening such as this, when she was dancing, or kissing a handsome stranger in a dark garden. He never took every jewel a lady had on, or even the most valuable piece she wore. He could, of course, if he'd wished to do so, but it would be dangerous. Someone might recall his face, or the fact that he'd danced with the victim of the theft and had left early. He took enough to pay for his rooms, his food, his clothes, and no more.

Tonight, the baroness's diamond bracelet would be more than sufficient. She could keep the gaudy ruby necklace she'd dared to wear in Paris, of all places, where ruby necklaces still recalled the terrors of revolution, and the other kind of scarlet necklaces left by the guillotine.

The curtains brushed his pant legs with an encouraging caress as he waltzed the lady out of the heat of the ballroom and into the cool of the summer evening. He could smell roses, real ones now, subtler and better than the inexpensive and imperfect copy of their scent that the baroness wore. He breathed deeply, clearing his nostrils, and didn't stop dancing until they had reached the end of the terrace, a dark and perfect place for stealing kisses and jewels.

He didn't hesitate. He swooped in for a kiss, and she gave a token squeak of protest before she clasped her arms around him and pressed her breasts against his chest.

He cupped her cheek, relieved her of one diamond earring and pocketed it.

"What a lovely evening, in such charming company," he said, running his hands along her arms, his fingertips raising gooseflesh. He bent for another kiss, his hands poised on the clasp of the bracelet as she gasped delightedly at his audacity.

Instead of swooning in his arms, she grasped his lapels and hauled him closer. A moment's fear rushed through him as he thought himself caught. He let go of the bracelet and resisted the urge to push her away, to leap the balustrade into the garden and flee. Instead, he smiled at her and waited, caressing her hands, her wrists, the bracelet.

"Come to my rooms," she murmured, her eyes half closed. "I'll pay you."

Now he did step back, shocked at the bold offer of payment for services rendered, the bracelet entirely forgotten. "I think you have mistaken me, my lady."

Her eyes opened fully, passion gone, shrewdness replacing it. "Have I? You are an attractive man, but your cuffs are frayed. My guess is that you were born well but have fallen on hard times. I assumed you were interested in me for my money, sir, since I am a decade older than yourself. Even my husband never smiles at me the way you do, not even on our wedding day. What else could you want but my money?"

She was at least *two* decades his senior, and he was appalled. Appalled that he had fallen to such a point that a woman like this one assumed he was—a vile taste filled his mouth—*for hire?*

He would not stoop that low. He still had honor, scruples, manners. He flicked a glance at the edges of his cuffs, at the monogrammed linen of the finest quality, which was indeed fraying after so many months of wear. At least he used to have honor. He'd discovered the hard way that a man cannot eat honor.

He gave her an aristocratic, go-to-hell-smile and bowed crisply. "As I said, you have mistaken me, madam. I am merely a foreigner here in Paris, like yourself, glad to see a fellow traveler from England. If my courtesy has left you with an impression of me I did not intend, then I apologize, and I shall bid you good night." He turned on his heel and left. She did not call him back or follow him. Was she embarrassed, angry? God, he hoped so, because that was precisely how he felt. He walked briskly down the steps and let himself out the side gate, onto the street.

Her earring burned in his pocket like shame.

He walked the dark streets at an angry pace, his heels ringing on the greasy cobbles. He needed more pleasant company. For that, he had been seeing Millicent Carlyle for some weeks while she and her husband spent the summer in Paris. She was young, her husband old. She had a soul like Thomas's own, out for pleasure, without a care for tomorrow. While her husband visited the brothels of Paris, she invited Thomas to dine with her in the evenings. It was an uncomplicated relationship, without demands or awkward questions. They drank champagne in her boudoir, made each other laugh, and ended up in bed. She didn't notice his frayed cuffs. Millicent was easy company, and she made him forget what he'd become—a thief, a scoundrel, and a liar.

She'd sent him a note this afternoon, inviting him to come and play once her husband had left for the evening. How could he resist?

He knocked softly on the door of her hotel suite in the English fashion. French lovers scratched on the panels, and he did not want her to mistake him for someone else.

She opened the door and gave him a slow smile when she opened her robe to show him she was naked underneath. She didn't want to talk tonight, or drink champagne. Wonderful, perfect Millicent! Thomas took her in his arms with sigh of relief and slipped the silken garment off her shoulders, letting it drop to the floor as he pressed his lips to her exposed flesh.

Millicent pushed him away, her nose wrinkling. "You smell of roses! Have you come to me from another woman?"

The baroness's cheap perfume. He forced himself to grin. "It's summer in Paris. The roses are blooming.

I must have brushed past a blossom or two on my way here."

"And you did not think to pick one for me?" she pouted.

She led him to a screen in the corner and pointed to a basin and pitcher. "Wash off the scent, if you please, or I will be suspicious all night. Use my soap. It is made with jasmine."

She went to lie naked on the bed, spread invitingly. "Hurry."

He could hear her beyond the screen, writhing on the sheets in anticipation. He lathered his face and neck, and the scent of this woman's perfume replaced the last. How had he come to this, the son of an earl, the brother to another?

He'd been disowned, that's how. And the irony was that while he had been guilty of many sins, he was innocent of the one his brother accused him of, he thought bitterly. His brother's young wife, his new countess, had stood wide-eyed before her husband and said nothing, allowing him to take the blame for her sin. He gritted his teeth at the memory. That had been the last time—if one excluded his encounters with Julia Leighton—he'd behaved with chivalry.

He froze when the door opened.

"Jonathan!" Millicent cried. "You're back."

"Is it a crime in Paris for a husband to come home early?" her husband demanded gruffly, and Thomas waited, motionless, for him to ask his wife why she was stark naked. "Were you waiting for me?"

"I just finished my bath. I was about to go to bed," she said breathlessly.

"Then I'll join you. Do I smell roses?"

Millicent trilled a nervous little laugh. "It's summer in Paris, and the roses are in bloom," she parroted Thomas.

Thomas listened to the rustle of Lord Carlyle's clothing being discarded, heard the Englishman grunt as he mounted his wife. He listened to the rhythmic creak of the bedsprings and rolled his eyes, waiting.

He remembered the night his brother had thrown open the door to his bedroom and found Joanna there, half naked. He was in bed, had just woken at the sound of her entrance, but his brother suspected the worst. He didn't wait for an explanation, hadn't wanted one. And Joanna didn't say a word. He remembered how she came to see him the next day with tears in her eyes—and bought his silence with her earrings—his mother's earrings, actually, and before that his grandmother's, and most recently Edward's wedding gift to her. She needn't have bothered. He would have kept his silence for honor's sake alone, but he took them anyway.

Beyond the screen, Lord Carlyle grunted again, reminding Thomas that at least this time he was actually guilty of the sin, even if he hadn't been caught. Yet.

He looked around his hiding place as he buttoned his shirt. It contained hooks for her clothes, a copper hip bath, and the washstand. Three bars of jasmine-scented soap lay in a crystal dish next to the basin, and beside that he saw a little porcelain trinket box. He stared at it while fastening his flies, then opened the box. It contained a few bits of jewelry, including a simple pair of garnet and pearl earrings, and he took one, a parting souvenir. It would pay for a bottle of champagne or two.

Carrying his coat, he tiptoed out from behind the screen. The gray-haired lord was pumping heroically into his pretty wife. He had a red birthmark on his broad backside. Millicent's blue eyes widened over her husband's shoulder as she caught sight of him, and he blew her a farewell kiss as he opened the door silently and slipped out.

"Two earrings? Is that all? They don't even match!"

Thomas opened his eyes the next morning and glowered at his valet.

Patrick Donovan wrinkled his nose. "And you reek of perfume. What kind of flower is that?"

"Jasmine," Thomas muttered. "Or roses. Get me a bath."

"I should say I will," Donovan grunted.

"Then you can break up the earrings and sell the stones. They should fetch enough for breakfast at the very least."

"Bread, cheese, and olives yet again," Donovan muttered. "I miss a good English breakfast. A beefsteak and some sausage—"

"Then go back to England, my friend, by all means," Thomas snapped.

"And leave you to hang for your crimes? Which you will, if some husband doesn't shoot you between the eyes first, or between the—"

"Is this the part where I say you mean far more to me than a mere servant?" Thomas asked, pushing back the sheets. They positively stank of cologne. He didn't much care for the perfumes ladies drenched themselves with—rose, lavender, lily-of-the-valley, gardenia, jasmine. In his opinion, the artifice of cheap scent mocked both the flower and the lady who wore it.

Except violets. Violet perfume smelled like a garden after the rain, sweet, innocent, yet tantalizing, and . . . He rubbed his eyes, trying to remove the image of the one woman he knew who wore violet scent from his mind. The lovely Julia Leighton had been a lady to her fingertips, and she was probably married by now, a lofty duchess who had forgotten him entirely. He'd be willing to wager *she* was enjoying a fine English breakfast at this very moment. His mouth watered—but for her, not the beef.

He got up and crossed to the basin, wanting the insipid scent of his almost-lovers off. He would never see either lady again.

He sank into the bath while Donovan busied himself preparing the shaving kit. The silver handles and leather case were still monogrammed with Thomas's family crest. He'd pawned it and redeemed it a dozen times, but couldn't let it go permanently. It reminded him of who he'd been on the days he could not bear to think of what he was now.

He shaved himself while Donovan pried the jewels out of their settings and held them up to the light.

"The diamond is nice. So are the pearls with it. You should have taken both earrings."

"Against the rules," Thomas muttered as he drew the razor over his cheek.

"Your rules," Donovan muttered. "We need a necklace, or a tiara, or both, if you're to end this."

"It will end when I say so," Thomas said, and hissed when he cut his chin.

Donovan tossed him a towel. "You're the one always going on about finding a better life, not me. Ah, well. I should be back within the hour, since there is so little to haggle over."

Thomas dressed himself and stood in the open window, looking out over the city of Paris. It was touted as the most magnificent city in Europe, filled with everything and anything a man could want, if that man had the price, the guile, or the right friends to get it.

He had the guile, and when that succeeded, the price, but he was friendless, except for Donovan, and that's the way he liked it. Still, he'd been in Paris long enough, and he couldn't wait to leave. But where he might go next was the problem. He couldn't go back to London, and he had no interest in joining the Grand Tour of Europe or seeing German spa towns. He was a man without a home, like a mongrel dog.

He looked down at the street below and watched a coach drive by, the horses' hooves clattering on the cobbles. If he leapt from this window, he could land on the roof, knock the driver off his box and steal the vehicle. He'd drive it to the sea and take the first ship going to—

It was a game he played, like sticking a pin in the map. He imagined traveling to the first place that came to mind, but the trouble was, there was nowhere he wanted to be.

He turned away from the window and picked up the newspaper. It was days old. Donovan insisted on keeping up with London news, in case their crimes were ever discovered and it became necessary to flee, or in the vague hope that Thomas's brother decided to forgive him and welcome him home, or dropped dead and left an inheritance. Donovan still believed in miracles. Thomas did not.

He flipped through the yellowed pages. There was no mention of her. He'd gone for months without looking at a newspaper, afraid to read Julia Leighton's wedding announcement. Now he looked for items of society news that mentioned her. There weren't any. Had Temberlay shut her away on some country estate for her sin? He wondered what she'd told her husband on their wedding night, or if he'd even noticed. He shut his eyes and saw her face, glazed with passion, heard the soft sighs she'd made as he loved her, smelled the sweet, maddening, luscious scent of violets.

He was a cad, and a fool.

He'd wanted to see her again, even after she'd made it clear that she didn't need him.

Even now, when he should have long since forgotten her, he was letting himself be distracted, to feel something a man in his position couldn't afford to feel. He had no right, not where Julia Leighton was concerned. Yet no matter how hard he tried to tell himself she was better off, or to convince himself that she had used him for a momentary thrill, the hard edge of longing never quite went away.

He'd decided to leave London when he found himself standing outside Carrindale House, staring up at her window for the fifth night in a row, sure it was the only way to stay away from her. He'd departed for Paris on the very day the papers announced that Napoleon had been defeated.

A breeze came through the window and riffled the pages of the newspaper. He caught it and laid it flat on the table again.

An announcement caught his eye. It was an invitation, every bit as grand as the ones he used to receive by post when he was Viscount Merritton, a respectable earl's son and an eligible catch for a peer's daughter. This invitation came from the Austrian emperor, and was addressed to Europe's crowned heads and diplomats. There was to be a peace conference in Vienna, and a grand celebration of the end of more than twenty years of war. The sober task of dividing up Napoleon's conquered territories would be undertaken, of course, along with the difficult task of returning—or not—the priceless art treasures, crown jewels, and estates that Napoleon had stolen.

Crowned heads and jewels. Thomas grinned. It was almost too easy. In the crush, there would be dozens, even hundreds of thieves. A few big pieces and he'd be free of this life. He frowned. Or he'd be part of it forever. Either way, it was somewhere new, somewhere different, where things just might be better, and he might find a way to be happy, if there was still a possibility of that.

Donovan returned with two bottles of champagne under his arm.

"Pack everything. We're going to Vienna," Thomas ordered.

"Vienna?" Donovan said. "You don't speak whatever it is they speak in Vienna. You barely speak French."

Thomas passed the newspaper to his valet, pointed to the invitation.

Donovan read it and grinned, his green eyes lighting. "When this is over, I want enough to buy a horse farm in Ireland," he said.

"We'll part ways," Thomas agreed. "Each of us rich."

"And where will you go?" Donovan asked as Thomas opened the first bottle of champagne. Froth spilled over the table, and he hastily rescued the newspaper.

"Italy," Thomas said, testing it on his tongue. "Or India, perhaps."

But neither one sounded right.

Chapter 5

Brussels

Stephen watched as Julia Leighton helped his sister out of the coach. Dorothea was pale from the journey, and she leaned heavily on Julia, who bore her weight without comment or demure, blocking the cold wind between the vehicle and the inn's front door with her slim figure, taking the full blast of it herself. He tried not to feel admiration for her kindness.

It was, after all, her job.

He hadn't known what to expect when he agreed to take on a fallen woman as Dorothea's companion. Julia Leighton had a child by a man she had yet to name, conceived, if scandal was to be believed, at her own betrothal ball. He sometimes found himself staring at the child, looking for features he recognized in the infant's face, trying to guess his sire's identity, but the boy looked like every other baby, including his own nephew, Doe's lost son.

He'd only agreed to hire her as a favor to a friend—

well, two friends, really, if you included his debt of honor to James Leighton, as well as the favor he'd done for Nicholas Temberlay—and he'd done it knowing that employing such a woman might prove dangerous to his career. Really, how could a diplomat take a notorious lady of dubious morals to the most important peace conference in history? Yet here she was, and he'd found himself more intent on watching her for signs of impropriety than in doing his job. She'd done nothing as yet but still might prove him an even bigger fool than he felt. Once they reached Paris, surely people would recognize her as Carrindale's ruined daughter, and his career would be over. He was glad that Dorothea had refused to any attend official state functions in Paris, since it would mean her companion would have to stay at home with her.

And there was the issue of Julia Leighton's unruly physical passion. What could he expect in that regard? Would she try to seduce him? He shifted uncomfortably. She was pretty enough, but he couldn't afford such a mistake.

Not that she'd tried, of course. She had been the very picture of propriety, the perfect peer's daughter, treating him with cool politeness. What a duchess she would have made, yet she had taken on the role of a servant with remarkable grace. He frowned. There was that damned grudging admiration again, and she had yet to fully earn it.

It began to rain, a sudden, coursing downpour, and Dorothea cried out at the icy deluge. Julia quickly wrapped her own cloak around Doe and hurried her toward the inn, careful to find solid footing in the slippery mud of the yard.

Stephen reminded himself it was not his place to step forward and help her, and moved under the protection of the eaves to watch the men unloading the coaches and baggage wains. They stopped to look at Julia as the rain pasted her gown to her legs, revealing the long, lean shape of her limbs.

He felt a moment of panic. He should send her home now, before they joined the rest of the British delegation, but he'd promised to give her a chance to prove herself—or do the opposite.

He'd given his word to Nicholas, and James Leighton had known Nicholas as well, and given his life to save theirs. James had been as heroic as his sister was notorious. Julia was here as Stephen's way of repaying his share of the butcher's bill. If he were forced to send her home in disgrace, he wouldn't hesitate. She could not count on her brother's reputation to save her twice.

Without her cloak, the rain soaked her gown, flattened her hair, and clung to her lashes. She had endured everything thus far, even Doe's seasickness, without a word of complaint.

It appeared to Stephen, at least at first glance, that Julia Leighton was just what Dorothea needed. Doe had not been well since Matthew and her infant son had died. Stephen had feared the very sight of Julia's child would send her back into the dark days of madness she'd endured during the worst of her grief. He wondered if she would ever be able to overcome her loss, resume her life.

Doe had known Julia slightly before tragedy touched both of them, and apparently liked her. She had agreed at once to take Julia as her companion on the journey to Vienna, without any questions at all. He hadn't explained about the scandal, not knowing how to tell his delicate sister such a tale. He was certain she had seen the baby among their party, and Julia with him, but Doe looked past the infant as if he were invisible. He should be grateful, he supposed. Without Julia, he would not have been able to make this trip, since Doe could hardly remain in London alone.

Julia got Dorothea to the door and turned her over to her maid. To his surprise, Julia took her sodden cloak back and returned to the inn yard to direct the unloading of Doe's luggage, insisting on her feather bed first, which was wrapped in oilcloth to keep it dry, so Dorothea could rest properly.

She stood in the rain directing things with little care for herself, and it grew more difficult for Stephen to squelch his admiration. The more he looked, the less he saw the fallen woman and the more he saw the lady, soaked to the skin and still smiling. He left his post under the eaves, gasped at the icy downpour, and crossed the cobbles to assist. They spoke only French here, and perhaps she needed his help after all.

But Julia was giving orders like a duchess—and giving them in perfect French. He skidded to a stop and watched. Every servant jumped to obey, despite the weather.

"You speak excellent French," he said, and she turned with a polite smile. She looked pretty in the rain, with crystal drops on her dark lashes, her lips moist.

"Bien sûr," she replied. "My grandmother insisted that I must have a first-rate education, including Fre—"

A porter screamed a warning as a heavy trunk slipped from wet hands, tumbling off the roof of the coach. Stephen caught her shoulders, pulled her back against his chest just in time. The trunk landed in the mud where she'd been standing seconds before. Muck splashed her skirts, but she ignored it, looking up at him in surprise, her hazel eyes meeting his—wide, beautiful, very wary eyes. A shock went through him. Good God! Surely she didn't think that he— He set her on her feet at once and stepped back.

"Watch what you're doing!" he snapped at the porters in English.

"Take it upstairs, third room on the left," Julia said quietly, ignoring the stains on her gown and the obsequious apologies of the servants. She drew her dignity around her like a cloak and moved away from him, concentrating on the rest of the trunks.

He didn't take her arm when they finally went inside out of the rain, once everything had been seen to. Instead he clasped his hands behind his back, walked beside her. She was soaked to the skin, her jaw clenched to keep her teeth from chattering. "Would you like something warm to drink?" he asked.

"Thank you, but I had better go upstairs, see that Dorothea is settled." She met his eyes, her hazel gaze unapologetic, bold. "And my son." The reminder—the warning—was clear.

"Of course," he said, feeling his cheeks heat at the rebuke. "Order what you like, have it sent upstairs. Good night, *Miss* Leighton." He stressed the word Miss.

"Good night, Major Lord Ives."

He watched her go, a lady to her fingertips.

Yet she wasn't.

The very fact that she had been seduced, had given in to passion and possession, suggested she had a sensual side. It was intriguing, even if he must ignore it as her employer.

He was still a man, and as curious as the rest of the *ton* about the affair.

He looked away from the slender figure of the enigmatic Lady Julia.

Like she did, he had duties to attend to before he could rest. They had at least a month of hard travel ahead, and anything might happen on the road between here and Vienna.

He had to be on his guard.

Chapter 6

Paris

Dorothea's face was as white as the lace handkerchief she held over her nose. "How horrible this city smells!" she cried. "Make the coachman go faster!"

But there was no way to do that. The narrow streets and the crowds hemmed the vehicle in, and no one paid any attention to the coachman's orders to move aside. The city was mad with the celebration of the Feast of St. Louis. Wine, song, and laughter flowed freely through the streets, even if the coach did not.

Julia's eyes strayed upward to the gargoyles that adorned a church. The devilish faces grinned down at them, more puckish than wicked to her eyes, but Dorothea recoiled. "How frightening!" She gasped as grinning faces danced past the windows of the coach, singing. "They look as ugly as the gargoyles, and the buildings are so black, so dirty!"

To Julia, the people looked happy, celebrating the end of two decades of war. The gargoyles looked like they were laughing at the celebrations, as if they wished they could descend from their perches and join the fun.

Soot and grime had indeed curled up in the nooks of statues, embedded itself in the carved doorways, but the windows and balconies were decked with flowers, and the sky above the city was the bluest Julia had ever seen. There was color everywhere, red, blue, and yellow, even in the black silk of the Seine.

She pressed her face to the window of the coach and gaped like a tourist. "My grandmother used to say that every city had its own charm, like a woman, or a handsome man. There is a unique scent, a particular flavor, a distinctive color to the light, which gives each place its own special magic and makes you fall in love with it. She said the first thing to do when you arrive in a new place is to smell it like a rose, find the scent of it." Dorothea kept her handkerchief firmly over her nose.

Julia smiled sympathetically, but to her Paris was a marvel, a grand old lady who might have seen better, brighter days, but still enjoyed life to the fullest nonetheless. She took a deep breath. She could smell garlic and fresh bread, and the heady perfume of the flower market as they passed. There was wine and sweat and darker odors too, of course—the smell of life.

Dorothea cried out as several urchins climbed onto the coach and peered boldly into the windows. *"C'est Wellington?"* she heard one ask, but they dropped away, their faces twisting with disappointment when they realized the coach carried only two ordinary English ladies, and not the famous Duke of Wellington.

"They've gone now," she assured Dorothea. Outside their little sanctuary, the merriment went on, with everyone making the most of the celebration. Julia supposed the fact that Napoleon had been sent into exile on the tiny

Island of Elba, and a Bourbon king sat once more on the throne of France, was secondary to the people's joy that the fountains ran with wine instead of water.

The British delegation was here at the express invitation of King Louis XVIII. He had spent the last years of the war in luxurious exile in the English countryside, and now, restored to the French throne, he wanted every foreign lord, officer, diplomat, and aide to don their finest dress military tunics and most elegant evening clothes to attend the gala celebrations.

As a mere servant, Julia would not attend formal events unless Dorothea intended to go and needed her company. Even then, her place would be in the shadows, watching from the sidelines. But at the thought her dancing days might be over, she still longed for the pleasure of seeing great events unfold. Someday, she'd tell her son about these heady days of celebration.

Except Dorothea refused to leave her room to attend the balls and dinners, and Major Lord Ives went alone.

He told Dorothea and Julia all about the parties over breakfast each morning. While Dorothea could not bring herself to go out, pleading the fact that she was still in mourning, she wanted to know every detail.

"Tell me what they are wearing in Paris now," she begged as Julia poured the tea and tried to contain her own eagerness to hear Lord Stephen's response. It had been many years since Paris fashions were available in England. Not that English ladies of fashion didn't manage to smuggle in Belgian lace and French pattern books, along with the French brandy their lords illicitly imported. It was quite illegal, and unpatriotic, but no lady of fashion would allow *that* to deter her.

Stephen's eyes widened in vague horror. "Isn't it customary to say good morning first?"

Dorothea sent him a quelling look. "Not when there is important information to impart, brother dear. Did you say good morning before a battle?"

"No, but war is not nearly as serious as fashion," he replied.

Dorothea rolled her eyes. "You're stalling. Don't tell me you didn't notice what people were wearing!"

Stephen waited as a footman set a plate of food in front of him. "Er, well, everyone was wearing *clothes,* if that's what you mean."

Dorothea gasped. "You'll shock Julia with that kind of innuendo! Of course they were wearing clothes!"

Julia felt her skin heat as Stephen's mouth tightened for a moment. Was he thinking that she could not possibly be shocked by such a mild comment, or perhaps that for her clothes at a ball were optional? She concentrated on buttering a triangle of toast.

Would James have noticed what the ladies at a ball were wearing? Not likely. He would have danced with the prettiest girls, and spent the rest of the evening making morning appointments for male pursuits like hunting, or riding, or boxing.

Yet there *were* men who noticed a lady's appearance. She recalled Thomas Merritt's appreciative appraisal of her gown, her hair, her jewels. David had barely glanced at the dress it had taken weeks to select and have made, but Thomas said she was beautiful, made her feel it from her coiffed hair to her embroidered dancing slippers. She pushed the image of his smile away, the admiration that had been clear in his eyes, and took a forkful of ham. No one would look at her again that way—not without thinking of the scandal, and how easy it might be to seduce her in a dark corner.

"Come now, surely you remember *something*!" Dorothea insisted.

"Well, most ladies seemed to be wearing gowns with, um . . . kind of—" Stephen set his fork down and described a narrow, form fitting gown by waving his hands in the air.

"A high waist, fitted to the body?" Julia guessed. She had seen ladies on the streets in similar day dresses.

"Yes," Stephen said gratefully. "But with more . . . um . . . frills, or furbelows, perhaps? I have no idea what the correct term is—than one might see in London."

"I suppose he means more ruffles at the hem," Dorothea said to Julia. "Oh Julia, if you'd been there, you could describe every detail to me properly! I cannot picture how anyone looked from Stephen's description."

"Some dresses had more than just ruffles at the hem," Stephen forged on bravely, doing battle with the problem very diplomatically indeed, and Julia hid a smile at his kind attempts to please his sister. "There were some gowns with sparkling trims too. Glass beads, perhaps?" He put his hands on the shoulders of his military tunic. "Here," he said, "and here." Then he drew two fingers swiftly across his chest. The gesture looked more like a sword slash than the path an elegant fringe might take along the edge of a lady's bosom. "And at the floor as well. It clattered dreadfully when they walked or danced, making it sound like a herd of sheep was trotting across the marble floors on pointed hooves."

Julia hid her laughter behind her napkin. Dorothea nudged her knee under the table, and Julia knew she was enjoying her brother's torment.

"Sheep?" Dorothea said. "You are comparing the most elegant ladies in Europe to sheep? Oh, Stephen, how unchivalrous, and most undiplomatic!"

He blushed, his freshly shaven cheeks as scarlet as his jacket. "I did not say it to their faces! I am simply no expert on fashion." He ran a hand through his blond hair.

"Many ladies wore feathers in their hair, which made it rather difficult to see around them, and ticklish if one was not careful when he bowed to the lady's curtsy. I think some ladies dipped their heads intentionally to torment gentlemen with those feathers. Why, one chap in our party was stabbed in the eye with a particularly long bunch of peacock plumes, and had to retire for the evening to bathe his wound."

"Does that count as a battle scar, since he is in the service of his country?" Julia asked.

Stephen sniffed indignantly. "It most certainly should."

"And what colors were the ladies wearing?" Dorothea forged ahead. "Was one color more popular than the rest? Who wore the most shocking color?"

Stephen's throat bobbed, and Julia noticed a thin sheen of perspiration on his forehead under his sister's merciless grilling. "Um—many colors. White, perhaps? Pink? With colored ribbons tied here—" He delicately indicated his ribs with manly hands, pinkies outstretched, and Dorothea nudged her again, hiding a smile, obviously enjoying teasing her brother so wickedly.

Julia felt a twinge of sympathy for the poor major. He would probably take his meals with the other gentlemen after this, and that would be a pity. If she could not see the events for herself, she was glad to have him to describe them. Stephen Ives was probably extremely eloquent when asked to describe a battle or a military maneuver.

"What did you eat for supper, my lord?" she asked, changing the subject to one more dear to a man's heart than feathers and frills.

He visibly relaxed. "Oh, there was chicken, and a wide assortment of pies—and snails done in garlic and butter," he said, his eyes twinkling as he embraced the topic. He held up a hand at Dorothea's grimace. "Snails are called escargot here, and they are quite delicious, as were the frog's legs—and there was a marvelous dish of apples in cinnamon and cream, and a selection of cheeses, and the cakes . . ." He rolled his eyes in rapture, looking at them with boyish delight.

Dorothea swatted her brother's arm gently. "Snails? You can remember how the snails were dressed for dinner, yet you cannot recall a single detail of how *people* were adorned?"

He grinned. "I wore my uniform, and so did many other gentleman. I can quote you the ranks and regiments present, if you wish."

"Yes, yes—*of course* you and every other military gentleman cut a dash as always, and the officers put the men in ordinary evening wear to shame, but what of the ladies' hair styles?" Dorothea demanded, nibbling on the corner of the same bit of toast she'd been worrying at for the past half hour. She hadn't touched the rest of her breakfast, Julia noted.

Stephen's smile fell once again, and he raised his hands above his head and wiggled his fingers like grass in the wind. "Tall," he said. "Tied up with, um, ribbons, a few with jewels?" He shot a pleading look at Julia as Dorothea sighed.

"You are dreadful, Stephen. Thanks to you, I have a picture in my mind of sheep wearing feathers on their heads and dancing with handsome officers in uniform," she quipped. "Why, I feel as I might have been there myself!"

Julia laughed before she could stop herself, and Stephen looked at her, trying not to laugh himself. "My sister is a great wit." He set his fork down carefully. "You will have to see for yourself, Doe, if my descriptions do not satisfy you. There is a performance at the opera tonight. It wouldn't be too taxing, and you could see firsthand what the ladies are wearing."

Dorothea's mirth faded. "No, I couldn't. You could take Julia."

Julia's throat closed in shock at the suggestion. It would hardly be proper for a diplomat to escort his sister's paid companion to an official event. Stephen Ives studied his fingers, and an awkward silence fell over the table.

"Was there anyone of particular note in attendance last night, my lord?" Julia asked hurriedly, to change the subject.

Stephen met her eyes, his relief evident, but all merriment gone. "The Duke of Wellington was there, of course. He was escorting Princess Pauline de Borghese, one of Napoleon's sisters. And of course King Louis was present, and our own Lord Castlereagh, His Majesty's foreign secretary and the ambassador who will represent us in Vienna."

Dorothea gave a shocked gasp. "Wellington and Borghese attended together? Can one defeat a lady's brother, throw him off his throne, and yet have the gall to woo his sister? They are both married!"

Julia wondered at Dorothea's reaction. The duke's affairs were well known, and had been a source of gleefully wicked gossip in London, as was Princess Pauline's scandalous conduct.

"I daresay His Grace is simply being polite," Stephen soothed. "It's useful to have friends, Doe, and we still must keep tabs on Napoleon, even if he says he's content on Elba. Perhaps Wellington is merely hoping to gain information from his sister."

"Or perhaps he is simply being gracious to our enemies now that we have vanquished them," Julia suggested. "The princess would require an escort of a rank equal to hers."

Stephen looked surprised. "A very diplomatic observation, Miss Leighton," he murmured.

Dorothea sniffed. "His Grace could not have chosen a woman more shockingly indiscreet! And what of his poor duchess? Kitty is a lovely person, even if she isn't as flamboyant as her husband."

Stephen smiled fondly at his sister. "Kitty is your friend, but I believe she is more accepting of her husband's behavior than you are, Doe. Best to leave it be." He got to his feet. "If you'll excuse me, I have work to see to. Miss Leighton, try to convince her to come to the opera tonight. You used to love the opera, Doe—"

Dorothea shrugged and picked at the edge of her napkin. "That was before," she murmured. "I loved it because Matthew enjoyed it so very much. It would be unbearable now."

Julia's heart went out to her. "We shall go shopping," she said cheerfully, "or have pattern books brought in to us, so we'll know exactly what to order to take to Vienna."

Stephen sent her a grateful smile as he left the room.

Julia read to Dorothea while the rest of their party went out that evening, Lord Stephen to see to his official duties at the opera, and the servants who could be spared to the taverns and the parties on the streets.

"Is there any laudanum?" Dorothea asked, lying on the bed with a cool cloth on her forehead. "It's so hot and my headache is unbearable."

"None," Julia said firmly. "But we have chamomile tea or some feverfew for your head."

Dorothea regarded her fiercely. "That's not medicine! I will never be able to rest. We must find a doctor, get some laudanum at once, I say."

Julia ignored the order and crossed the room to dip a

cloth in cool water. She bathed Dorothea's temples, but Dorothea snatched the kerchief and flung it aside peevishly. "It doesn't help!" she said.

Julia felt the pain of Dorothea's endless grief, but she could not give in. Dorothea was dependent on the drug, and Stephen feared it was making it impossible for his sister to recover from her loss. He had instructed Julia that Dorothea was forbidden to have any more laudanum.

Julia herself knew the harm it could do. Her own mother had slipped into the drug's dangerous embrace for weeks after James died. Laudanum dragged its victims into a sleepy twilight, where they lived without pain or emotion of any kind, only half alive. She knew that Stephen hoped good company and new places would replace Dorothea's craving for the drug and improve her spirits, but her longing for laudanum continued.

She remembered Dorothea as a young bride, vibrant and witty, her eyes bright, the life of every party she attended. Now she lay in the dark, dull, listless, and afraid. She rubbed Dorothea's wrists, anointed her temples with attar of roses, and wondered if she might resort to laudanum too, if she lost Jamie, or a beloved husband.

She would probably never marry now, or be any man's beloved. That was a pain and a pleasure that she would never know.

"I cannot rest!" Dorothea sobbed, clutching Julia's hand on a fierce grip.

"I'll open the window, let the cool air in," Julia said. "Try to sleep."

"No! Leave it closed. The air smells of sweat and garlic and piss, and the street is too noisy. I won't have the window open, d'you hear?" Dorothea said sharply, moving restively on the sheets.

"Then I shall read to you," Julia said calmly.

Gradually, as Julia read, Dorothea drifted off. She moaned in her sleep, her brow furrowed as her ghosts haunted her.

At last the clock struck eleven, and the door opened with a soft creak. Dorothea's maid tiptoed in, back from her night out. "I'll keep an eye on her now. You get some sleep," she said kindly, and Julia went to her own rooms, and opened the door of the small antechamber where her son slept in a cot near his nurse.

He opened his eyes and smiled at her, waving his arms to be lifted, and she picked him up and crossed to open the window, letting the cool night air flow over them both. There were fireworks bursting in the sky above they city, great blossoms of red and yellow, and she watched the colors reflecting in the baby's wide eyes and against his soft flesh. He reached out a chubby hand, and she smiled and kissed the soft curls on his head.

Jamie was her whole world. She had lost everything but gained her son, and he was enough.

She hugged him tightly, and he made a soft exclamation, his fingers coiling in her hair. She kissed him again, breathed him in. She would devote herself to him, be father, mother, and friend, protect him with her life if she had to. On days when she wanted to break down and cry for all she'd lost, she had Jamie to console her, the miracle—never the mistake.

She gazed up at the fireworks. Where was Thomas Merritt now? Far from here, no doubt, unaware that he had a son. He'd probably forgotten *her* altogether. Jamie cooed as a new burst of scarlet petals filled the sky, and Julia smiled down at him.

He was her son, and no one else's.

The coach came to a stop on a hill just outside Paris as the fireworks began.

Donovan whistled as he looked out the window. "Look at that!" he said, staring at the colored lights bursting over the dark city. "We should have stayed an extra day or two, had some fun."

Thomas barely glanced at the sky. He wasn't interested. He wanted to be gone from the city, on the way to somewhere new, someplace that might offer him—well, whatever it was his restless soul was looking for. Even he didn't know. He was beginning to fear he'd spend his life wandering aimlessly from place to place, never finding a home. It made him angry, irritable.

"We have work to do," he said to Donovan. "And if we want a decent place to stay in Vienna, we'd best get there before everyone else."

"I know, I know," Donovan sighed. "The longer we wait, the more a place to stay will cost, if you can't find a landlady to charm into letting us stay for free."

Thomas knocked on the ceiling of the coach. But the coach didn't move. The coachman was probably watching the fireworks, couldn't hear over the booms and whistles. "We will need to appear to be entirely respectable and start forming social connections as soon as we arrive, make friends, earn the trust of people who count, and they'll provide us invitations to the best parties, the finest balls."

"And access to the best jewels," Donovan added eagerly. "To be delicately plucked from the prettiest necks, wrists, and earlobes."

Thomas glanced at the grinning face of his valet, glowing devilish red for a moment in the light of the fireworks. Donovan was starting to enjoy this life. He liked stealing from the rich who had been his masters all his life. For Thomas, it was a matter of survival and nothing more, but Donovan was in danger.

"Once we are done in Vienna, we'll both find a quieter life," Thomas said firmly. He would take just enough to send Donovan home, then he'd gather the last shreds of his honor and dignity and face what was left of the ruins of his own life, make some decisions.

Vienna was simply one last, great chance to make his fortune by stealing it. He tried to see it as revenge—since that's what made it necessary for him to stoop to stealing in the first place—revenge on his brother, his duplicitous sister-in-law, the society that shunned him without bothering to ask for his side of the tale. But revenge didn't make this life any more palatable. Of course, if his brother were here at this very moment, with their father's gold watch in hand, the familiar ruby pin in his cravat, his signet ring on his finger, and his duplicitous wife with him, draped in his mother's jewels, Thomas knew he wouldn't blink, wouldn't hesitate. He'd take it all, leave them naked and bleeding, the way they'd left him.

He knocked again, more forcefully this time, and the coach lurched grudgingly on, the driver's gaze torn from the fireworks as the last one fizzled over the silver ribbon of the Seine.

"Then are we to have no fun at all?" Donovan grumbled.

"Later," Thomas replied. "First, we make our fortune."

Chapter 7

Vienna, September 14, 1814

"Look, Dorothea, it's Vienna at last," Julia cried, struggling with the latch on the coach's dust-dimmed window.

But Dorothea was asleep, worn out by hours—weeks—of jolting over rough roads. She was pale and sweat had pasted her hair to her forehead. The dust kicked up by the horses had folded itself into creases in her skin, left a coating on her skirt and bonnet. Julia knew she looked every bit as travel-worn herself, and wished for a moment she had a mirror.

"Almost there," she murmured, and turned to stick her head out the window. They had been through five countries in a month, including France, Switzerland, Germany, Bavaria, and Austria. As much as Dorothea had hated the long hours of travel and the hardships of the road, Julia had loved them. She didn't miss England at all, while Dorothea constantly bemoaned the lack of English comforts, manners, and food. Julia had hidden her enthusiasm for Dorothea's sake, but she adored the dark forests of Germany, the glorious peaks of the Swiss Alps, and the ripe golden fields of France. The signs of twenty years of war had been visible too—deep scars across the landscape, burned villages, ruined manors. The people they passed on the road and met at the inns showed the ravages of war as well, their gazes narrow and suspicious as they watched the strangers pass.

The wayside inns had been rough places, the food coarse and unfamiliar, but the British ambassador, Lord Castlereagh, had been in a hurry to reach Geneva, where his wife Emily was waiting to join the delegation. Then, he wished to get to Vienna as quickly as possible, to set up his embassy and take the measure of the place before the conference officially began.

Dorothea had been terrified by the rumors of bandits on the roads, and insisted that Stephen give her a pistol, which he refused to do. He gave it to Julia instead, discreetly and out of Dorothea's sight, and she kept it in her reticule under the seat.

He showed her how to use the weapon while Dorothea napped one afternoon. "Not that we aren't as safe as could be, with a detachment of troops riding with us," he said. "I just don't want Doe to get so frightened she shoots a farmer, or Lord Castlereagh's valet."

"Aren't you worried that I might shoot someone by accident?" she'd asked.

"You hardly strike me as the nervous sort, Miss Leighton. Still, handle it with care, won't you?"

Since then she had only considered using the weapon once. Lord Castlereagh's infamous half brother, Lord Charles Stewart, joined the party with Lady Castlereagh at Geneva. He was a brash soldier who had fought bravely on the Peninsula with Wellington and was now officially in charge of the delegation's security, and other matters, which weren't discussed. Stephen introduced Lord Stewart to Dorothea, but Julia had noted that he was much more interested in *her*. She read the knowing look in Stewart's dark eyes, the way he smirked when he caught her eye. He'd been in London during her scandal, and of course he knew the gossip.

From that moment, she'd felt his eyes following her, had read speculation and obscene invitations in his gaze. She was careful to avoid him, kept her door locked and stayed away from Stewart as much as possible.

One morning as she was supervising the provisioning of Dorothea's coach, he caught her unawares. She turned a corner and nearly walked into his broad chest.

"Lord Stewart, I didn't see you there!" She'd gasped, her stomach rising into her throat as he caught her arms. Instinctively, she stepped back, and retreated right into the side of the coach, trapped.

"I've been wanting a word, my dear Julia," he said. He reached out a hand, drew his finger over her cheek. She turned away, felt sickness and fear rise in her throat. "I think we should become better acquainted, don't you?"

If she had still been an earl's daughter, he would not have dared to touch her, or to stand so close, or to make such a suggestion, but she no longer had the protection of a title, or even respectability. She fixed him with her best lady-of-the-manor glare, which once would have left him cowering. It had no effect at all now.

"I have duties to see to, my lord. I have very little free time to converse with—"

He laughed. "Oh, I'm not interested in conversation. I'm interested in visiting your room tonight—or you could come to mine if you prefer," he said boldly.

Fear turned to fury. She raised her chin, met his eyes. "Please excuse me at once," she said coldly.

"Of course, forgive me—you like to be seduced, don't you? You like a crowd nearby, the thrill of getting caught adds spice for you, doesn't it?"

She tried to push past him, but he blocked her way, put one hand on the side of the coach, gripped her jaw in the other, pushing his mouth against hers. She turned her head away from the obscene kiss, shoving at him, but he was like a rock, unmovable. He pressed against her, grinding his erection into her hip.

"No!" she said, shoving harder, using her fists to pound on his chest, swinging at his head. He laughed as he ducked the blow, caught her fist in his.

"There's no need to be like that. We both know you like it. Come now, lift your skirts for me." He pawed her breasts, thrust his hand between her legs. Panic seized her. She felt the pistol in her pocket and jammed it into his belly.

He looked down in surprise, then met her eyes, his lust extinguished. "What's that?" he asked, but she could see he knew exactly what it was.

She jabbed harder, and he grunted, then stepped back at last. "If you ever come near me again, I shall not hesitate to shoot you."

He forced a smile. "So you prefer it rough, do you? If you like games, I'm willing to play—"

"Julia?" Stephen came around the coach, his gaze swiveling between Julia and Lord Stewart. He took in the man's heavy breathing and her disheveled hair. "Doe is looking for you, *Miss Leighton*," he said sharply, his eyes hard, his suspicions about her clear.

Julia felt her skin heat. He hadn't seen the gun, had simply imagined that she would— Her anger flared again.

"If she is ready to go, the coach is prepared for her," she said drawing herself up. She felt the little pistol in her hand. She should shoot both of them for the insult, first Stewart, then Stephen bloody Ives. If she were a man—like James, for example—she could draw off her glove, call them both out with a slap, and defend her honor.

But she was only a woman, and a ruined woman at that, forever to be regarded with suspicion. She'd seen it in Lady Castlereagh's eyes, and even in the eyes of her ladyship's servants. She put the weapon back into her pocket and turned away, moving woodenly toward the inn to find Dorothea.

"Is there a problem, my lord?" she heard Stephen ask, his tone brittle.

She heard Lord Stewart laugh again. "Not at all. I was telling *Miss* Leighton how nice it is to have a pretty face on the journey," he drawled. "As I'm sure you've noticed yourself by now."

Julia pressed a hand to her hot cheek at the innuendo and kept walking.

After that she'd kept the pistol loaded and made certain she was never without a maid close by when she was not with Dorothea. She did not even glance at Lord Stewart when she was in his presence, but she felt his gaze crawling over her.

But now they were here, in Vienna, and Stewart was riding far ahead with his half brother, the ambassador.

She held her bonnet against the sluggish breeze and stared at the city, still distant, but close enough that the church spires were visible, floating above the golden cloud of dust. The channels of the River Danube wove through the landscape like dark ribbons. It was early afternoon and the sky was a clear and cloudless blue against the dusty earth. It was impossible not to feel joy.

She took a deep breath, trying to catch the perfume of the city itself, the signature scent of the place, but it was still too far away, and all she could smell was dust.

Stephen rode up alongside. "Vienna at last," he said, his eyes on the city. He had been cool and correct and distant since the incident at the inn, nearly silent during meals.

"How marvelous it looks," Julia replied.

"But the Danube isn't blue," he said. The wind blew a lock of fair hair over his forehead, making him look young and wistful as well as handsome on his tall black horse.

"No, it's more purple, perhaps, or even—" She bit her lip. *Indigo, like his eyes, as he shaded them against the sun.* Like Thomas Merritt's eyes had been by starlight, though they were gray in candlelight. She turned away to look at the river again.

"At least it isn't the greenish brown of the Thames," he finished for her, studying her face. Her cheeks were hot and she was sure she was blushing.

"A real bath," he murmured.

"Pardon?" She looked up at him in surprise, and wondered if she had dust on her cheeks. She resisted the urge to wipe her hand over her skin, but he smiled, the first genuine smile he'd given her in days. The thrill of arrival was contagious, it seemed.

"I mean that's what I'm looking forward to when this journey finally comes to an end."

She drew a breath. "Oh, yes. Dorothea will also be pleased to arrive. She has heard that Lady Castlereagh has insisted on bringing an English cook."

"She has indeed. What would you have him make for you?" Stephen asked.

Julia rolled her eyes. "Scones with clotted cream— though I hear that Vienna is famous for apple strudel and chocolate confections."

"So they say," he laughed. "Are you game to try the local delicacies, then?"

"I have heard the way to know a city best is to taste it." Once you knew it by sight and scent, of course.

"I think you may be right. Who could understand Paris without tasting the bread, or the chicken cooked with apples and garlic?"

"Or the snails," she teased, and wondered if she were being too forward. "And the cheese, and the butter," she continued quickly, aware that she was babbling. "Though English strawberries are much sweeter than the French ones."

He smiled at her as if they were meeting at tea, conversing as equals, and she was still an earl's daughter, a lady of consequence. She lowered her eyes. It was his training as a diplomat, she thought, to give the speaker his attention, encourage them to talk, while he remained cool and charming. She ran a hand over her cheek after all, felt the grit on her skin. Yes, a bath would be very nice indeed.

"I know Dorothea is looking forward to a good English breakfast," she said, "and a proper cup of tea made in a china pot."

"We shall do our best to give her all the comforts of London, but we'll have to encourage her to 'taste the city,' as you put it, to try new things while she's here. I wish she'd see this as you do, as an adventure. She has not enjoyed the journey."

"Not at all," Julia agreed. "But we're here at last, and no doubt she'll find things more pleasant when she is settled. I shall do all that I can to make her comfortable."

His smile faded and he nodded crisply, the moment of connection passed, and she was merely a servant once again, with responsibilities to see to. She drew her head in, focusing on Dorothea, who had yet to wake, and he rode on, spurring his horse to a gallop and disappearing in a cloud of dust.

Julia could not resist one more look at the distant city, which was coming closer by the minute. Her toes curled inside her half boots. Even if she must tread the careful path of a servant, she would savor every moment of her time in Vienna.

Chapter 8

"**C**an we afford such a grand place?"

Thomas smiled grimly at his manservant as they stared up at the facade of a fashionable town house by Vienna's city walls. "Can we afford *not* to take it? We will have the second floor. The top floor will probably be rented by another threadbare gentleman, or perhaps a pair of genteel ladies—maybe a mother looking for a rich husband for her daughter."

Donovan laughed. "Best be careful she doesn't snag you, imagining you've got money. Which, hopefully, you will have before our time here is done."

Thomas eyed the building's yellow and white facade. "Such a woman will be canny enough to know I am not wealthy enough for her purposes, or I would be at least two streets closer to the palaces where the ambassadors are lodging. Once the scramble begins for places to stay, we may find ourselves with a junior diplomat, or even a displaced lord who couldn't find better accommodations, living on the first floor."

"And how do you know all this?" Donovan marveled. "I wasn't aware you'd done the Grand Tour, or traveled widely, even before you were disowned."

Thomas set his top hat on his head. "I've been to Brighton at the height of the summer. Every mama with a marriageable daughter, every lord who needs a favor, is there to be close to the Prince Regent. Bath, I hear, is much the same. There are subtle clues to one's respectability based upon the street your lodging is in and the view your windows afford—of people, that is, not scenery. An eligible bachelor with money and a title learns to spot predatory mamas and hopeful debs early, and to identify the young ladies with rich dowries and high connections. The goal is to make a marriage and the best connections possible. It is a skill that has become inbred in the upper classes."

Donovan scratched his head. "What about looks? Don't they count? I wouldn't want an ugly wife."

"It doesn't matter what she looks like. It's the family she comes from, the lineage she will give to one's heirs, her dowry and lands, and the goodwill of her titled relations. Being lucky enough to find a beauty with all those characteristics is a rare thing indeed." David Temberlay came to mind as the exception to the rule—a man lucky enough to get dowry, connections, land, and a beautiful bride to boot.

Donovan still looked baffled. "The upper classes never fail to amaze me. No wonder there are so many ugly earls and hideous heirs to dukedoms, and it all just leads to more ugly brides, doesn't it?"

Thomas sighed. It would never be his problem now. "See to the trunks, Donovan, and try to look like a servant for the next ten minutes, will you?"

Donovan pulled his forelock sarcastically. "Aye, milord. And what shall I call you?"

Thomas considered. "Viscount Merritton should do."

"Until someone who knows you remembers you aren't a viscount anymore."

"I doubt my brother will be here to tell, and we won't be mixing with the British ambassador and his friends," Thomas said coldly, pulling on calfskin gloves and straightening his coat.

"You would still be a viscount, wouldn't you, if you'd spoken up properly, or let me do it."

Thomas tightened his lips. "We've had this discussion," he said in a bored tone.

"A lady's honor," Donovan sneered. "As if *she* deserved your regard." He growled. "She's a lying bill o' goods, that one, for all she's a countess."

Thomas ignored Donovan's indignation. It was too late for regrets. He'd made his choice. Even if he hadn't been guilty then, he was guilty of other seductions, other sins, both before and after Joanna.

"Let's go in," he said, dismissing the matter from his mind. From somewhere nearby, one of the grand bells in a grand Viennese church tolled the hour.

Chapter 9

⌒⌒✎⌒⌒

The palace on the Minoritenplatz had been chosen especially by the British ambassador for its strategic location in proximity to the residences of the other great powers. It was an elegant, sober edifice with a gray facade that brooked no nonsense from the more impressive palaces nearby. The offices of Prince Metternich, the Austrian foreign minister, were in the nearby Hofburg Palace, where Tsar Alexander had an entire floor at his disposal, as did the kings of France and Denmark. The king of Bavaria had taken over the Reichskanzlei, and the French ambassador, the wily Prince de Talleyrand, was directing French interests from the Kaunitz Palace. Their host, the Austrian emperor, presided over everything from the magnificent Schonbrunn Palace, located on the outskirts of the city and set in hundreds of acres of parkland. In fact, the entire city seemed to be set in a park, with trees and gardens everywhere.

"Isn't it beautiful?" Julia asked Dorothea as they explored the high-ceilinged rooms they would occupy on the palace's second floor. Plaster cherubs watched their arrival from the corners of the rooms with mischievous smiles, their chubby cheeks shining with gold leaf. Dorothea glanced up at them as she tested the mattress. "Far less intimidating than the gargoyles in Paris, at least." She made a face anyway. "They call this the Yellow Room. It is one of my least favorite colors."

"We can change the counterpane on the bed," Julia replied. "What color would you like?"

"Blue," Dorothea said. "My husband loved it." She smoothed her hand over the blue traveling dress she wore, as far from the half-mourning colors of gray and mauve as she ever strayed. "Best have the draperies changed as well. Where are your rooms, Julia? Close by, I hope."

"Of course. There is a sitting room between us, and a small dining room where we shall take our meals, but my bedroom is just along the hall."

Her room was done in soft shades of green, with a connected dressing room that would serve as nursery for Jamie.

She crossed to the windows in Dorothea's suite and opened them to let in the early fall breeze. There was a lovely view over the tiled roofs of the houses that squatted beneath the walls of the city's great palaces and churches, and the lovely parks beyond that. There were trees everywhere, making the city fresh and green. In a few weeks, if they were still here, the fall colors would be glorious.

She closed her eyes and took a breath. Vienna had a crisp, dry scent, with a hint of old roses and sugar, an elegant fragrance that suited the lovely city.

She turned at a knock on the door and crossed to open it to a procession of liveried male servants carrying Dorothea's luggage. "Please put the trunks in the dressing room," she directed. A maid was already there, setting out the small things, waiting to unpack the trunks.

"Well hello, sweetheart. Have you been assigned to these dull English ladies?" one of the porters boldly asked in German as he entered the dressing room.

"Hush, Hans. You must be more discreet!" the maid warned, casting a glance at Julia, giving her a flat imitation of a smile. "What if they speak German?"

Julia's senses warned her, and she gave no indication she understood them for the moment. In her time as a servant she had been surprised to find out just how outspoken those hired to serve were about their masters. They gossiped like the most expert *ton* cats and knew far more damaging secrets. She waited to hear what their Austrian servants had to say about the new arrivals. If the conversation grew too bold, she could reprimand them in German, but something told her this wasn't ordinary servants' gossip. Perhaps the quick, furtive glances they cast at the papers on the desk or the interest they took in Dorothea's trunks suggested they were more than mere footmen and maidservants.

"Why should I be careful?" Hans asked insolently. "Are these women important?" He turned to look at the crests on Dorothea's trunks.

"Well, they are not princesses or countesses or royalty, if that's what you mean," the maid sniffed. "I believe this lady is merely the sister of a mere assistant to the ambassador. This is quite a dull assignment for me. I was promised a post with a Russian princess." She sighed and ran a dismissive hand over the first trunk. "Ah well, perhaps I will unpack some elegant clothing or jewels of note, but I doubt it. These English do not know how to dress."

Hans chucked her under the chin. "You do not speak Russian, *liebchen*. You speak English, and you must keep your eyes and ears open. You never know what this lady might hear from her brother or his fellows and repeat while she is— What *do* English ladies do to pass the time between balls?"

"They embroider, I hear, or write long letters complaining of the food, the weather, and the local customs and saying how bored they are. Hans, I shall go mad with boredom myself!"

"Just do your job," he said dryly. "I shall be down-stairs, doing the same. If you hear anything of interest—" The maid giggled.

Julia had heard enough. With shaking fingers she opened the door fully. They spun to regard her with sharp eyes for a moment, then the porter bowed and the maid dipped a respectful curtsy.

"Can I help, madam?" she asked in accented English.

"Would you see that Lady Dorothea's own maid is sent up?" Julia asked in English. "Then you may go."

The Austrian girl reddened. "But she will need help with all the unpacking, and I have been assigned to assist you."

Julia stepped aside, brooking no arguments, and indicated the door. The maid could do nothing but bob another curtsy and go. The porters followed. Julia followed them to the door as they left, and listened.

"Do you think she understood what we were saying?" the maid asked breathlessly.

"Impossible," the first porter grunted. "English ladies do not speak German."

"Such an odd sounding language, don't you think?" Dorothea mused behind her, and Julia turned. "I wish I understood what they were saying. If they are to serve us, I suppose we must ask that they do their best to speak English, or there will be no communicating at all. I am glad I brought Ellie. She knows what I want without my even having to ask, and so do you, Julia. I'm so glad you're here."

Julia wondered if she should warn Dorothea to be careful of what she said. She glanced around the room, chilled by the idea there might be spy holes, or someone listening even now. The lovely palace suddenly felt sinister.

"Oh, Julia, my shawl!" Dorothea said, looking around her. "I must have left it downstairs in the salon when we arrived. It was a gift from Stephen, since all the ladies in Paris were wearing them. Can you go and find it?"

"Of course. Shall I order tea?" she asked.

"Yes, thank you," Dorothea replied, drifting toward the window. "And some biscuits, if they have them. Do you think they will?"

"Of course. The pastries in Vienna are famous." Julia smiled and slipped out the door.

The whole palace seemed alive with whispers and echoes as she reached the grand staircase. At the first click of her heel on the marble step, the sounds ceased. Icy fingers of unease climbed her back, and she felt unseen eyes watching her. She forced herself to keep her pace sedate, her expression placid, to hum a carefree tune as she descended the steps.

"Who is she?" an unseen German voice asked softly.

"No one important," was the ghostly reply.

She gave no indication she understood, or had even heard.

Julia was breathless by the time she reached the salon, where they had been welcomed with tea upon their arrival. She didn't knock—she grasped the brass handles and opened the elaborately painted doors that soared from floor to ceiling just wide enough to slip inside, then shut them behind her with relief, cutting off the whispers.

"I doubt the staff understand English, so we should be quite safe from eavesdroppers," a male voice said. "But we shall have to take precautions with our correspondence."

She watched in horror as Lord Castlereagh's eyes swung toward the door, his brows raised at her intrusion. He lanced her with a sharp stare.

"Lady Julia—Miss Leighton. Do come in," he said, recovering quickly, his expression becoming blank and correct, all emotion tamed and concealed. The two other men in the room rose to their feet.

To her horror, she recognized Lord Stewart. Stephen was the third gentleman. He was frowning at her unexpected appearance at what she realized was most certainly a private meeting. She colored at the appraising look Charles Stewart gave her. And surely Lord Castlereagh knew of her scandal as well, since he was an acquaintance of her father's.

She curtsied. "Please forgive my intrusion, my lords. Lady Dorothea has misplaced her shawl and wondered, perhaps, if she had left it here in the salon when we took tea with Lady Castlereagh. I had not expected the room to be occupied." She cast her eyes desperately around the room, saw the blue cashmere shawl on a distant chair.

The gentlemen waited silently as she crossed the room to retrieve it, following her with their eyes. Her footsteps on the soft carpet and the swish of her gown sounded like thunder in her ears. She felt her face heat.

Stephen picked up the shawl and tucked it into her hands "Settling in all right?" he asked quietly, his fingers brushing hers.

"Yes, thank you." She tightened her grip on the soft fabric and took a deep breath. "Please, my lord, I hope you won't think me forward, but I couldn't help overhearing your conversation," she whispered to him. "I believe the staff do indeed speak English. In fact, they understand everything we're saying." Stephen raised his brows in surprise, but she held his gaze. "I have overheard some of their comments to that effect since our arrival—"

"What's that?" Lord Stewart said loudly, approaching. "Did I hear you say the Austrian servants were speaking *English*?"

Julia resisted the urge to look around the room to search out the spy holes. Was that a mouse hole in the skirting board, or was there an ear pressed to the other side?

"No, they spoke in German," she said softly. "They assume we do not understand them, you see, and speak quite candidly about—"

Stephen's jaw dropped. "You speak German," he said. "As well as French?" She colored, but Lord Castlereagh came to her rescue.

"Lady Arabella Gray was your grandmother, was she not, my lady?" he asked.

She looked at Britain's foreign secretary, the head of the English delegation. He was a handsome man, and a brilliant if stubborn politician too, if her father's assessment of him was to be believed. He spoke little and almost never smiled. He wasn't smiling now, but there was a keen light of interest in his eyes.

"She was, my lord," Julia replied, squaring her shoulders.

"As in 'Ottoman' Gray?" Lord Stewart demanded, reddening. She had heard he was not a man who liked surprises of any kind. He was prone to tantrums if things did not go as he expected. She nodded again.

"Yes. Lord Gray set many of the diplomatic protocols we continue to use today, many, in fact, of the very ones we shall employ here in Vienna," Castlereagh mused. "I recall meeting Lady Gray, though she had remarried by then, to your grandfather, and was Countess of Carrindale. One of the most fascinating ladies I've ever had the pleasure to converse with." He was regarding her with interest, his gaze almost soft at the memory, though he remained a safe distance across the room, his hands clasped behind his back.

Julia gave him a genuine smile. "Thank you, my lord. She was an amazing storyteller."

"Did she teach you to speak German?" Lord Stewart demanded.

"She insisted upon hiring the governess who did."

"And do you speak other languages besides German and French?" Castlereagh asked.

"A little Italian," she said, feeling her skin heat under the stunned scrutiny of three gentlemen. "And a few words of Arabic." Very few indeed, and none repeatable in polite Arab company, but her grandmother thought a lady should be able to express herself with a suitable set of curses that no one else understood. It offered a discreet outlet for frustration. Julia bit her tongue and hoped she wouldn't be asked to repeat them here.

She looked around. Stephen Ives was staring at her as if meeting her for the first time. Lord Stewart was looking at her with narrow-eyed suspicion, and Lord Castlereagh was regarding her with a penetrating stare, as if the veracity of her claims was printed on the inside of her skull and he was reading them right through her skin.

She lowered her eyes. "If you'll excuse me, my lords, I shall return the shawl to Lady Dorothea."

"Thank you, Lady Julia," Lord Castlereagh said, using her title. She held her breath and waited for Stewart or Stephen to correct him, but they did not. "I look forward to speaking more about your grandmother. Perhaps over tea some afternoon?"

Julia curtsied, and the gentlemen bowed. She colored.

The respectful gesture surely was habit only, a mistake. They would not bow to a servant. She slipped out the door and fled up the stairs, followed once again by the dreadful whispers.

"Three languages?" Stewart whistled as the door closed. "Pity. But what would a girl do with an education like that, a mere maidservant? And even if she'd become a duchess—"

Lord Castlereagh put a finger to his lips.

"Perhaps it is to our advantage that she is not a duchess after all," he said quietly. "Nor is she a mere maidservant, Charles." He turned to Stephen. "We shall discuss this later, I think. In the meantime, please see that all the staff our hosts have kindly provided us with are replaced with our own people."

Chapter 10

Thomas entered the dark recesses of the rough tavern and looked around him, his nerves tensed, ready to fight if he had to. He was aware of the weight of the pistol in his pocket, the chill of the knife in his belt. Some of the patrons regarded him with open suspicion, some with no expression at all. The ones with sly smiles were the most dangerous ones—the kind who'd grin at you, take everything you had, and continue to look pleasant as they stuck a knife between your ribs. He took a table where he could keep his back to the wall.

He was here at Donovan's insistence, because his man-servant had said they needed to make connections of an entirely different sort than Thomas had described. They needed to know the people who ruled the underbelly of the city, who could help them profit from their visit. "We need to know where it's safe to sell stolen jewels," Donovan had told him. "I've heard the Austrian police have spies everywhere, thief-takers too."

"Who told you that?" Thomas asked.

"Does it matter?" Donovan had replied. "You bring me the jewels, let me worry about the rest. It's a dangerous place, and there's people just like you, upper class, who'll turn you in for the reward if they can. Doesn't matter to them where the profit comes from. This isn't London, or even Paris, where we can deal with Englishmen. We're foreigners here, and we'll have to be careful till we find the right connections on this end of things." He'd made a grisly face and drawn a finger across his throat to demonstrate his meaning, as if Thomas needed a demonstration. The warning was clear enough in the hooded gazes around him.

Now, Donovan was nursing a large stein of the local ale at the bar. Thomas ordered schnapps when the barmaid shuffled over to him, her eyes dull and disinterested.

He sipped his drink and tried to look like he was comfortable in such a place. He even forced himself to smile and nod at those staring at him. They did not return the gesture. He put his glass down. He was deuced uncomfortable and ready to leave. There must be another way.

Thomas glanced at Donovan, but his valet was staring at an elderly gentlewoman who had entered the tavern. Her clothes, once stylish and expensive, were now years out-of-date and shabby. The only finery she wore was a simple gold cross around her wrinkled neck. It was studded with three tiny pearls and a minuscule garnet, worth very little to anyone but her.

Thomas looked at his manservant again, and his stomach tensed with distaste as he read the avarice in Donovan's eyes, saw him mentally calculating the value of the necklace the way he assessed the price of the jewels Thomas brought home. Thomas looked at the necklace again. It wasn't worth more than a few Austrian shillings, which would buy nothing more than a loaf of bread or a bottle of passable wine.

He watched the old lady preen, stroke the necklace with her fingertip, like a talisman. To her, it was priceless. He glanced around the room, hoping she'd come to meet someone, had a protector of some kind. There were a number of people staring at her, their expressions a mirror of Donovan's. It would be easy to take the necklace from her and everyone in the tavern knew it, except for the lady herself, apparently, or she would have worn it inside her clothing, kept it hidden.

Donovan caught his attention and jerked his head toward the woman. Did he really expect Thomas would be willing to charm her, steal from her? He wasn't sure which of them was the most pathetic—himself, Donovan, or the old woman who trusted that the Christian symbol would protect her in this hellhole.

Thomas's stomach turned. Had he really come to this, stealing from those who could least afford to lose? He got to his feet so suddenly that every eye in the place turned on him. He picked up his hat and strode out, aware that Donovan was staring at him, incredulous. He didn't draw a breath until he was outside, moving swiftly down the street.

"What's wrong? Did you see something?" Donovan asked, catching up, looking back over his shoulder nervously.

"Nothing," Thomas growled.

"Looked to me like there were a few useful coves in there, should we have need of them," Donovan said.

"No."

"No?"

Thomas stopped walking, and Donovan took a few more paces before he realized it. "Would you have taken her necklace?" Thomas demanded.

Donovan grinned. "The old woman? Aye, maybe, for a bit of practice."

"But what of *her*, Donovan? Did you look at her?"

"Too old to seduce, if that's what you mean." His face hardened. "She should stay out of such places if she wants to keep her jewelry."

Thomas shut his eyes and wondered what the necklace meant to her. Perhaps it was a memento of happier times, the one thing she could not bear to pawn or sell, or the last thing she had to save her if she did have to sell it.

"There are other ways," he said, looking at Donovan as if seeing him for the first time. Once, he'd been a respectable young man, a servant who worked his way up from footman to valet, held himself and others in high esteem. What the hell had happened? Thomas felt a pang of guilt. *He'd* happened. Donovan had wanted to stand by him, even knowing the truth, proud of the fact that even under impossible circumstances, Thomas had acted with honor. He realized he hadn't seen admiration in his valet's eyes for a very long time. Did either of them have any honor left?

Donovan's puzzled expression suddenly cleared and he grinned. "Oh, I understand. You want to do it *honorably*, remain a gentleman."

Yes, Thomas thought, hope surging.

"There are richer folks, with better jewels, right?"

Hope sank to the cobbles and died. *No.* He felt helpless. How else could they survive, make their way out of this life? *Would* it be easier to take advantage—steal—from someone who could better afford to lose their jewels? What of gems that had been in a family for generations and were irreplaceable? Why did that bother him now? He'd taken his share of his mother's jewels when he left, sold them without a qualm, relishing the revenge, knowing Joanna would not dare to report them stolen.

The ability to steal without qualms had ended with Julia Leighton. He pictured her at the ball, glittering under the weight of her mother's heirloom jewelry. He hadn't been able to take them from her, not then, and not after he realized what he'd done. She was more than the jewels. She was a creature of grace. She had not blamed him for what happened between them. She had let him go with dignity, though he'd taken the most valuable jewel of all. Since that night, he hadn't been able to steal anything without a twinge of conscience. He found himself hesitating more and more often, wondering what the jewels meant to the lady who wore them.

For some women, jewels simply marked them as their husband's possession. They were badges of ownership, and if lost, the lady faced the wrath of the giver. Like Joanna, and like Julia's father.

Some—the luckiest ones—wore jewels given to them with love. Those jewels were part of who the lady was, something she wore often, whether it matched her outfit or not, because it was a symbol of a deep emotion. If lost, the sentiment would forever remain, and the missing jewel thought of merely with regret.

And there were, of course, women who wore jewels they had earned. They let their gazes flick over the necklaces and diamond bracelets of other females, calculating the worth of those gems compared to their own, imagining what their rivals had done for such a prize. Those jewels served as surety for a comfortable old age.

And which of these women deserved most to be preyed upon, to lose her jewels to a man like him?

"The Emperor's ball is next week," Donovan was saying, rubbing his hands together. "Aye, that's it—just a few big stones, some really fine ones, and we'll be set. All we need are the invitations, and I've no doubt you can arrange those. I'll find the buyer."

A few big stones—perhaps a ruby or two, or an emerald,

or a diamond of flawless quality. The kings and queens of Europe were all here, with their jewels. State jewels, not personal ones. It would make it easier, wouldn't it? And he'd become good at it. His victims never knew until he was long gone. How many times had a lady accused her maid of losing a precious earring, or blamed her for not noticing that the clasp of a bracelet was loose? And all the time it was him.

Viscount Merritton had become Tom the Thief.

And yet, a few big stones, as Donovan put it, and he'd be back among the class he was born to, the gentle folk. Respectable again.

Except he wasn't one of them anymore.

Chapter 11

Stephen found Julia in the garden. Actually, he heard her laughing before he saw her.

She was sitting on the grass playing with her son, her face rapt and loving. It was for this very reason that he had objected, as diplomatically as he could, to Castlereagh's suggestion. But the future of Europe, the prestige of England, hung in the balance, and under those ponderous circumstances there was little he could do.

The child's nurse looked up, catching sight of him before Julia did. Stephen waited, cringing a little inside as she alerted Julia, loath to interrupt such a happy scene.

Julia looked up at him, her eyes wide, lips forming an *Oh* of surprise, her face flushing as she picked up the child and rose from the grass.

Stephen's breath caught in his chest. The autumn day was mild, and Julia glowed in the warmth of the late afternoon sun. She was embarrassed at being caught playing in the garden, and her blush put the late blooming roses to shame. She rested the child on her slim hip and waited for him to traverse the cinder path to reach her.

He recalled how Doe had carried her child like that, smiled at him with the same maternal love, made a beautiful mother just like Julia did. He glanced at Julia's boy, who had turned to watch him approach, trying again to recognize the child's father in the round baby features, but he looked like every other infant, and most especially like the plaster cherubs that adorned every single corner, doorway, and pillar inside the palace.

Julia kissed the baby's forehead and handed him to his nurse.

"I wish to speak to you," Stephen said, more crisply than he'd intended, all too aware that he was interrupting. He stopped a short distance from her and folded his hands behind his back as the nurse strolled along the path with the child.

Julia folded her hands at her waist. "I am sorry for intruding on your meeting, my lord. I didn't think the room was occupied. I assure you it will not happen again."

She thought he'd come to reprimand her. He unclasped his hands and waited until the maid had moved out of earshot. "You didn't tell me you spoke so many languages," he said, and realized he sounded peevish now. He smiled, but it felt like a grimace.

She caught her lower lip in her teeth. "I didn't think it was important."

"Not in London, perhaps." Or for an earl's daughter, or a duchess. "But here, well . . ." He straightened his shoulders. "You see, a peace conference is a delicate thing. Knowledge is power and leverage. Do you understand what I mean?" He could see she did. She was clever. And beautiful—though he tried to ignore that—and she was Arabella Gray's granddaughter. He rattled on. "Part of our diplomatic mission here in Vienna includes doing our best to gather knowledge of what the other delegates want, so we know ahead of time how they will vote on an issue we hold dear, and if they might be convinced to change their vote if it does not fit with ours." He waited to see if she understood.

"I see," she murmured.

"In the next few weeks there will be a great many private meetings before and after the public ones. Forming alliances in peace talks, I daresay, is nearly as important as having allies in war. More so, since we cannot simply shoot those whose opinions we do not like." He was babbling, but how did one ask a lady to be a spy? Lord Castlereagh imagined it would be a simple matter of appealing to her sense of patriotism. Lord Stewart, who was in charge of such unsavory things as espionage, had simply wanted to order her to do it. Stephen had suggested he might speak to her more gently, convince her to offer to help them.

He met her eyes, hoping to see understanding in their hazel depths, but she was studying her fingertips.

"I do understand your concern, my lord, and as I have said, I will be certain to knock before entering a room from now on, but you may be assured of my discretion."

His stomach fell to the cinder path. He hadn't been clear at all.

"Our letters will be intercepted and read," he said.

She smiled tentatively. "I have no one to write to, and I do not keep a diary."

"Our conversations will be monitored, reported—"

She looked around the garden in alarm, but the paths were empty, except for the nurse and baby some way off. As she turned, he noticed the way the sunlight played on her dark hair, lighting strands of gold and copper, and the delicate bones of her jaw, the muscles of her neck. She was so slender, so delicate, a lady, not a hardened spy, no matter what stories her grandmother had raised her on or what deeds Charles Stewart thought her capable of. Moreover, as his own employee, she was under his protection.

"There wouldn't be any danger." She turned to look at him, her brows flying toward her hairline like frightened birds, and he realized he'd spoken aloud, though he hadn't meant to. He was a diplomat, a man of words, yet Julia Leighton, this whole situation, made him feel tongue-tied.

"Danger?" she gasped.

"I—We'd—like you to help, as a kind of listener," he said. "If others are listening to us, then we must also have eyes and ears, and since you speak so many languages—"

"Me?" she said. "But I'm not . . ." She paused, shut her eyes. "I am merely a servant. There must be better people to assist with such things, people who are trained, or better suited to—"

He held up a hand to stop her. "We need you to be more than a servant—which you are, of course. You were—are—an earl's daughter . . ."

She shook her head, her expression closing. "What if someone recognized me, *knew*? I cannot—"

"Every diplomat in Vienna has a hostess. Tsar Alexander has Countess Sagan, for instance. She holds salons and parties, charms Austria's foreign minister, Lord Metternich, flirts with him, and she offers an ear to anyone who might wish to confide in her. Lord Talleyrand has his niece here for the same purpose. She is young, pretty, charming—"

"And we have Lady Castlereagh."

He made a face, and immediately smoothed his expression. "Yes, of course, but she is as taciturn as her husband, and slightly deaf. Her salons promise to be dull affairs, all whist and small glasses of sherry, with only the most superficial and banal conversation—not the kind of event likely to embolden people to make the sort of indiscreet comments we can use. You wouldn't be a hostess, of course. Lady Castlereagh would never—"

She turned as scarlet as the autumn leaves. "She's quite correct. My . . . notoriety . . . would not serve you well. It may work against you, if the truth was discovered," she said carefully. "There are people here who know me, know my father."

It was becoming increasingly difficult for him to look at Julia Leighton and see a ruined woman. "His lordship thought you might say that. Yet Countess Sagan is a married woman, and is known to have any number of lovers. Quite scandalous, but her salon is one of the most widely attended."

She looked at him fiercely. "I am not interested in taking 'any number of lovers,' my lord. If I have given that impression, then I can only say you are grievously mistaken."

He felt himself blush, and ran a finger around the collar of his tunic. "I am not explaining myself very well at all." He caught her hands, held them in his. "We—I—would never ask you to compromise yourself in such a way. You are my sister's companion, and as such, you are under my protection. Every maid, every coachman, every waiter, and footman in town—save our own, of course—reports to the Austrian emperor. We have you to thank for the fact that our conversations will remain private. But you must understand that no one in Vienna goes completely unobserved. We simply want you to listen to conversations in crowds, at parties, at the theater with Doe, and tell us what you hear. As Doe's companion, you will be able to attend official functions as part of our delegation. The French, the Austrians, the Russians will also attend the same balls and parties, and in such a relaxed atmosphere, who knows what confessions might come out, in French or German or even Arabic?"

She blushed. "I haven't a suitable gown to wear."

"I—We—will take care of that."

"And Dorothea—"

"Will be fine. It will do her good to get out and attend parties again. I shall insist."

She withdrew her hands from his, stood back, staring down the path in the direction the nurse had gone with her son. "How will I know what's important? What would you like me to report on?"

"Somehow, I think you'll know, just the way you knew it was important to report that the servants understood our conversations. I trust your judgment. Just tell us everything."

Chapter 12

The lady's light laughter floated across the park on the breeze, making heads turn. "Flatterer!" she said, swatting Thomas playfully.

The park, located in the center of Vienna, amid the grand palaces and official embassy residences, was the perfect place to watch royalty promenade, or to be noticed yourself. Today, the paths and manicured gardens were filled with people out enjoying the lovely fall weather, including Thomas and the lovely Russian princess Katerina Kostova.

The princess wore red from head to toe, from her jaunty feathered hat to her handmade and lavishly embroidered red leather boots. If her red velvet habit and the gold lace tassels on her fox fur muff were not eye-catching enough, her beauty and her lavish jewelry alone would have caused heads to turn, but she made the most of his compliment by laughing out loud, making heads swivel, garnering the admiring glances of a dozen other gentlemen besides Thomas.

He didn't mind. People were looking at him too, wondering who he might be and what special charms he possessed to have the lovely Russian princess hugging his arm and gazing up at him with playful adoration.

"It's not idle flattery in the least," he insisted with a rakish grin. "Look around you. Every other woman in the park today is wrapped against the wind, wearing dull woolens and warm hoods. It is impossible to see the glory of *their* hair, or their faces." He touched a gloved fingertip to her upturned nose. "Of course, the wind has probably reddened their noses and made their eyes water, so it's for the best, but not you—you put the autumn leaves to shame, grace the park with your beauty and live to enjoy the weather."

The lady cast her stunning blue gaze around the park, checking to see if his assessment of the other ladies was true. She smiled when she saw he was in earnest, and took a deep breath of the crisp fall air, expanding her lungs, and filling her red jacket to eye-popping proportions. "The weather is not cold at all! It is warm to me, but I am Russian, and we love the cold."

"Have you a choice?" Thomas quipped, and she laughed again.

She leaned in closer, her breast resting on his forearm. "You do not know the glories of a Russian winter, my dear viscount. Have you ever made love on a winter evening on a bed of soft fur?"

He gave her a slow grin. "Not yet." He cast his eyes over her as she laughed, from the huge brooch that adorned her hat—a pheasant with ruby eyes, a vast pearl for a breast, and feathers of rubies, diamonds, and emeralds—to the jeweled tassels on her boots.

She was the wife of a great Russian general, nobly born, and she was reputed to be one of Tsar Alexander's many lovers. Since both general and Tsar were busy, she was looking for distraction. She wore a fortune in jewels wherever she went, and rumor said that she'd brought a bag of diamonds to Vienna simply to use for wagering at the card tables.

"You amuse me," she purred. "Attend my salon this evening." She made it a command.

"Of course," he murmured. People begged for invitations to Princess Kostova's salons. He held his smile, comparing her, as had become his habit with women, to Julia Leighton. He had to learn not to do that, since he was most unlikely to ever see Lady Julia again. He pushed the image of her just-kissed face away and concentrated on the princess. She wore the heavy fragrance of gardenia like another garment. It entered a room before she did, announced her arrival, filled any space she inhabited, and insisted people look at her. The heady scent lingered long after she was gone. There was nothing subtle about her perfume, but it suited her well, he thought.

"I shall send my carriage for you at eight o'clock."

He pretended to be surprised. "But your salon does not begin until midnight."

"Then we shall have to find ways to amuse ourselves, *non*?" she said with a wanton smile.

"I shall bring a pack of cards," he suggested, and her laughter rang out again.

A dozen pairs of eyes turned to see who had amused the princess so. And a dozen people sent servants running to discover the handsome gentleman's name.

Chapter 13

Julia's stomach tied itself in knots as she entered the Hofburg's magnificent ballroom—one of three massive rooms being used for tonight's ball. The room was dazzling. Thousands of candles hung in crystal chandeliers high above the floor, their light reflecting off white and gilt walls. A king's ransom in jewels filled the room with colored stars as the ladies who wore them caught the light whenever they laughed, or danced, or waved their hands. It was breathtaking.

She stood at the top of the stairs and waited while the majordomo announced the most important members of the British delegation, Lord and Lady Castlereagh, Lord and Lady Stewart, Major Lord Ives and Lady Dorothea Hallam. As a servant, her name was not announced, and the majordomo gave her little more than an impatient glance before taking the invitation of the Bavarian ambassador behind her, next in a long line of important guests waiting to enter.

As she descended the steps behind Dorothea, she scanned the room for Thomas Merritt, the way she did in every crowd, but as usual he wasn't here. How foolish. Why would he be? Would he recognize her if he was?

Probably not. She didn't look anything like she had at her betrothal ball. Her gown tonight was simple blue muslin, borrowed from Dorothea, with a bit of lace and a ribbon sash hastily added to make it suitable for such a grand event. Unlike her betrothal ball, she wore no jewels at all aside from a simple pair of garnet earrings she'd had since her sixteenth birthday. Not as eye-catching as the Carrindale diamonds, but they were hers. Perhaps she would give them the grand title of the Julia Garnets. She tossed her head a little, wondering if they cast a sparkle, but no one looked her way. She was simply an anonymous servant, and no one bothered to look at servants. She was once considered one of the prettiest girls in the *ton*. She would have been much courted if she hadn't been betrothed to David. Having made her curtsy to the queen at seventeen, she was allowed to attend the parties and balls that Season, but aside from general admiration and a desire to make the acquaintance of the future Duchess of Temberlay, no one had ever flirted with her.

Until Thomas Merritt.

Would he flirt with her now, a mere servant, if he were here? Of course not. She tilted her chin higher. She was not the same silly girl she'd been then. She was a grown woman, a servant, a mother.

And a spy.

She smoothed a hand over her borrowed gown and willed her stomach to drop back to the place it belonged, so she could breathe. She didn't know where to put her eyes, who to look at among the hundreds—thousands—of people who filled the vast room. She heard snatches of German, French, English, and Italian among the banal banter that passed for conversation at any ball, but surely such ordinary talk would be of little interest to anyone. She stopped where she was, looked around. Where should she begin? How?

Stephen looked back over his shoulder and caught her arm with a smile, guiding her along with Dorothea through the crush to a row of chairs beside the dance floor.

"There is so much chatter that I can barely hear the music," Dorothea said, almost yelling to be heard above the din.

Julia swallowed. How was she to listen to private conversations in such a place? The dancing began, and the sibilant swish of silk, the clink of dress swords, the hiss of dancing slippers on the wooden floor added to the cacophony. Dorothea grasped her arm and leaned toward Stephen. "Look, on the dais—Stephen, who are they?"

"The Empress of Austria and the Russian tsarina are seated in front, and behind them are the Queen of Bavaria and the Tsar's sister, Grand Duchess Catherine."

"I have never seen anything so magnificent," Dorothea said, taking in the glitter of the state jewels and the lavish elegance of their gowns. Golden cloth shone, sliver thread sparkled, tiaras and diadems sent out beams of light as each lady sought to outdo her fellow monarchs. Julia wondered if it would be fair to single out just one as the most glorious lady among the group. This was a peace conference, after all. She wondered if the glittering orders they wore pinned to their bosoms were military, tokens of war, reminders of their nation's prowess against Napoleon. Lady Castlereagh was wearing her husband's diamond Order of the Garter Star in her hair, like a kind of tiara.

Stephen leaned close to Dorothea. "I met the Grand Duchess Catherine last spring, when she visited London with the Tsar, do you remember?"

Dorothea's gaze clouded and her blue eyes turned vague, then filled with pain. "Last spring—" she began, her hand coming to her throat. "I don't remember last spring."

Julia squeezed her hand, glanced at Stephen and read concern tinged with impatience in his gaze.

"Look there, Doe," he said, distracting her from her anxiety. "That's the Princess Esterhazy. I overheard someone say her gown alone is worth six million francs, and the value of her jewels is incalculable."

He'd *overheard* it? How, in such a noisy place? When? Julia frowned. Would she be able to do this job after all? She followed his gaze to the princess. She sparkled from head to toe. Most of the eyes in the room were fixed on her.

Julia looked around her at the other dignitaries present. The papal delegate was recognizable by his scarlet robes. The bearded gentleman in the turban, his ears, fingers, and caftan dripping with gems, must be the representative of the Ottoman sultan.

There were surely a thousand people in her line of sight, all dressed in a hundred different uniforms, or wearing elegant evening clothes studded with honors and orders. Everyone seemed to be whispering in someone else's ear. Were these the secrets they wished her to overhear?

She imagined sneaking up behind people, leaning over their shoulders, pressing her ear into the conversation while trying to appear inconspicuous.

"Do you think Napoleon's empress is here tonight?" Dorothea asked. "I hear that Marie Louise did not join her husband on Elba as she promised, but came home to Vienna at her father's insistence."

"Where did you hear that?" Stephen asked. "I thought you hadn't been out, Doe."

"It was in the park the other day. Julia insisted we must sample the air." He shot a look at her, sending Julia a conspirator's smile as Dorothea rambled on. "There were some people talking, that's all. It is nearly as noisy there as it is here tonight, but I must say the paths are lovely in Vienna, especially at this time of year. Much nicer than Hyde Park," she mused. "Remember how I used to love the gardens at Matthew's estate? And it used to be said that I have an ear for the best gossip. There is no shortage of it here. One promenades in the park, looks at others, and is looked at in return. The social order is rather muddled at the moment, I think, but it will soon sort itself out into the right kind of people"—she counted the rest on her fingers—"followed by those who will serve to amuse the right kind of people, and lastly, everyone else." Her hand fluttered like a bird and landed on her lap. "Just like London."

Stephen smiled at his sister. "And which are we?"

"Oh, the right kind, of course, though rather invisible. We will do to speak to if no one of better pedigree arrives."

"Just like London," Julia repeated again, and Dorothea gave her a wan smile.

"Exactly."

He glanced from Dorothea to Julia. "Is English society truly this complicated?"

"Yes," they said at the same moment, and giggled.

"Then I stand corrected on thinking the English are a simple race—I thought if you gave us good beef, a few hundred acres of prime land, an heir, and an income over a thousand pounds, that we would be content. It appears not." He sketched a mocking bow. "Since I am standing, corrected or otherwise, would you care to dance, Doe?" he asked, bowing low and presenting his hand.

Dorothea drew back and ran a hand over her lavender half-mourning gown. "No, but you might ask Julia." She gave an exasperated sigh when he hesitated. "Come now, we both know Julia is not really a servant. She is as much a lady as I am, and I'm sure she waltzes better than any other woman here."

"I doubt the Austrian empress—or any other Austrian lady for that matter—would agree with you," Julia said to break the tension, but Stephen was looking at her, his eyes unreadable. Her stomach tensed again. "Since the Austrians invented the waltz, I mean," she finished lamely.

"Shall we try to outdo them?" He extended a gloved hand to her, and she stared at it for a moment before taking it. Was it proper, a servant dancing with her employer, a fallen woman waltzing with a diplomat? She let him lead her out, aware of the heat of his arm beneath her hand, staring at the scarlet dress tunic he wore. Was there a man born who was not more handsome when dressed in a military tunic? She had been unable to see James as a boy any longer, as merely her brother, when he donned his uniform. He'd been transformed into a hero, and Stephen Ives was every bit as handsome. Any lady would be proud to be seen on his arm.

He set his hand on her waist, his touch warm through her gown, and expertly spun her across the floor as the music began. She'd almost forgotten how very much she loved to dance.

She tried not to think of the last time she'd waltzed—the only other time in her life. Stephen was not quite as tall as Thomas Merritt, and he moved with graceful, dignified restraint, where Thomas had been more flamboyant, making her breathless—

"Tell me who is important," she said, her eyes darting over his shoulder, taking in the crowds. "Where should I begin? Did you say there are two other ballrooms filled with just as many people as this one tonight?"

He smiled down at her, his eyes creasing at the corners. "Yes. They had to open two more large reception rooms and the Spanish Riding School as well to accommodate everyone. Now let's see who's here." He looked around the room as she had. "Ah, there's Baron von Geritz, behind you. He's a minor secretary from Bavaria. He enjoys schnapps and champagne, and he likes to flirt with women far younger than himself. He thinks he is far more important than he is," Stephen said lightly. "If he knows anything important, he will crow it to anyone who'll listen."

"Then it won't be a secret," Julia said, discounting the baron. "Do you remember Viscount Reedsdale?" she asked, watching the Bavarian secretary strut before a young lady.

Stephen nodded. "Of course. He was a fixture at every hostess's party, wasn't he?"

"Yes. And he was exactly like the baron—he liked to pinch young ladies in dark corners at parties. My mother warned me about him before my debut, but he supported the same issues as my father did in Parliament, so I was advised to be charming and sweet, but to stay out of the corners at all costs."

"Then you already know how to play this game," Stephen said.

Did she? She had learned who to cultivate and who to avoid as a debutante, hadn't she? She hadn't put a foot wrong until she flirted with Thomas, let him take her into those forbidden dark corners. She stiffened at the memory, stumbled a little, and Stephen righted her, swept her onward. She forced a smile. She had learned her lesson, and would never make a mistake like Thomas Merritt again. So, she thought, relaxing a little, perhaps she knew how to proceed after all.

"There's the Prince de Ligne," Stephen said. "He is an aristocrat of the old world, a soldier, courtier, and bon vivant. He's charming, witty, and he loves to gossip. Mind you, at his age some of that gossip is fifty years out of date, but still fascinating. He is most worth knowing. Shall I introduce you?"

She regarded the prince, wearing a powdered wig and a silk coat two decades out of style, but he was speaking with a lady who seemed delighted with his company. Her laugh rang out like the tinkle of crystal.

She smiled at Stephen. "Perhaps you could waltz me past him now and I could contrive to lose my slipper at his feet. As a gentleman, he would have no choice but to return it, and beg an introduction."

Stephen tilted his head, his gaze admiring. "You play this game well, Julia."

She felt her heart swell at the praise, and realized she was enjoying the evening.

Thomas Merritt bought a forged invitation to the grand ball—one of hundreds that were circulating in the city—and slipped in late. The room glittered, all sharp edges and brilliant lights that made his eyes hurt. Every lady present was dripping with jewels, glamorous in satin and lace, each trying to outdo the others, more for the sake of feminine pride than patriotism. The miasma of a hundred perfumes mingled with the odors of sweat, pomade, and shoe black.

He leaned on a pillar and looked around. What would these grand people say if they knew they were mingling with pirates, thieves, and con men who had slipped in with false credentials and stolen invitations?

He thought of the last ball he had attended in London. He hadn't been invited to that affair either. Julia Leighton's betrothal ball had been a polite, elegant party, unlike this frantic circus, but he'd attended for the same purpose he was here tonight—to steal a fortune. Instead, he had lost his heart.

Or very nearly.

He looked around the room, seeking her, but she wasn't here, of course. She was probably tucked away at one of Temberlay's country estates, playing the perfect wife, embroidering a sampler of the ducal crest by the hearth.

He straightened his cuffs—new, and of the best linen this time, and pushed the thoughts of Julia out of his mind, concentrating on the swirling crowd, looking for a place to dive in, a friendly face, a lonely lady, but the room spun in an impenetrable wall of gaiety. He took a glass of champagne from a passing footman, then another, and stood back to watch. Faces blurred. Every woman was Julia, smiling and lovely, and every gentleman became his brother, sour and superior. He set his glass down on the nearest table and turned away. Perhaps he had made a mistake in coming here tonight.

"Not in the mood to dance?" a thick German accent asked, not unpleasantly, at his elbow, and Thomas turned. The man bowed stiffly, clicking his heels as he extended a hand. "Captain Franz von Jurgen. Bohemia."

Thomas found his hand captured in a firm grip. "Viscount Merritton. English," he said.

"Ah, then you are with the British delegation, perhaps?" von Jurgen asked.

"I'm just a tourist," Thomas replied, taking another glass of champagne from a footman's tray—how did such skinny lads manage to carry the heavy trays so gracefully through the crowds without dropping them, or spilling the golden liquid over naked shoulders and silk gowns?

"There are a great many tourists here," von Jurgen said. "Did you know that Vienna currently holds twenty times her usual population? Everyone wants to see how the peace will play out. I myself am here to see to family interests. Petty in the grand scheme of things, perhaps, but Napoleon's *grande armée* marched through my fields, burned my home, and stole nearly everything. Then the Prussians came and took the rest."

Far from bitter, the man was smiling, tapping his foot in time to the music. Thomas frowned, and von Jurgen chuckled. "I will petition the Congress for compensation, but if that fails, maybe I will find a wealthy wife. Plenty of pretty ladies here, eh?" He pressed an elbow into Thomas's ribs. "I should be choosing one I like and wooing her, yet I find the task daunting in such a crush. I understand there is a card room, with cigars and schnapps, which I far prefer to champagne. If you are of the same mind, shall we go and find this room and leave the delegates here to strut?"

That suited Thomas well enough. Within an hour he had won enough money to pay for a month's lodging, a new coat and boots, and enough good meals to keep even Donovan happy. He looked at the pile of coins—an exotic mix of florins, francs, zlotys, and pfennigs, and smiled. He hadn't stolen a thing. Between the winnings and the schnapps, he felt happier than he had in months.

"One last bet," a wild-eyed gentleman from Venice begged. The man had lost everything, even his cuff links. Von Jurgen had those, and Thomas held his last handful of coins.

Von Jurgen leaned forward. "Have you anything left to bet with, *mein herr*?"

"This." The man laid a gold watch on the table, a lady's watch, engraved, delicate, expensive, with a single diamond set in the center of the case. Thomas picked it up and opened it. The tinny notes of a familiar English lullaby played. Behind the time piece itself there were a pair of miniature portraits, a gentleman and a child, also very English, though the owner—if he was the owner—was obviously Italian.

"A family heirloom," the man said with a sly smile, and Thomas knew he was lying.

He laid down his cards, and the delicate little time-piece was his.

Chapter 14

Stephen stirred his tea with a flourish the next morning, wide-awake, though he hadn't been able to sleep a wink.

She'd been magnificent. Even Charles Stewart had looked impressed, though he hadn't actually said so.

Julia had charmed the Prince de Ligne and a dozen other people who'd had the luck to make her acquaintance. When the time came to leave in the wee hours of the morning, she had a dozen invitations to tea and lunch, which she neither accepted nor declined. When gentlemen asked to call upon her, she merely smiled politely and changed the subject. He'd led her out of the ballroom on his arm while another aide escorted Dorothea, and felt envious glares like daggers in his back.

He'd yet to figure out how she had done it, and he'd been watching her all evening—just to make sure she didn't get into any trouble. She listened more than she spoke, smiled charmingly, and made witty comments at precisely the right moments, always in English. Was that all there was to it, or was there something extraordinary about Julia Leighton? Her upbringing, of course, had a great deal to do with her social skills. If only she were not . . . He frowned.

He wasn't married, mainly because he had never found a woman who interested him enough. Until now.

He sighed as he took a forkful of eggs and sausage, grinning like a fool as he chewed. The footman, a proper English chap, shifted uncomfortably as he watched.

Once they arrived home after the ball, Stephen had taken Julia in to see Lord Castlereagh. She perched on the edge of a settee and advised him that a number of delegates were feeling slighted by the accommodations provided to them by the Austrians, or at the order of precedence they'd been assigned in meetings and assemblies. She had not said it outright, since it was not her place, but she hinted with the utmost delicacy that a kind word or offer of assistance from Britain's envoys might sway lesser delegates to side with England on contentious issues in return.

Castlereagh had put Stephen in charge of seeing what might be done, then thanked Julia and bid her good-night. "Perhaps," he had suggested, "you might encourage Lady Dorothea to cultivate the friendship of Prince Talleyrand's niece. She is serving as his official hostess."

Stephen chuckled out loud over his breakfast, remembering how Julia had curtsied to his lordship and told him she would see what she could do in that regard. The footman looked sideways at him again.

"More tea, Major?"

He nodded absently.

If Julia could charm the wily old French ambassador, it would be a coup indeed. Talleyrand held the lion's share of secrets.

Stephen dug a spoon into a frothy cheese soufflé and considered the matter again. No, he was quite certain he had never met a woman like Julia Leighton. He'd put his plans to seek a wife on hold when he joined the army, then again when Dorothea needed him, but those were simply convenient excuses. He was beginning to think he was a confirmed bachelor, the kind of man who would dandle his nieces and nephews on his knees and tell them stories of long ago wars, his glory days. No heirs, no cares. Yet now—

He put his spoon down and frowned.

"Something wrong with the soufflé, Major?" the footman asked.

"No, not at all," Stephen said, looking at the dish. It was almost empty, but he didn't remember tasting a single bite.

What the devil had gotten into him? He could never *marry* Julia Leighton. He added a spoonful of sugar to his teacup, unsure if he'd already done so or not, then grimaced at the oversweetness of the tea.

One thing was certain—Julia Leighton would have been wasted on Temberlay. He'd met David Temberlay on several occasions and found him as dull and stolid as his brother, Nicholas, was flamboyant and bold. He recalled now that Nicholas had actually proposed to Julia after his brother was killed. He'd returned from war to assume his brother's title and discovered Julia with child, disowned by her family. Stephen had wondered why any man would do such a foolishly honorable, reckless thing, but that was before he met Julia. She had refused Nicholas, determined to make her own way in the world.

He poured thick yellow cream over a bowl of late blackberries and let the sweetness of the berries fill his mouth.

Did Julia regret her actions, miss her old life? She could have been a duchess, yet she carried the role of companion like a queen. He smiled again, and a cream-covered berry rolled off his spoon onto the pristine tablecloth. He and the footman both stared at it for a moment.

Julia looked to be enjoying herself immensely last night, her face glowing, her eyes bright. He'd been enchanted, even though he knew the truth about her.

He could see now that the truth was that she was beautiful, charming, elegant, and smart.

Of course she was passionate too. She'd proven that in her folly, but also in her devotion to Dorothea, her son, and the new tasks they'd given her.

He felt a stir of desire, and swallowed a blackberry whole. It stuck in his throat for a moment. Perhaps there was another way.

He'd never had a mistress. He never had time, or found a woman who attracted him enough, or who was equal to his intellect in the drawing room as well as good in bed. He imagined taking Julia to bed, then waking up and actually enjoying *talking* to her.

He shifted in his chair and added another spoonful of sugar to his tea.

A diplomat could never travel with his mistress. It would be scandalous.

He set the spoon down. Yet if Doe continued to travel with him, and brought Julia as her companion, everything would look quite proper. Dorothea had been remarkably happy last night on the ride home, her eyes bright as she chattered about fashions, food, and music. She'd hugged him when he asked her if she enjoyed the ball, and bid him good-night with a kiss on the cheek. Perhaps she might enjoy travel with him on future missions—and that meant Julia would be there.

The door of the breakfast room opened and he looked up as Julia hurried into the room. He rose to his feet with a genuine smile, his heart missing a beat as she hurried across the room.

She was wearing the same blue muslin gown she'd

worn last night to the ball, wrinkled now, and stained. Her eyes were red-rimmed, shiny with tears. She looked as if she'd been through a battle. His smile faltered.

"What's happened?" he asked, throwing down his napkin.

"My lord, Dorothea has taken an overdose of laudanum."

Chapter 15

The curtains actually shrieked as Donovan opened them with a flourish, letting the afternoon sun stream into the room. "'Morning, my lord, or rather, good afternoon," he said with jaunty sarcasm. The light pierced Thomas's aching head like a bolt of lightning, and he shut his eyes and rolled over, cursing his valet with every colorful phrase he could think of. His stomach heaved and he swallowed bile.

Donovan whistled and nudged the chamber pot nearer to the side of the bed with his foot. "Must have been some party. You came home drunk as a lord—well, a lad who used to be a lord—and you're as green as the damned wallpaper now."

"Go 'way," Thomas managed. What the hell had he been drinking last night? He hadn't been this drunk in years. He'd learned to be careful, canny, let other men do the drinking while he stayed sober and alert.

He cracked his eyes open when Donovan picked up his coat and breeches from the floor and began going through the pockets, and chuckled as he scooped three handfuls of coin onto the table with an ungodly clatter.

"What have we here? Is this a souvenir?" Donovan said

when he found the watch. "I thought you stuck to earrings to remember your conquests." He opened the watch and the lullaby played. "I hope you didn't go to a lot of effort to get this. It's too personal to be of any value. Someone's bound to recognize the portraits, and we'll never be able to sell it. It's the kind of thing people go looking for when they lose it."

"It's not for sale," Thomas muttered thickly. "Get me something to drink, water, tea, I don't care." But Donovan had noticed the diamond embedded in the case. He examined it, letting the jewel catch the light and throw it into Thomas's eyes like a handful of needles. Donovan whistled again, the thin, high sound every bit as painful as the light.

"This stone should fetch a few quid. Maybe more." He took a knife out of his pocket.

"Don't—" Thomas began, but it was too late. The diamond popped out and Donovan held it up, murmuring praise.

Thomas wrapped the sheet around his waist and rose, managing to cross the room and snatch up the watch from where it lay on the table. He collapsed into a chair, shielding it in his hand against further damage. He didn't need to look at the portraits again. He knew them by heart, having stared at them for hours last night before he passed out, trying to conjure an image of the lady who owned the watch. The dainty timepiece had been a gift from her husband, perhaps—the man in the portrait—and the child was doubtless their son. The perfect English family.

He envied them. Were they in love, happy? Did the lady hum the lullaby to her child as he slept? The gentleman's painted face reeked of starchy nobility, but there was something else in his expression as well, a gentleness, a look of love that Thomas had almost forgotten existed.

By the time his coach had rolled to a stop outside his door at dawn, he'd decided he would try and find the owner and return it. No doubt the lady was here in Vienna. How else could such a personal treasure have ended up here, in his hands?

He sat on the edge of the bed now and stared down at the scratched case, at the gouge where the diamond had been. Would she—whoever she might be, and if he ever found her—still be glad to have the watch back again, even without the diamond?

He thought of his own family. They were not the kind to give each other portraits of loved ones. The Earls of Brecon married for position, profit, and power, but never for love. They lived grand lives and painted grand portraits of themselves to hang in the hallowed halls of Brecon Park, or they had their likenesses carved in marble, which was fitting, given the hard, proud, unfeeling nature of his kin.

There would be no portrait of himself in Brecon's hallowed halls. His brother Edward had promised to strike his name from the family records, remove all trace of him from their lives.

To Edward, or even their mother, the diamond would have been the most important aspect of the watch, an expensive gift that conveyed the giver's wealth, and consequence, one that she would have preferred untainted by cumbersome emotions and fond portraits.

This watch, with its sentimental pictures, sweet music, and tender engraving, *Ever and always,* spoke of a family that treasured each other. His gut tensed with a wave of longing for that kind of connection with a woman, a family. Try as he might to picture someone else, when he imagined the owner's face, he could see only one woman's face in his mind. Julia . . .

He snapped the case shut. Yes, he decided, whoever the lady was, she would definitely want her watch back. The parts she would find most precious were still intact, and whether it had been lost or stolen, she would be most glad of its return.

All he had to do was find her. He stared at the wall, his aching head spinning, and wondered how to begin.

"**H**ow is this possible? Where did she get the laudanum?" Stephen demanded as they hurried through the corridors to Dorothea's room. His harsh whisper echoed off the walls, his anger emphasized by the ring of his boot heels.

He wasn't really angry with Julia, just angry he had forgotten that her prime responsibility was to take care of Dorothea. How must it have looked to Doe, Julia dancing and flirting at a ball, while he hadn't been able to take his eyes off her? Doe was astute and would have noticed that. Was this his fault? He had decided once they left London that Dorothea would not be allowed any more laudanum. He thought her strong enough to face life without it, especially with Julia by her side and himself to protect her. He'd thought that enough time had passed to dull the pain of her grief without the drug. He was wrong about everything. His throat closed, thickened at the thought of losing her.

"I don't know how she got it," Julia said. "The doctor is with her now."

Dorothea's door was ahead, and he stared at the blue and white panels, the brass latch. He stopped, unable to go on, to enter the room, if—

He stood in the middle of the hall, his fists clenched, his jaw tight. Breakfast roiled in his belly, and he had the same feeling of dread he got before a battle.

Julia stopped by his side and waited. "My lord?" she asked.

"Will she live?" he asked tightly, unable to look at her. He was a man used to death, a soldier. He knew how fragile the human body was, how easily it shattered, fell prey to disease. One day a man might be whole and healthy, the next— He swallowed. His sister wasn't a soldier. She'd been a fragile creature already when she lost Matthew and her child. He shut his eyes, ready for bad news.

Julia squeezed his arm. "The worst has passed. I didn't want to fetch you until the doctor was certain." He met her gaze, seeing the truth there. She was tired, bewildered, but she gave the last of her fragile strength to him.

"When did . . . ?" he asked, the rest of the sentence stuck behind the lump in his throat.

"Dorothea dismissed her maid when she returned from the ball, said she was tired and wished to go straight to sleep. Fortunately, she left the window open, and the maid felt the cold air and came to shut it. She noticed the vial on the floor by the bed. She came to get me, and I sent her for the doctor. I've been with her ever since. She *will* live, my lord," Julia said fervently, as if she could feel the fear in him.

He searched her eyes, read compassion in the hazel depths, determination. He felt the shame of the situation, his own weakness, his inability to help Dorothea past her grief.

Julia should have been watching Dorothea, protecting her. But she'd been playing games, spying. They both had.

Stephen closed his eyes, imagined the scandal this would cause. Was it wrong, wanting to protect his own reputation now that he knew Doe would survive? His career was everything to him.

Angry at the whole situation, he shook Julia's hand

off his arm and walked on, grasping the brass latch and twisting it, throwing the door open, leaving her to follow.

Dorothea lay on the pillow, her eyes half shut, as pale as the linen beneath her. The doctor rose from a chair beside the bed.

"Good morning, Major. I'm Dr. Bowen," he said.

"You're English," Stephen said, surprised.

"I'm part of the delegation, here to tend anyone who might fall ill. I'm Lady Castlereagh's physician in London."

Stephen felt his skin heat. Surely when her ladyship heard, she would insist that he be sent home in disgrace. He ran a hand through his hair, seeing disaster.

Dorothea moaned and her head lolled on the pillow, and Stephen stared down at her. The physician patted her hand, gently tucked it under the blanket. "You needn't fear, sir. Lady Dorothea is out of danger."

The ache in Stephen's chest didn't ease. He sat on the edge of the bed and touched her cheek. It was cold as ice.

"Doe," he said, more sharply than he intended.

She opened her eyes and looked up at him. "Stephen— I'm sorry, Stephen. Dear, dear Stephen."

"Who gave you the laudanum?" he asked.

She smiled weakly. "No one you know. You needn't call anyone out or fire anyone on staff. There was a man at the ball last night. He had some laudanum in his pocket. I traded my watch for it."

He felt his stomach clench. "The watch Matthew gave you?" he asked. She hadn't let the timepiece out of her sight since her husband's death. She listened to the lullaby a hundred times a day, kissed the painted faces good-night, whispered to them when she thought no one was looking.

"I thought I wouldn't need it anymore, you see," she

murmured. "The laudanum lets me see them just as clearly as I see you. I thought if I had enough—or a little more than just enough—I'd never have to let them go at all and I could be with them again." Her face crumpled, and he gathered her into his arms as sobs shook her and tears slid over her cheeks, wetting his face too, and glistened silver on her gray skin in the mid-morning light.

He'd been wrong. The grief had not passed at all. How could it ever pass, the horror of such a loss? *He* wasn't enough to ease the pain. He looked up at the doctor, the question in his eyes.

"She'll need watching," Dr. Bowen murmured.

"I'll stay with her," Julia said at once, stepping out of the shadows.

"Not today, my lady. You need rest yourself," Bowen objected. "You've been a great help, but perhaps her maid—"

Stephen looked up at Julia. Her hair was disheveled, long dark locks drooping over her shoulder. There were deep hollows under her eyes, though her mouth was set in a determined line, her eyes bright. She stood by the bed like a sentry, ready to object to the doctor's refusal of her help. Her continued help, rather. He noted the stains on her gown, and knew she'd stayed with Dorothea through the worst of it, held her while they made her sick, forced her to expel the drug from her body. He felt a frisson of admiration pass through him.

"Who knows about this?" he asked, still aware that disaster loomed, even if his sister had survived her attempt to take her own life. It would mean gossip and scandal for the entire British delegation when word got out, and most especially for himself. Bowen would have to make a full report, of course. It was protocol. They lived and died by protocol.

The doctor glanced at Julia. "No one knows, sir. Just myself, Miss Leighton, and Lady Dorothea's maid."

"I didn't think there was any point in waking Lord Castlereagh, especially once the crisis had passed," Julia said. "This is a family matter, and Dr. Bowen agrees that it should remain so."

Stephen stared at her for a moment. Of course Julia understood all this. She had faced her own scandal, must have tried to keep that secret too.

"These are important times, my lord, for England, for you, and for Lady Dorothea," Dr. Bowen said. "I don't see any need to report this officially. It would only distract Lord Castlereagh, which is obviously unnecessary now. Lady Dorothea will need a few days to rest and recover. I will tell Lady Castlereagh that she has a head cold and must remain in her rooms." He turned and smiled at Julia, admiration clear in his eyes, as if they were meeting in a salon. "Lady Julia makes a fine nurse, but we shall take turns watching Lady Dorothea. It will be good for her to wake up and find people she knows by her side."

Stephen undid the top button of his tunic and sat down. "I will take the first watch," he said, and turned to Julia, meeting her eyes, unable to speak, to thank her. "Go and rest," he said gruffly.

She nodded and moved toward the door. The doctor went to pack his equipment into his bag.

"Julia?" Stephen said, stopping her. She turned to look at him, her hand on the door latch. "I owe you my thanks."

"Not at all," she murmured. "I am only glad—" Tears formed in her eyes, and her mouth crumpled. She fled before the first drop could fall.

He watched her go. In that moment Julia Leighton ceased to be notorious. She was perfect.

Chapter 16

⁓⊙⊙⁓

The intimate supper at Princess Kostova's lavish apartments turned out to be for four, not two.

Katerina greeted Thomas at the door with a warm embrace and a promising kiss, then stepped back, running her hand over his lapels.

"My oldest and dearest friends have arrived, and I could not turn them away." She kissed him again. She tasted of champagne, smelled like gardenias. "I think you will like them. Come." She clasped his hand in hers and tugged him toward the little dining room, since the big dining room was being set to accommodate the luminaries who would attend her salon later that evening.

An elderly gentleman stood as they entered, his dark eyes assessing Thomas at a glance.

"You have a new gentleman, Katya. How delightful. We shall grill him like a squab and devour him. I do hope you're up to it, *monsieur*."

"Behave yourself, you old roué," the princess admonished gently. "This is Viscount Merritton. Thomas, this is the Prince de Ligne."

"Ah, Thomas is it? First names already," another voice purred. "Then he is more likely to be dessert than the main course." Thomas turned to look at a large woman reclining on a chaise longue, her eyes bright, her smile suggestive, though she was old enough to be his grandmother. Thomas's eyes popped. The woman's bulky figure dripped with jewels, from the tiara on her gray head to the waterfall of diamonds, rubies, emeralds, and pearls that flowed over her vast bosom.

"This is my godmother, and my mother's oldest friend, Madam Anna," Katerina said.

"Charmed," the jeweled lady said with a thick Russian accent, letting her eyes wander over him as if she were indeed contemplating dining on him. She extended her hand to be kissed. Every finger bore a glittering ring. Thomas smiled.

"Likewise charmed, madam."

The prince nudged him. "Be careful, Viscount. Anna and I met many years ago in Russia, at the court of Catherine the Great. I was bewitched by her beauty and her wit, and I have been under her spell ever since."

Anna grinned, her jewels twinkling with delight. "I have a penchant for military men. So did Empress Catherine. I was the empress's 'tester.' Does that shock you, young man?"

Thomas's brows rose. "You tasted her food?" He took a seat near the chaise.

The prince chuckled. Madame Anna purred. Katerina smiled behind long fingers.

"It's nothing to do with food at all, Thomas," Katerina began. "When the empress admired a certain gentleman—"

Anna took over. "Oh, they weren't all gentlemen. In fact most were not—not even nobly born. She liked soldiers best of all. Are you a soldier, Viscount?"

"He would be in uniform, Anna," the prince said gently. "When Catherine the Great admired a certain gentleman, Anna had the great responsibility of testing his, um, sexual prowess, before he was invited to the imperial bedchamber."

Thomas's surprise must have shown on his face, for everyone laughed.

"I see you are shocked indeed," Anna said. "But it was a privilege, you see, a great honor, and—" She sighed, and trailed a be-ringed finger over her finery with a wicked smile. "Each time I recommended a man to the empress and he pleased her, she would reward me with a bauble." She ran a long rope of pearls through her fingers and gazed lovingly at the ruby pendant on the end. "I have named all my little trinkets for the talented gentlemen who were unknowingly responsible for them. The pearls are called Lieutenant Dashkoff, and the pendant—oh the pendant!—that is General Semyon."

"And where is your emerald pin, the Sergeant, tonight?" Katerina asked.

Anna pursed her lips. "Alas, he is away on duty at present. Of course, the sergeant himself was hardly one of my favorites, nor Catherine's—though he pleased her for a night or two—and a lady needs to eat."

Katerina patted her hand. "I will send someone to buy the pin back for you."

"Oh would you, my dear?"

The prince smiled at Thomas. "All very baffling, *non*? It is a game they play. When one is . . . How do you English say it? In Queer Street? Without blunt? One must do what one needs to survive. Anna refuses to accept charity. Instead, she pawns her jewels, and her goddaughter buys them back."

Thomas knew exactly how that worked.

At the delicate chime of a bell, a set of damask curtains at the end of the room parted, revealing an intimate table set for four. The prince escorted Katerina, and Thomas offered his arm to Anna. She squeezed his bicep, as if she were testing him too. She sniffed his cologne and nodded approvingly. Katerina raised one eyebrow and smiled fondly at the old lady.

"Well?" she asked.

"He will do, but let us see how he eats."

"It is a theory that Catherine had," Katerina whispered. "If a man enjoys his food, he will enjoy a woman similarly." The table was so small her knee rested against his under the long white cloth.

Thomas stared at the variety of food. The table positively groaned with roast pheasant, caviar, and chicken. An equally eye-popping selection of chocolates, cakes, and fruit waited on the sideboard. He raised a glass of red wine, sparkling like Anna's ruby in the glass.

"And yet, if a man ate so much, would he be able to perform to any woman's satisfaction?" he asked.

Madam Anna looked pleased. "You have passed the second test as well, dear viscount. A man must savor, not gobble, his meat." She waved her hand over the lavish meal as if casting a spell. "He must choose what to enjoy, do so slowly, appreciatively. Between courses, he must cleanse his palate, heighten his senses for the next dish."

The prince chuckled. "I told you she was bewitching, did I not? You will never look at a chop or a bit of liver pâté the same way again, will you?"

"You will taste every mouthful," Katerina said in a low purr, taking a spoonful of caviar.

"Especially dessert, the sweetest course—the rich cream, the tartness of the fruit, the smooth gloss of chocolate, and the pungent nip of cinnamon that comes at the end," Anna added.

"Praise the Lord it comes," the prince sighed, and

mockingly fanned himself with his napkin. Katerina nudged Thomas's knee under the table, rubbed it intimately, a promise of sweetness.

The prince raised a toast as the second course was served, chicken in a fragrant sauce, rich with garlic and wine. "I will now do my best to change the topic of conversation, so the viscount may eat his meal without having his bedroom skills analyzed. I encourage you to eat as you please, sir. Pick up a chicken leg and gnaw on it if you wish, spread the caviar on bread, and let these hussies wonder what it means. It would give Anna great pleasure indeed to watch you, try to puzzle out if you like to start, so to speak, at the head or the tail."

"Your toast, old roué?" Katerina reminded him.

The prince raised her hand and kissed it. "Firstly, to the lovely company we find ourselves in tonight," he said, nodding to the two ladies. "Secondly, to the great pleasure of meeting new people," he said to Thomas. They drank deeply, and a footman stepped out of the shadows to refill their glasses. Anna held the servant's sleeve as she drained the glass, and smiled as he immediately filled it again.

"Tell me, Viscount," the prince said. "How do you come to be in Vienna for this great and auspicious event? My old friend Rousseau, the king of philosophers, would have said such a confluence of emperors and kings is rarer than the conjoining of stars in the heavens. He would say it means the end of the world. What say you to that?"

Rousseau? "I am simply a tourist," Thomas said.

De Ligne leaned forward. "Ah, on the Grand Tour, perhaps! I am pleased it is back in fashion. I took the tour myself, many years ago, before all the best places were spoiled by Revolution, and Napoleon's *grande armée* trampled all the rest. Which country did you enjoy most?"

Thomas met the old courtier's eyes, still sharp and dark as marbles. It was easy to imagine him as a great general, reading the battlefield, making tactical decisions based on what he saw. His gaze took a man's measure, Thomas realized. As surely as Anna had her method, de Ligne had his. Thomas held his gaze, resisted the temptation to look away. Could the prince see what he was, what he'd become, what he feared most?

"Belgium," he replied to the prince's question, knowing the prince had been born there. "Brussels is lovely in the spring." He could hardly say he had yet to truly find a place he loved above all others, a home.

The light in the general's eyes went out. He shook his head, disappointed. "You try to flatter me, I think. Yet it is not necessary. I have no power now. I am simply an old man with interesting tales to tell, and so I am invited to dine by lovely ladies like Princess Kostova."

"You are my old roué," Katerina said, leaning over to kiss his cheek.

De Ligne grinned at Thomas. "She does it too, flatters me, but I will indulge *her*. Ah well, good manners insist that I return the favor and say that I enjoyed my time in London, though I could never understand the intricate etiquette of the upper classes. So many rules makes one stiff and dull. I was regarded as an oddity, a social buffoon, always putting a foot wrong. The English have no sense of humor at all, and I, as you have seen, cannot help but speak my mind. If something is amusing, I must say it is so."

"You are notorious *everywhere* for speaking your mind, dearest, not just in England," Katerina said lightly.

"And you are notoriously charming, Princess," he said. "Would you have invited me tonight if I did not say the outrageous things I do? We amuse each other, charm our friends, and shock those who do not know us well, as it should be. Do you not agree, Viscount?"

"He learned this naughty banter from his dear friend Casanova," Anna whispered. She laid her hand on his, and he stared down at a pearl ring the size of a quail's egg. "Captain Starensky," she introduced the pearl. "I gave him a very good report, and so did the empress. By now the captain himself is long since dead, or old and ugly, but his namesake will keep me warm forever."

How easy it would be to slip one of the rings off the old lady's wrinkled fingers, Thomas thought. She would probably forget she'd worn it tonight, wonder if she'd pawned it. She would not suffer for the loss of it—the princess would see to that.

Still, he hesitated. He was enjoying the company and loath to spoil the evening.

"One thing I liked about England were the ladies," the prince mused as the footman filled their glasses with wine the same color as Anna's yellow diamond earrings.

"Better than Russian ladies?" Katerina demanded, her blue eyes flashing fire.

The prince winked at Thomas. "Better than Austrian ladies, at any rate," he said. "Are you married, Viscount?"

Thomas shook his head.

"Why?" Anna demanded. "You are so—" She squeezed his hand again.

"I have been traveling, and I haven't met a lady I want to wed," Thomas said, giving the usual excuses.

"A pity Katerina is already married," the prince sighed. "But what is your taste? A proper English lass, perhaps?" He glanced at the princess and Anna. "Englishwomen are taught the feminine graces, but nothing more intellectual. It is a rest for the mind to spend time conversing with an English lady."

"How very dreadful you are tonight!" Katerina said, laughing.

Thomas thought of Julia. She was anything but restful or soothing.

"You, for example, Princess," the prince went on. "You speak three languages, read widely, and you consider yourself quite independent of your husband's authority. You are a handful, my dear, and you know it. I daresay Kostov is sating himself on a buxom little tavern wench who doesn't speak a word of any language other than German, and even that not well, so he does not have to think of anything witty to say."

Katerina sniffed. "He is more likely to be closeted with the Tsar and his companions and advisors. Not that they are conversing about anything. They are probably enjoying the favors of two dozen buxom little wenches." She gave Thomas a brilliant smile. "He has his amusements, I have mine."

"It's much the same in England," Thomas said. "The upper classes marry strangers of similar pedigree, breed blue-blooded heirs, and find their pleasures outside the marriage bed."

"Then perhaps the English are not as different from Europeans as I thought," the prince said. "Is that the kind of marriage you look forward to?"

"Not at all," he said, feeling the watch in his pocket, hearing the lullaby playing in his mind.

"Is it possible," Anna said, "that you are promised to some English lady, and merely touring the Continent to sow the last of your wild oats, as the English say, before settling down to the dull task of getting heirs with a woman you do not enjoy?"

"Oh, do tell me about her!" Katerina said, a sharp edge to her tone. Thomas glanced at her. Was she jealous? Her expression was unreadable in the candlelight.

"There's no one," he said, though it was a lie. Julia's face invaded his thoughts again. "I am a confirmed bachelor." She had become the hallmark by which he judged every woman he met. He remembered her—whether his memory of those few short hours in her company was accurate or not—as the most beautiful, charming, desirable woman he'd ever met. She'd been unskilled and inexperienced as a lover, but her response to him had been genuine. Regret filled him again, and he tightened his grip on the delicate stem of his wineglass.

"Ah, there is someone I think," the prince said, watching him. Thomas forced a carefree smile.

Katerina tilted her head. "Should I worry? Is she here in Vienna, waiting to scratch my eyes out for taking you from her company?"

Thomas took her hand and kissed it. "There is no one but you, Princess, at least tonight."

The prince barked a laugh, and raised his glass. "And that is all we have, *mais non?* Tomorrow is very far away indeed."

"What are Englishwomen like in bed?" Anna asked. "Or English *men* for that matter?" She waggled her gray brows and her tiara twinkled. "No, don't answer, darling viscount—I shall leave it to Katerina to tell me tomorrow."

As Katerina gently scolded her godmother again for her boldness, Julia's face filled Thomas's mind, the softness of her sighs as he loved her, the way she'd caught her bottom lip in her teeth as he kissed her breasts. Did she think of him as she lay with her duke, striving to breed an heir? Did she enjoy Dull David's touch, or recoil from it?

"You are embarrassing my guest, Anna," Katerina said, bringing him back.

"Not at all," he said lightly. "But I'm afraid I can't offer much illumination on the subject. I have been on the Continent for over a year. I cannot recall the last time I even spoke to an English lady." He recalled every word that he had spoken to Julia. He winked at Anna. "Or an English gentleman."

The prince looked surprised. "You have not dined with anyone from the British delegation?"

Katerina sniffed. "Lady Castlereagh is exceedingly dowdy, and her husband is as stiff as a statue."

The prince took a spoonful of caviar and rolled his eyes with pleasure. "But there are other members of the delegation, much more pleasant company. For example there is a young lady—"

Anna interrupted. "I have heard Castlereagh's half brother is quite a scandal. What he lacks in charm, he makes up for in drunken persistence. Reminds me of Captain—"

The prince set his spoon down. "I was speaking of the ladies, Anna!" he scolded her interruption mildly. "Some of them are quite charming. For instance, there was a very lovely lady at the Emperor's ball the other night—"

Katerina's eyes widened in surprise. "Were you there, my roué? I didn't see you! How could I have missed you?"

He patted her hand. "With several thousand people there, half of them eating, half of them dancing, all of them talking at once, who could find anyone? This is much better, an intimate dinner, good conversation. Quality, instead of quantity."

"Never mind the flattery, old friend. Tell us all about the ball," Anna sighed. "Alas, I was unable to secure an invitation. I would have worn the General . . ."

"Which one is the General?" Prince de Ligne asked.

"My other tiara, the one with the emeralds."

"Are there very many ladies traveling with the British delegation?" Thomas asked, thinking of the watch.

The prince pursed his lips. "Yes, a few. As I was saying, I met a charming lady at the ball named—"

Katerina laid a finger on his lips. "You shall not speak her name here! He is *my* guest, and tonight I want him to think only of me."

Anna gave Thomas a knowing grin. "She means to have you, Viscount, even untested."

"Pity you did not think to bring letters of reference, my friend," the prince said, raising his glass. "Ah well, we shall meet some morning in the park and compare all the women we have known and loved, though I daresay my list will be far longer, simply because I outrank you in age."

Thomas raised his glass in return, conceding the claim.

"Oh, do tell us now," Katerina encouraged him. "Of all your tales, I adore the ones about your amours most of all."

The prince let the footman refill his glass, then grinned. "Let me see . . ." he said, rubbing his lower lip thoughtfully. "Ah yes, Versailles . . ." He leaned in and filled the room with salacious tales of his romantic adventures, and Thomas realized he was enjoying himself for the first time in a very long time.

Chapter 17

"No," said Lady Castlereagh, glaring down her long nose at Julia Leighton. "Charles, send her away. I won't have her near me."

Julia bit her lip as her ladyship's horse sidled anxiously as if it too was loath to be near a fallen woman. Charles Stewart smirked at Julia before he turned to whisper in his sister-in-law's ear. Lady Castlereagh listened a moment, her jaw dropping with surprise. Her pitiless gaze fell on Julia again, raked over her riding habit, took note of every detail of her appearance. "What d'you mean, Castlereagh *ordered* that she ride with me today? This is a royal hunt! It would look as if I condone her behavior!"

Julia felt her skin turn as crimson as the autumn leaves around her.

Her ladyship waved her hand dismissively, as if shooing away a stray cat. "If she must be here, she will ride at the back of the pack, far from me."

Lord Stewart looked around, probably to see if anyone was listening. Well over a hundred people were gathered for this morning's hunt in the magnificent grounds of the Schonbrunn Palace, including the Emperor of Austria, the Tsar, and the King of Bavaria, and each came with his own entourage of grooms, servants, translators, and beaters, making the party large and loud enough to frighten any game for a hundred miles. Stewart beckoned to a uniformed officer, who nodded smartly and rode over to Julia.

"My lady—"

"*Miss* Leighton!" her ladyship snapped.

The officer's cheeks colored as red as his tunic. "Miss Leighton, if you would fall back to the end of the queue."

Julia nodded, her cheeks filled with hot blood. She had not wanted to come this morning. She had spoken to Stephen, asked him to relieve her of her extra duties as a listener. Her primary responsibility was to Dorothea, especially now, but Lord Castlereagh had refused to release her, believing that Dorothea was merely sick with a head cold and could easily spare her companion for the morning.

He'd given Stephen another lecture. Everyone on the delegation must do their duty as required, and Julia was proving useful. If Dorothea was ill, she required a nurse, not the services of a woman who could be doing much more important work elsewhere. Julia was assigned to join the hunt as one of Lady Castlereagh's attendants, with instructions to keep her eyes and ears open.

She had done her best to refuse; graciously, of course. She was being thrust into the spotlight when she longed to cling to the shadows, to avoid unpleasant situations like this one. It was to be expected, she supposed. Lady Castlereagh was an old and dear friend of the Countess of Carrindale, Julia's mother, and knew every detail of her shame.

Julia turned her mare's head toward the back of the pack.

"Would you mind if I ride with you?" a pleasant voice

asked, and Julia turned to find a young woman in a blue riding habit by her side. "I cannot abide hunting, but I love to ride, and the day is too lovely to stay indoors."

"Of course," Julia said. "I—"

The lady smiled. "Oh, I know who you are." Julia's spine stiffened and she clenched her teeth. "You are the lovely Lady Julia, the one Prince de Ligne cannot stop talking about. I have been hoping to meet you. I am Doro-thée de Talleyrand-Perigord."

Julia's mouth dried. The French ambassador's niece-by-marriage? The lady who served as his official hostess here in Vienna had wanted to meet *her*?

"Good morning, Madam de Talleyrand," she croaked, and braced herself for the usual questions about the scandal.

"Please call me Diana. My uncle says it suits my personality better—it is the name of a goddess of the moon. He is a dreadful flatterer, but I am growing to enjoy being called after a goddess."

"Please call me—" Julia began again, and hesitated. She wasn't Lady Julia any longer, though some insisted on using her former title.

"Lady Julia!" another voice cried, and she turned to find the Prince de Ligne riding toward her. "How pleased I am to meet you here today, and Diana, my dear. Have the two of you been introduced?"

"We're just getting acquainted," Diana said.

The horn sounded to start the hunt, and the pack of riders began to move forward. "Let us linger," the prince said. "My old bones cannot keep up with the young bucks at the front, and I shall have the two prettiest ladies here all to myself if we wait."

Diana giggled. "Flatterer! You are as bad as my uncle! But I agree with you. It is too nice a day to rush pell-mell over the countryside. Let's ride that way." She pointed in the direction opposite to the one the hunters were taking.

The day was crisp and cold, and a glittering crust of frost clung to the grass in the shade. Julia took a deep breath. She used to race James to the ruins of the old castle at Carrindale on days like this, riding neck-or-nothing over the frosty fields. They would return to raid the kitchen for apple tarts, still warm from the oven. She felt the sting of regret that she would never experience those pleasures again.

They followed a path through thick stands of pine trees, which gave way to a lake and a magnificent view of the palace.

"How lovely!" Diana cried. "It reminds me very much of Versailles."

"Do you miss home?" Julia asked.

"I miss my children," Diana said. "But I am needed here, and Vienna is lovely."

"Speaking of children," the prince said, "did you know Napoleon's son, the little King of Rome, is here at Schonbrunn?"

Diana's eyes widened. "I had heard rumors, but no one has seen the French empress or her son at state events. My uncle has made official inquiries, but his attempts to visit and pay his respects to her as the French ambassador have been rebuffed."

De Ligne made a wry face. "Pity. I believe she could do with the company, but her father is the Austrian emperor, and he prefers she remain incommunicado for the moment, perhaps for fear her presence might influence the proceedings of the Congress. She is quite a pitiful figure, is she not, the empress of a fallen nation, an innocent girl forced to marry a man now considered a monster? Think how her tearstained face might sway opinion. And the lad—he is a charming boy! His grandfather is quite right in keeping him here. He does not deserve to be a pawn." The prince straightened his shoulders. "I saw the little one only yesterday. We sat on the floor and played with his toy soldiers."

Diana clasped her hands to her chest. "Truly? How wonderful! But how did you come by such a privilege?"

He spread his hands wide and grinned at her. "I am harmless. Prince de Talleyrand is not."

"And the Empress Marie Louise? Have you seen her too? I had heard she wishes to return to her husband on Elba."

The prince looked horrified. "What? Give up this grandeur to play Robinson Crusoe with Napoleon?" He beckoned them in to whisper. "There is a rumor that she has taken a lover, and that is why she will not go to Elba. But there is also a rumor that it is her father who keeps her here, and has forbidden her to ever see Napoleon again. He has petitioned the Congress on her behalf to grant her the Duchy of Parma as a bribe to ensure her good behavior and cooperation. I've heard she is watched day and night, mostly by her lover, who follows her everywhere like a devoted puppy."

He shook his head as he met Diana's rapt expression. "I know that look, Diana. Don't imagine I'll help you pass notes from your uncle, my dear. I am a neutral party here." He took a deep breath of fall air. "I enjoy the parties, the gossip, and an occasional game of toy soldiers with the King of Rome. Nothing more. I am too old for intrigue."

"I would simply offer her feminine company, a kind shoulder, if she wished a friend to confide in," Diana sniffed. "How sad she cannot even trust her lover, since he is devoted to her father."

De Ligne laughed. "Ah, the French. You must have love, mustn't you? Very well, they say she is indeed in love with her count, and he with her, and why not? She loved Napoleon, did she not, and how unlikely was that? An Austrian princess, forced to wed her country's conqueror? Perhaps she has the ability to fall in love easily, like many women—and men like myself." He turned to Julia. "Are you in love, my dear, or are you merely married?"

She blushed. "I am . . ." she began, and paused. How could she explain what she was?

Diana tilted her head. "Have no fear of us, my dear Julia. One hears rumors, of course, but this is Vienna, not London. Things are different here."

"My word, yes!" the prince agreed. "The more scandalous you are, the better for you! And speaking of scandal, did you see Princess Bagration's gown at the last ball?" he asked, returning to gossip, his favorite subject. "Where it was not low-cut, it was sheer as the air itself. They are calling her the 'naked angel.'"

Julia realized that no one cared about her affair. There were far more interesting things to discuss. No one was shocked or horrified—outside the British delegation, of course. She looked around her, wondering if perhaps she could make a life here, once the conference ended.

The prince nudged her. "I met the most charming Englishman the other night at Princess Kostova's salon. A viscount. He is not part of your embassy—like me, he is merely here to watch this great bumbling spectacle unfold. I could arrange an introduction, if you wish to fall in love while you are in Vienna. A love affair is good for the soul as well as the heart," de Ligne said. "I daresay Katerina will find a new passion within the week, and the viscount will be left lonely. She is nothing if not fickle, and Anna did not care for the fact that he does not like caviar."

Julia laughed. "I have no idea what that might mean, Your Highness, but for the moment, sir, I am quite done with love."

"I detest caviar myself," Diana added.

"Is there someone else?" the prince asked. "Forgive me, but I am quite aghast that a single lady as lovely as yourself would turn down a handsome viscount, equally single."

She thought of Jamie and smiled. "There is indeed someone else, and he is the love of my life."

Chapter 18

⌒⌒⌒

"**Y**ou still have the watch, I see," Donovan said, removing the contents from Thomas's pockets, folding his clothes. "I never thought of you as sentimental."

"I'm not," Thomas said, looking up from his book, taking the watch from the valet's hands, tucking it into his waistcoat pocket, out of sight.

"Did you by any chance bring home anything we can sell? We cannot eat sentiment, if I may be so bold."

"You have always been bold," Thomas said, shifting uncomfortably. "Even more so recently, if *I* may be so bold." But Donovan was right. He hadn't brought anything home for nearly a week, not even a paste garnet set in tin. The money he'd won gambling at the ball was almost gone.

He would need to find another game, or work up the nerve to steal another jewel or two. Or more.

Donovan leaned against the bedpost and looked at him. "One needs to be daring. I've even been so bold as to make a few contacts on my own. There's a gent who lives in the park, has a few followers. He fancies himself a kind of Robin Hood, except he steals from the rich and shares only with a very select group of friends."

"Is this your way of giving me your notice?" Thomas asked.

Donovan studied his fingernails. "No, not yet. They want information, contacts, times and places, you see. They need someone on the inside, someone who is invited to the grand parties, knows the best people—the rich and gullible ones."

Thomas felt his stomach tense. He didn't like what was coming. "Donovan . . ."

His valet held up a hand. "No, hear me out. It will be easy. They have an ear to the ground, these lads. They aren't stupid. They've heard the stories of the parties you've attended. They know you've seen the jewels, had access to them." His face turned hard, his hand became a claw. "They were in your grasp!"

"Tell your friends—and I doubt they are *anyone's* friends—that I'm not interested."

Donovan stared at him. "Suddenly you're back to honor and high-minded ideals after all this time? Men with high ideals and no friends starve, *my lord*. What will you do, work for a wage? Maybe we could trade places, eh?"

"Don't be impertinent," Thomas said, but it sounded weak, especially since Donovan was right. Would he survive on the charity of lovers like Katerina until he got too old to appeal as a casual bedmate? He imagined living like the Prince de Ligne, counting on the stories of his glory days and his ability to amuse the rich to keep himself fed.

He turned on Donovan, angry now, and threw the book across the room. "And what can they give me in return?" he demanded. "What will my share be?"

The valet's eyes flared with surprise at his violence, then he smiled slowly. "What do you want?"

A way out, but they could not give him that. He would be drawn ever deeper into their world of the shifting shadows, trapped in the sucking tides of a disreputable life, without a shred of honor or dignity left. He would become a man who would do anything, take anything, to survive, as far from the genteel English life he'd been born to as it was possible to get. He reached into his pocket, took out the watch. It had become the symbol of everything he'd lost, everything he regretted. "I want to find the Englishwoman who owns this watch, can they give me that? She is somewhere in Vienna."

Donovan looked stunned. "That's it? You could name any price for your help. You needn't even get your hands dirty. Just point the way for them."

And how would they take the jewels, the gold, the art, they wanted? By violence. His hands would indeed be dirty then. "This is enough," he said, clutching the watch stubbornly. "For now."

Donovan studied his face, still baffled. "D'you know what *they* want? They want the tiara Lady Castlereagh was wearing at the Emperor's ball. They want that old Russian whore's necklaces and rings and bracelets. Everyone knows about her. Someone will steal them eventually. Why shouldn't we benefit? The price they'd bring would free you from this life, buy you all the honor and sentiment you could want. You could buy Brecon Park right out from under your brother's arse."

Thomas shut his eyes, imagined Anna toying with her "soldiers," her pride, her delight. What would she be without them? And he didn't want Brecon Park at any price.

"What is it you want, Donovan? I thought you wanted to go back to Ireland, buy a farm, settle down."

His valet gave him a feral grin, all teeth and cold eyes. "That was before I saw the possibilities."

Thomas suppressed a shudder of revulsion, at Donovan, and at himself, but it seemed there was no other way out.

"I'll find a way," he said aloud, fervently.

"Good," Donovan said, mistaking his meaning. "I'll tell my friends you're in."

Chapter 19

"**M**ore tea, Stephen? Actually, do try one of the apricot tarts. They're delicious."

Stephen watched as his sister poured more tea for him. She was dressed in a new gown of pale green wool, instead of her usual dark mourning garb. They were taking tea together in her sitting room after nearly a month of hurried visits in the hushed twilight of her bedroom.

He hadn't quite known what to expect when he received her note inviting him to tea, but here she was, looking much better. Almost—well, *happy*. He accepted one of the dainty tarts and let the tang of the fruit and the richness of the buttery pastry fill his mouth.

"Aren't they wonderful? Peter brought them for me."

"Peter?" he asked in surprise, trying to swallow and speak at the same time. She handed him a napkin.

"Peter Bowen, the doctor," she said, as if that explained why a physician was bringing his patient pastries. But it could mean that the good Dr. Bowen was— He gasped, and the crumbs shot down his throat, making him cough. She slapped him on the back.

"The *doctor*? Peter Bowen?" he repeated like an idiot, gaping at his sister.

"He's been so kind, and I've enjoyed sitting and chatting with him."

"I suppose he's the only visitor you've had," Stephen said sharply. "Of course you'd enjoy his company." He'd have to speak to the doctor, especially now that Doe was well again, tell him that his services were no longer needed.

Doe tilted her head and laughed. "You used to get that exact same look when Matthew began courting me, all indignant brotherly concern."

He set his plate down, the tarts spoiled for him now. "Do I have anything to be indignant about? Is Bowen courting you?"

"It's a friendship, nothing more," she replied. "And he is not my only visitor. Julia is here constantly, and she tells me about the balls and parties she's been to." He caught the question in her eyes, shifted uncomfortably in his chair and concentrated on his tea for a moment.

"She's part of the embassy," he said. "Most of the other delegations bring ladies to the balls and parties. It ensures there are enough dance partners for the gentlemen, who, as you can imagine, far outnumber the ladies here in town."

"I see." She set her own cup down. "You should know I've had a note from Lady Castlereagh herself, complaining about Julia." She pinned him with a look, an older sister brooking no impudence from her younger brother. "What is Julia really up to, Stephen?"

He held his breath and picked up his cup, hiding behind it, wondering if he dared to tell her the truth.

"Is it you, Stephen? Do you have feelings for Julia? I assume you are her escort when she goes to these parties."

He dropped his cup in surprise, and spilled tea across his lap. He leapt to his feet, mopping at it with the napkin. "Of course not!" he spluttered.

She calmly offered him another napkin. "Really? A lovely young woman like Julia, intelligent, witty, charming, and you have no feelings for her? I despair of you, brother dear."

"Don't be ridiculous, Doe! We all have a job to do, and Julia is merely doing her part. Lady Castlereagh can go and be hanged!"

"Shh," Doe cautioned. "Peter says we must be careful what we say. Ironically, private conversations are not private indoors. One must go to the park for intimate conversation." She sighed. "How fortunate the weather is still so lovely right now."

He glanced at the window. "It's raining," he said.

"Yes, today it is," she said with another sigh. "But yesterday was lovely."

"You were in the park yesterday?" he asked, surprised yet again.

"Yes. I went out with Peter, and of course Julia. I would have invited you too, if I thought you had time. Now that I know you don't fancy Julia, I'm glad I didn't."

"I do not . . ." He paused. But he did, and the look in Doe's eyes confirmed that she knew it too. He stopped talking.

She righted his cup and poured him more tea with a knowing smile. "I wonder if you—or she—knows how lucky you are?"

Was he? He was beginning to think that it had been good fortune indeed that brought Julia into their lives.

"Doe, I cannot simply—"

She laid a hand on his sleeve. "Yes, you can. You must, Stephen. Tell her how you feel. Don't wait. Life is much too short."

Chapter 20

"There's something I wished to, um, speak to you about," Stephen began, and Julia turned to look at him.

"Oh?" It had become the habit among the residents of Minoritenplatz Palace, and at almost every other embassy in the city, to walk outdoors if there was something private to discuss, away from potential listeners. People crowded the park, some speaking in low tones with their heads together, others craning their necks to catch whispered secrets.

The crowds were somewhat thinner today, given the distinct possibility that there would be rain, or even snow, before evening, and any gossip and intrigue that could be saved for a warmer afternoon had to wait. Still, there were several small well-wrapped groups strolling in quiet conversation. Less hardy souls rolled by in closed coaches, the horses blowing frosty mist.

Julia felt the cold creeping up through her boots as they walked along the cinder path, but it was nice to be outdoors in the fresh air. She waited for him to speak, but they walked on in silence for a few minutes. Was he upset about something she had done or failed to do? She was doing her best to balance her duty as Dorothea's companion with her activities as a listener. She cast a glance at his face. He looked pensive, thoughtful.

"Is this possibly about the fact that Dr. Bowen is spending so much time with Dorothea?" she asked, thinking perhaps he was worried that his sister was not recovering and still needed the doctor's care even weeks after the overdose. "You needn't worry. He believes she is quite out of danger, but we thought a few more days in his company might be a good idea, in case someone began to ask questions as to why he was visiting her so often. Giving the appearance of a friendship between them seemed the perfect idea . . ."

Stephen stopped in his tracks. He looked horrified as he turned to face her. "*You* arranged for Bowen to befriend her?"

Julia clasped her hands together inside the thick woolen muff she carried. "Yes, along with Dr. Bowen himself." She faced him. "There was a flurry of notes from Lady Castlereagh last week. She wished to know why Bowen was spending so much time with Dorothea if she was entirely well again. Her ladyship suggested another doctor should examine her, make sure she didn't have anything catching. Dorothea was horrified, of course, both by the suggestion that she was contagious and by the thought of another doctor. She likes Dr. Bowen. And so, Dr. Bowen and I thought a—friendship—might offer a reason why he was still visiting her." She was babbling, talking too much and too fast, and he was staring into her face as if she were a stranger—a very daft, very talkative, very annoying stranger.

"And what will happen when Dorothea realizes that he is simply visiting her to cover for me, and you, and the whole damned British delegation, that it's all politics, not friendship at all?" Stephen demanded. "She'll be heartbroken. You are not doing her a favor at all. It's cruelty."

Julia felt her smile slip in the face of his anger. He was protective of his sister, gentle and kind, and she admired that, but why would he disapprove of Dorothea enjoying a simple friendship? Dr. Bowen had been happy to have a reason to keep visiting Dorothea, liked her company. Would Stephen not be pleased if Dorothea found new love, a way forward with her life? Perhaps he feared that Peter Bowen was not suitable for his sister, the widow of a viscount, the sister of a baron.

"Have you not noticed how happy Dorothea has been of late?" she asked. "Even if she cannot walk in the park with Peter, she walks with me, or her maid—"

"You call him Peter?" Stephen demanded, his brows drawing together, colliding.

She felt her face heat despite the cold. What was he suggesting? "He has given me permission to do so."

"Do you meet with him to discuss my sister often?" My, but he was stiff this afternoon. He was scanning the park, looking at everything and everyone but her, his tone brittle. He had stopped in the middle of the path, his hands clasped behind his back, at attention. A pigeon flapped overhead, and she wondered if the bird would land on him, mistaking him for a statue. He'd sunk his chin into his greatcoat, oblivious to the fact that his nose and cheeks were reddening from the cold.

Julia raised her chin. "No. He visited Jamie at my request. His teeth are growing in, and he's fractious. I was concerned that his crying might disturb someone." She had been up at night for weeks, walking the floor with her son until he slept at last. "Peter—Dr. Bowen—was the one who mentioned the notes from Lady Castlereagh, and her fears about Dorothea's health." She assumed a similarly stiff posture to match his. "Perhaps I should mention that Dr. Bowen has invited Dorothea to attend the symphony tonight. There is to be a performance of Beethoven, and the maestro himself is conducting. She is most excited to go, but if you think it best that she stay at home, you should speak to her."

He popped his head out of his greatcoat like an angry turtle. "I will indeed. I won't have anyone using my sister as a pawn, Miss Leighton. What will happen when Bowen decides she can do without his company? He'll grow tired of her, and then what? Dorothea is already beginning to imagine that he has feelings for her, and she most certainly has feelings for him."

Julia felt her heart melt, and she smiled. "But that's wonderful!" He was still frowning. "Isn't it?"

He began walking again, in long, angry strides she struggled to keep up with. "Dorothea is a fragile creature. Bowen doesn't know her as I do. Only a year ago she lost everything she loved. Do you expect me to stand by and allow her heart to be broken again?"

She caught his arm. "But what if it isn't? And she didn't lose everything. She had you."

He stopped again, and studied her face, looked at her hand on his arm, his eyes softening at last.

Was he remembering that her own world had also collapsed a year ago, that she too had lost everything? If not for her own strength, and for this job, where would she be now? Seeing Dorothea happy again, hopeful, had given her hope as well, but if he didn't approve of his sister finding love again, he would hardly think it appropriate for her. Would anyone? Would she only ever have memories of that one, brief, frenzied night to keep her warm?

She withdrew her hand and stepped back, continuing ahead, measuring her distance from him in the crunch of her footsteps on the cinder path. Perhaps there was no hope for her to find redemption after all. She hadn't just *lost* everything—some would say she had thrown it away, and did not deserve a second chance. Perhaps Stephen Ives thought so, would forever see the taint upon her.

She looked up at the bare gray limbs of the trees, felt tears fill her eyes but blinked them away. There was no room, no time, for self-pity. If she could go back now and change everything, would she?

As long as she lived, even if she spent the rest of her days alone, she would never forget the admiration in Thomas Merritt's eyes, and the way he made her feel like a woman for the first time. She could not have married David after that night, even if pregnancy had not prevented it. They would not have made each other happy, or ever had any more than vague regard for each other—and even one night of passion was better than a lifetime of vague regard.

She'd often wondered if it had been a trick of fate that had turned Thomas Merritt's footsteps toward her in the park, brought him to her betrothal ball. What if, like Dorothea and Dr. Bowen finding joy in each other after such a dreadful introduction, her meeting with Thomas Merritt had been a kind of salvation?

She heard Stephen following her, his footsteps matching hers as he caught up. "Julia, wait, please—this isn't what I wanted to speak to you about at all," he said, and she shut her eyes. Yes, she thought, as she waited for him to speak, if the chance to love someone came along, she would take it. She wanted a man to love her, a father for Jamie. She did not want to spend her life alone after all.

"Julia, I'm sorry. I cannot bear to see her hurt anymore."

"But that isn't your choice. If you chase away any chance for happiness that comes her way, she *will* be hurt, don't you see?"

He studied her face. "I think that perhaps I should—"

If he was intending to apologize, the shout that rang out stopped him.

The thunder of hoofbeats trampled the quiet afternoon, and the air filled with the objections and surprised cries of those who suddenly found themselves dodging a pack of unruly riders.

"Stand!" screamed a voice in German, and Julia gasped at the sight of the gray afternoon light glinting on the barrel of a pistol pointed at a coach. The person holding the gun was masked, clad in black like death himself. Only a pair of ferocious dark eyes showed. His horse danced nervously as the vehicle's occupant, a woman, screamed.

Two horsemen wrested the reins from the frightened coachman's grip and pulled the team to a stop, and the woman's scream rang out again as the black rider pulled the door open and pointed the pistol inside. She began to sob and plead, but he yelled for silence in German.

Other riders trained their pistols on the crowd.

Julia gaped in stunned silence until Stephen gripped her arms and thrust her behind him. He reached for his sword, drew it from the scabbard, but the hiss of the metal made one of the gunmen swing his pistol in Stephen's direction, point it at his chest.

"Raise your hands!" he screamed in English. The gun shook in his grip.

Stephen did so, dropping his sword. "Julia, don't move," he muttered.

"Money, jewels, everything!" a guttural German voice shouted at the occupants of the carriage, and the woman pleaded for mercy.

A robbery? Julia stared at the scene before her, at the guns, the masks, the frightened faces of the bystanders, the hard eyes of the thieves. She drew a breath—highwaymen, here in Vienna's most elegant city park, the park where Jamie walked with his nurse, where Dorothea strolled with Peter Bowen, where countless others spent pleasant hours in the sunshine. She stared at the gun pointed at Stephen's chest, saw the gunman's pale eyes through the ragged holes of his makeshift mask. Would he shoot? She had no doubt he would.

The woman screamed again, and a bystander cried out as one of the other riders cuffed him for daring to protest. The gunman holding Stephen looked away for a moment, his gun wavering in his hand, his finger twitching on the trigger. Julia felt a flash of anger. The damned fool was going to shoot someone by accident. Or entirely on purpose. This was not a play or one of Dorothea's gothic novels. It was real, and dangerous. She looked around at the faces of the bystanders, saw only numb fear in their eyes. They would do nothing, *could* do nothing without risking their own lives. She looked down the path, but there was no one coming to the rescue. The lady in the coach was begging for her life in German as they tore the jewelry from her throat, demanded her wedding ring.

Indignation burned in her breast. Someone had to do something.

Behind the cover of Stephen's back she reached into her reticule for the pistol he had given her in case this very situation should occur on their journey here. She'd kept it, carried it still, in case she happened to run into Lord Stewart again, or someone else who imagined a fallen woman might be easy prey for a little rough seduction.

She'd never imagined that she would actually meet a highwayman—or seven highwaymen. She wasn't afraid—anger and indignation filled her. How dare these men put people's lives at risk, terrify them, steal from them? It was not to be borne.

She felt the solid weight of the pistol in her hand, the cold metal radiating through her thin leather glove. She took a breath as she stepped out from behind Stephen and aimed at the nearest rider.

Everything happened at once. Stephen called her name as she pulled the trigger, turning toward her, diving for his sword with one hand, grabbing for her with the other.

She heard the rider scream, saw the mist of blood fill the air as the bullet hit his leg. His horse lifted him into the air, kicking out in fear, and he was tossed like a bag of meal in the saddle, holding on but dropping his gun.

She was lying on the grass, breathless, Stephen stood over her, his sword in hand, shouting orders to stop, to surrender, and suddenly everyone was moving. Gentlemen drew their swords as the riders set their heels to their horses and fled pell-mell, desperate to escape now that everything had gone wrong.

Julia watched the chaos, her hand aching from the recoil of the gun. The man she'd injured was clutching his leg, blubbering and bleeding, trying to turn his horse, to ride after the rest. One of his fellows grabbed his reins and dragged the horse away. Within seconds they'd vanished into the trees as quickly as they'd come.

"Are you hurt?" Stephen asked, helping her to her feet, but she shook her head.

"The lady in the coach—" she began, and he nodded, then ran to the vehicle and looked inside.

People were crowding around Julia now as well, looking into her face, touching her, speaking to her. She couldn't hear a word.

Stephen helped a portly woman in a fur-lined cloak out

of the coach. She was crying, tears flowing over her red face as she clung to his hand. Her neck was bruised where her missing necklace had cut into her skin. Her maid followed, crying hysterically, her mouth bloody. The pitiful sight started several other women wailing too, realizing the danger they had all been in.

Julia stared at the pistol, then at the blood on the grass, and tasted bile. She felt light-headed but resisted the urge to faint. An arm came around her, holding her upright, and she was bundled toward a bench. "Sit down," a man ordered in French. "I doubt I could catch you if you fainted." He pressed a flask into her hands. "Drink," he commanded, and she did so. Her eyes watered and she coughed as the heat of the spirits crept down her throat and through her limbs. He patted her back. "Well done, *mademoiselle*. Very well done," he said. "This could all have ended rather badly, if not for you. If you were not English, I would compare you with Joan of Arc."

She looked up at the gentleman leaning on an ornate cane, wearing a heavy cloak lined with thick fur. His sharp eyes took in her face, her clothes, everything, in a single sweeping glance.

"*Merci, monsieur*," she said as she handed back the flask, and her voice came out a hoarse croak.

He pursed his lips. "*You* are thanking *me*?" He looked around. "Now that the excitement of the afternoon is over, I believe I shall go back to my lodgings and enjoy a hot cup of something well laced with brandy. I suggest you do the same, *mademoiselle*." He bowed and walked away with a heavy limp.

Stephen came to find her, his face filled with concern. "I'm quite all right," she managed. "Is everyone . . . ?"

"Yes, thanks to you." He looked around the park. "Five

of these people are actually Austrian policemen, all sent to snoop for secrets, and yet they were of no bloody use at all for anything else, it appears." He held out a hand and she took it, surprised at how wobbly she felt. He tucked her hand under his arm and smiled, and she read pride in his eyes, admiration, and felt her cheeks flame. "The lady in the coach wishes to thank you," he said, leading her in that direction.

"It isn't necessary," Julia said. "I just want to—" She wanted to go home and hold her son, kiss his soft curls, curl up and sleep, thankful it was over and everyone was safe. She looked at Stephen. "You weren't hurt?"

His mouth quirked to one side in a wry grin. "No. You were very brave."

"Was I? Foolish, perhaps," she murmured.

"It's what James might have done, if he'd been here," he said, scanning the activity in the park as they walked toward the coach. "It seems I am beholden to yet another heroic Leighton."

"James?" She felt her heart contract.

A liveried servant bore down on them over the grass, a man who had been on the coach. "Madam, the countess is most grateful," he said stiffly in accented English. His eyes roamed over Julia as if she were one of the wonders of the world.

Like James.

"She begs you to name your reward," the servant said, taking out a notepad and a stub of a pencil. He beamed at her hopefully, his brows raised in readiness.

Julia stared at the end of the pencil. Did he expect—hope—that she would ask for rubies, diamonds, emeralds? A king's ransom in gold? Wasn't that what the highwayman had demanded? She shook her head. "Nothing," she said.

His face melted and his jaw dropped. "But my lady is the wife of the Bavarian ambassador! You must!"

There was blood on the gray November grass, bright as roses.

Julia felt tears spring into her eyes. "The man I shot, is he—" she began. Stephen and the servant both turned to look in the direction the thieves had fled.

"No, unfortunately, they all got away," the servant said. "There are men looking for them, have no fear, dear lady."

"I'm not afraid!" she said fiercely. She was relieved. She had not taken a life. She turned to Stephen. "I must get back. Dorothea will be waiting and I have duties to see to." She simply began walking, ignoring the quivering of her legs.

Stephen caught up with her. "Are you quite all right?" he asked. "You're as pale as a sheet."

"Yes," she said. "At least, I think so. I have never shot anyone before."

He chuckled. "You did very well. What did Prince de Talleyrand say to you?" he asked.

She looked up at him in confusion. "Who?"

"The gentleman with the cane. He's the French ambassador. Lord Castlereagh refers to him as the Old Fox."

She blinked at him. Bavarian countesses, the French ambassador—was there anyone in Vienna who hadn't been in the park this afternoon?

She swallowed, tasted the brandy on her tongue. "He thanked me, and gave me brandy to drink, said it would calm my nerves."

He guided her homeward in silence, too stunned, perhaps, to speak of ordinary things now.

The palace came into view, yellow light spilling out over the blue shadows of twilight. She would go in, ask for a hot bath, see her son, and do all the ordinary things that needed do be taken care of. Dorothea wanted a pattern book from Paris. She wanted pastries ordered from a little café where she had taken coffee with Peter Bowen . . . She glanced at Stephen Ives's shadowed profile, felt the warmth coming from his body next to hers in the chill evening, watched the way their footsteps marched together. Had she fallen in with his pace, or he with hers? Like soldiers, marching, as he might have marched with James. She realized that he had not told her what he'd wanted to say to her, that the events of the afternoon had interrupted him. That conversation had been the point of their excursion, the reason why they were in the park at all. It suddenly seemed very important to know what he wanted to discuss.

"What did you wish to speak to me about, my lord?" she asked as they reached the steps of the palace. She held her breath, hoping it was a task that would take her mind off the events of the afternoon, something mundane and dull and—

Stephen turned to look at her in the soft blue light of the evening, his eyes in shadow. "I—" he began, then swallowed audibly. "I wanted to say—oh, bugger it!" He pulled her into his arms, and his mouth descended on hers, his lips warm against her wind-chilled skin. His mouth slanted over her as if he were starving. Surprised, she held onto his lapels and allowed the kiss, felt relief in it, the antithesis of fear. Their warm breath rose around them, misty in the cold. He kissed her until they heard footsteps coming along the street toward them and he was forced to stop, and reluctantly stepped back. She stared at him in the light from the doorway, too stunned to even nod as Stephen tipped his hat to the passerby. She raised her gloved hand to her lips. Why on earth would he—

He brushed a lock of hair out of his face and watched the figure disappear into the twilight. "We'd better go inside."

She hurried up the steps and into the warm glow of the foyer. Servants arrived at once to take their coats. "I must see Castlereagh," he murmured to her. "Make a report of what happened. Go upstairs and rest. I shall see you at dinner." He paused. "No wait, I have an official engagement this evening. Later, perhaps? Or at breakfast?"

He looked boyishly eager, his eyes and cheeks and lips bright with the cold, and the kiss.

She nodded, still unable to trust her voice not to shake. It had been the stress of the moment, the aftermath of the frightening events in the park. He'd wanted to soothe her, offer him his thanks. It was the shock that had made him kiss her like that.

He was probably mortified he'd gone so far, kissed a ruined lady, a servant.

But when she met his eyes, she read his desire to kiss her again—a warmth in his eyes, a longing that made her breath catch in her throat and stick there. He turned to the servants, asking them to fetch tea and sherry and send it upstairs to her room at once, before he strode off down the hall toward the ambassador's study.

"Was it cold outside, miss? Cook says it's going to snow tonight. He says his bunions are never wrong," the footman said, and chuckled.

Was it cold out? She felt hot all over. Couldn't they tell he'd kissed her?

But everything was perfectly normal, exactly as it had been when they'd left, scarcely two hours earlier.

How was that possible?

Chapter 21

Thomas arrived at the dowdy inn on the edge of the city just as Donovan screamed as they dug the bullet out of his leg. The valet had sent a tavern wench to fetch him, and she'd babbled the incoherent message that the Irishman was dying.

It turned out the shot had simply ruined Donovan's boots and buried itself in his calf muscle, but missed the bones and vital tendons. He was laid out on a table, writhing in pain as they removed the ball.

"A pint of rum. Half on the wound, half down his gullet," the rough surgeon said, and the barkeep had laughed.

"Aye, listen to Hans. He's the best vet in town!"

"Vet?" Donovan moaned, and fainted. Thomas winced as he watched them pour the rum into the wound and bandage it.

"What the hell was he doing?" Thomas demanded, looking at the blank faces of the men who sat around the scarred table that had served as a makeshift operating theater.

Another man came into the circle of lamplight that surrounded the table, wiping his hands, his face freshly shaven, his clothing clean, an eagle among vultures. "A robbery in the park, gone wrong." He made it sound like a child's prank, a skinned knee.

He held out a hand to Thomas. "My name is Erich. I'm glad to meet you at last, Herr Merritt, even under such circumstances. I have been waiting for a chance to speak to you for some weeks, and you have refused all my invitations. I am sorry it took this to bring you here." Erich looked down at Donovan's unconscious form without an ounce of pity in his gaze.

Thomas felt unease prickle at his scalp. Of course, he should have recognized the man from Donovan's descriptions. Vienna's King of Thieves, and his merry men, though not one of the mongrels surrounding the table looked merry in the least. They were downtrodden, whipped dogs. He didn't bother to take the man's hand. "You're Donovan's Robin Hood," he muttered. "Is this how you thought it best to get my attention, to shoot my valet?"

Erich's lips quirked as if Thomas had said something funny, but his eyes remained cold. He repeated the comment to his fellows in German, which Thomas didn't understand, and there was a brief round of forced laughter at Thomas's expense.

"I didn't shoot him. A woman did, in the park. She had a pistol in her purse." He indicated a seat. "Is this a usual habit with English ladies? Come and sit down, have a drink."

Thomas's skin prickled again. "She was English?"

Erich shrugged. "She was with an English officer, so I assume she was. Anyone you know?"

Thomas frowned. Would the lady who owned the watch, such a sweet, sentimental token of love, carry a pistol? It didn't fit. Lady Castlereagh herself would be well guarded, with a whole platoon of crack shots, meaning she wouldn't need to carry a gun. "No."

Donovan stirred, groaning. "Give him the rum now," the vet ordered, and took a swig from his own pint of grog. The tavern wench propped his head on her shoulder and fed him sips of rum.

"Merritt. You came. I wasn't sure you'd bother," Donovan muttered. "Shall I make the introductions?" His face was white and drawn with pain. A slick trail of rum flowed over his chin.

"We've all met," Thomas said. "What the devil were you doing? Do you even know which end of a pistol the bullet comes out of?"

Donovan managed a pained smirk. "Someone's got to earn a living. Did Erich tell you?"

"Tell me what? That you've traded your valet's coat for a bandit's mask?" he said. "It doesn't suit you, Patrick."

Donovan smiled wanly at the use of his first name. "Ah, so we're friends again. You've barely spoken to me for weeks, and after I made all the arrangements you wanted."

Thomas frowned. "What arrangements?"

"You were looking for an English lady," Erich said. "Donovan told me you wished to return something to her."

Thomas gave him the most aristocratic glare he could manage, damning the criminal for his impudence without saying a word, though his heart hammered against his breastbone.

Erich grinned, all teeth and malice, and Thomas half expected them to drag the poor Englishwoman out of the back room, bloodied and broken. Instead, the thief merely took a place across the table from him. They stood facing each other and Donovan lay between them, a living, battered border between the worlds of good and evil. Thomas wondered which side of the border his valet resided on now. "Sit, drink," Erich invited him again, but he remained standing, his posture stiff.

Erich snapped his fingers and the wench brought him a glass of schnapps. He quaffed it at a gulp, and she poured another.

"I shall tell you what I know, then," Erich said. "All the English ladies with the British Embassy have apartments on the second floor of the palace on the Minoritenplatz. The ambassador and his wife live on the third floor, and the first floor serves as offices and reception rooms. There, I have given you something you wanted. Does that help you?"

Thomas kept his expression blank. "Not at all. Why should it?"

"The watch. You said you wanted to return it, wanted to find the lady," Donovan reminded him, as if he were an idiot, the rum taking effect now. "Well, she's likely in there, on the second floor, now isn't she? You'll have to get inside, at night. Erich thought you might climb through a window on the second floor."

Climb through a window? "Why?" Thomas asked again.

Donovan tsked drunkenly. "Because you can't simply walk up to the door and pay your respects, demand to see what's-her-name who lost the watch with the bloody huge diamond on the case. Especially since the diamond is long gone, and there's bound to be some awkward questions 'bout that. 'Sides, Lord Stewart is in there. You remember him, don't you? Good friend of your brother's, better friend of his wife's?"

Thomas felt his legs turn to water, and he took the offered seat at last. He felt the thief's eyes on him, and kept his expression flat. Stewart. He'd heard that he was in Vienna, had known he would be. Donovan was quite right. It was a reason to steer clear of the British Embassy altogether. But the watch was in his pocket, waiting.

Erich simply began talking, as if Thomas had agreed to something he hadn't. Yet.

"There is a wide ledge around the second floor. You can get in at the back, where there aren't any guards, because those rooms are right above the stables, where the guards are housed. If you're careful, they won't see you in the dark." He grinned. "Are you careful? Donovan seems to think you are a master thief indeed."

He wasn't. He'd climbed trees and hills, but never walls. Thomas folded his arms over his chest, tried to look like he knew exactly whet they were talking about. "Go on."

"Once you are inside, you can find the lady, or leave the watch where it will be located and returned to her by someone else, if you prefer," Erich said. "The staff will probably be blamed for the loss of the diamond. You'll have to be careful after that."

"After that?" Thomas asked.

Erich smiled coldly. "A favor for a favor, Herr Merritt. I have given you something you want, now you must give me something I want. The English guard their palace as if the crown jewels of England were inside." He smirked. "If they are, I want you to bring them out."

Thomas gaped at him. He could charm a lady, purloin her earrings, slip a ring off her finger in the heat of passion, but he wasn't a housebreaker. He glanced at Donovan, who knew that he had dared to lie, to increase his stock with this man by embellishing tales about Thomas's skills as a thief. His valet just shrugged, then winced at the pain.

"They want the Order of the Garter Lady Castlereagh was wearing as a hat at the Emperor's ball," he said.

"Tiara," Thomas corrected him. "I have no idea where, or even how—" he began.

Erich laughed, a low mirthless growl. "But you are English, raised in a noble home. You know the kinds of places where English lords hide their valuables, do you not?"

"'Course he does," Donovan said. He grimaced as he tried to sit up, then fell back, too drunk or in too much pain. "It will be the easiest thing in the world. Erich's lads will create a distraction so you can slip inside. Once there, leave the watch and take the hat. Simple as that."

Simple as that. So was a hanging.

"And if I don't?"

Erich sighed, took a pistol out of his waistband and laid it on Donovan's chest. "We'll have to shoot you, my friend. We'll shoot you in the leg, like Donovan here. Then we'll leave you where the authorities can find you. The Bavarian ambassador wants the man who attacked his wife. There's a warrant out for a man with a bullet in his leg, and a substantial reward. He won't care if it's the wrong man. Everything about this damned conference is all for appearance anyway, truth and justice be damned. And since you don't speak any German to defend yourself—" He shrugged expressively and ground his thumb into Donovan's wound, making the valet scream. "Meanwhile, Herr Donovan would be entirely expendable."

"God, Merritt, do as he says!" Donovan panted, clutching at Thomas's hand, leaving a smear of grime on his skin. Tainted, Thomas thought, staring at the mark, just like Donovan or Erich. As bad as they were.

Thomas met Erich's cold smile, and felt a bead of sweat roll down his back. He had no choice. He couldn't let Donovan die of stupidity, since that's what this whole thing amounted to. When—if—they got out of this, he'd . . .

What? Dismiss the fool without references?

Erich's glare was burning a hole in his forehead. Planning a suitable punishment for Donovan would have to wait until he'd saved his life.

"Tomorrow night," he said, feeling as if he was sitting on a shifting pile of sand in a snake-infested river.

"Tonight, I think, would be better," Erich said. "There's no moon."

Thomas had no argument for that logic. He nodded, a brief jerk of his head, and Erich extended his hand, his smile cold. This time there was no choice but to take it.

Chapter 22

Julia hurried down the hall to her room, her footsteps echoing through the marble corridors, her cheeks burning.

It had been quite a day. She had shot a man in the leg, almost killing him—probably. Someone had returned the pistol to her, and she'd tucked it back into her reticule. She tossed the bag into the corner now, not wanting it near her.

Stephen had been wrong. She wasn't anything like James. James was brave and smart, and he wouldn't be hiding in the dark of his bedroom trembling like a leaf.

She forced herself to cross the room and light a candle. She caught sight of her pale reflection in the mirror. Was she different? Her eyes were deep hollows, her cheeks lean and reddened by the wind. Would James even recognize her? She was not the little sister he'd known.

Not only had she shot someone today. She'd allowed Stephen Ives to kiss her.

She put a hand to her lips, touched the still-tingling flesh tentatively.

It hadn't been a brotherly kiss, or the type of kiss given in thanks for a kindness.

It had been the kiss of a man who admires a woman,

desires her. Even with her limited experience of kisses, she knew that much.

Her first kiss, at her betrothal ball, had altered her life forever. And her second one, Stephen's kiss? "Impossible," she murmured.

She felt a frisson of shock that a man like Stephen Ives—a gentleman, a diplomat, an officer, someone who knew the worst of the tales about her—had kissed her! It wasn't like Lord Stewart's kiss, forced upon her, a hard, cold parody of affection.

Nor was it like Thomas Merritt's kiss. Would she forever compare all other kisses to his?

She tried to leave Thomas out of her analysis of the situation. She had to, if she was going to make any sense at all of it.

Stephen's kiss had been a comfort, a soothing balm after the events of the afternoon. She wanted to sink into his arms and not remember that she'd shot someone. She hadn't seen stars. She'd felt safe in his arms, yet unsafe. She was treading on dangerous ground yet again.

Julia watched herself in the mirror as a bloom of color rose over her cheeks. She genuinely *liked* Stephen Ives. He was kind, charming, intelligent, and handsome, but she had never considered him in a—well, a *kissing* kind of way before.

What could he have been thinking? Horror struck her, and she met her gaze in the mirror, saw her own mother's accusing eyes, filled with scorn and shock. Did he assume she might be willing to— No, he'd been perfectly correct in every way with her until now.

It *must* have been shock, gratitude, or some other emotion that made him do it.

The door opened and she spun around, wondering if it were Stephen come to kiss her again, or worse, beg forgiveness for being so rash. But it was Dorothea. Her eyes were bright, her cheeks glowing, and she was smiling like a cat with a canary in her teeth. Julia felt hot blood fill her cheeks again. Had Stephen told her about the kiss, or had Dorothea heard that she'd shot a man in the park? Surely she wouldn't be smiling about the latter.

"I'm having supper with Peter tonight," Dorothea said. "Alone, in the small dining room downstairs, before we go to the concert."

"Oh? Did you want me to join you?" Julia asked, wondering if she needed a chaperone, but Dorothea giggled.

"Quite the opposite! I *do* want you to help me choose a dress—something bright and pretty—but I was hoping you would be otherwise engaged this evening."

Julia had nothing planned. The Castlereaghs were attending a formal dinner at the home of the Austrian ambassador, Prince Metternich. She had not been invited to the important and exclusive function, of course. "I'm not—" she began, interrupted by a knock at the door.

Her chest tightened. What if it was Stephen? Dorothea was sure to ask why he was coming to her room. She had a way of reading the truth in her brother's eyes. Julia imagined him standing in the middle of the rug, his hands behind his back, looking more like a chastised schoolboy than a lord major as Dorothea put him to the question. *I kissed your companion,* he might tell her, *and now I've come to—*

To what?

"Aren't you going to answer the door?" Dorothea asked, going herself.

A liveried footman bowed. "This arrived for Miss Leighton. The courier asked that it be delivered at once."

Dorothea took the envelope off the tray and glanced at it. "Prince de Talleyrand?" she said, her brows rising.

"How do you know the French ambassador, and why on earth is he sending you messages?"

Julia crossed to take the letter, a prickle of surprise crawling along her spine, but it had been a day of surprises. "It is probably from his niece, Diana. We've met several times in the past few weeks."

"Truly?" Dorothea asked, sitting down to wait while Julia opened the letter, her eyes alight with curiosity. "What did you talk about?"

Julia turned the envelope in her hands, glanced at the seal. Not Diana's. And the script that addressed the letter was bold and masculine, not Diana's delicate hand. "Oh, we—gossip, mostly, I suppose."

Dorothea smiled. "I can't wait to hear! Peter brings me stories, but not from the niece of the French ambassador! Do open it."

Julia broke the seal, scanned the enclosed message and nearly dropped the letter. She stared at it, read the polite note again. It was written in French, and bore the unmistakable tone of a man certain his order would be obeyed, even if it was disguised as a very kind invitation to a birthday dinner for Diana. "It's an invitation," she said to Dorothea. "Apparently, Diana's birthday is tomorrow, and the prince is having a supper party for her this evening. He is sorry for the lateness of the request, but asks if I might attend."

"Truly?" Dorothea gushed again, and held out her hand. Julia put the letter into her palm and crossed to the desk. "Why on earth?"

There was yet another knock on the door. "And who might this be, the Tsar of Russia?" Dorothea quipped, but a mere maid entered with clean linens and a pail of kindling.

She curtsied and set her burdens down before turning

to Julia. "Oh, my lady, the tales of your bravery are all they're talking about in the servants' hall!"

"Her bravery?" Dorothea asked, looking from Julia to the maid and back again. "What does that mean?"

"Lady Julia—Miss Leighton—shot three robbers in the park! They were trying to steal the crown from the Austrian emperor himself!" the girl gushed.

Dorothea's eyes widened. "Truly? What on earth were you doing in the park?" she asked Julia.

"I was walking."

"Alone?"

"No, she was with Major Lord Ives," the maid said, bending to lay the fire in the grate. "He killed six robbers himself, and climbed a tree to retrieve the crown."

"Stephen climbed a tree?" Dorothea gasped. "He hasn't done so since he was eight. As I recall, he got stuck and had to be rescued by his tutor."

"He carried the crown in his teeth!" the maid said.

Dorothea looked confused. "All this happened while I was napping?"

There was another knock, and this time a footman entered, carrying a scuttle full of coals for the fire. "If I may be so bold, we're all proud of you, Miss Leighton, below-stairs, saving Major Lord Ives's life like that," he said.

Dorothea turned. "Did you catch him as he fell from the tree?"

"Tree?" the footman said. "He was facing almost twenty men, my lady, all armed with pistols, and he had naught but his sword. If Lady Julia hadn't shot eleven men, he'd have perished there in the park."

"You shot eleven men with a single pistol, Julia? I thought it only held one bullet!"

Julia's cheeks warmed. "It was only one man, and I merely grazed him. Everyone else ran off unharmed."

The footman's mouth twisted as he stared at Julia. "D'you mind if we tell it our way, m'lady? It makes a better story."

"It's a lovely story," the maid added. "You could dine out for weeks on it, as Lady Castlereagh might say."

Dorothea rose. "Yes, well, Lady Julia is to dine out tonight, as a matter of fact, with the French ambassador, and she must dress at once." She made a shooing motion with her hands, and the servants bowed, glancing adoringly once more at Julia as they left.

Julia crossed to the desk and took out a sheet of writing paper. "I wish you hadn't told them that. It will be all over the kitchen that I'm having dinner with the Emperor, or the Tsar, or both!"

"What are you doing?" Dorothea asked.

"I'm sending my regrets to Prince de Talleyrand," Julia replied.

"Of course you're not! Once you have told me the whole story of this afternoon's escapades, you simply must go!"

Julia regarded her with a half smile. "I am a servant, Dorothea. It is not my place to attend supper parties with the French ambassador and his niece, especially without permission."

Dorothea waved her hand. "You have *my* permission. Is it that you don't have an escort?" She pointed at the pen in Julia's hand. "It would be better if you sent your acceptance, then wrote a note to Stephen to ask if he could escort you." She snatched the pen from Julia's hand. "Better yet, I shall do it for you, so he cannot refuse. Not that he would, of course. He is fond of you, and he would gladly lend you an arm to lean upon, especially now that you've saved his life."

Julia felt her skin turn crimson again at the idea of

spending such an evening in Stephen's company. How might such a request look—*or feel*—especially now, so soon after the kiss?

"I believe he is attending a state dinner with Lord Castlereagh tonight—" she began.

"Then we shall send one of Castlereagh's aides to escort you to the door of the French Embassy. You shall not go unchaperoned."

Dorothea grabbed Julia's hand as she opened her mouth to protest again. "Come with me," she said. "I just know you were about to say that you have nothing to wear, but we shall go at once and raid my wardrobe for pretty dresses for both of us to wear tonight, you at your French ball and me at my far more intimate meal. Who knows whom you might meet—a handsome French diplomat, a charming prince, a lord or two, even. You must dress tonight the way you did in the days when we both attended London parties and danced and flirted the nights away." She picked up the vial of perfume that sat on Julia's dressing table, the last of her favorite perfume, which she had not worn since she left her father's home. Dorothea opened the stopper and sniffed deeply.

"Hmm. Yes, wear some of this too. You are too good to be a servant, Julia, though I adore your company. It will do you good to go out into the kind of society you should be mixing with. I won't hear any more excuses. It will be perfectly all right—more than all right. Now come and help me. I need something especially nice to wear tonight, perhaps pink? And you should wear green, to bring out the color of your eyes. I would suggest blue, but perhaps it would appear too French? Perhaps not . . . we shall see." She swept Julia down the hall to her rooms, calling for her maid.

Dorothea sent Stephen a note, and he sent one back.

He could not change his plans for the evening, being officially required as Lord Castlereagh's aide. After another insistent note from Dorothea, he agreed to arrange a coach to take Julia to Kaunitz Palace. Despite appearances and propriety, which demanded an unmarried lady needed a chaperone, Julia realized that she was outside the bounds of such precise etiquette. Stephen had probably agreed to let her go in hopes that she might overhear something of use. She no longer needed instructions. She simply reported what was useful, and had become quite good at discerning useful tidbits among ordinary chatter.

Several hours later Julia was dressed in a pale gold silk gown, her hair elegantly styled by Dorothea's maid. She hurried down the grand staircase to the front door, where the arranged coach awaited her.

"Well, well, what have we here?" Lord Stewart's voice rang through the foyer, stopping Julia where she stood on the steps. Her stomach clenched as he crossed the hall to stand at the bottom of the stairs, blocking her way to the door. He gave her an insolent look of appraisal. "The plain workaday pigeon is a peacock by night, I see. Where are you sneaking off to?"

She raised her chin. She wished she had the daring to sweep past him without a word, to let him watch her get into the coach and wonder, but she did not. As a mere servant, he would never let her pass. "I have Lady Dorothea's permission, my lord."

"An errand, at this hour, in that grand dress? No one alerted me that you would be out of the palace—" He made a show of looking behind her. "—and quite unescorted. I am responsible for the safety of this delegation, and that includes knowing where everyone is, servants and underlings included. Especially you, given your reputation for—"

"I am attending a birthday celebration," she interrupted.

"Ah, but whose birthday is it?" he asked, setting one booted foot on the bottom step, leaning against the balustrade, his eyes roaming over her.

"I am going to visit—" Julia swallowed the rest. Would he approve or disapprove if he knew she was going to spend the evening at the French Embassy? If he forbade her to go, she would be forced to return upstairs, Dorothea's permission or not.

"You know, my dear, despite Castlereagh's satisfaction with the scraps of information you've brought him, Lady Castlereagh is pressing to have you dismissed," he said. "She doesn't believe it is wholesome to have a woman of your reputation here among the honorables and worthies of our delegation. Seeing you here, dressed so fetchingly, and about to slip out into the night, I must say I'm inclined to agree. A word from me to Lord Castlereagh and you would be gone." He took another step up toward her, then another. Julia resisted the urge to back up. "I'm sure you realize just how easily I could ensure that will happen . . . or not." Julia held her ground. She didn't have her pistol now. All she had was a fan. A debutante might get stellar results by rapping an impertinent swain on the wrist with her fan, but a servant would not.

His slick leer made her stomach turn. He was five steps away from her, then four . . . "If you might be so inclined to show your appreciation for my silence, then perhaps—"

"Julia?" Stephen stood at the bottom of the steps, glaring up at Lord Stewart. He was also dressed for the evening, elegant in his dress tunic, glittering with braid and gold frogs. He came up the steps, past Stewart, and took her arm. "The coach is outside. I will see you safely to the Kaunitz on my way to Prince Metternich's," he said.

Stewart looked at her again, and this time his eyes were sharp with suspicion. "The Kaunitz?"

"Oh, she's not going to sell secrets, if that's your concern, my lord," Stephen replied. "She is a dear friend of Talleyrand's niece, and has received an invitation to dine. Even you cannot object to that, having failed to win such an entrée into Talleyrand's company yourself."

Charles Stewart looked stunned for an instant, then suspicious. "Does the prince know about her?"

Stephen's brows rose into his hairline. "Know about her?"

Stewart's smirk was back. "Yes, *know,* that she's ruined, disowned by her own mother for her wanton ways."

Stephen tilted his head. "Oh, that. I thought you meant her heroic actions in the park today. I gave a full report to Lord Castlereagh just an hour ago. Have you not heard the story?"

Stewart looked confused. "In the park? I have been otherwise occupied this afternoon. I haven't seen his lordship yet."

Stephen took Julia's hand and placed it on his sleeve. "I'm sure you'll hear the story before long, and then I'd really start to worry about Lady Julia's skill with a pistol if I were you. And as for Talleyrand, you can be sure he *knows* everything about every member of this household, down to the lowest scullery maid. He was in the park this afternoon, by the way, watching."

Charles Stewart was staring at her now with quite a different expression—awe.

"You can be sure I will speak to my brother," he said, "and I will expect a full report on everything you see and hear tonight, Miss Leighton."

Julia inclined her head obediently. The danger had passed, the lion's teeth had been pulled. She was grateful to Stephen. "Of course my lord. I shall describe every plate of food, every bubble in the champagne. I will be sure to count the hairs in every gentleman's moustache, and recount every birthday toast right down to a detailed report on who does not like strawberry gâteau. Will that do?"

He flushed deeply but didn't reply. Julia felt his eyes burning into her back as Stephen escorted her to the coach.

In the darkness of the vehicle, she waited for her heartbeat to slow, and tried to calm her indignation and anger. How dare Charles Stewart assume she would ever agree to a casual tumble? His reputation was far worse than hers, and he had done nothing but cause trouble since his arrival in Vienna. It was well known that the British ambassador's half brother had a taste for whores, fighting, and drink. And yet Lady Castlereagh despised her, when she had done nothing even the slightest bit shocking—at least in the past hour or two. Julia bit her lip. What would her ladyship say when she heard about the incident in the park?

"You look beautiful tonight, Julia," Stephen said, after they had ridden in silence awhile. "I daresay that's what prompted Stewart to behave the way he did. You should be careful. You cannot afford to offend him."

Her indignation roared back, multiplied. "Are you suggesting that I should encourage him?" she demanded.

"Of course not!" he said. "He's dangerous, that's all, a boor, but a boor with power. He's used to getting what he wants with threats, or even force if necessary. He thinks you are easy prey because—" He stopped.

"Because of what?" Julia demanded. "Because I allow

my passions to rule my head? Is that why *you* kissed me? Because you think I might—" She didn't go on, felt a lump of shame and misery rise in her throat. Despite the chill of the evening, her face burned.

"Julia, I kissed you *despite* all that!" he said. "I've discovered that I don't *care* about any of it. I see you, Julia, your gentleness, your beauty, your wit, and how very brave you are. I think . . ." He paused, and leaned forward across the slight width of the coach, found her gloved hand, held it in his. "I think I may be falling in love with you, and try as I might, I cannot find a single reason why I should not do so."

Julia's mouth dried, making speech impossible, and her thundering heart stopped dead in her chest. The only sound was that of the horse's hoofbeats on the cobbles.

He was falling in love with her?

"Believe me, I wanted to punch Charles Stewart in the mouth for speaking to you that way, or challenge him to a duel, but this isn't the place. The rules are different here because of the conference." He gave a harsh laugh. "I have been through wars, fought in battles, faced terrible danger, and lived through it all, but nothing has ever scared me more than this. My feelings for you have caught me by surprise. I am not the kind of man who falls in love. I never have before, and I always considered myself more sensible than that. That's why I became a diplomat, because I believed I had the intellect and the sense to remain cool, unaffected by passions of any kind, like Castlereagh. But you've proven me wrong. I—I thought I was fully capable of controlling my emotions. Until I kissed you. No, until I met you, I think."

When the coach drew up at the grand entrance of the Kaunitz Palace, a footman stepped forward.

Julia watched him approach, knowing there were only

seconds before he opened the door, and she had no idea what to say. No one had ever loved her. Well, her brother had, and Nicholas and David—also like brothers. Thomas Merritt's attentions had been borne of exactly the kind of unruly emotions—passions—that Stephen spoke of.

"My lord, I—" she began, but he put her gloved hand to his lips and kissed it gently.

"Come, you've a party to attend, and I am off to a state dinner. We can talk later."

He really was very kind, and handsome, and charming. She felt a wistful yearning to be in love with him too.

"Go on, go and dazzle Talleyrand and his guests."

She got out of the coach, and he waited until she reached the door and it had opened for her before he ordered the coachman to drive on.

Chapter 23

Julia was ushered into an elegant drawing room filled with music, light, and people. A bust of the French King Louis XVIII looked down on the party with bland benevolence from a prominent pedestal. In fact, all the art in the room was French, right down to the Aubusson tapestries that adorned one entire wall, portraying the Goddess Diana hunting with Apollo.

Diana de Talleyrand looked up with pleasure as Julia entered and hurried across to greet her with a kiss on both cheeks.

"Dearest Julia, my uncle was just telling our guests about your adventure in the park this afternoon. How brave you are!" Julia felt her skin heat, especially when light applause broke out and she looked up to find everyone staring at her.

"But this is your night to celebrate, Diana. I wish you a very happy birthday," Julia murmured.

"Thank you," Diana twinkled. "It is all the happier for your presence. My uncle enjoys heroic tales, and you have brightened his day."

Julia was introduced to army officers, counts, baronesses, a charming Russian general, and a number of other people who were utterly delighted to make her acquaintance. She felt the way she had when she made her debut and people rushed across the ballroom to make her acquaintance as the future Duchess Temberlay, a lady worth knowing. It was seductive, this feeling. How easy it would be to have that life back again, here on the Continent. There were admiring gazes from several gentlemen, and one asked to whom he might apply for permission to call upon her formally.

She merely laughed. She had no idea.

She strolled in the prince's picture gallery, enjoying some of the marvelous paintings he had brought from France. Many were being brought home, a gesture of goodwill, since they had been taken from their rightful owners by Napoleon's troops.

"A lover of art as well as a heroine, I see," Prince de Talleyrand said, appearing at her elbow. "Come and see the very finest ones." He didn't wait for her to agree. He tucked her hand under his arm and set off, leaning on his cane. The ivory tip was silent in the halls of the Kaunitz Palace, which had been fitted with priceless carpets and tapestries to eliminate any noise. Julia felt a prickle of unease creep up her spine. She had grown used to listening to the sound of footsteps in the corridors of the Minoritenplatz. She could read them—fast steps meant news, slow, muffled ones eavesdroppers. There were the various sounds of soldiers' boots, ladies' slippers, and the servants' shoes. But here, in the deep silence, how would anyone know if there was someone approaching? They passed another tapestry, this one showing Joan of Arc crowning the Dauphin, and she realized that anyone might be hiding behind it, watching.

Talleyrand paused and swept the edge of the tapestry back, revealing a door. She wondered if there were other hidden doorways behind the draperies. Her heartbeat quickened as the door opened to reveal a small private chamber, brilliantly lit with candles, lighting the paintings that adorned every wall. A vast inlaid desk stood in the center of the room, with a single chair, but there was no other furniture.

She glanced at the pictures. Marie Antoinette smiled down at her from one wall, and Julia drew a breath. "Oh, my."

"Beautiful, aren't they? These are French paintings, meaning they were not looted by Napoleon. They are to be presented to His Majesty, the Emperor of Austria, when the time is right," Prince Talleyrand said. He pointed to a placid pink-cheeked lady with a plump baby in her arms. She gazed out at Julia with vague blue eyes. "That is a portrait of Napoleon's second empress, the former Austrian princess Marie Louise. Do you think her father will like it?"

Julia thought of the portrait Carrindale had ordered of her, painted just after her debut. Where was it now? Had he burned it, or did it merely lie in the attics of Carrindale House, moldering and forgotten?

"What father would not love such a portrait?" she asked. Talleyrand regarded her with pleasure. His eyes were so sharp she could almost feel them, probing her skull, reading her thoughts. And yet, he gave nothing away of his own thoughts, like Castlereagh.

"She is not the first Austrian queen we've had in France," he said, his eyes returning to the wall. "Though after what we did to the last one, poor Marie Antoinette, I'm surprised the Austrians allowed us to have another." He turned to look at her. "But I suppose when one has been conquered, everything goes to the victor. Napoleon wanted a princess of impeccable royal blood to give him an heir, and so this poor lady became a prize of war." He tilted his head. "Yet she came to love him. Tell me, do you think her a victim or a conqueror? Napoleon certainly loved her, once she had given him a son."

"And now she is kept away from her husband," Julia said softly. Did she miss him, dream of him, or had she forgotten him in the arms of her lover?

"Oh, it is better that way, I assure you. Do you not think Napoleon deserves to suffer?"

"Is that not what this Congress will determine?" Julia said carefully.

He smiled, pleased by her answer. "In part. They can make him suffer all they wish, but I am here for France, and France must not become the scapegoat for Napoleon's sins." He pinned her with another razor-sharp look. "And yet, as much as Napoleon suffers, I fear that poor little boy is the one who will suffer most. He will be a prisoner for the rest of his life, and there is little I or anyone else can do about that. He is most dangerous, like a small dog that might bite, or stir up trouble, and must therefore be kept locked up, just in case." He paused only a moment before asking, "I understand you also have a son, my lady. Is he enjoying Vienna?"

Julia hid her surprise at the question by moving forward to look at another painting, this one of a young boy sitting in a prison cell, hollow-eyed and haunted, the roses gone from his cheeks. He was Marie Antoinette's son, once the heir to the throne of France, and now dead. Her maternal heart went out to the poor child.

"He is too young to know, Your Highness," she answered Talleyrand's question.

"So innocent. Keep him so for as long as you can, my dear," Talleyrand said, looking briefly at the portrait of the little prince before moving on to a painting of a garden in Paris.

"I brought this one with me so I would not forget my beautiful city, and France, and why I came, while we diplomats plot and try to seduce each other at the peace table."

"It is a wonderful city," Julia murmured. What did he want from her? He was watching her reaction to every picture, hanging on her polite comments, waiting for something. She clasped her hands in front of her and studied the painting more carefully, as if it were the most fascinating landscape on earth.

"I think, if I could, I would have your portrait painted, my dear Lady Julia, to remind me of what beauty looks like, and bravery."

"Not at all. I am not usually so bold," she said, feeling a blush sweep from her toes her hairline.

He gave her an enigmatic smile. "There's no need to be modest—I admire bold women, especially when they are sensible as well, which I believe you are." He sighed. "I have a problem, my lady, and I thought you may be able to assist me with it."

Julia turned to regard him. "I? I am only a companion, a servant, Your Highness."

He laughed softly. "We both know you are more than that. Isn't everyone in Vienna more than they seem? I have been looking for a way to give Lord Castlereagh an important message, but it is so difficult to arrange a private word without being hamstrung by protocol and involving a dozen people in a sensitive matter that I would prefer was not misinterpreted as anything but a kindness."

Julia glanced at the door. The sound of voices and laughter was entirely absent, the party far away. She was entirely alone with the French ambassador. A knot formed in her throat, and she swallowed, but he merely pointed at another portrait, this one of a lovely woman with a winsome smile on her face. She wore a low-cut gown embroidered with gold, a frame for a magnificent collar of emeralds. A sparkling tiara sat on her dark curls.

"Have you heard of Princess Pauline de Borghese?" he asked, studying her painted face as if he were enchanted. "She's Napoleon's youngest sister. She adores her brother, and she adored being the most scandalous lady in France while he was on the throne, knowing even the Emperor himself could not control her wild behavior. She took lovers, gambled away fortunes, and did exactly as she pleased. She is quite magnificent, I think. A lady who refuses to play by the rules—a different kind of heroine, if you like."

Julia recalled the rumors she had heard in Paris, that the Duke of Wellington had fallen in love with Pauline, and she was leading him about on a leash, so to speak. Dorothea had been scandalized by the tale. Julia looked up at Pauline de Borghese's knowing smile.

"She is quite lovely," Julia said, unsure of what else to say about her.

"She is clever," Talleyrand corrected her. "Very clever indeed. She wants her brother back on the throne of France, and she is willing to do whatever she must to put him there."

Julia felt a thrill of shock run through her.

"There are rumors, for example, that she is on her way to Elba to deliver a fortune in gold. British gold, my lady." She gasped in surprise, and he smiled at her reaction.

"You see, she has been telling friends that a certain British general has approached her, pining for his enemy and the glorious days when he had a worthy foe. That general admired his adversary so much that he was willing to pay to see him back as Emperor. Oh, not to fight him again, but because he admires him."

Wellington. She kept her face blank.

"You must see, dear Julia, that having Napoleon back would be the worst possible thing for France. He won't remain a silent symbol like Louis XVIII, the poor Bourbon resting his aging paunch on the throne now. Napoleon will want it all back again, the power, the majesty, everything. And that will plunge Europe back into war." He paused and regarded her with his needle gaze.

Julia swallowed. "I know very little of politics," she said, managing a light tone despite the knot in her throat. She began to move toward the door, but he stopped her with a laugh.

"Come now, Lady Julia. You are a diplomat's grand-daughter. It is in your blood. I met your grandmother many years ago, at the court of King Louis and Marie Antoinette. I've been at this game too long not to recognize a fellow player. You remind me of Lady Arabella. She was charming, and she knew how very powerful women can be in the undercurrents of politics. I think you understand politics well enough."

He picked up a candle and walked toward the desk. The polished surface reflected the light like a mirror. "You play the game charmingly, by the way, listening and reporting. I can see your subtle influence every time Lord Castlereagh adjusts his strategy. I know he's heard things—things you are telling him."

She didn't deny it. There was no point. She stood and waited, her mouth dry.

He moved in front of the desk, leaning on the cane, the candle at his back, so she could not read his face. "Imagine how grateful Lord Castlereagh would be if Princess Pauline's plot could be thwarted? If it could not, Britain would face an enormous scandal, and will be seen as the cause of our return to war, which is sure to happen."

The lump in her throat grew larger, and her stomach ached.

"You see, Pauline got that fortune in gold from Lord Wellington, her lover. He supposedly bought a palace in Paris that she owned, but she is still living there, available to him night and day. She is party to his secrets, reads his letters—even secret official dispatches, I'm told."

She thought of the security measures that Lord Castlereagh had in place. Not a single scrap of paper, even a laundry list, made it out of the embassy. Official dispatches were guarded, and burned as soon as his lordship finished reading them.

Talleyrand went around the desk and unlocked a drawer. He took out a leather folder and opened it. He laid out the pages precisely, side by side, and beckoned her forward to look at them. She approached with dread.

"You see, here I have one of the letters Wellington wrote to Pauline, offering to pay whatever price she named for her house, as long as she came with it." He pointed to a particular paragraph. "It is very passionate reading. Here he swears to give her whatever she wishes, do whatever she wants, as long as he can possess her. I do hope I am not shocking you, my dear."

He moved to the next document, this one adorned with several wax seals. Wellington's was among them, along with his signature.

"This is the bill of sale for her house, and one must assume at such a steep price the lady was indeed part of the bargain." Julia's eyes widened at the amount.

Talleyrand merely pointed at the last letter, as if he were loath to touch it, and frowned. "And here is a letter from Pauline to her brother, on his own gold edged stationery, no less, informing him she is on her way to Elba with that exact sum in British gold paid to her for her house. She tells Napoleon that they can count on the support of—how does she put it?" He looked closely at the letter, then pointed out the paragraph to Julia. "Ah yes—that they can count on the support of an old enemy, now a friend and admirer of Napoleon's."

Julia could see how damning it looked, how easily an enemy of Wellington or Castlereagh could use the letters to discredit the British peace efforts. She felt the blood leave her limbs.

"I can see you understand politics after all," he said softly.

She looked at the prince, her mouth dry. "What do you want?"

He looked surprised. "I? Do not mistake me, my dear. I want nothing at all for myself. What I ask is for the good of France, and Britain. I do not want Napoleon back. I'm sure Lord Castlereagh and every peer in your House of Lords would agree with me. I wish to thwart this ridiculous plot, and get on with the important business of helping Lord Castlereagh to forge the best peace we can."

He began to gather the letters, placing them precisely into the folder in order. "I understand Castlereagh is trying to solve greater problems than his mandate allows. He hasn't got the permission of his government to address the topic of slavery, for example, but he feels most strongly about it. There are other such issues too. If his masters in London learn of his activities too soon, he will be recalled to London." He shrugged. "Who knows who would replace him? I would rather deal with the devil I know."

"I don't see how I can help with anything so grand, Your Highness," she interrupted, drawing herself up and raising her chin. "I am a mere servant. I believe you have mistaken my importance."

He smiled fondly. "I do not make mistakes, my dear. I am asking a favor of you, a simple thing, a trifle."

She swallowed. "What do you want?" she asked again.

"I wish to send Castlereagh a message, a private, friendly word. I wish to meet with him, to discuss this, and how we can squash it before it becomes an issue that other delegates here in Vienna might misinterpret. Is that so much?"

Julia shut her eyes. It sounded so simple, so easy. Too easy. She wished Stephen were here, or even Charles Stewart. She looked up at the paintings, but the laughing faces offered no assistance. She was out of her depth.

"Tell me, what will you do when this conference is over, and your mistress goes home to England?" Talleyrand asked. "You cannot go back there, and you cannot remain here in Europe without the money to live and raise your son. Imagine how good it would be to have a house of your own, some land, a dowry, perhaps, in case you decide to marry."

A bribe. Julia let him read the disdain in her eyes. "I cannot help you, Your Highness."

He made a soft sound of sympathy. "I hope you do not feel I am asking you to be dishonest or to betray your country! I too am a patriot. I am merely asking you to tell Lord Castlereagh what I have told you tonight, let him know that I offer my hand in friendship."

He smiled reassuringly as he came around the desk. He patted her shoulder, a kindly, grandfatherly touch. He smelled of cloves and orange flower cologne. Julia resisted the urge to flinch, and met his eyes boldly. "There now—I have engaged the bravest, most clever lady in Vienna to ensure that peace is far more probable now," he said, as if she'd agreed to help him.

She stared at the bare surface of the desk, the locked

drawer. "What will you do with the letters if I do not . . . ?"

He smiled sadly. "I was on my way home from the park this afternoon, and I happened to see you with Castlereagh's aide in front of the British Embassy." He sighed. "A perfect place for a tryst, Vienna. The passion in that kiss made me wish I was in love myself, but I am far too busy, though never, ever too old." He smiled at his own joke, but Julia felt her knees weaken, her stomach roll.

"It isn't like that. He is my employer," Julia said stiffly. "He was just—" Her tongue tied itself in a knot.

He sent her a knowing look. "I understand Lady Castlereagh is looking for a reason to dismiss you. I imagine your young major would also be sent home in disgrace, his career ruined." He tilted his head, feigned avuncular concern. "Then what would become of you, my dear? Usually, ruined women find only one path open to them, and not a pleasant one, I'm afraid. How would your son grow up then?"

Julia put a hand to her throat, scarcely able to breathe. "This is blackmail," she whispered.

"It is *diplomacy*, since we are working toward our mutual benefit. France needs friends, my dear, as do you. This is a partnership, nothing more. No one wishes to be embarrassed by little indiscretions, but sometimes . . ." He shrugged. "Well, you know that all too well, don't you?"

She blushed scarlet.

He opened another drawer and handed her an envelope. It was addressed to Lord Castlereagh, the seal plain. "Deliver this. In exchange, I will be most generous. You could afford to raise your son to be a gentleman, with lands of his own. Who knows? Perhaps he will be a diplomat as well."

She fervently hoped not.

She had no choice but to reach out and take the letter,

and he looked pleased. He made a show of glancing at the clock. "We've been gone almost too long. We must rejoin the party before there is gossip. I would find it delightful, of course, but I doubt it would please you." He took her arm, escorted her toward the door. "Now, I'm sure Lord Castlereagh will need time to consider my offer. It is a busy time for all of us. I will wait for . . . three days? That should be sufficient, *mais non?*"

Julia stared at him. Talleyrand was called Europe's master diplomat, the man everyone feared most, after Napoleon. But the Emperor was safely locked away on Elba, and Talleyrand held the power to bring governments and ordinary lives toppling into disaster—even hers. And he did it with a smile. He held her future and the fates of those she loved in his perfumed hands. She felt sick, the way shooting the man in the park had made her feel. He smiled as if they'd had the most pleasant conversation in the world, and gallantly led her back to join the party.

Chapter 24

"We must guard against the influence of the French, I believe," Prince Metternich said at dinner. "Talleyrand says he would not see Napoleon back again, but I believe he intends to see that France maintains the power Napoleon stole." A rumble of anger passed along the length of the table, and Stephen did his best to look interested in the political discussions that whizzed back and forth across the table like musket balls.

Nothing was new.

Weeks after the formal peace discussions were supposed to have started, they remained stalled, since no one could decide on even little details, like the format the conference should take. Some believed every delegate with a grievance should have a seat at the table. Others thought the decisions should be left to the four major allies—England, Prussia, Austria, and Russia. And while the diplomats wrangled over the shape of the conference table and shuffled and reshuffled the seating charts, everyone attended endless balls, parties, hunts, soirees, salons, and interminable dinners like this one. It was like the London Season, but without any end to the exhausting whirl of merriment.

Stephen stifled a grimace as the next dish was placed in front of him, merely the fourth of twelve courses planned for the lavish meal.

Tonight he was only interested in one discussion, one decision.

He'd told Julia that he loved her. He hadn't even realized how deeply his regard for her ran until this afternoon. He'd been terrified for her safety in the park, and decided then and there that he could not enjoy life without her. From a diplomatic point of view, his blurted confession—not to mention the kiss—probably hadn't been the smartest plan of campaign.

He shifted uncomfortably.

"Lovely chairs, but the carving is digging into my spine too," the wife of an Italian baron seated next to him said, noticing his movement. He smiled and nodded.

Had he shocked her, moved too quickly? Meaning Julia, of course, not the Italian baroness. Perhaps he should have wooed her more slowly, sent her flowers, written her poems.

He took a bite of veal in a red wine sauce. He'd never sent a lady flowers. He'd sent lilies to a funeral or two . . . and he'd never under any circumstances written a poem—the draft of a treaty, yes, poetry, no.

"Lord Metternich has a lovely way of putting things," the Italian baroness mused. "Normally, I find political discussions dull, but I hear he writes poetry to the beautiful Countess Sagan." She cupped a hand to his ear. "They say he is courting her to be his latest lover," she whispered.

"And what is her response?" he asked hopefully.

The baroness sighed. "They say she is quite immune to him, and all his lovely words."

Stephen felt his stomach sink to his evening shoes. The

lady leaned closer. "She fears, so I understand, that he wants only one thing, and once she has given it . . ." She gave an expressive shrug. Stephen felt a frisson of horror.

What must Julia be thinking? He should have been more specific. How was she to know if he wanted marriage or some other form of relationship? He swallowed without chewing, and grabbed for his wine, coughing. The baroness helpfully thumped him on the back.

What *did* he want from Julia? He wanted to kiss her again, that much he knew. But the rest—wife, mistress, or whatever else—was as baffling as the politics of the conference.

"I don't like it one bit!" cried the Prussian ambassador, shooting to his feet in reaction to a comment, attracting every eye in the room.

Had Julia liked it when he kissed her?

"Yes, more please," the baroness said, and he turned to find the footman refilling her wineglass with ruby liquid.

She hadn't objected to his kiss. Desire stirred, a hopeful erection rising, even here, in the Austrian ambassador's dining room, miles from her. He smiled at his own foolishness, and the baroness smiled back. Desire diminished at once.

As another course arrived, this one chicken, or pheasant, perhaps, in a sauce made with blackberries, he realized that he could hardly wait to see Julia at the end of this evening. Sometimes in diplomacy one must simply present one's case and wait for a response. A diplomat must be patient. He frowned. A diplomat must also be prepared for the worst possible news, and receive it without emotion.

"Patience is indeed the most trying virtue, wouldn't you say, my lord?" the baroness asked, regarding the next course that arrived.

"Do you not care for haricots, baroness?" he asked politely, identifying the vegetables under their shroud of cream sauce.

"They are quite delicious. It's just that dessert is so very far away, and that is what I want most. It makes it hard to wade through endless plates of vegetables."

"Four, no at least six courses yet to come," he sympathized.

"Interminable!" she said, rolling her eyes.

Indeed it was. Stephen ate without tasting anything, made polite conversation, and waited until he could be with Julia again.

Chapter 25

The rest of the evening passed in a blur, and at long last Julia sat in stunned silence in the coach on the way home. It had been quite a day. She'd shot a man in the park, allowed her employer to kiss her, and now the French ambassador was blackmailing the entire British Embassy, from Lord Castlereagh and the great Duke of Wellington, the highest members, to Stephen and she herself, the lowest of all.

She was tempted to glance out the window to look for a full moon, or a passing comet, or some other portent of evil tidings and disasters.

What would Castlereagh do when she handed him the letter she carried? If he ignored it, the British stood to be tarred as villains, not heroes, when Talleyrand spread the shocking innuendos about Wellington. If the ambassador accepted Talleyrand's friendship, the British would fall under a pall of suspicion from other delegates. All the goodwill and connections that Lord Castlereagh had spent the past months building up would come crashing down under the weight of accusation and suspicion. It was quite extraordinary what harm a few documents and letters, and a well-placed rumor, could do if brought together and presented in a particular way. There were many here in Vienna who resented Britain's power. If this did indeed lead to war, as Talleyrand predicted, it would look entirely like the fault of the British.

And Stephen would be in the midst of it all, disgraced, as ruined as she. She'd been responsible for enough pain—David was dead because of her foolish desire for a simple kiss. Now, Stephen stood to be destroyed too.

Was the world fated to end every time she kissed someone?

She shut her eyes and pressed a hand to the icy lump of dread in her chest that refused to melt. She knew what it was like to lose everything. Stephen didn't deserve such a fate simply because he had kissed her on the spur of the moment, simply because he thought he loved her. Did he really? He would not love her now.

There had to be a way to outsmart Talleyrand.

But she was just a humble listener, and a ruined woman.

Even so, this time she could not, would not, let it end in disaster.

Chapter 26

It had started to snow, and Thomas felt the icy flakes melting against his cheeks. He'd be happier at home with a large whisky right now, but Erich was by his side, and he didn't doubt the King of Thieves carried a brace of pistols in his pockets and a knife in his boot, and there was Donovan to consider.

"Are you ready?" Erich asked, his tone pleasant, as if this was a holiday instead of an excursion that could get Thomas shot—or worse. "As soon as the sentries look away, slip in and go around back. There's a terrace, and you can climb to the second floor—"

"I've got it," Thomas growled, though he wasn't at all sure he did. How difficult could it be? He'd opened his brother's safe, tucked behind a family portrait in his study. Every lord in England had a safe hidden behind a family portrait—usually his own, or a dull landscape. He doubted the British ambassador had brought a portrait of himself to hang in the embassy, not when there were so many top painters in Vienna and so many official portraits being painted.

It would be a matter of simply finding the right picture, and opening the safe behind it, Thomas told himself, hoping it would indeed be that easy.

"Once in the library, look for the safe," Erich persisted with his instructions.

Except it wouldn't be in the library. It would be upstairs, in Lord Castlereagh's private quarters, hopefully in a sitting room and not his bedchamber. He imagined his lordship sitting up in his bed to regard him with his famous sober silence as he watched him search the room for the hiding place.

Erich believed that Thomas understood how the English aristocracy thought, where they were most likely to hide their valuables, and Thomas did nothing to dissuade him from his opinion—it was keeping Donovan alive. But this was different—there were *secrets* to be protected here, not just jewels, and secrets were far more valuable. If Erich knew that—

"If there are any official looking papers in the safe, bring those too," the Austrian said casually.

Thomas didn't reply. He felt a trickle of sweat roll between his shoulder blades, despite the cold.

"Do you have the watch?" Erich asked, making conversation. "Can I see it?"

Thomas couldn't bear the idea of the perfection of the little family's portraits clutched in the hands of the thief.

"Why, do you want to know what time it is?"

Erich grunted. "I just wondered why a man would go to such trouble, take such a foolish risk for someone he doesn't even know."

"I thought Robin Hood was chivalrous to ladies and the poor?"

Erich laughed coldly. "I am a practical man. Chivalry can get you killed. Think of all the dead heroes on the battlefields who fought and died for chivalry. Fools, every one of them."

"Were you a soldier?" Thomas asked.

Erich chuckled. "Donovan was right. You are clever. Yes, I was a soldier. I fought at Jena, Austerlitz . . . so many other places over the years."

"Then why turn from honor to crime?"

The thief shifted, and Thomas heard the slosh of liquid in a metal flask as Erich drank. He didn't offer him any. Thomas could smell the schnapps on the thief's breath. "Honor? Why are some men so obsessed with honor? This way—my way—is the only way ordinary men will get justice at this peace conference, by taking our share of the spoils. Why should the kings and the princes get it all? We were the ones who did the fighting and dying, and we've been dismissed and forgotten while they dance and flaunt the spoils we took. Forget the honorable ways. I will take my share by force."

"I'm not a housebreaker, Erich," Thomas said, hoping one last time to avoid this futile excursion.

"Oh? Donovan told me you broke into your brother's homes, both in the country and in London. You opened his private safes and left them empty."

He had taken a small amount of cash and some of his mother's jewelry, which he would have inherited anyway. He'd left everything else. "I was a member of the family," he said. "No one was surprised I was in the house. I didn't expect a bullet in the back if I was caught."

"A bullet?" Erich said. "Here they'll probably hang you. At least if you're caught, the fact that you are English, speak the language, look the part, may help you."

Thomas doubted it. Every foreigner in Vienna feared thieves and spies. There probably wasn't a lady in this embassy or any other who didn't sleep with her jewels under the mattress and at least a very sharp letter opener beneath her pillow.

The scream of horses rang out, then shouts, as two coaches crashed in front of the palace.

Erich looked on calmly. "There's your cue." He pointed to the small side gate where the sentry had already stepped away from his post to see the accident. "Don't even think of coming back empty-handed. Your friend's life is in your hands."

"And a good valet is so hard to find," Thomas quipped, and slipped silently through the gate.

In moments he was moving along the terrace that ran the length of the back of the palace and overlooked the garden, wincing at the crunch of the dry leaves beneath his boots, trying to avoid the light from the stables where the guards were housed.

He swore as a light appeared above him, and jumped back into the shadows as it illuminated the dark terrace. He pinned himself against the smooth stone of the building, waiting for a shout as they saw him, but there was only silence. He waited until his heart stopped trying to pound its way out of his chest, and looked up again.

Someone was still awake upstairs, and bound to hear him. He swore again.

He couldn't turn back now. He looked along the facade of the building, trying to find another way. The rest of the windows on the second floor were dark, and he chose the last one, as far from the lighted room as possible.

He took a deep breath and began to climb.

Chapter 27

⚛

"**M**ajor Lord Ives left word that he wished to see you in the sitting room when you got home," Jamie's nurse Mrs. Hawes said, waking when Julia tiptoed into the little nursery off her own bedroom to kiss her son good night. "He's been a bit fractious tonight with his teeth coming in, but Lady Dorothea rocked him to sleep."

Julia looked up. "Lady Dorothea?"

"She sang him a lullaby, and he was out like a snuffed candle, the little lamb."

Dorothea had scarcely acknowledged Jamie in all the months they'd been in Vienna. Julia assumed it was the pain of losing her own child that made other infants, including Jamie, invisible to her.

"Does she visit often?"

"No, just recently," the nurse said. "She's quite taken with him. There's no need to worry, though. I'm with him all the time. I know some mothers give their babes a drop or two of laudanum to stop the crying and make them sleep, but I would never allow such a thing."

"Laudanum?" Julia's heart stopped in her chest for an instant. She looked down at her son's peaceful face, the long lashes resting on plump cheeks.

"I would never allow her to give him any, my lady," Mrs. Hawes said again.

Julia managed a smile. "Of course not. Go back to bed. No doubt Jamie will be up early." She tiptoed out and shut the door of the nursery quietly.

She glanced at the little clock on the desk. It was nearly three. She bit her lip.

She should go to the sitting room and give Talleyrand's letter to Stephen at once, let him decide if it would be necessary to wake Lord Castlereagh now or if the matter could wait until morning, but she hesitated.

A kiss given in the heat of a frightening and stressful moment might be explained away as gratitude, but a midnight tryst could not. How many others besides Talleyrand's spies saw that kiss, thought the worst?

No, the letter could wait until morning. She would see Stephen at breakfast, with Dorothea present, everything as correct and polite as could be. Still, she stood looking at the letter in the dim light, the dark lines of the ink crawling over the surface like spilled blood.

She pushed it under her pillow and crossed to open the curtains, not bothering to light a candle. The faint light from the city would be enough, since she only needed to undress and climb into bed. She stood by the window for a moment. It was snowing softly, and the bare black limbs of the trees were limned with white.

Plucking the pins out of her hair one by one she dropped them in a porcelain bowl, and shook the careful curls loose, letting the dark waves fall over her shoulders.

She heard a sound then, a thump, and froze. Was Talleyrand watching her, even now, in the privacy of her bedroom? How ridiculous she was. With all that had happened today she was likely to have nightmares anyway, and there was no point in adding to them with imagined fears.

She began to undo the pearl buttons on her gown, then turned, and gasped at a shape looming over her. The skeletal clothing rack reached for her from the corner, looking remarkably human in the dark.

"Twaddle," she murmured, took off her gown and tossed it over the clothing rack, vanquishing the monster. There was no one here. She was perfectly safe in her own room, and the embassy was under guard. There was no safer place. No one was lurking in the dark, waiting to judge her, or blackmail her, or charm her. Tomorrow, in daylight, all that had happened today would be less frightening. She squared her shoulders.

Bold, decisive action. That was what was needed— with Prince de Talleyrand, with Lord Stewart, and with Stephen.

And yet, her mother always said she was too bold, and had often predicted it would get her into trouble someday. Julia's actions at her betrothal ball had certainly proven her mother right, and seeing off a pack of robbers in the park had most definitely been bold.

Overbold and unladylike, she heard her mother's voice in her head.

She sat down to remove her stockings, her legs long and white in the dimness. She thought of her brother, James. He'd stood before the enemy guns, boldly screamed a warning, knowing he would die. He *must* have known. Or did he have hope of salvation? He'd done what was necessary, stepped out of the safety of the shadows to save the day.

But she was a woman, and a fallen woman at that. She *belonged* in the shadows. She stepped into the pale puddle of light that came through the windows. In the

morning she would ask Stephen to make an appointment
with Lord Castlereagh, and simply explain to his lordship
everything she had heard and seen. It was her job to do so.
Then she would have to speak to Stephen, tell him someone had seen them kissing and how the consequences
might play out if it continued. Surely he would see—

A shadow passed by the window, blotting out the light
for a moment, and Julia gasped. A cloud passing in front
of the moon, perhaps?

But it was a moonless night. She moved toward the
window, then stopped in her tracks, her eyes widening.
The black silhouette of a man's body moved across the
panes. She blinked, her heart faltering.

Impossible. They were on the second floor. Her heart
began again, thundering against her ribs. Perhaps it was a
bird, come to roost out of the snow, and her imagination
was making it more than it was . . . she was hallucinating.
In a moment the bird would fly away into the night, go
back where it came from.

But the bird quietly opened the window, and a booted
foot invaded the room.

She backed into the shadows beside the bed, half
hidden by the bed curtains, and held her breath, her mind
racing.

A robber—the highwayman himself, perhaps, come
for revenge. Her heart died of fright in her chest, dropped
into the pit of her stomach.

She glanced at the door of the nursery, her eyes burning like brands in the dark. Her son was asleep in the
next room, in danger. Surely once he'd dispatched her, the
thief would look there next.

The figure paused. She held her breath.

What if it was Lord Stewart? She'd heard salacious
tales of his daring seductions and bold escapes from irate

husbands that included exactly this, a convenient window and a dark night.

Fear knifed through her as the intruder stood for a moment staring at the empty bed. Who would believe her if she said it was rape, not seduction, that the man had climbed the outside of the building to have his way with her in the very sanctuary of her bedroom? She had not even locked her door. She scarcely dared to breathe. In a moment he would see her, and then—

He began to cross the room, but instead of dragging her from her hiding place, he sank into a chair, his outstretched limbs a scant few feet from her own. He rested with a sigh. With a flare of anger, she hoped he was comfortable. He probably thought she had not returned yet, and was waiting for her to walk through the door. She scowled at the shadowy figure.

Then he bent over, his head down as he struggled with something, grunting like a bear. The hair on the back of her neck rose. He was releasing something—a dog, perhaps, some sharp-toothed creature that would attack her while she stood here wearing nothing but her shift.

She curled her bare toes into the carpet, waiting for a bark, the impact of teeth in her flesh, but the room was silent except for the rustle of his clothing, the sound of his breath.

He let out a long sigh, and dropped something heavy on the floor.

The next thought flared in her breast, bringing an instant of heat and fury. Obviously he wasn't a burglar or Charles Stewart. It was one of Prince Talleyrand's agents, come to steal more secrets he might use against the British. Did he think she would cooperate? Is that why he'd chosen her window?

She would not.

She reached out a hand, seeking a weapon, anything sharp or heavy within her reach. Her hand tangled in the bed curtain for a moment before it closed on the long handle of the copper bed-warming pan, standing cold and empty against the wall. She gripped it, felt the wooden handle warm beneath her palm.

She waited until the intruder rose to shut the window, and then took a breath and leapt forward. He was spinning now, turning back to face her, his countenance a dark blur, his gasp loud in the dark as she brought the bed warmer up and swung it with all her might.

It connected with his head, ringing like a gong.

He grunted and dropped heavily to the floor in a lifeless sprawl.

She stood over him with the pan raised, ready to hit him again if he dared to move. He didn't. She felt panic fill her. Had she killed him too? This was becoming a dreadful habit.

Dropping her weapon, she knelt beside him, carefully feeling for a pulse under his chin. He didn't move a muscle. She bent closer. He was breathing, at least. She could feel the warmth on her cheek.

There was no time to wonder what to do next. The door to the nursery opened and Mrs. Hawes came out. "My lady, I heard a sound—" Her scream split the night, and Jamie woke and began to cry too. Within seconds there were footsteps in the corridor, then the bedroom door was thrown wide against the wall, light invading the room, making her squint.

"Get some light!" She heard Stephen order. "Julia? What on earth—"

Light flared, chasing the shadows away, revealing everything.

The man was sprawled on his back, arms and legs

spread wide, filling the room. He looked for all the world as if he were sleeping.

Julia watched as Stephen assessed the situation at a glance, took in the body on the floor as she kneeled beside it, only half dressed. Her breath caught in her throat as she watched suspicion bloom in Stephen's eyes. Not worry or love now—he thought the worst.

The man groaned, and she looked down at him. He had a purple lump on his forehead that was getting bigger by the moment.

She felt the shock of recognition rush through her limbs as she stared down at the familiar face. Surely it couldn't be—

But it was.

She hadn't seen Thomas Merritt for over a year, yet here he was, lying unconscious on her bedroom floor.

Chapter 28

He'd run into a wall in the dark. Or a door, or a battering ram. How stupid of him.

Thomas tried to open his eyes, but searing light forced them shut again. Perhaps he was dead—shot, after all. His head rang like heavenly bells, but how likely was that? He should be feeling the crackle of flames licking his feet.

A soft, cool hand touched his face, and he could smell violets. So it was heaven after all, he decided, but then a scream split his skull all over again. The pain was excruciating.

"Hush, Mrs. Hawes! You'll wake the baby!" a woman's voice whispered.

Baby? What *baby?* The child's wail rose in the distance.

"Is he dead?" another female voice warbled.

"Of course not, he's breathing, see?" Fingers poked at him, and the violets assaulted his senses again. There was only one woman he knew who smelled of violets . . .

"I don't like the look of that lump," the sharp-voiced one said. "What did you hit him with?"

There was no answer. He felt fingers probing at a hot

place on his forehead and saw stars for a moment. He gasped as the pain shot through his brain, tried to turn away.

"Lie still, Mr. Merritt," she murmured.

He frowned, and discovered that hurt too. He'd heard that voice before, but he couldn't think of where it might have been. Then he heard footsteps, felt them pounding through the floorboards under his head, and men shouting.

"Julia? What on earth is going on here?" a male voice demanded.

"Julia." His mouth formed the word, and it came out as a croak. He forced his eyes open and saw her above him. There were cherubs behind her too, hovering over her hair, which hung over her shoulders in dark waves to caress her breasts, which were clad in the filmiest lace.

He *was* in heaven, after all. What on earth had he done to receive such a reward? He tried to smile at her as he reached out a hand to touch her cheek. Her skin was as soft as he remembered, heated by a deep flush as he spoke her name again. She flinched, and he let his hand drop away.

"Do you know this man?" a man asked, his voice starchy with indignation.

"Dull Duke David," he muttered, making an assumption as to his identity.

Rougher hands gripped his jaw, twisted his head, probably to identify him, or to check the wound. Was it as bad as it felt? He squinted up at the face above him but didn't recognize the man.

"I've never seen him before! He's an intruder!" the screamer warbled as if she'd been asked. "If her ladyship hadn't laid him low with the bed warmer, he'd have murdered us all in our beds!"

"Would he, Julia?" the man demanded, and Thomas watched his eyes flick over Julia's scanty garments.

She sent him an indignant glare, one he remembered well from the day he'd met her in Hyde Park. How long ago that seemed, how very far away, and yet that expression was as familiar as if it had been yesterday. She rose to her feet to retrieve a blue robe, and buttoned it right to her chin, her white fingers moving like angry spiders. She tied the sash with such fury it nearly cut her in two, and then she stood before the man like a queen, though her feet, planted beside his own head, were bare.

"His name is Thomas Merritt. He came in through the window. I had no idea who he was when I hit him."

"She saved us all," the screamer added. Thomas turned his head to see the bed warming pan on the carpet beside him, sprawled like a second victim.

He tried to sit up, but the room spun, and he sank back to the carpet. With a whimper, the screamer grabbed for the warming pan, but Julia stopped her. The man put his foot in the center of Thomas's chest. "Don't move," he ordered. Thomas stayed where he was.

"Do go back to bed, Mrs. Hawes, we're quite safe now," Julia said calmly.

"Are we?" she asked.

"Lord Stephen will take care of everything," Julia soothed, and the woman withdrew.

Lord Stephen? What happened to Dull Duke David? Thomas squinted at the man. Definitely not David Temberlay. This man was tall and fair-haired, and glaring down at him as if he'd like to finish the job Julia had started.

"He's not wearing his boots," Lord Stephen said, making it an accusation, his expression hard as stone, his eyes suspicious.

Of course he wasn't. He'd taken them off so he could move more quietly over the marble floors. Did thieves not usually take their boots off when they broke into a house? He sent Lord Stephen a rueful smile, which hurt like the devil. The man's face darkened with anger. "Why is this man half undressed in your room?" he demanded.

"I have no idea," she replied, her tone cutting, aristocratic. She held the lord's eyes boldly, indignation clear at his insinuation.

Lord Stephen looked away first. "Tie him up, search his pockets," he ordered, stepping back. Other hands grabbed him roughly, bound him with the ties from the curtains, and he winced as his head bounced against the carpet. He felt hands in his pockets, robbing him, instead of the other way around. They dragged him up and propped him against the foot of the bed.

"There's only this, Major Lord Ives."

They laid the little gold watch in the man's palm, and Thomas squinted at him. Whoever he was, Lord Stephen wasn't the man in the portrait.

He looked down at Thomas in surprise. "Where the hell did you get this?"

"Won it," Thomas managed, his tongue thick. "Who are—"

"I'll ask the questions," Lord Stephen snapped, his fingers closing over the timepiece, and Thomas frowned at the loss of it. "Who the devil are you?" he asked Thomas twice, once in English, and again in German.

"Nobody," Thomas replied in English, though his voice was so slurred it might have been any language. He glanced at Julia, who stood silently behind the man, staring down at him, her face white. She was as beautiful as he remembered. "I simply came to return—" he began, but Lord Stephen raised his hand to strike him, and Thomas braced for the blow. It didn't come. Julia caught his hand.

"He's English. His name is Thomas Merritt," she supplied for him.

He gave her a lopsided grin, though it hurt. "Forgive me for not bowing, Your Grace."

She colored to a deep shade of scarlet, and his breath caught. No, she wasn't as beautiful as he remembered, she was even prettier—with her hair loose around her shoulders and her bare feet.

"Take him down to the guard room," Lord Stephen ordered.

"Dr. Bowen, would you take a look at his forehead first?" Julia asked breathlessly, turning to one of the other men who stood in the room. The third appeared to be a footman.

Thomas turned to regard his captor. "A doctor?" he asked, but the good doctor was looking at Lord Stephen for confirmation of Julia's request.

"Please, my lord. I fear I may have injured him—"

Judging by the look on his face, Thomas was sure Lord Stephen would refuse, order him taken to the lowest dungeon, if the grand palaces on the civilized Minoritenplatz had such things, but the man nodded at last. "Take him to the sitting room. I'll be there momentarily."

They grabbed his arms, hauled him to his feet and dragged him toward the door. "Boots," he said, but they ignored him, left his footwear lying by the window. He glanced over his shoulder at Julia. She was staring at him, and Lord Stephen was staring at her. Then he was in the hallway, sliding over the icy marble tiles in his stocking feet.

Why on earth would the Duchess of Temberlay be in Vienna? he wondered.

There was something definitely wrong here, and as soon as his head stopped pounding and he had his wits back, he'd figure out just what it was.

Of course, he'd probably wake up in the morning a corpse in a ditch, next to the cold dead body of Patrick Donovan.

He almost laughed at the foolish idea of waking up dead, but it hurt too much at the moment.

His captors yanked him into a well-appointed sitting room gleaming with polished wood, plush with comfortable furnishings, and shoved him into a chair. More curtain ties bound him to it. He looked longingly at the crystal decanters that sat on the delicate side table.

The doctor poked at his wound and winced. "She has a good arm," he said, shaking his head. "But you'll live."

He'd live—at least until they hanged him, or shot him, or turned him over to Erich, who would do both.

He laid his head back and shut his eyes, trying to still the wave of dizziness.

At least he'd had the opportunity to see Julia Leighton once more before he met his end. The familiar ache passed through his breast, a feeling he'd come to associate with her. Now it was even stronger, knowing she was in the very next room. Whatever the reason she was here, he was glad that she was.

Seeing her once more might just be worth the pain he was about to face.

Chapter 29

$\sim\!\!\infty\!\!\sim$

Stephen went downstairs to find Charles Stewart. The first question he wanted to ask was how the hell the man in charge of ensuring that the embassy was guarded day and night against intruders could have let this happen. Julia might have been—

He stopped on the staircase and stared into space, and considered, felt another emotion stir in his chest, this one unfamiliar.

Julia *knew* him, this Thomas Merritt. He had found his way into her room by climbing the side of the building in the dark. She'd been undressed, half naked, tantalizingly clad in a mere slip of silk and lace, completely different than the prim Miss Leighton. And Thomas Merritt wasn't wearing his boots. What kind of thief, if that's what he was, took off his boots? He gripped the banister hard as jealousy tore at him. He might if he wasn't planning a quick escape, or he intended to stay the night. Had she met him at Talleyrand's, agreed to a tryst?

While he'd been waiting for her in the sitting room.

He reminded himself that she'd hit Merritt hard enough to leave him senseless on her bedroom floor, just steps away from her sleeping son. What kind of woman did that to a lover?

He knocked briskly on Charles Stewart's bedroom door. A sleepy manservant answered.

"Wake him. I need him upstairs at once," Stephen ordered, not bothering to be polite.

"I would, but he isn't here, Major. He's out for the evening, and I don't expect to see him until tomorrow."

Stephen punched the door frame, and the man flinched and stepped back. "Do you know where he is?"

The man gave him a wry smile. "I'm sorry, Major Lord Ives, but it's four in the morning. I doubt by now even Lord Stewart himself knows where he is."

Stephen turned away. It wasn't protocol, or his place, but he'd interrogate Thomas bloody Merritt himself.

But first he had a few questions for Julia.

She was dressed when he knocked on her door, wearing a prim and sensible gown of moss-green wool, her hair plaited and bound as tightly as the prisoner. Her hazel eyes were sober as she regarded him, her cheeks stained a guilty pink—or was it anger?

"Did you meet him at Talleyrand's?" he asked without preamble.

She looked surprised for a moment, then lowered her gaze. "No, I knew him in London," she said.

"Why is he here?" he demanded, and she met his eyes again, her brows rising.

"Why was he in my bedroom in the middle of the night, or why is he in Vienna?" she asked quietly. "I'm afraid I don't know the answer to either question, Major Lord Ives."

He swallowed. They were back to Major Lord Ives, were they? Then he recalled she had never actually used his Christian name. Had she called the intruder by his name?

He retreated to safer, more sensible ground. "He had Doe's watch in his pocket," he said, and drew it out to show her. She hesitated a moment before she took it from him and opened it, letting the familiar notes of the lullaby play.

"I thought she said she'd sold it for—" She paused, looked up at him with sudden realization, coloring anew. "Thomas Merritt gave Dorothea *laudanum*?" she asked, her brow furrowing. "But that's entirely—" She stopped and swallowed, snapping the watch shut, cutting off the tune.

"Is it?" he asked.

Her brow furrowed as she studied the watch, ran her fingers over the damaged case. "I don't know," she said at last. She bit her lip, as if dreading something. "I suppose Dorothea could tell us if he was the man who gave her the drug. I—I didn't see him at the ball that night."

"Are you defending him?"

She looked surprised. "No, of course not."

"How well do you know him?" he demanded, his hopes pinned on her answer.

She turned pink again. "Not terribly well. We met only—briefly."

He had the urge to pull her close, kiss her again, see if he could taste the truth on her lips, read it in her eyes, but she stepped back, wary, folding her arms across her chest in defense against such intimacy.

What on earth was he doing? He had never, ever been jealous of any woman before, never acted on emotion as he was doing now. But Julia wasn't any woman. He had kissed her, told her he loved her.

He took the watch back, the brush of her fingertips against his sending shock waves through his body. He straightened himself, took control.

"I'll speak to Dorothea when she gets up. For now, I have questions for Thomas Merritt."

"I'll come with you."

"I think not," he said coldly.

She leveled a determined look at him. "I shot a man yesterday, my lord. Then I knocked Mr. Merritt senseless. I have no wish to make harming people a regular activity. I wish to make sure I have done no permanent damage, since I cannot ascertain whether or not the man I shot is dead. I too want to know why he came here."

There was no passion in her eyes, no feminine fear for a lover, merely determination. Still, he was inclined to refuse, to tell her to wait in her room and not dare to stir until she was summoned to give an official account of herself before himself and Lord Castlereagh.

But he wanted to see her with him, watch her as she looked at Merritt, see the truth. He nodded.

She picked up Merritt's boots and followed him down the hall to the sitting room.

Chapter 30

Thomas Merritt dwarfed the dainty side chair they'd tied him to. He'd filled her bedroom as he lay sprawled on the floor, and he filled this room too, though he took up only a corner of it. Julia drew a breath at the sight of him. He was still as devastatingly handsome as she remembered, though his hair was longer and he needed shaving. The stubble, and the dark clothing he wore, made him look like a pirate. So did the terrible bruise that marred his forehead.

She felt a shock of recognition as he looked up at her, his eyes carefully blank. She winced at the lump, and he smiled wryly.

"Don't worry, Your Grace. It only hurts when I curtsy. Do forgive me for not getting up and doing so." She noted the incongruous gold silk tassels that hung from his wrists. One leg was crossed over the other, as if he were holding court. Even in his stocking feet he looked danger-ous, and she took a seat well across the room from him.

"I trust Dr. Bowen has looked at you?" she asked, not bothering to correct him as to her title. He obviously as-sumed that all had been well after they— She felt a surge of physical awareness pass through her, a memory of every touch, every caress they'd shared. It left her breathless. And if he had no idea that she hadn't married David, then he knew nothing of Jamie, her son—and his.

Stephen drew up a matching side chair and sat down in front of Thomas. "You were carrying a lady's watch," he said, his tone deceptively calm. She knew him well enough to hear the steel in his voice, read the tension in his body.

She saw interest bloom in Thomas's gray eyes. "I didn't steal it, if that's what you're thinking."

Stephen's eyes were rapier sharp as they bored into his prisoner's, and Julia held her breath. "No, my sister sold it several weeks ago."

Thomas's eyebrow quirked, but he shook his head. "Not to me."

"Then how did you come by it?" Stephen demanded.

She stared at Thomas Merritt as he faced Stephen, looking for signs of Jamie in his face. There—in the shape of his jaw, and in the dimple in his cheek. She felt dizzy.

"I won the watch in a game of chance."

She almost winced at his tone. It was the same soft, insouciant way he'd spoken to her, charmed her. Her body responded even now, over a year later, opening feelings she'd locked away when they parted in the darkness of her father's library. He glanced at her, and their eyes met for just an instant, and she felt the full knowledge that he also remembered every detail of that night.

She jumped to her feet and crossed to pull the bell. "Tea," she managed to say around the lump in her throat when both men looked at her. "Or should I order breakfast?"

"Oh, breakfast, if you would be so kind," Thomas said. "I have not eaten a good English breakfast since I left London."

"And when was that?" Stephen leapt on the statement.

"Over a year ago. How was the old place looking when you sailed?"

Julia held her breath, and wondered if Stephen was doing the arithmetic in his head. Jamie was seven months old, nearly eight.

"Why did you leave England?" he asked instead.

Thomas slid his eyes to hers, another brief glance that hit her like a touch. "Adventure."

"You came to Europe looking for adventure *after* the war was over?"

Thomas shook his head. "Not at all. I came to get away from it."

Her heart flipped in her chest, and she sat down again.

"You were going to order breakfast, Your Grace?" Thomas prompted.

She lifted her chin as if she *were* a duchess. "I have rung the bell. Someone will arrive momentarily."

"Do you use laudanum, Mr. Merritt?" Stephen demanded.

Thomas swung his gaze from Julia to Stephen. "No, why?"

"Someone sold my sister laudanum in exchange for her watch. Do you know who might have done so?"

Julia searched Thomas's face. There was a flicker of surprise, quickly suppressed. He kept his expression flat. "No."

"Then I can assume you weren't here to give her more of the drug? For that, at least, I'm glad," Stephen said sarcastically. "Now we need only find out why you *did* come."

Julia reminded herself yet again to breathe. Thomas studied his opponent's face, then smiled. "You're assuming I came to visit Her Grace."

"Did you come to visit *Miss Leighton*?" Stephen asked.

Thomas looked at her then, his brows flicking upward in surprise, and hot blood flooded her cheeks. She held his gaze and said nothing. His gaze moved to her naked ring finger, then returned to Stephen.

"It was quite by accident that I landed in that particular room. While it is always pleasant to see an old acquaintance—"

"Get on with it!" Stephen snapped. Was he recalling how she'd been dressed when Thomas Merritt arrived in her bedroom, she wondered, when *he'd* arrived? She raised her chin, noted the hard set of Stephen's jaw, the way his fists were clenched.

"Then why exactly were you here, Merritt, at three o'clock in the morning?"

Thomas met his eyes. "I came to steal a tiara."

Chapter 31

Now why in the hell had he said that? The blow to his head must have done more damage than he thought.

Ives was regarding him dully, the superior look of a gentleman who would never, ever do a wrong thing.

Thomas clenched his fist, but it was the truth. He'd spent months denying it, but he was, indeed, a thief.

Perhaps it was the look on Julia's face that made him admit it aloud. She sat there watching him, not quite able to disguise her interest, though she tried. Her face turned pink, then red, then stark white in turn. Then there was the look on her face when Ives corrected him the second time he'd called her "Your Grace," downgrading her to a simple miss. He felt somehow—no, he knew *exactly* how—that was his fault.

Had David Temberlay found out?

Anger flared, and he'd suddenly been afraid that she would expect him to make it right, even after all this time, to rescue her from her disgrace. Then in one single ferocious glance Julia had told him silently she expected nothing of the kind, and he knew he wasn't worthy of Julia Leighton, and could never be.

He was a thief.

But now that he'd made the admission about coming to steal the tiara, the shock in her eyes made it worse, not better. If she held any fond memories of that night at her betrothal ball, he'd squelched them utterly—stolen them, even. He smiled wryly at that.

"You're a thief?" Ives said, as surprised as Julia, it appeared. "They hang thieves in England, or transport them," he continued, as if considering which punishment to inflict in this instance.

Thomas felt the skin on his neck tingle, as if the noose was already in place. He forced a carefree smile. "And yet we are in Vienna, and you'll recall that I have, in truth, not actually stolen anything."

"Yes. You came simply to return a valuable watch, didn't you?" Ives asked sarcastically. "Now why would a thief do that?"

Donovan. Thomas remembered suddenly. He glanced at the windows, saw the faint pink glow of early dawn beyond the lace curtains, and his stomach clenched. Was Erich still outside, waiting for him to emerge, triumphantly waving Lord Castlereagh's jeweled Order of the Garter star? Or had he already given him up and gone back to cut Donovan's throat?

Thomas tugged at the silk ties binding his hands. "Have you ever heard of Robin Hood, stealing from the rich, and—um, doing good deeds?" he asked. "Returning the watch is my good deed. The only thing I took was a nasty blow to the head, which I assure you was punishment enough," he said, his eyes on Ives.

Even if Ives jumped up and released him this minute, which he showed no signs of doing, he might be too late to save his valet's life. Even if he wasn't, he'd failed. He had nothing but words to convince Erich to let Donovan—and himself—live.

He glanced at Julia. She frowned back, her eyes narrowed. If it were up to her, he'd suffer all the punishments of hell. He silently cursed her. Honor and good deeds be damned. He'd let her keep her jewels that night, returned her earring the next day, but he'd take them from her now, teach her a lesson. Except she wore no jewels at all, not the massive Temberlay betrothal ring, not even a wedding ring. So he smiled at her, and robbed her of her composure instead as he watched her blush rise like the dawn in the window behind her.

"Have you been well since we last met, my lady?" he asked her.

Ives swiveled to look at her. "When exactly was that?" he demanded, turning the interrogation upon the lady. He looked suspicious, Thomas thought. No, he looked jealous.

He tugged at his bonds. Was there something between good Lord Stephen and Julia? What was she to Ives? Not his wife, since he called her *Miss* Leighton. Her blush deepened under his scrutiny.

"It was a very long time ago, in England," Julia said lightly.

"You were betrothed to His Grace of Temberlay, I believe," Thomas said.

She sent him a quelling look. "And you, Mr. Merritt, other than beginning a new career since we last met, I trust you've been well?"

She sat with her hands resting neatly in her lap, her back stiff, looking as if she were interviewing a new spit boy for her kitchens, not meeting an old lover. He twisted his hands again, but the knots held. "Save for the headache, I've never been better."

The first sharp gold shafts of sunlight were edging the buildings and the trees outside, limning her hair with light. Erich wouldn't wait long now. Someone might see him, and he was a creature of the night. He turned to Ives again. "Look, I have an appointment with my tailor this morning, and with so many gentlemen in Vienna just now, and all of them needing tailoring themselves, you can understand why I am so anxious to arrive at his door on time. I'd hate to miss a fitting so close to the Emperor's next ball."

He watched Ives consider whether he had enough reason to detain him further. He looked less certain now. Thomas did his best to look harmless, yet haughty, a British gentleman mistakenly caught in queer circumstances that weren't entirely his fault.

Ives rose. "Yes, I suppose there's no reason to keep you," he said. He stepped behind Thomas to undo the knots.

Thomas felt a prickle of unease. It was that easy? Ives wanted him gone, away from Julia, that much was clear. He sent Julia a long, inquiring look as he rubbed the circulation back into his wrists. She sent back a flat stare, offering him no information at all, but the pulse at her throat throbbed above the fine wool of her high-necked dress. That spoke volumes. The tension in the room made it hard to breathe.

When he was free, he pulled his boots on, a difficult task with no valet to assist him. Then he rose and bowed to Julia.

"Good day," he said, as if he were taking leave after tea. "It was pleasant to see you again." He did not bid Ives farewell. The major stood silently, watching him. Clearly, Ives wasn't releasing him out of gratitude for the return of the watch, or kindness, not when he obviously would rather hang him, preferably after a long morning of bloody torture. Ives would no doubt send someone to follow him, see if he led them to the nest of thieves, or Erich, perhaps. Did they know about Erich? Capturing the King of Thieves would make Ives a hero, especially in the eyes of the woman he wanted to impress most. But Ives was on his own when it came to that. He wouldn't help him. He'd stay well away from Erich until he knew it was safe, for Donovan's sake.

Thomas shook off the raged little teeth of jealousy as he glanced at Julia once more when he reached the door, until he was forced to step aside for the little parade of footmen entering with his breakfast.

"Leave that and escort Mr. Merritt to the front door," Ives ordered. "See that he keeps his hands in his pockets on the way out. In fact, I'll see him out myself."

Thomas smiled coolly. He deserved that.

He was a thief, after all.

Chapter 32

Julia's breath caught in her throat as he cast a glance over his shoulder while they escorted him out. Was it wistful, or simply insolent? They were very broad shoulders. How had he fit through her window at all? Would Jamie look like that when he grew to manhood? He'd certainly be handsome. Devastating. And if she had a chance to do everything over again— She shut her eyes, stopped those thoughts right there.

He was a thief.

Perhaps he always had been, and she'd been too foolish, too charmed by stars and champagne, to notice. The familiar burn of shame filled her. Not for what she'd done, but because in her heart of hearts she knew she'd probably do exactly the same thing, even now.

She crossed to the window and hovered behind the lace curtain, waiting for him to emerge from the gates. He strode away without looking back, tall and dark against the snow, not at a run, but not slowly either, as if he was indeed a gentleman with an appointment to keep. He moved with confidence and aristocratic grace.

Her heart quickened, and she reminded herself again that he was a thief and a rogue. How ridiculous she was, sighing over him like some silly chit who read too many novels and imagined that highwaymen and pirates were romantic and daring. She recalled the thieves in the park, the terror they inspired. There was nothing charming about *them*.

She was still watching when a second figure left the embassy, following Thomas Merritt's footprints in the snow. She felt a frisson of surprise. Stephen was having him followed. Perhaps that was why he let Thomas go at all, so he would lead them to his lair, a cave of wonders or a woodland hideout filled with stolen goods. Then he'd hang Thomas Merritt.

She was being silly yet again—a terrible habit where Mr. Merritt was concerned. Stephen would not let a man go only to trick him, would he? He had done a kindness. Dorothea's watch sat on the table where Stephen had left it, and she picked it up and ran her thumb over the place where the diamond had been. He could have thrown it away, but instead he'd risked life and limb climbing the side of a well-guarded building. She frowned. "Why on earth?" she murmured.

She thought back to their meetings in London. He'd been kind then too—Robin Hood indeed. He'd been cool, dangerous when Stephen questioned him, but when he'd kissed her, made love to her, he'd been tender, gentle, and sweet. She would have sworn his passion was honest, if she'd had more experience of such things. And he hadn't stolen a single thing that night, except— She blushed.

She opened the watch and stared down at the painted faces of Dorothea's husband and child. The familiar tune of the lullaby began to play.

"Where on earth did you get that?" Dorothea asked from the doorway, her hand clenched over her heart, her eyes haunted in a way Julia hadn't seen for weeks. Julia shut the watch, cutting off the tune. "Mrs. Hawes said we had an intruder in the night," Dorothea said.

"Yes, a housebreaker." She stumbled over the word. "He said he came to return your watch." Julia looked at the breakfast trays. "Come and have some breakfast."

Dorothea took the watch from Julia's hand. "A housebreaker, you say? Yet he comes bearing gifts. How odd. I had thought this was gone forever."

Julia lifted the lid on a tray filled with pastries. Lady Castlereagh's English cook was slowly conforming to local customs. He made a lovely cherry strudel, which she served now.

"Apparently, this housebreaker was here to steal a tiara."

"Was he?" Dorothea asked blandly. "Even stranger. Did he plan to leave a note with my watch, explaining why he wished to do such a kind thing?"

"No," Julia said. "He's been compensated for his good deed. Lord Stephen let him go." She poured Dorothea a cup of tea.

"How sad. I would have liked to meet him. One does not often meet such a chivalrous criminal."

Julia hesitated a moment before she took Dorothea's hand. "Is he the one who gave you the laudanum?" she asked.

Dorothea met her eyes. "Was he small and balding, with a mole next to his nose, just here?" She pointed to her own nose.

"No, nothing like that. His name is Thomas Merritt. Do you know him?"

"No, I don't think so." Dorothea frowned. "But I've met a good many people in Vienna I don't recall. I can't imagine why any of them would break into this house in the dead of night to return my watch. Have you met him?

Well, I suppose you have, since it was your room he broke into, according to Mrs. Hawes."

Julia concentrated on stirring her tea. "I knew him slightly in London. I met him at a ball."

Dorothea smiled. "Really? How surprised you must have been to have him show up here!" She bit into her strudel and rolled her eyes with pleasure. "It's as if the stars had all aligned to bring it about. How many ladies in Vienna have thieves climbing through their windows in the dead of night, only to discover they not only know the man, but he is English too? And let's not forget his real mission—to bring back my watch."

Julia felt her heart lift at the romantic image, though she knew it was false. "He came to steal, Dorothea."

Dorothea smiled knowingly. "Perhaps, but I haven't got a tiara. Nor does her ladyship, or any other lady in the delegation."

Julia frowned. Why would he lie about his reasons for breaking into the embassy? Then again, why wouldn't he? He'd given no indication he'd been looking for *her*. Indeed, he seemed surprised to see her. Her stomach knotted. He'd done a good deed in Hyde Park, and again at her betrothal ball, and after—if flattering her, and noticing that David had no regard for her was a good deed—making her feel beautiful, admired, loved. But she'd made a dreadful mistake in letting a simple kindness turn into disaster.

She resisted the urge to leap from her seat and race to the window, to see if she might catch a last glimpse of him, for surely it would be the last time she ever saw him. Instead she concentrated on the amber depths of her tea, saw his face, that devilish grin and the welt on his forehead. Whatever Thomas Merritt was, he was kinder than he let on.

She felt a surge of longing, and clenched her fist to stem it. Why was he here in Vienna?

"Did he leave his direction?" Dorothea asked.

Just footprints on the snow. "No, of course not."

"Pity. I should like to thank him."

Julia looked at her in surprise. "I doubt Stephen would permit it. Thomas Merritt is a dangerous man."

"All the same, he has done a kind deed, thief or not, and I shall not forget it, if I am ever so fortunate as to be able to repay him."

Could anyone ever forget Thomas Merritt?

Chapter 33

Stephen looked up in surprise as Julia entered his study. "My lord, there's something I need to speak to you about."

He was writing a report about Thomas Merritt. He'd started over twice, not sure how to describe the unusual situation. Nothing had been stolen, nothing broken, though the warming pan was badly dented, and no one had been hurt but Merritt himself. And there was the inexplicable fact that he'd returned Dorothea's watch. Doe was filled with happiness at having her watch back, asked him to find out where she could send a note of thanks, and babbled nonsense for half an hour about fate, kindness, and unlikely heroes.

Merritt was not a hero. He was a thief, albeit an unusual one, but nothing more. Some criminals had unusual quirks. Obviously Thomas Merritt was one of those. When he discovered where to find Merritt, he wouldn't tell Dorothea. He'd hang him. He didn't doubt for a moment Merritt had dark sins on his conscience. He'd put that into the report, and taken it out again. His suspicions smacked of jealous twaddle rather than clear, professional judgment of the situation.

She knew him. Julia knew Merritt. Would he wonder every time she even looked at another man?

She came forward to put a letter on his desk. It was addressed to Lord Castlereagh. "What's this? Tell me Merritt didn't leave it."

She clasped her hands and stood stiffly before his desk. "Prince de Talleyrand gave it to me, last night." Ah, so her visit was official, not an apology or an explanation.

He studied her face. She looked grave, almost afraid. He felt a frisson of warning. "Do you know the contents?"

"Yes."

She explained the details, and Stephen felt his stomach sour at the wily Frenchman's plot. "I thought you could explain it to his lordship, but I have an idea. Mr. Merritt—"

"Oh?" He still stung with jealousy at the sound of Merritt's name on her lips. "What's he got to do with this? Was he there?" He watched her color. She pursed her lips and didn't continue.

He ran a hand through his hair. "This couldn't have come at a worse time," he said, glaring at Talleyrand's letter. "I think you'd better explain this to his lordship yourself, and explain what exactly the prince said to you."

Her eyes flew to his, panic in their hazel depths. "Surely I cannot be of any use in something like this!"

"Talleyrand obviously wants you involved." He rose to his feet. "Come on. Lord Castlereagh must see this at once."

The clock ticked as Lord Castlereagh read and reread the letter in silence. Julia perched on the edge of the leather chair in front of his desk, her stomach twisted into a tight coil while Stephen stood by the window, looking grave.

At last the ambassador set the letter down and regarded Julia carefully.

"One does not receive notes of this kind every day. Would you like to tell me just how your involvement came about? I have, of course, had a note from the Bavarian ambassador describing the events in the park yesterday and offering his official thanks for your service to his wife, but to hear your praises from the French ambassador as well, and especially in such a letter as this, requires explanation." He glanced at Stephen. "I had no idea Miss Leighton's connections were so—auspicious, shall we say?"

Julia felt her skin heat. "He asked me to deliver the note to you, my lord. I had no idea of the exact contents."

"But he says you have seen the documents, can verify their existence, that you—how did he put it?" He picked up the letter again. "Ah yes, here it is. That you understand how dangerous scandal can be, and how helpful it is to have good friends." He laid the letter aside again. "Can you tell me what that means in this instance, Miss Leighton?"

"Blackmail," she murmured.

"An ugly word, but accurate enough. I've been Foreign Secretary for many years, served as a diplomat, and now I am His Majesty's representative here in Vienna. I have never found myself at a loss for words prior to this moment. I was surprised to hear of your actions in the park yesterday. You are a heroine to the Bavarians, and they wish to offer you a post in the royal household. Now, the French ambassador is offering similar rewards for your assistance. Joan of Arc, he calls you, and Boudicca."

Julia swallowed, studied her fingertips.

"While your glorious ascent is quite refreshing, this

matter could not have come at a worse moment. I have been recalled to London. The Duke of Wellington is to replace me as ambassador. Imagine the scandal. He—We, England—would have no credibility left if this was made public."

Julia looked up. "I have an idea, my lord. What if Prince Talleyrand did not have the documents? What if they were lost or . . ." She took a deep breath around the lump rising in her throat. " . . . stolen?"

She heard Stephen gasp, and turned her eyes to him. He shook his head, coloring. "I forbid you to go any further with this, Miss Leighton."

"But if there *were* a way to remove the prince's threat, would that not be best?"

Stephen strode toward her. "If you say one more word, I will dismiss you!" he threatened. She half rose to her feet, the lump in her throat huge now.

"And have her go to the employ of the Bavarians, or the French? Let Talleyrand ruin our credibility?" Castlereagh said. "I believe we must listen to all options, whether we agree or not. Now, what were you about to suggest, Miss Leighton?"

"If there was a thief, perhaps, someone who could slip into the prince's palace and take the documents . . ." she babbled breathlessly. Castlereagh's brows flew into his hairline at her suggestion. Had she gone too far? "If there was such a man, would it solve the problem?"

Castlereagh turned to Stephen. "Does she mean you by any chance, Major Lord Ives?"

"I mean a man named Thomas Merritt, an Englishman, here in Vienna, who just happens to be a—"

"Thief." Stephen finished for her.

"Can he do the job?" Castlereagh asked, his eyebrows rising, a hint of hope in his tone.

"I think so," Julia said. "He broke in here last night, despite all the security measures, and the guards."

Castlereagh looked at Stephen, who confirmed it with a nod. "Where is he now?" the ambassador asked.

"I let him go," Stephen said stubbornly. "He took nothing."

"But you had him followed. You know where to find him."

"He's an adventurer, a vagabond. I should have turned him over to the Austrian police, let them hang him for his crimes."

"What crimes?" Castlereagh asked.

Stephen raised his chin. "I don't know, but I don't doubt he's guilty of something."

Castlereagh folded the letter, put it back in the envelope. "Then use that. Get him back. Tell him if he assists us, he will be excused for his crimes. If not, we'll hang him. Surely that, if not patriotism, will motivate him. Tell him he can keep whatever valuables he finds, but only if he retrieves the letters." He turned to her, his eyes cool. "Miss Leighton, you will tell him where to find them, keep an eye on him, make sure he doesn't betray us." He rose and tossed the letter into the fire, and watched it blacken, flare, and curl into ash. "Talleyrand means to make this peace conference a statement of power—not French power, but *his* power. We are the victors, we won the war, but Talleyrand means to win the peace. I cannot allow that. I want this matter settled before I leave for London." He looked at Stephen, read his expression. "Do you feel this is dishonorable, Major?"

"I do, my lord. Theft is a crime."

"And sometimes it is, perhaps, the only way."

"What if we are caught?" Stephen asked. "Would that not be more embarrassing?"

"Mr. Merritt has no official connection with this embassy. We will disavow any knowledge of him," Castlereagh replied.

"And if he is successful?" Julia could not help but ask.

"I will arrange a pardon. One more question, Miss Leighton, and you will forgive me for being indelicate, but what did Prince de Talleyrand promise you for your help?"

"Land. A home for my son, money," she said softly.

"The old fox," Castlereagh murmured. "He knows exactly what each person wants. I wish I knew how he did it. He is the ultimate politician. Did he ask for further—services—from you to earn your reward?"

Julia raised her chin at the suggestion. "I was simply to impress upon you that he wished to be your friend. I have no intention of accepting—"

"You should, you know," he said. "He's a very rich man. Get the deeds in writing, though. It is more than our government will ever do for you." He turned to Stephen. "I want to hear nothing more about this, is that clear? I will leave the matter in your hands, Major. Officially, this conversation never occurred."

Stephen bowed and opened the door for her. For a moment, as they walked along the marble hallway, she listened to the echo of their footsteps.

"Why didn't you speak to me first?" he demanded in a whisper as they passed a footman standing at his post.

She shot him a glance. Would he have listened? She was tired already of the suspicion in his eyes every time Merritt's name was mentioned. "There really wasn't an opportunity. I just thought Thomas Merritt might . . ." She paused. Do what, rescue her again, and the whole of England with her?

He stopped in his tracks, and when she stopped too,

turned to her. "Julia, who the devil is he to you? Is he the one who—"

She met his eyes, read the question there, the agony, and felt her heart contract. He had confessed he loved her, had kissed her, made himself a target for disgrace and ruin. And now, if they failed—if Mr. Merritt failed—what would become of his career? Surely he deserved at least to know the truth. She had never told anyone.

"Yes."

Chapter 34

He pawned his shaving kit to buy Donovan a reprieve. While it was not nearly as valuable as Lord Castlereagh's jeweled Order of the Garter, it proved to be enough for the moment.

Erich took the money. "Got caught, did you?" he asked, looking at the bruise on Thomas's forehead. The tavern was dark and shuttered, lit by a candle that did nothing to dispel the gloom. Outside, the city lay pristine under the glistening blanket of new snow. Inside, Erich's den stank of stale beer and sweat. "And yet you got away."

"I fell in the dark, hit the edge of a bureau," he lied. "The good lady woke up and screamed before I could reach the safe."

Erich had a smile like a lizard, cold-blooded and mirthless. Thomas half expected his tongue to flick out to test the truth of his statement, but the thief continued to shave pieces off an apple with a long thin knife without looking at it, popping the flesh into his mouth. "Then we will have to go back. It should be easier now that you know where to go, and where the bureau is placed in the room. You can step around it and get to the safe much faster. I nearly froze my balls off waiting for you to come out. Donovan was awaiting my return, and I didn't want to disappoint him." He chewed a slice of apple, his eyes hard on Thomas.

Thomas felt his skin prickle. He should have known it wouldn't be so easy to gull a man like Erich. He'd been living in the demimonde long enough to recognize danger. He wondered how many of the wretches littering the room, drunk and asleep on tables and the floor, were beholden to Erich, so deep in debt to the thief lord that they could never escape him. He felt a moment's panic. Where the hell would he find the kind of loot that would satisfy his own debt?

"We'll go back tonight," Erich said. "I'll send someone in with you."

"Fine. I'll take Donovan. In fact, if he's well enough, I'll take him now. No one ties a cravat like he does," Thomas joked, though his gut was tight with fear that Donovan was already dead. "Where is he, anyway?"

Erich smiled his reptilian smile again. "Not here in the tavern, but he's quite safe. We're enjoying his company too much to allow him to go just yet, especially since you have not fulfilled your end of our bargain. You will have to find a sailor to tie fancy knots for you. If you need an accomplice, I will provide you with a good man."

Thomas's skin prickled. "No, I work better alone."

Erich stuck the knife into the table, where it quivered. He rose. "Very well. I shall expect you to visit again once you have what I want. Send a note, and I will come and meet you here, alone, of course."

Thomas got to his feet, felt the bruise on his forehead throb, and picked up his hat. It would be some days before he could wear it. The lovely Julia Leighton had a powerful arm for so delicate a lady.

"Viscount?" Erich called out as Thomas reached the

door. He shut his eyes. He should have known it wouldn't be so easy. He turned to regard the thief king.

"I forgot to mention that the price has gone up. The price of Donovan's accommodations, fees for the doctor, and so on. You understand."

Thomas tightened his hand on the door latch. "What do you want?"

"The old Russian whore. She wears a ruby pendant nearly as big as this apple. I want that. In addition to Lady Castlereagh's tiara, of course."

Madam Anna's favorite, General Semyon. Even Katerina wouldn't be able to replace it.

Thomas kept his face carefully blank. For a moment he was tempted to correct the thief, tell him it wasn't a tiara at all, but a star, a symbol of honor he didn't deserve, but he refrained. "It will take a few days," he said.

Erich looked coldly sympathetic. "But no longer, I hope. Patrick's expenses are mounting."

Thomas forced his hat onto his head as he opened the door, wincing at the pain, hoping it would help him think, spark a brilliant idea, but it just stung with every step.

He was a thief. Why should he be surprised to be treated as one? He could still walk away, of course, but he imagined his valet locked in a dank, dark cellar with a pair of burly guards at the door, well armed and ruthless.

Knowing Donovan, the valet was cursing his name as loudly as he could manage, his Irish baritone growing weaker with every curse, fading as fever overtook him and the bullet wound became corrupted.

If he didn't stay, do his best to save him, he would live with Patrick Donovan on his conscience for the rest of his days.

Along with all his other sins.

"Mr. Merritt?"

Thomas looked up. He was steps from his lodgings, but there were five red-coated soldiers between himself and the door. Behind them stood Stephen Ives.

"What now?" he asked. He was too tired to fight. His head hurt and he needed food, a bath, and sleep.

Stephen Ives came forward. "You bastard—you're under arrest."

One more sin, it appeared, had been added to the list, and he could only wait and see what it might turn out to be.

Chapter 35

Stephen had never hated a man like he hated Thomas Merritt. He had not been able to get the image of him with Julia out of his mind. He imagined her kissing him, holding him close, allowing him to—

"Did Merritt kill Temberlay?" he'd asked her as she stood before him after her admission, her chin high, waiting with dignity for whatever scorn he would heap upon her. He didn't have the words to express the pain he felt. He wanted to step away, run, never look at her again, but he just stood there and stared at her, thinking her beautiful even as hatred for her seducer built with every second. She'd looked surprised that his first question should be about Temberlay.

"No. He'd left England by then. He couldn't have."

"And does he know about—" He felt bile fill his mouth and he swallowed it. " . . . about the child?"

Her gaze turned ferocious, as protective as a mother tiger. "No. I had no way to tell him, nor did I wish to."

"You didn't trust him?" he asked, and choked out the next question, his fists clenched. "Was it rape?"

She blushed scarlet. "No! I simply had no intention of forcing him to do the honorable thing and marry me.

There would have been no dowry, and my father would still have disowned me. Jamie is mine."

"Then you don't intend to tell him, even now?"

"Especially now," she insisted. "He has not yet agreed to help us. Do you think he would, if he was suddenly faced with—"

"He has very little choice in the matter," Stephen said through gritted teeth, meaning the mission. Merritt could be forced to that at least, but she mistook him.

She lifted her chin, her eyes ferocious. "There is always a choice, my lord, and this one is mine alone to make."

She'd spun on her heel, her head high, her back straight, leaving him standing in the hallway staring after her, hating Thomas Merritt.

And now Merritt sat in the coach with him, on his way back to the embassy. Stephen glared at him, the thief, the rogue, the debaucher of innocent ladies. He clenched his fists until his gloves squeaked, wanting to lunge across the small space and clamp his hands around Thomas Merritt's throat and squeeze until he stopped breathing.

It had not been rape.

"To what do I owe the honor of this rather elaborate summons?" Merritt asked, his eyes half shut, meeting Stephen's glare. The dark bruise shadowed his broad brow, made him look dark and dangerous. He was, Stephen supposed, exactly the kind of man a woman would find attractive, even injured.

Especially injured.

He had a brash charm even men would find appealing in a companion to spend an evening drinking or gaming with—someone quick with a joke, clever. He wondered what Merritt would be like on the battlefield, under fire, where charm didn't matter.

"I suppose the lady who owned the watch wishes to

thank me personally, is that it?" Merritt continued in a bored tone when Stephen didn't reply, though his gaze was sharp enough. "She could simply have sent a note, or invited me to tea. This—abduction—was hardly necessary. I am always glad to bow to the whims of ladies."

Was it Julia's whim or his, that night at her betrothal ball? She'd been innocent, young . . .

She said it had not been rape, but would a well-bred lady as young and sheltered as Julia know the difference? He felt anger flare.

"The lady in question is my sister, and I would not allow her to sully herself with any kind of contact with a thief and a liar and a—"

Merritt's eyes opened fully, glittering with interest. "A what?" he asked, bidding Stephen to continue, but Stephen clamped his mouth shut, and imagined calling Thomas Merritt out for his various sins and shooting him between the eyes.

Merritt sighed. "There really is nothing to fear, Major. I mean your sister no harm. I returned the watch because I thought it was the kind of thing a woman might miss, a gift from a devoted husband, a keepsake of a fleeting moment of childhood. I want nothing from her, and I don't expect a reward."

"Good, because you'll get none," Stephen snapped. "Just how did you come by the watch again?"

"As I said, I won it gambling at a ball. I don't recall the man's name, if that's your next question. It was a good night, actually. I went home foxed with a pocket filled with my winnings, including that watch."

Stephen sent him a steel-edged glare. "And you decided out of the goodness of your heart to return it? How did you know where to find her? There are thousands of ladies in Vienna."

"True, but the man in the portrait is wearing a British uniform, like most of the Englishmen in town for the conference, including yourself. I assumed the owner was with the embassy."

So he was smart as well as charming. It didn't make Stephen like him any better.

"Why not simply come to the front door, hand it over?"

Merritt looked away. "Call me sentimental. I wished to give it back to her personally."

"A knight errant on some chivalrous quest. Robin Hood, wasn't it?" Stephen mocked. "Let it go, Merritt, and stay away from her—and Julia Leighton as well."

Merritt pinned Stephen with a pointed look at the mention of Julia's name. Stephen glared back, letting him know that she was under his protection, safe from the likes of him.

"That would be easier if I wasn't on my way to the British Embassy, wouldn't it? Not by my choice, of course. So why am I going a-visiting so early this morning? It's hardly the polite hour for calls."

"I'll explain when we arrive."

Merritt gave an exaggerated sigh. "Then I'm not to be hanged for my crimes just yet. If I were, I have no doubt the ambassador would simply have sent you to carry out the command. Or we'd be on the way to an Austrian prison, not a palace."

"Unfortunately, it's not my choice," Stephen replied, his mouth twisting. He imagined pulling the noose over Merritt's head, wiping the smirk off the bastard's face as he tightened the rope against his throat. Stephen's foot twitched as he imagined kicking the stool out from under him.

He turned away, looked out the window at the sugary dusting of snow that made the city look pristine and soft, when it was anything but, in his opinion. It was a den of thieves and liars, without an honorable man among them. They passed the rest of the journey in stony silence.

When he glanced at Merritt again, the man was fast asleep, as if he had nothing at all to fear.

Chapter 36

Julia set the pen down and rubbed her eyes. Try as she could, she couldn't stop thinking about Thomas, how he'd looked, what it felt like to be in the same room with him again. She'd been staring at the chair he'd occupied for half an hour, when she was supposed to be writing a very important note.

How long did it take desire to sicken and die?

He was a rogue, a scoundrel, and a thief.

"Who are you writing to?" Dorothea asked. She was sitting by the window, playing Patience.

"To Diana de Talleyrand, to thank her for inviting me last night." Diana would tell her uncle she'd received Julia's note, and he would understand that Julia had delivered his message. The prince would expect to hear from Castlereagh, think he'd won.

"How kind of you. Perhaps we should ask her to tea. What is the correct diplomatic protocol for asking an ambassador's niece to tea?" Dorothea mused. "Will it matter which chair she is offered, or from which side we pass the cakes?"

Julia bit her lip. "I don't know." She would undoubtedly lose Diana's friendship entirely when the theft was discovered. She was sorry about that.

"Lady Castlereagh would know, of course, but she would also wonder why we wish to pursue Diana's friendship," Dorothea mused. "It would not occur to her we simply admire her, and have no political motives at all. Her ladyship is a political creature, and a suspicious one at that."

Not to mention that Lady Castlereagh would hardly approve of a woman like herself mixing with the upper echelons of the diplomatic circles for any reason. She imagined her ladyship perched in her private sitting room like a vigilant bird of prey, waiting for word of any impropriety she might commit so she could swoop in for the kill—in this case, Julia's dismissal. The events of yesterday had been improper indeed. If Stephen had assumed the worst when he saw Thomas Merritt sprawled on the floor of her room, what would Lady Castlereagh make of it? And Lord Castlereagh would surely help his wife toss her out if this plan failed. And what would become of Thomas Merritt? Surely people would guess the truth when they heard she'd known him in London.

Ruin, all over again.

A jolt of horror passed through her, and she jumped to her feet. Dorothea looked up at her. "I'm going down to ask someone to deliver the note," Julia explained.

Dorothea set her playing cards aside.

"Yes, do." She looked out at the snow. "It looks cold, doesn't it? Even if the snow is rather pretty. I suppose we must stay indoors today, wait and see if it will melt or stay. Could you bring me a book from the library? Poetry, I think. Something bold, heroic, and romantic."

"Of course."

As the clock on the mantel chimed the hour, Dorothea

picked up the watch and compared the time with a smile.

Julia's quick footsteps echoed all the way along the hall and down the stairs. Lady Castlereagh had insisted that carpets be installed in the wing of the house she occupied, saying the clatter of boots on stone made her fear the palace was being overrun. The rest of the corridors remained unadorned, and even the soft hiss of a lady's slippers filled the air like a malicious whisper.

Where was Mr. Merritt now? she wondered as she entered the library and began to search for a book for Dorothea. Was he thinking of her the way she was thinking of him?

He'd probably forgotten everything about that night. Would she have forgotten too, if things had turned out differently, if she had not quickened with his child, if David had lived and she'd become Duchess of Temberlay?

Of course she would have, she lied to herself. She would be at Temberlay this very moment, overseeing the day's meals, or planning a dinner party. No, she could never have married David. Not after Thomas.

She scanned the shelves, finding books in German and French, which Dorothea could not read. Then at last, in a corner, tucked away on the far side of a mahogany shelf, she found a volume of poems by Lord Byron. If Dorothea wanted words to warm her in the depths of a winter's day, this would certainly do it. She recalled the salacious pleasure of gossiping with London ladies over tea about the wicked poet. He did as he pleased, lived beyond the pale of good manners and good society, and if his poems were any indication, he enjoyed every moment.

Just like Thomas Merritt.

The door opened, and her ears pricked. Was she eavesdropping? Was it better to come out, make herself known, or to wait until whoever it was departed and then make a quiet exit? What if it was Charles Stewart? She clutched the book to her chest, peered carefully around the shelf and stifled a gasp.

It was worse than Charles Stewart. It was Thomas Merritt, and Stephen.

"In here will do," Stephen said, his tone harsh.

"Indeed. Looks much more comfortable than a dark dungeon. Does this palace actually have a dungeon?"

A shiver rushed through her at the sound of Thomas's deep voice, and the hairs rose on the back of her neck. She couldn't move.

"Sit down, Merritt. I've sent for Miss Leighton to join us."

Julia's eyes widened in dismay. It would certainly look odd if she popped out from behind the shelf now.

"Any chance you might consider sending for tea, and a scone or two? I was about to have breakfast when you apprehended me, and I'm fair starving now."

"Later," Stephen snapped.

"Then will this interrogation take long?" Thomas asked calmly.

"You aren't going anywhere."

"As you wish, but your hospitality leaves much to be desired, Major."

The door opened again. "Yes?" Stephen said impatiently.

"Lord Castlereagh wishes to speak with you in his study, Major Lord Ives," a servant said.

"Come along, then, Merritt, on your feet—" she heard Stephen order.

"No sir," the servant interrupted. "Just you. The gentleman is to wait here."

"I promise to behave myself. Is there any silverware or valuables in the room you'd prefer to lock up before you go?" Thomas said lightly.

"Lock the door behind me," Stephen ordered the servant. "If he tries to leave, shoot him."

"I haven't got a gun," the man complained, and Thomas's sudden burst of laughter startled her.

"There's a rather lethal looking letter opener here on the desk," he offered.

"Just guard the door," Stephen said, and she heard the door close, the jangle of the key, then silence. Her heart sank. She was locked in with Thomas, and how would *that* look when Stephen returned? She would have to stay here all day, she supposed, hiding. His presence sent pins and needles through her limbs. She wanted to sit down, or to run.

How silly she was! She would step out, cross the room and leave. It was as simple as that. She took a breath and came out from behind the shelf. He was standing by the window, staring out as if he was considering plunging through the panes.

"I was wondering if you would make yourself known." He smiled apologetically. "I smelled violets."

"Were you planning to escape out the window?"

His eyes roamed over her, and she clutched the book against her chest like a talisman against his allure.

"Would you stop me?" he asked. She looked pointedly at the letter opener.

"If I had to."

He crossed his arms over his chest and grinned, and her heart turned over at the memory of what that smile could do to a lady's composure and good sense. "Then I'll stay. What shall we talk about? Shall I start by saying you look well? Vienna agrees with you, but the air is so much healthier here than in London, is it not?"

Hot blood crept into her cheeks. He was mocking her. She looked at the bruise on his forehead.

"Does it hurt?" she asked.

He raised a brow. "Proud of that, are you? No. It only

hurts when I wear my hat." His mouth quirked to one side, and her heart skipped a beat. How many times had Jamie given her that exact smile? She tightened her hold on the book.

"I had no idea it was you when I hit you."

The grin deepened, showing the dimples he'd passed on to his son. "Then I might have expected a different greeting if you had recognized me sooner?"

She leveled a quelling gaze at him. "Not at all."

"You probably would have hit me all the harder," he said quietly, sobering.

She glanced at the door. Where on earth was Stephen? Would he leave her locked in here all day? The room was overly warm, and she had things to do upstairs. Dorothea was waiting for her to return, and she could not simply stand here with the charming Mr. Merritt, wishing . . . Wishing what? That he would come closer, or step back, or kiss her again so she could see that it truly wasn't the way she remembered it and stop thinking about him? She looked at the window, tempted to open it herself, push him through it, get him out of her life for good.

"Does my presence here this afternoon have anything to do with you, my lady?"

Warning tightened her skin. "Why would you think that?"

"A vague hunch."

"Do you imagine I have the power to order people arrested on a whim?" she demanded.

He tilted his head and grinned. Jamie again. A jolt of awareness frayed her nerves.

"I don't know. Do you? You were never good at hiding your emotions, my lady. They show on your face, in every line of your body, at least as I recall. So why am I here?"

She felt her skin heat another degree, remembered the

feeling of his body against hers as they danced, kissed, made love . . . he was coming toward her, prowling like a panther, still dressed in the same black clothing he'd worn last night. He looked thoroughly disreputable with the bruise marring his face, dangerous. Better, even, than she remembered him. She resisted the urge to step back, faced him with determination and cold hauteur. Let him read what he wished in that.

He reached out and she drew a sharp breath, waiting for his touch, but he merely took the book from her hand. "Yes, indeed. I can read you like a book of—poetry?" He glanced at the cover and back at her. "Julia, you know why I'm here. Care to enlighten me?"

She was not so transparent as that, was she? Oh, please, not with him, not now! She straightened her spine, drawing herself up as tall as possible. He was far taller still, and so close she had to tip her head back to meet his eyes.

"Of course I know," she snapped. "You are here at my suggestion. Major Ives wanted to turn you over to the Austrian authorities, but there is a matter that we—"

"Ah, so he's Major Ives to you, is he? Not Stephen, or darling, or—"

She snatched the book out of his hand and spun on her heel, heading for the door without another word.

" 'When we two parted in silence and tears, half broken hearted to sever for years . . .' " he said, and she stopped in her tracks, turned to face him.

"What?"

"Byron's poem, 'When We Two Parted.' I've always had a penchant for his writing. Every young buck in England secretly wishes he were Byron. He's quite a rogue, yet women adore him, sigh for him," he said, scanning her face.

Did he expect her to sigh? He was about to be disappointed. She tucked the book behind her back. "I detest Byron," she lied. "The book is not for me. A friend requested I bring it upstairs for her. Not that it's any of your concern, Mr. Merritt."

He tilted his head. "Why, you've become as prim as a governess since we last met, my lady. I think I preferred the blushing debutante."

She flinched at the assessment, far too close to the truth. He reached out and touched her cheek, drawing his finger down the curve of her face. Fire transferred from his touch, and heated her skin, the simple caress burning all over her body.

"Ah, there she is," he said, his whisper vibrating over her senses. "The debutante, I mean."

She could smell the faint hint of his soap, the still-familiar scent of his body. Had she not forgotten even that? She remembered how his hands felt on her body, the champagne taste of his kiss, the sound of the whispered endearments and charming compliments . . . Her mouth watered, and she moved back, retreated, not daring to take her eyes off him, not wanting to, but knowing if she stayed, if he touched her again, she would never, ever be free of this man.

Her cheek still tingled, and she resisted the urge to touch the spot. She backed toward the door. "If you'll excuse me, I have things to do," she managed in a breathless rush. "I'll bid you good-bye."

"This time for good, eh?" He was advancing toward her, taking one step forward for every step she took back. "Since we likely won't see each other again, perhaps you will do me the kindness of satisfying my curiosity?"

"As to what?" she croaked.

"Ah, Julia, you were once entirely honest in your speech, your actions, your passions. Has that changed? It would be a pity, because that was what I liked best about you."

Her blood flowed hotter still, and the tingle on her cheek spread. "I'm surprised you remember," she said tartly, but it came out a husky purr. She couldn't seem to look away from him. His gray eyes were as deep as a well. She felt as if she was about to fall in and drown, and it wouldn't be a terrible fate at all.

"I remember," he said, his meaning clear. "I also remember you were about to marry a duke. What happened after I left that night?"

The pain returned, like hitting the cold water at the bottom of the well, bringing with it the regret, the guilt. She tore her eyes from his. "He—died."

She glanced up as a flicker passed over his face. Horror, perhaps, or was it merely pity? She didn't want his pity. Anger flared.

"And you, Mr. Merritt, were you a thief even then?"

He smiled ruefully. "I'm afraid so. I was hoping to steal your mother's tiara that night."

She felt something snap inside, a thread of hope, perhaps. He hadn't cared a whit for her, not while he danced with her and flattered her, not when he kissed her, and not when he made love to her in her father's library. And in the park, when he rescued her, made her feel feminine and beautiful? Just part of the ruse, no doubt.

"I see," she said coldly. "You said you came to steal Lady Castlereagh's tiara too. Do you specialize in tiaras?"

He looked appreciative of the jest. "I got neither one. I'm sure if you ask your mother, she will confirm that her jewels are exactly where she left them, as are Lady Castlereagh's."

Ask her mother? "That would make you the worst thief

in Christendom!" she said, her heart sinking. She had promised Lord Castlereagh he could— Oh, no.

"And beyond," he agreed easily. "How did you end up in Vienna?"

Julia blinked at the question. "I—I came with the embassy."

"Why?" he shot back.

"I wanted an adventure." It was partly true. That adventure that started the moment she laid eyes on him in her father's ballroom.

"An adventure," he drawled. "With—" He jerked his head toward the door. "What *is* Ives to you? A replacement for Dull Duke David?"

Indignation closed her throat, kept her from a tart reply. "Major Lord Ives is a gentleman and a diplomat," she said, telling him nothing at all that he didn't know.

He smiled at her again, a mocking smile, touched with a little sadness. He raised his hand to touch her again, but she moved out of reach, and he dropped his hand. "Not a thief. Whatever he is to you, he's a lucky son of a—"

She gasped at the jangle of the keys and turned to look at the door. Stephen entered.

"Here you are. I was looking for you," he said, and glanced suspiciously at Thomas Merritt. "What are you—"

"I was hoping you were the footman with tea," Thomas quipped, distracting him, rescuing her once again, stepping in front of her, blocking Stephen's view of her flushed face so she could compose herself. "Might I have some stale bread and moldy cheese, at least, or whatever it is you feed condemned prisoners here?"

Stephen smiled coolly at him. "You're not condemned, Mr. Merritt. In fact, you're about to be offered a reprieve. I suggest you take it."

Thomas raked her with a glance, then turned back to Stephen. "What the devil does that mean?"

"Sit down. We have a lot to discuss."

Thomas stared at them as if they were mad. Julia was perched on the very edge of the settee across from him, her lower lip caught between her teeth, nervous, unsure of his response to the odd—and dangerous—request. Only it wasn't a request at all. Ives's cold glare dared him to refuse the proposition, hoped he would.

Thomas sat forward. "You want me to break into the Kaunitz Palace, the most carefully guarded building in this city, and steal some papers?" No one moved. "And if I won't do it?"

"You'll hang," Ives said pleasantly. Thomas waited for more. "Surely this is not a difficult proposition. You're a thief. We have something that requires stealing."

Thomas felt Julia's gaze on him like a touch. His fingers still burned from touching her cheek. "Have you no patriotism?" she asked.

He laughed at that. "Patriotism? England has hardly been a friend to me."

"Do you believe in nothing, then?" she said softly.

"I believe in preserving my own skin." She looked at him as if she suspected that wasn't true at all, knew it in her heart. He frowned at her, but she held his eyes steadily, giving him no choice.

Stephen Ives got to his feet, began to pace. "This is pointless. Will you do it or not?"

Julia didn't look away, and Thomas held her gaze. This was a fool's errand, certain to get him killed. And yet how could he say no? "I have conditions of my own," he said instead.

Ives stopped pacing. *"Conditions?* Isn't letting you live enough?"

"You'll have a full pardon," Julia said. "You could, if you wished, go back to England."

He laughed again. "No, thank you." When had Julia become a spy? She was good at it. He hadn't suspected a thing until she breathlessly outlined her plan. He felt a surge of admiration. She wasn't the blushing debutante now. She'd grown up since he last saw her, and he wondered again what the hell had happened to her, and how she'd ended up here, with Ives.

"What conditions?" she asked. He read the fear in her eyes, at what he might ask.

"Freedom, first of all," he said. He watched her shoulders drop a little with relief. "I wish to return to my own lodgings, comfortable though your dungeon might be. You have my word—if you meet the rest of my conditions— that I will not try to flee."

Julia nodded agreement, but Stephen Ives shook his head. "I'd be a fool to agree to that. You're a thief, Merritt. Why should I trust you?" he demanded.

Thomas shrugged. "Then I'll stay here, but I want a room on the second floor, a bedroom with a sitting room, and . . ." He slid his eyes ever so slightly toward Julia, and watched Stephen Ives turn purple. Ives did not want him anywhere near Julia.

"You may remain in your own lodgings, but under guard," Ives said stiffly.

"That is my second condition," Thomas said. "No guards."

Ives snorted. "You have a very long list of demands for a condemned criminal."

" 'Condemned' being the important word," Thomas said. "This job could get me killed. You might decide to hang me anyway once the documents are retrieved and the job is done."

"Major Lord Ives is an honorable man," Julia objected, but one glance at Ives's dark scowl, and Thomas knew he'd gladly betray this agreement—even go so far as to hang him personally. For Ives, this was entirely about Julia, he realized.

He wondered if Ives knew what had occurred between himself and Julia. Would she have told him? Pillow talk, perhaps. Apparently she did not know Ives as well as she thought. Under his shining, righteous honor, jealousy made Stephen Ives as ruthless as any other man. He felt a frisson of his own jealousy.

"I want Castlereagh's Order of the Garter star."

Julia gasped, and Stephen gaped at him. "If you can't steal it, you expect me to hand it over to you?" Ives demanded.

"Why?" Julia asked. "You could never sell such a thing."

He raised one eyebrow, surprised that she knew that. Her lips parted and she blushed at the gesture, looked away. Now what did *that* mean? "Call it part of my reward for contributing to the successful conclusion of peace in His Majesty's favor, if you wish."

"Anything else?" Ives asked sarcastically. "The Crown jewels, perhaps?"

A large ruby on a gold chain might help, he was tempted to say. "Money," he said instead. "Enough to leave Vienna and go where I wish when this is done." If he rescued Donovan, he'd dismiss him, send him home with the price of a horse farm in his pocket. *If* . . .

He watched Julia frown at the crass demand. What did she expect from a man she was hiring to steal? "I want all of this in writing," he said.

Ives folded his arms. "Impossible. This is a secret mission, Merritt, and time is of the essence. We cannot simply draw up a formal agreement."

"Then I will take your vowel, Major, since you are a gentleman."

Ives looked surprised, but Thomas let him read the fact that he didn't really care if they hanged him or not.

"Agreed." He watched Stephen Ives cross to the desk to find a piece of paper.

"Money and a souvenir," Julia said softly. "I had not imagined it would be so cheap a price."

Damn her. She had no right to mock him, look down on him. Anyone else, but not her, not now that he'd agreed. He wouldn't have, except for her.

"Ah, but there is one more condition, this one just between you and me."

He watched her throat bob, and the smugness went out of her hazel eyes. She glanced at Ives, but he was all the way across the room. "What?" she asked in a husky whisper, but she knew. He could read it in her eyes, fear—and desire too.

"You. One more night together."

She shut her eyes. "I cannot—"

Ives was coming back. "Say yes, or I shall tear up the vowel," Thomas whispered.

"Why?" she pleaded.

He wanted to step over the tea table that separated them, take her into his arms and show her why. She felt it too, the unfinished desire between them. She stared at him, her eyes wide and dark, her lips parted, and he stifled a groan and curled his hand on his knee, almost wishing he hadn't said it.

"Do you agree or not?" he asked.

She sent him a desperate, wordless plea as Ives arrived

behind her, but he held her gaze, his desire naked in his eyes.

"Here you are," Ives said. "But if you betray me, I will hunt you down and put a bullet in your brain, is that clear?"

He didn't even glance at Ives as he took the note, held it between his fingers, daring her to refuse.

At last she nodded, an almost imperceptible jerk of her head.

He put the vowel into his pocket and rose to his feet. "We're done here, then. I shall return tomorrow night," he said, and strode toward the door.

One more night. One more chance to hold her, touch her skin. If, of course, he survived breaking into the French Embassy and stealing secret documents. Could he do it?

For one more night with Julia, he would break into hell itself and come back alive.

Chapter 37

Julia couldn't breathe. She watched Thomas leave the room, the house, without a backward glance.

He wouldn't hold her to it, surely. It was just a game.

"My God, he's cocky. He won't hold us to any of those agreements," Stephen said. Julia turned to look at him.

"What?" Surely he didn't mean to hang Thomas Merritt anyway, even if he succeeded? The look on his face spoke of hatred. It made her shiver.

The door opened again, and Julia's heart leapt into her throat, but it was Dorothea, not Thomas.

"Ah, there you are. I met your Mr. Merritt on his way out."

"He's not my Mr. Merritt," Julia said.

"Well, your housebreaker," Dorothea said. "He's charming. He reminds me of someone, though. I wonder if we've met before?"

Stephen sniffed. "He hardly travels in the same circles you do, Doe."

"But Julia knew him in London," she said. "Perhaps I met him too."

"That's quite impossible. Anyway, he won't be in Vienna much longer," Stephen said.

"Then I'm glad I invited him to dine with us tomorrow evening," Dorothea said. "To thank him for his kindness in returning my watch. He accepted."

"What?" Stephen gaped at his sister.

"I think I will ask Peter to join us as well."

She turned to Julia. "The afternoon has turned sunny, and the snow is almost gone. Mrs. Hawes is preparing Jamie for his walk, and I thought I'd go along for some fresh air. Would you like to come too? You look rather flushed. Are you well?"

"This room is—rather warm," Julia managed. Dorothea had never shown the slightest interest in walking Jamie in the past. Why now?

She went upstairs to get her bonnet and gloves. Mrs. Hawes was wrapping Jamie in shawls and blankets, and Dorothea looked on, laughing, and bent over to tie his bonnet herself.

"Oh, Julia, he's a lovely child. He *is* strong, isn't he?" Julia caught a flash of sadness in her eyes.

"Of course he is," Julia said, looking at her son's rosy cheeks. He had Thomas Merritt's eyes, her own snub nose. She drew a shaky breath.

"Life is so fragile, isn't it?" Dorothea said, then smiled. "All the more reason to enjoy every moment, don't you think?"

Julia stared at her, but her eyes were on Jamie, bright with unshed tears. Jamie cooed, and Dorothea laughed, the tears disappearing. "I feel so happy today!"

Chapter 38

Princess Kostova's footman was waiting for Thomas at his lodgings. Katerina didn't bother with notes—she sent servants to recite her invitations.

The man snapped to attention and bowed as Thomas approached him, waiting on the steps, and carefully delivered his memorized message. "Her Highness wishes to inform you that her—no, *our*—dear friend the Prince de Ligne is ill, and a visit from you would cheer him considerably. Will you come? I am to wait for your answer, and remind you that he is a very old gentleman, and not strong, and if necessary escort you to his lodgings."

"You may tell Princess Kostova that I will come," he said. "But I will need to change my clothes and bathe first."

The Russian bowed. "I will wait."

Thomas gave him a few coins. He must already have been waiting in the cold all morning. "Go and get a drink in the tavern. I'll find my own way to the prince's lodgings."

He climbed the stairs to his flat. The place was empty without Donovan's cheeky presence, and he bathed quickly and did his best to shave himself with a borrowed razor. He stared at his battered face in the mirror. He'd have to make up a story to tell. Katerina would immediately suspect it was another woman, especially since he hadn't been to see her recently. He'd become so obsessed with the watch that he'd been avoiding her. Every time he saw her, Donovan had expected him to return with her jewels. Thomas began to spend his nights in gaming hells instead of attending her salons and parties, earning enough to cover his expenses without stealing.

He'd never been a very good thief, and now his future depended on it, and that of England, if Julia was to be believed. He had no reason to doubt her. She had told the story of the French ambassador's blackmail with fear in her eyes, afraid for her country, perhaps, but there was something else.

If she knew his one and only attempt at housebreaking had ended with him unconscious on her bedroom floor, she'd be afraid indeed. He couldn't afford to fail this time. Lives hung in the balance, including his own.

He tied his own cravat with less efficiency than Donovan would have and picked up his coat. He'd worn it to break into the embassy, and it still smelled faintly of Julia's perfume. He held it to his nose, felt a powerful surge of lust that stopped his breath.

Why on earth had he demanded she spend the night with him? He'd been carrying around an obsession for a woman he couldn't have for too long as it was. If she honored the bargain, it wouldn't make it better. She belonged with Stephen Ives, an honorable gentleman, a diplomat with a title and a future beyond tomorrow night.

But he'd never felt about any woman the way he did about Julia Leighton. Tomorrow night he'd do his best to break into the French Embassy and steal the documents. His success would gain Stephen Ives recognition, promotion, and Julia would benefit by that—and he'd get to live another day, and hold Julia one more time. If he held her to the agreement, of course.

And beyond that?

He turned away from the mirror.

There was nothing.

Chapter 39

"There's a letter for you," Stephen said when she arrived back at the embassy, her cheeks still pink with more than the cold. She hadn't been able to stop thinking about Thomas Merritt's "condition." It was impossible.

And yet, he was risking his life, and she had agreed. There was no choice but to fulfill her part of the bargain.

She took the letter from Stephen's hand. "It's from Diana Talleyrand," she told him, and opened it. "It's an invitation to attend her salon tomorrow night," she said breathlessly, and grinned at him. "It's perfect, a way in—"

He took her hand, kissed it. "Perhaps this will be easier than we thought."

"Yes," she said. "Or perhaps not. Will Prince de Talleyrand expect me to deliver some kind of message from Lord Castlereagh?"

"If Merritt is successful, that will be message enough."

She paced the room, measuring the rug. "Yes, I suppose so. What will happen if we fail?"

He looked away uneasily, hiding something. "We can't. It's too important."

He came to stand in front of her, to stop her from

pacing, and put his hand under her chin, raising her face to his. He kissed her gently on the lips.

"You're a remarkable woman, Julia. When this is over—"

She pressed her hand to his chest, gently. "Wait until then," she whispered.

"Knowing about Merritt hasn't changed my mind about what I said, Julia." He stepped back. "I can't go with you tomorrow night. I've been ordered not to."

"By Castlereagh?" she asked.

He nodded. "I am a recognized member of the British delegation. If Merritt fails and I am there, it will be impossible to deny our involvement."

She felt her heart sink. "Then what will happen to him?"

He frowned. "That won't be our concern."

"But he agreed to help us!"

"For a price," he said fiercely. "For jewels and money, not for any love of king or country or—" He stopped before he said it, but she understood. *You.* As if Thomas Merritt might care about her beyond the pleasure he'd already had.

"And what of me? I'm to go with him, show him where the documents are," she said, breathless. He looked pained, came and touched her cheek, his own skin flushing, his eyes bright.

"Don't fail, Julia. You can't. Get out if things go badly."

"Or what?" she asked, but she already knew. She was as disposable, as expendable, to Castlereagh as Thomas Merritt was. Her heart climbed into her throat.

There was a knock at the door, and he sprang away from her and took a seat on the other side of the room, as if she had already failed, was already tainted.

"Another letter for Miss Leighton," the footman said, entering.

She took it and saw Diana's neat script. What now? Had Talleyrand heard somehow?

"Another invitation?" Stephen asked, returning to her side once the servant left the room.

"No," she said. "News. A mutual friend is ill, the old Prince de Ligne."

"Sorry to hear it. The old fellow has been a fixture at the courts of Europe for half a century."

She folded the letter. "If Dorothea doesn't need me, I think I will go to see him."

"You are very kind," he said. "It will take your mind off—things. I'll see you at dinner."

Chapter 40

The Prince de Ligne had lodgings near the old city walls. He cheerfully referred to his modest home as his "birdcage" since it was so small his bedroom doubled as his salon.

"And how very convenient that is, when one is confined to one's bed," he said, greeting Julia as she arrived in the crowded room, which was already filled with visitors. "How wonderful that you've come today, my dear. There is someone I've wanted to introduce you to for a very long time. Viscount, here is the lovely English rose I told you about."

Julia turned to find Thomas Merritt standing near the window where the light shone on him, illuminated him like a dark angel. The lady next to him assessed Julia with a narrow-eyed glare.

"Miss Leighton and I have met, Your Highness," Thomas said, regarding her with sardonic amusement.

"*Miss Leighton?* Oh no, among friends she is Lady Julia. Especially now," de Ligne said. He held out his hands. "Come and stand here by the bed, both of you. There now, didn't I say they would make a dazzling couple?" he asked his guests.

"Not at all, in my opinion," the beauty by the window said in accented English, to ensure Julia understood.

Julia took in the emerald green military spencer the lady wore, cut to show her lush figure to perfection. Her eyes matched the hard glint of the emeralds in her ears and adorning her saucy little cap. She came to stand next to Thomas, his dark handsomeness the perfect foil for her blond beauty.

De Ligne chuckled and blew her a kiss. "No, you would not see it, my dear Princess Kostova. But Vienna deserves to be a city of love as much as Paris does. Forgive me, my dear, but a little matchmaking now and then keeps me young, especially now that I am past the age of participating in love affairs in any other way."

The princess's face softened to a smile as she straightened the shawl around de Ligne's shoulders. "You old roué, you will always be my first love."

"I had no idea you knew de Ligne," Thomas said to Julia in a low voice, drawing her into a quiet corner. "But then I had no idea you knew Talleyrand, or Castlereagh, or Stephen Ives, for that matter."

He sounded almost peevish. Julia looked again at the lovely Russian princess. "Is she your lover?" she asked boldly.

He raised his eyebrows. "How surprising. I doubt the demure Julia Leighton I met in London would ever have asked such a bold question. She was a lady to her fingertips."

"And innocent," she said, meeting his eyes. He colored slightly. No, she was no longer the pampered earl's daughter, no longer a virginal English lady. That had all changed the moment she set her hand in his and let him waltz her out the French doors of her father's ballroom, and straight into scandal. Truth be told, it irked her—just a little—to imagine him with the vivid blonde.

"Since we are sharing our deepest secrets, is Stephen Ives *your* lover?" he asked, though he hadn't answered her question about Kostova.

Anger flared, and she scanned the room to see if anyone was listening, but the prince was spinning one of his fascinating tales, holding his guests in thrall. "Do you imagine I would ever have agreed to your—" She tripped over the word, a prim earl's daughter after all, perhaps. "—'condition' if he was?"

"Ah yes, my condition," he drawled.

"Surely you didn't mean it," she said in a breathless rush. He filled their quiet corner of the room, and by necessity she was standing so close that her skirts brushed his trousers and his face was mere inches from her own. She could feel his breath on her cheek, see the flare of his pupils at the question. She held her breath. Could he still make her see stars if he kissed her now? Her body tingled.

"Didn't I?" he asked, yet another question to avoid answering her. "Do you ever think about that night at your betrothal ball?"

She glanced at his cravat, inexpertly tied. Her hands itched to straighten it. "Of course not," she said, her voice a husky murmur. She met his eyes, her gaze locked with his.

"I remember every detail. Your dress was blue, and you wore diamonds in your hair—" He reached up to coil a lock of her hair around his finger, indicating the place on her head the diamonds had been. "Here, and here. You wore violet perfume." He leaned in and sniffed, then smiled to see she still wore it. "I remember the exact feel of your waist under my hand as we waltzed, the taste of champagne on your lips, the sound of your sighs when I—" He stopped and let his eyes drop to her lips. Her mouth watered.

"Surely you've had dozens—hundreds—of other, um, encounters, since then," she said, the pounding of her heart making her breathless.

"As have you, no doubt," he said.

She looked away. "Of course."

"My God, you haven't, have you?"

She stared at him ferociously. "Just because I do not make a habit of going about seduci—" She choked on the word.

He looked contrite for a moment. "I didn't realize until after that I was the first. I would not have—"

"That's why you came to see me, on Bond Street. It wasn't to return my earring, was it, which I assume you—took—on purpose?" She couldn't say "stole."

His lips tightened. "I wanted to be sure you were—unhurt. I feared I might have been too rough." Was he *blushing*? She should be the one to blush!

Did his bedmates usually announce such facts? She had no idea of the etiquette for illicit seductions.

He looked at her as he had that night, his eyes gentle, lit by an internal fire that set her own blood alight.

He caught her hand in his. "Forgive me, Julia. I am not usually so—"

"What are you two discussing over there?" The prince's voice rang out. "Come and sit here on the bed beside me, Lady Julia. There are some people here even more sheltered than I. They haven't heard the tale of your heroic actions in the park. I daresay there are a lot of rumors and half-truths surrounding the encounter, so you must tell us the true tale—or embellish it further, if you prefer—so long as it is a good story."

Thomas watched Julia blush, felt his heart turn over in his chest. How long had it been since he'd seen a genuine blush? She was still as innocent as she'd been that night. Almost. He felt frustration that their conversation had been interrupted, and yet he was intrigued that she had yet another adventure to recount. Did she make a habit of daring escapades?

Escapades like him. He felt a surge of desire.

"There's not much to tell, Your Highness," she said, smiling at the prince. "Just some robbers in the park."

De Ligne gaped at her. "*Some* robbers? I heard there were twenty men, armed to the teeth. They shot four bystanders and swarmed over the coach carrying the imperial jewels of Austria—the empress had ordered them fetched from the vault buried deep under the Hofburg Palace so she could wear them at a ball at Schonbrunn. Lady Julia disarmed one of the thieves, and used his own pistol to shoot him and four more of his fellows."

"Doesn't a pistol hold just one single shot?" Kostova asked blandly.

A robbery in the park? Thomas felt his stomach clench. *Donovan's* robbery? He stared at Julia in stunned silence—and he'd been afraid she was too fragile to withstand his rough seduction.

He assessed the delicate lines of her body, the slim fingers, soft skin, demure blush.

The woman was an Amazon.

He watched as she gently corrected the story. She had shot one man, not four, and only in the leg. The coach had contained the wife of the Bavarian ambassador, not the Austrian crown jewels. She told her tale modestly, hoped she hadn't killed the man, even if he was a criminal. He noticed she carefully avoided using the word thief, and did not look at him as she told the story.

By the end of the tale it was perfectly clear that Lady Julia Leighton had shot his valet. He stood and stared at her, numb.

She was not the woman he'd thought she was—she was more. More complex, more intriguing, more womanly—and he wanted her more than ever.

Chapter 41

Dorothea waited until Mrs. Hawes stepped out of the nursery to go down to the kitchens. She slipped into the nursery and stared down at the baby asleep in the cot.

How beautiful he was, how much like her son, William. Will, Matthew had called him, saying he was far too small for such a long and princely name as yet. He was only a few months older than Jamie when he died.

Children were so fragile. Life itself was fragile. She touched the baby's plump pink cheek, checking for signs of fever, but he was perfect, and healthy, and beautiful.

She smiled at him with tears in her eyes and reached into the cot to pick him up.

He stirred, cooed, as she rocked him, humming the familiar lullaby.

Chapter 42

Dorothea looked beautiful tonight, Stephen thought as he watched her at dinner. She'd planned a private supper in the small dining room, like the intimate parties she used to give when Matthew was alive. He hadn't seen her sparkle so brightly since before her husband died.

He sipped his soup and looked up as Julia laughed at some comment Dorothea made to her, and his breath caught in his throat at Julia's beauty. The two women genuinely liked each other, it seemed to him, and if all went well tonight at the French Embassy, he intended to formally ask Julia to marry him. If she succeeded, performed such an important service to Castlereagh and her country, no one would dare to call her a fallen woman.

He wondered if he should tell Dorothea of his plans to marry. Surely she wouldn't object. He watched as his sister leaned over to speak to Peter Bowen, brushing his hand with her fingertips, their eyes meeting as they smiled at each other. He felt a frisson of irritation. Perhaps Dorothea should be speaking to *him*, but surely she didn't intend to marry Bowen.

He watched the good doctor with narrowed eyes. If it did not go well tonight, he would be unable to marry

Julia, but as long as Dorothea was traveling with him, her brother, he could make Julia his mistress, but that would be impossible without Doe. Julia turned to him and smiled, her eyes sparkling in the candlelight, and his heart turned over in his chest. Yes, he loved her. He smiled back, and wondered if she was nervous about the mission tonight. He most certainly was. He'd almost gone to a jeweler today, but hesitated. Tomorrow he'd buy a betrothal ring if all went well.

Julia's pulse was racing. She barely tasted the soup. She was aware of Thomas Merritt's presence across the table from her and of Stephen's eyes on her. Were they thinking abut the mission that would take place later tonight? She laughed at something Dorothea said without really hearing it.

Thomas Merritt was watching her, his eyes roaming over her borrowed gown—yellow tonight. His expression was unreadable. He was staring at her as if she were a stranger. Had the tale she told at Prince de Ligne's shocked him? He'd left the prince's birdcage without even saying good-bye. Surely he would not hold her to his "condition" now. She looked at him, trying to read some clue, anything, in his eyes. There was none of the searing heat that had so stunned her that afternoon. He looked devastatingly male in his evening clothes, dark and dangerous, the way she remembered him. He trapped the light, held it.

In contrast, Stephen's fair hair shone in the candlelight and his scarlet military tunic glowed like honor itself. She could read his thoughts easily enough. He didn't approve of Dorothea's budding romance with Dr. Bowen. Quite the opposite. Then his face softened as he looked at her, his eyes gleaming, his smile intimate and meant for her alone. It made her stomach tremble.

She looked away from both men, concentrated on going over the plan for the evening in her mind. She would attend the salon with Thomas by her side. He would be introduced as a new arrival from London, someone who had come with diplomatic papers for Lord Castlereagh and an old friend of Julia's. When the party began, they would slip away to Talleyrand's secret office. Thomas would pick the locks and take the documents. She took a long sip of wine, but it didn't melt the knot in her throat. If they were caught—and her limbs trembled at the very idea—she would simply say she had wanted to show Thomas the paintings that graced the private little room, and the door had been open.

She wondered what the punishment was for espionage, and touched her neck.

She slid her eyes to Thomas once again, smiling now at something Dorothea was saying to him. Stephen was speaking with Peter Bowen.

Both men looked up at her at the same time. Thomas's grin faded to something dangerous. Stephen's smile flared as if the sun had just entered the room.

She had to remind herself to breathe.

Julia Leighton did not look capable of shooting a man, Thomas thought. Where on earth had she learned to use a gun? There were a lot of things about her he didn't know. Right now she looked harmless . . . well, certainly not harmless to his self-control, of course. She was dressed in a gauzy yellow silk that brought out the gleam of her dark hair, the golden light in her hazel eyes, the creamy perfection of her skin. She was indeed a lady, to her long, delicate fingers, looking for all the world like she was meant for decoration, not spying or shooting or vanquishing burglars with warming pans. He had a hard time paying attention to anyone else in the room. He was aroused at the idea of the condition he had imposed on her. She'd fulfill it if he insisted. She was brave—but would she do so willingly, or in tears? He watched her lift a hand to her throat, caress it, and he imagined her hands on his flesh, and his on hers, raising soft cries of desire from those perfect pink lips.

Of course, if he—they—were caught stealing documents at the Kaunitz Palace tonight, if he managed to get it all wrong and failed her, he would do his best to make sure she got out safely. Ives would be waiting outside, hidden in the dark. He'd insisted that the major be there, just in case. Thomas wondered if Julia had a pistol strapped to her leg under her elegant gown or a sharp knife in her stays. He wouldn't be surprised.

Then the door opened and everyone turned. Thomas's gut tensed at the sight of Lord Charles Stewart's all too familiar swagger. It was too late to hide and avoid the ugly scene that was about to occur. He could only sit quietly and wait for Charlie to notice him. His hands closed into fists in his lap.

This was going to be a disaster.

Chapter 43

"Well well, what have we here?" Stewart said. He was dressed in evening clothes, ready to go out, Thomas noticed, but he was already well past drunk. He leaned against the sideboard and regarded the assembled company from behind Thomas, who felt the man's presence like an icy wave about to wash over him. "I came to see Miss Leighton. Her ladyship summoned me from my bed this afternoon." He grinned. "Well, not my bed, but still—"

Stephen rose to his feet. "My lord, you are drunk, and there are ladies present. We can discuss this in the morning."

Stewart didn't leave, instead he began to circle the table, his footfalls soft on the carpet. Thomas felt his neck prickle.

"*Ladies*, Ives? I only see one, and a good evening to you, Lady Dorothea," he said. He pointed at Julia. "Her ladyship has had quite enough of *her* behavior. She's made a laughingstock of this embassy, shooting people in the park, and she is to be dismissed at once, without references. She sent me to see to it, now, tonight."

He watched Julia color, turning scarlet. Dorothea

gasped, and Stephen walked toward Charles, preventing him from reaching Julia. Good for him, Thomas thought. "*Lady* Julia received a commendation from Lord Castlereagh for her actions in the park, my lord. Have you spoken with him?"

"He's closeted with Metternich again," Charles said. "He's leaving as soon as the great Duke of Wellington arrives to take his place. Her ladyship wants loose ends tied up before she goes, won't have whores going around shooting people."

Thomas was on his feet in an instant. His fist and Stephen's hit Stewart's jaw at the same moment, getting in each other's way, making neither blow effective. Stewart staggered back, hit the sideboard, sending cutlery and crystal flying. He picked up a carving knife, and Dorothea screamed. Julia was on her feet, and Thomas wondered what the hell she planned to do.

"Charlie," he said quietly. Charles Stewart turned and caught sight of him then. His eyes widened and he dropped the knife in surprise. As he stared at Thomas, Peter Bowen picked up the weapon, took it out of harm's way.

"Tom Merritt?" Stewart said, and looked him over. "Tom Merritt, here?"

Thomas said nothing. His fist was clenched at his side. He'd dreamed of having Charles Stewart in front of him, thought of all the ways he'd kill the bastard.

Charles smiled slowly, the familiar obscene light filling his eyes. "Taken a wife lately, Tom? Who's wife was she?" He laughed alone at the old joke.

"You were my brother's best friend, Charlie," Thomas said softly.

Charles smirked. "You could have told him the truth, but you thought it would be honorable to keep her little secret, didn't you? D'you think I was the only one she was dallying with? Your brother married a whore, and when you refused her—you should have tried her, by the way. She was quite good in bed—well, hell hath no fury, isn't that what they say? And who would believe a swive-anything lad like you would turn down a beauty like Joanna? Not your brother."

The room was suddenly silent, fascinated. Thomas dared not look at Julia, or Ives, or anyone but Charlie.

Stewart lunged for the table, but only to grab Julia's glass. He drained it at a swallow, the red wine dribbling down his chin to stain his cravat.

"This is not the place for this," Stephen tried again, but Stewart turned on him.

"And how do *you* know the good viscount, Major Lord Ives? But wait, he isn't a viscount anymore. He slept with his brother's wife. Haven't you heard the stories? He was cut off by his family without a penny, cast out for his sins, his name stricken and forgotten."

Thomas felt every eye in the room turn on him. It didn't matter that he hadn't been guilty. He'd woken up as his brother's wife slipped into his bed, stark naked. And then the door had burst open.

"The vowel," Thomas murmured now. "The money you owed me? That was it, wasn't it? Why you did it?"

Stewart smiled. "P'raps. P'raps I just had had enough of your damned face, Tom. So had your brother, in fact."

Stephen Ives had stopped trying to force Stewart to leave. He was standing, watching, listening. And Julia too? Shame and anger warred in his chest.

"What a fool!" Stewart said, coming close, breathing sour wine into Thomas's face. "Get out. Her ladyship is a friend of your brother's, Tommy lad. She won't be pleased to know you're here, under her roof." He cast another look at Julia. "You can take that whore with you when you go."

Thomas didn't hesitate. He had defended Joanna, though his sister-in-law hardly deserved such chivalry. It hadn't been his fault, but this time, with Julia—he hauled his fist back and planted it in the center of Stewart's red face, putting all the force of two years of anger behind the blow. He heard the bone crunch, and Charles stared at him in dull surprise for an instant before he toppled like a fallen oak.

There was silence for a moment.

"Would someone please remove him? I won't allow him to ruin my dinner," Dorothea said tartly. "I daresay he's fortunate that Julia does not have her pistol this evening."

Thomas looked at Julia's scarlet cheeks, watched as she forced a smile, saw the glitter of unshed tears in her eyes. He crossed and rang the bell. When the footman arrived, the man gaped at Stewart's fallen form on the carpet. "We're finished with this dish," Thomas said, forcing a light tone, and Dorothea and Bowen raised their glasses in salute. Even Ives looked slightly envious. Julia looked thoughtful. He looked away. He didn't want her pity. There would be worse to come.

Charles Stewart had to wake up sometime, and now he knew that Thomas was here in Vienna.

Chapter 44

Julia clasped her hands in her lap as the coach set off for the Kaunitz Palace, trying to appear calm, though her heart was pounding. She would need to be very calm indeed once they arrived at Talleyrand's salon, try to look as if she did this all the time. They said Talleyrand could smell fear, taste weakness, and had not met an adversary he couldn't best with a simple cutting remark, delivered with such wit that the victim didn't notice the killing blow until it fell.

Across from her, Thomas and Stephen sat in uncomfortable silence. Stephen had changed into dark clothing, making him nearly invisible in the darkness, except for his blond hair. Thomas wore evening wear, well-cut and elegant, every inch the viscount he'd once been. He stared out the window, his profile lit by the lights on the street as they drove.

"Would you mind explaining what Stewart was talking about?" Stephen asked.

"Why do you wish to know?"

"I knew Edward Brecon. I had no idea he even had a brother."

"He doesn't."

"What did you gather, Julia?" Stephen asked her. "I heard that Thomas was having an affair with his brother's wife, and Stewart caught him and told Brecon, who disowned him."

She didn't get time to answer, but that wasn't what she understood at all. He'd rescued his brother's wife, saved her from disgrace of some sort. That part hadn't surprised her.

"It's none of your business," Thomas warned.

"But it is, you see. This is a very important job, and I wonder if I can trust you."

Thomas looked at him. "With Julia, you mean? She's safe."

"Are you sure? If anything happens to her, I'll hunt you down and kill you, is that clear?"

They had both missed the point of Stewart's unexpected visit entirely. He had come to remove her, on Lady Castlereagh's orders. They were about to come to blows over her now, tonight, when tomorrow it wouldn't matter.

"I plan to leave tomorrow morning," Julia said to no one in particular, her voice cutting through the argument.

"Don't be ridiculous. Where will you go?" Stephen asked.

"The Bavarian ambassador has offered me a place in his household." She watched Thomas's head turn toward her, but he didn't speak, and his face was in shadow.

"Look, Stewart probably won't even remember he spoke to you, or Lady Castlereagh, in the morning," Stephen said. "He'll wake up wondering how his nose came to be broken, and Lord and Lady Castlereagh will be gone within the week."

"He'll remember," Thomas said softly.

"Will he? Last chance, Merritt, to tell your side of the tale," Stephen said.

"I think it would be better if we concentrate on the business at hand, don't you?"

"Those were some rather strong accusations. Did you really sleep with your brother's wife?" Stephen asked.

"Does it matter?" Thomas replied. "It has nothing to do with stealing papers from an ambassador's desk."

Stephen laughed coldly. "You got caught. That's what worries me. And I caught you too, breaking into the embassy."

"Julia caught me, as I recall."

She wished they would stop arguing. She had butterflies the size of vultures in the pit of her stomach.

They arrived at the Kaunitz Palace before Stephen could reply. He grabbed her hand as Thomas got out first. "Be careful, Julia," he murmured. "Tomorrow this will be over, and we'll talk then. I intend to ask—"

"Julia?" Thomas's voice was sharp, and she turned to find him waiting to help her out of the coach, a gloved hand extended. She swallowed and set her hand in his, felt his fingers close. Stephen squeezed her other hand, and she was stretched between them for a moment before Stephen let go.

"I'll be waiting. Keep her safe, Merritt, or I'll hang you myself."

Thomas didn't reply. Instead he tucked her hand under his arm and turned away. "Are you ready?" he asked, and she swallowed. "Did you bring your pistol?"

She stumbled on the first step, and he put a hand on her waist to steady her, just as he had in her father's ballroom. "I thought *you* might be armed," she said.

"I? No. I find guns lead to trouble. Do you at least have a letter opener tucked into your garter, or a sharp hairpin?"

She glanced at him, saw the mirth in his dark eyes.

He was doing it again, rescuing her from her emotions by being charming, trying to make her laugh, just the way he had at her betrothal ball. "I am told I have a sharp tongue," she said.

He looked appreciative. "Dangerous indeed. Let's hope you won't need to use it."

She took a deep breath as the door opened and they were admitted. She saw Thomas look around as the butler glided forward, his eyes pausing on each statue and painting. Was he considering stealing those too?

"Miss Lei—" she began, but he interrupted.

"Lady Julia Leighton and Viscount Merritton," he said, and the servant led them into the brightly lit reception room and announced them.

"Julia!" Diana hurried across to kiss her on both cheeks before she slid an appraising glance over Thomas. "And who is this?" she asked archly.

"This is Viscount Merritton, an old friend from London. He arrived yesterday with some papers for Lord Castlereagh." He bowed over Diana's hand.

"I am most pleased you could join us," Diana said. "A new attaché to the embassy. My uncle will want to hear about your journey. Did you stop in Paris?"

"Of course, my lady," Thomas said.

"Then he will definitely want to hear any gossip you managed to overhear. He complains that official dispatches rarely contain the most interesting news from home."

"Indeed, and often public opinion is the most important news of all, is it not?"

Diana laughed. "Oh, my uncle is going to like you very much!"

Julia saw no sign of the French ambassador. "He is finishing some letters and will join us soon," Dorothea explained. "Come and meet our other guests." She looked around the room. "Now where to begin? The three officers in the corner are discussing the strategy used at the battle of Jena. Dull to everyone but themselves. The ladies in the opposite corner are talking of Princess Bagration's latest scandal of a gown, or her affair with the Tsar . . . Let's see, there's Count Razumovsky, the gentleman looking at the paintings. Do you like art, Viscount? He is quite a collector, and he was once the Russian ambassador to Vienna. Shall we start there?"

Julia felt her chest tighten. What on earth could Thomas Merritt have in common with Razumovsky? Yet within moments he was discussing the merits of Beethoven, Mozart, and Haydn, all of whom Razumovsky knew well, as if Thomas too had known them. He was charming and elegant. The gossiping ladies soon turned their attention on the handsome newcomer, casting coquettish glances at him and giggling together behind their fans.

She sipped champagne sparingly. They could do nothing at all until Talleyrand appeared. What if he was in his study, seated at the mahogany desk under the painted gazes of Pauline Borghese and Marie Louise? She felt a frisson of impatience, but Thomas laid a hand on her waist, lending her strength and patience as he steered her toward one of the magnificent landscapes in the room, following Razumovsky, who was comparing the work of French and English landscape painters. Thomas smiled down at her, and her heart leapt into her throat, and she had something else to occupy her nerves, the tingle that coursed through her veins.

"Ah, Lady Julia, how delightful that you could come this evening," Talleyrand said, kissing her hand, his eyes bright on her face, and then taking in every detail of Thomas's person as they were introduced. "I apologize for my lateness, but you are partly to blame, my dear. I just received a note from Lord Castlereagh, suggesting we meet."

Julia swallowed. It was surely part of the ruse. Once Castlereagh held the stolen documents in his hand, he would cancel the appointment. Until then, he had no choice but to play Talleyrand's game. She tried to look as if it wasn't a surprise. He drew her aside to look at another painting, a portrait of the King of France as a young man at his brother's court. "I must thank you for your invaluable assistance."

She felt Thomas's eyes on her, turned to see him watching her over the crystal lip of his champagne glass.

An hour later, as more guests arrived and the room became crowded, Thomas appeared at her side. "Everyone is watching you," she murmured, feeling panic like sharp little teeth. "How can we possibly—"

He bent to whisper in her ear. "Laugh, Julia. Look into my eyes."

His warm breath tickled, and he drew back and grinned at her, his eyes warm. She stared at him, felt her skin heat. "What are you doing?"

He stepped closer still, let his eyes fall on her mouth, and she felt hot color fill her cheeks.

"Flirt with me. No one will be surprised when we slip away to steal a kiss."

She stared at him. She couldn't seem to look away. "Have you lost your wits?" He was only looking at her, standing next to her, hadn't even touched her but she was on fire with longing.

"Tell me what you remember most about that night."

Stars. In the champagne, in the sky, in his eyes, in her blood. "I can't—" she managed.

He looked at the champagne in her hand. "You tasted

of champagne when I kissed you," he said. "I bet you'd taste of champagne now. Laugh, Julia."

She was shaking, but she drew a breath and put on the performance of a lifetime, staring into his eyes, waving her fan coquettishly, fluttering her lashes. She reached out and touched his hand, and he drew a long breath that wasn't entirely feigned. Her body buzzed with desire.

"Which hallway leads to the room he showed you?" Thomas murmured.

It was like a splash of cold water. "The door below the painting of the cavalier."

He glanced over. "Ah, the one by David. Did you know it's rumored that he is Talleyrand's illegitimate son?"

"Really?" she asked as he led her toward it.

"Yes. Does that shock you?"

She managed to shake her head. How could she of all people be shocked by that?

"Many people have illegitimate children, but Talleyrand was once a Catholic bishop, before he became a diplomat."

No wonder Talleyrand looked beyond her scandal!

They were under the painting now, by the open door. A long corridor led to Talleyrand's private office. It was unlit tonight, a subtle warning to guests that it was off limits.

She felt Thomas's hand on her elbow. "Come on."

"Someone will notice we're gone," she said as they slipped down the hall.

"They will expect it. You're an excellent actress. If Stephen Ives doesn't propose tomorrow, you might consider a career on the stage, or perhaps hire yourself out as a Bow Street Runner, or even a professional assassin."

"It may surprise you, Mr. Merritt, but I don't actually enjoy harming people."

He glanced at her. "Does that mean you'll accept Ives's proposal?"

She raised her chin. "Don't be ridiculous. He would never make such an offer."

He chuckled. "I thought women could read such sentiments in a man's eyes," he said. "Ives obviously has feelings for you. Will you say yes?"

"No," she said. "I mean, I don't wish to discuss it." They reached the end of the tapestry. "We're here." *Thank heaven*.

She lifted the edge of the tapestry to reveal the door. He grinned. "Clever. But every inch of this hallway is covered with tapestries. Are you quite sure?"

She glanced at Joan of Arc's woven face, gazing up at heaven. "Quite sure," she said. He tried the latch, but the door was locked. "Can you open it?" she asked, glancing down the hall. She cursed the thick carpets. They would not hear someone coming. The rattle of the lock as he worked at it was loud in the thick silence.

"Hurry," she murmured.

"Nervous, Lady Julia?" he asked. "And yet, you are without doubt the most daring woman I've ever met." The latch opened with a click, and he glanced at her, obviously as surprised as she was. The dark room loomed beyond the threshold.

"I am not nearly as bold as you might think," she whispered, hesitating.

"Nor am I. Let's get this over with," he said. "Our absence will assume scandalous proportions if we're gone too long." He stepped in and lit a candle.

The portraits regarded them with feminine surprise. Pauline Borghese stared at Thomas's broad shoulders as he gazed around the room. Marie Antoinette smiled archly. Marie Louise appeared to be watching the desk in horror.

"There—" Julia crossed to the mahogany desk and tried the drawers. "It's locked."

He was looking at the paintings, but he came to her side. "Which drawer?"

"This one," she said, aware of the closeness of his body, the warmth of his fingers as they brushed hers.

He began to pick the lock, his movements awkward, and Julia held her breath. "I used to take cigars out of a locked drawer in my father's desk when I was a boy," he explained. "He never suspected a thing."

She glanced at the door. Surely they would be missed by now and someone would be sent to search for them. What was the punishment for espionage and theft? Would they hang her?

The drawer popped, and she held the candle over the shadowed contents. The light gleamed on the familiar surface of the red leather folder, and she took it out, laid it on the desk and opened it.

The documents were all there. Thomas picked them up and glanced at them, scanning the contents. "A bill of sale and some love letters?" he asked. "That's what we came for?"

She nodded. He looked through the rest of the file. "There's one addressed to you."

She stared at the sealed envelope, at her name scrawled across the front in Talleyrand's unmistakable hand.

There was a noise in the hallway, the sound of swords clattering on scabbards.

Thomas grabbed her shoulders, spun her to face him. "Is this a trap, Miss Leighton?" he demanded, his eyes hard and shiny as marble.

"No!" Yet she replayed the consequences of getting caught. The English would disavow any knowledge of her, or Thomas Merritt. She blanched. It was indeed a trap, but not one of her making. They were coming closer now, and in a moment they would see the door was open.

"Kiss me," Thomas Merritt ordered, pulling her against him.

"This isn't the time!" she hissed, pressing a hand to his chest to push him away. She could feel his heart beating under the fine linen of his shirt.

"Trust me. Kiss me. You remember how, don't you?"

His mouth was inches above hers, the soft champagne of his breath on her lips, the scent of his soap surrounding her. She lifted her mouth to his and shut her eyes.

He groaned as he plundered her mouth, kissing her like a man starving—or a man about to hang. His lips slanted over hers, and he pulled her closer still, pressing her back against the desk. It all came flooding back— the desperate, impossible desire she'd felt for him the last time he'd kissed her. She didn't want to stop. She arched against him, losing herself in the kiss.

"Halt!" said a stern voice, and she snapped back to reality. She turned as the room filled with light and soldiers, stifling the desire to scream. Thomas kept his hand on her back, his touch firm, reassuring.

"Gentlemen," he said, his tone sheepish.

"What are you doing in here? Fetch His Highness at once."

Thomas grinned at the captain. "Is that necessary? We were merely seeking a moment's privacy," he said in English. "It's too cold to go out onto the terrace, and the door was open—"

"I wanted to show Thomas—the viscount—His Highness's paintings," she said. "You see, he knew several of these ladies in Paris, and—" She realized she was babbling. The soldier glanced at the walls, noticing the art for the first time, obviously unimpressed.

Julia's heart climbed into her throat. She wondered if it was too late to dive out the window, but there were ornate metal grills in place to prevent that. Pauline Borghese regarded her with mocking sympathy.

Talleyrand arrived. "Intruders, Your Highness," the captain said, snapping to attention.

Talleyrand's dark eyes took in the situation at a glance. "The door was unlocked," she began again. "The paintings—"

"Was it?" he said blandly. "How careless of me."

She watched his eyes flick over the desk, and waited for him to notice the folder, and the contents scattered over the surface. She looked down, but the desk was empty. She looked up at Thomas in surprise, but his expression was flat, giving nothing away.

Talleyrand tried the desk drawer and found it locked. He looked up at her with a sad smile, as if she'd failed to meet his expectations, and she raised her chin, felt hot blood creeping under her skin.

"What exactly were they doing when you found them, Captain?" the prince asked.

"He was—um, kissing her, Highness. Very passionately." Talleyrand grinned. "They said they were here to admire 'the art,'" the soldier added, more surprised by that, it appeared.

Talleyrand unlocked the desk and opened the drawer. Julia stifled a gasp of surprise. The red leather folder glowed like accusation in the candlelight. How on earth had Thomas managed that?

It didn't matter. They'd failed, and they would not get another opportunity. Defeat fell over her like a heavy blanket. Thomas didn't look at all perturbed. He was watching Talleyrand silently, with a bland expression.

"Will you say nothing, *monsieur le vicomte*?" the prince asked in French. "Will you not deny such a scandalous insult to a lady's honor?"

Still Thomas remained silent, and she felt mortification burn through her. She knew exactly what Talleyrand and the captain were thinking.

"Monsieur?" Talleyrand said again in French. Julia felt her limbs melt.

Would Thomas let them think she was a strumpet?

He shook his head. "I am sorry, sir, but I don't speak French."

Talleyrand's lips twitched. "The captain of my guards has accused the lady of bringing you here to my private office for seduction," he said in English. "What do you say to that?"

Thomas straightened his shoulders. "I suppose I shall have to call him out and shoot him," he said. "How do I say that in French?"

Talleyrand's brows rose. "How very English. Perhaps it would be better to tell him that you and the lady are old friends, and you simply share similar tastes in art."

"If you wish," Thomas said.

"In the interest of peace," Talleyrand said. He shut the drawer and locked it. "All is in order, Captain Dufour. Please escort my guests back to the salon."

The captain bowed crisply and led the way, with two soldiers in front, two soldiers behind them. Thomas kept his hand under her elbow, and she didn't dare speak. Had he saved her, or made things worse? Her mouth still tingled from his kiss. *Her whole body tingled.*

They reached the salon, and no one, it seemed, had even realized they were gone. The guards withdrew, and a footman offered them more champagne.

He stood quietly by her side. "It's over, Julia. You can breathe now."

She nodded to a lady going past, then turned to him. "How can you say that? We failed!"

He looked amused. "Did we?"

She shut her eyes, and he set his hand on the small of her back to steady her. "We won't get another chance," she said. "It will mean disaster—"

He leaned close to her ear. "I have the papers, sweetheart."

But she wasn't listening. "And now Lord Talleyrand has branded me as a—"

"I have the papers. They're in my pocket. I became quite expert at removing my father's cigars so he wouldn't know." He put his finger under her chin. "And Prince de Talleyrand is French. I'd say you've probably improved in his estimation. I daresay he wishes he were me, so he could kiss you."

She blinked at him. He was so close, his mouth inches from her own. Would he kiss her again, here, in the middle of the reception room? He stepped back.

"Your reputation is safe. Why would he spread a tale of anyone breaking into his private office, getting past not one but two locks, to steal secret documents? It would make him look like a fool."

"He could have arrested us," she whispered.

He frowned at that. "Yes, he could have indeed. It would have caused a scandal of quite a different sort, made England look—" He stopped. "Let's concentrate on enjoying the rest of the evening, shall we? We don't want Talleyrand to think it was anything other than a seduction, do we?" She shook her head. "Good, let's go in to supper."

"Stephen is waiting outside, probably freezing," she reminded him.

He grinned charmingly. "I know. "

Chapter 45

Stephen Ives took Julia's hand and helped her into the coach. His fingers were very cold.

"Well?" he asked when the coach set off.

"We have the documents," Thomas said. There was silence. "Are you surprised?"

"Frankly, yes. I had imagined that Talleyrand had better security than that. Where are the papers?"

Thomas took them out of his coat pocket, and Stephen put them into a pouch and set it on his lap.

"Aren't you curious? Aren't you going to read them?" Thomas asked.

"No, I'm going to place them in Castlereagh's hands as soon as we return to the embassy. Unread."

"And tomorrow?" Thomas asked.

"What of it?" Stephen demanded. "Your job is done, Merritt."

Except for their bargain, Julia thought. Surely Stephen would find a way to pay Thomas. And what of her bargain? Was the kiss enough? She glanced at him in the darkness. If she could kiss him again, do more than that—was he was watching her, thinking the same thing? Her heartbeat tripled, her body vibrated.

It was a relief when the coach pulled up in front of Thomas's lodgings and he got out.

"Good night, Julia. It was a lovely evening," he said with formal politeness, as if they hadn't kissed, hadn't been through an ordeal in the past few hours. "And Ives—congratulations. I have no doubt you will take the credit for everything, and rise far in the service of His Majesty on it." Then he was gone.

"Will we see him again?" Julia asked Stephen.

He sighed. "I suppose we must. There is the matter of his reward, the conditions he set."

"And will you meet them?" she asked.

He stared at Thomas's retreating back with narrow eyes. "I suppose that remains to be seen."

Chapter 46

Stephen came across the coach to sit beside Julia, and drew her into his arms. He turned her face to his, kissed her gently.

"Were you afraid?" he asked her. He could smell her perfume. She shivered, and he draped his coat over her shoulders.

"Yes. We were caught, my lord, but Thomas managed to—talk—his way out."

"Thomas?" he asked, feeling a flare of jealousy. "You call him Thomas, and still refer to me as 'my lord'? Call me Stephen, Julia."

"Stephen," she said. "Perhaps I *should* take my leave in the morning."

He put a finger under her chin. "No, my darling girl, you aren't going anywhere. Castlereagh cannot deny us anything now. You have triumphed, once again. Marry me, Julia."

She stared at him in the dark. "What? You know that's impossible."

"Not now. Merritt was right. These papers will make my name, Julia. I am set for life. We needn't return to England, at least not very often. I will be posted abroad as an ambassador, and no one will remember that Julia Ives was once—" He felt her stiffen in his arms and stopped. "No, that came out wrong. I want to marry you because I love you. I have never felt like this about any other woman. I don't think I can live without you."

She didn't immediately reply, and he kissed her, tasted the salt of tears on her lips.

"What about Jamie?" she asked softly.

Merritt's child. He felt a twinge in the pit of his stomach. "I hope we'll have children of our own. I want a son to inherit, of course. Perhaps our son will grow up to be an ambassador."

She was silent.

"Oh, I will care for Jamie," he said, "see he's well educated. He'll lack for nothing, and I'll raise him to be a good man, decent and honest." Unlike his father, though he knew he would see Merritt in the child's face every time he looked at him, remember how he was conceived. He'd try not to let it matter. He would ensure that Julia and the boy never saw Merritt again. It was, after all, for the best. Thomas Merritt didn't deserve Julia. He squeezed her hand. "Say yes, Julia. Make me the happiest man in the world."

She drew away from him. "It's been a very long day, Stephen. I need some sleep, time to think. Can I give you my answer tomorrow?"

He felt the sting of disappointment but forced a smile. "Of course. I must confess I hadn't planned on proposing to you tonight. I should be down on one knee, ring in one hand, flowers in the other. Isn't that how it's usually done?"

She smiled. "I don't know. My parents called me downstairs to the study on my eighth birthday and introduced David as my future husband. I had very little idea what that meant. There was no ring, no flowers. He did bring me a puppy as a birthday present, but I think it was actually from Nicholas, David's younger brother. He was such a good friend of James's, you see. My mother promptly turned the dog over to my brother and told me not to cry, because I would be a duchess someday, which was far better than having a puppy. Only—" She stopped. "I would have rather had the puppy."

Stephen smiled. "James, Nick, and I were friends in Spain. I seem to recall James rescuing a litter of puppies during a battle. The barn they were in was on fire. It took three trips to get them all. Burnt a hole in his new tunic, but he was a hero that day too."

"Will you tell me more stories about James?"

He kissed her forehead. "One for every day of our life together," he promised.

He helped her out of the coach, led her inside, escorted her to the door of her bedroom. "You're a remarkable lady, Julia Leighton, and you were very brave tonight. Rest and we'll talk tomorrow. I've got to go and see Castlereagh before I can find my own bed. Or . . ." He looked hopefully over the threshold.

"Good night, Lor—Stephen," she said, and firmly closed the door behind her.

Her bedroom was cold, and the curtains shivered in the icy wind coming through the open window. She hurried across to shut it, and turned to her bed. There, on the pillow, was the letter with her name on it that Talleyrand had left in the folder. She crossed and looked outside, but Thomas Merritt was nowhere to be seen.

Chapter 47

"**W**hat was Thomas Merritt doing here?" Charles Stewart's question stopped Stephen in his tracks. He was on his way to see Castlereagh, to give him the documents, to praise Julia, and to make a deal with the outgoing ambassador. He hadn't expected to see Stewart, who was leaning against the doorway of the library, a drink in his hand, his shirt stained with wine and his own blood.

Stephen winced at the man's appearance. His nose was broken and he had a black eye, swollen shut. He had to admit that he was almost pleased to see the damage.

He could afford to be pleasant. The future was secure, both his own and Julia's. "Don't you know why he was here, my lord?" he asked. "I thought you were in charge of the embassy's security. Haven't you been briefed?" He read the confusion in Stewart's one good eye.

"I've been—away—for several days. Business," Stewart lied. "I'm on my way to see Rob now," he said, referring to his half brother.

"Then you should ask him," Stephen said, and turned to walk away.

"Has Julia Leighton gone yet?"

"No. She's upstairs, asleep. You won't be able to get rid

of her now. She's done his lordship a favor." He waved the folder in his hands.

"What's that mean?" Stewart growled. He reached for the folder, but Stephen held it out of his reach.

"Sorry—classified. For the ambassador's eyes only."

"And this has something to do with Julia Leighton, and Tom Merritt?"

He was quick, Stephen would give him that much. Stewart was reputed to be an excellent spy when he wasn't drunk. He also hated Thomas Merritt. He wondered again just what Thomas had done to cross Stewart.

He hadn't missed the way Julia looked at Merritt as he got out of the coach. Did she still have feelings for him? He'd never been a jealous man, but he'd never been in love before. If Merritt was the reason Julia had hesitated in accepting his marriage proposal, then he would remove his rival by whatever means came to hand.

"I see you know Merritt, my lord. To me, he's merely a thief. We hired him for his professional skills, nothing more."

Stewart's brows rose, and he winced at the pain, crossed to pour a tumbler of whisky. "So that's what's become of him."

"Wasn't he a thief in London?"

Stewart snorted. "He was a fool when I knew him—a rake, a gambler, and a charmer of women, but he was a fool with morals. His brother married for love, but his bride married for money. Joanna lived for pleasure, wallowed in it, in fact. When she lost a fortune gambling and Edward cut off her allowance, she simply took lovers and made them pay, and when her husband discovered that, he banished her to Brecon Park. She wanted a playmate in her solitude, and she wanted to hurt Edward, so she sent for Thomas, and me. I was Edward's oldest and closest friend, above suspicion in his eyes, but if a woman offers . . ." He shrugged, and Stephen felt his gut twist.

"Joanna was in my bed one night, and Edward arrived at Brecon unexpectedly. We didn't know until we heard him coming up the stairs. There was no time to make it to her own rooms, so she ducked into Tom's rooms instead. That's where Edward found her, naked." He chuckled. "Joanna begged him not to tell. Tom saw me in the doorway when the shouting began and guessed the truth, but he'd given his word before he knew what that truth was. The chivalrous fool didn't defend himself, just let his brother disown him, cut him off without a penny.

"Joanna went to see him, days later, at some squalid hellhole he'd found in London. She offered him a pair of diamond earrings, Edward's wedding present, to keep quiet. He found out later just what she was, but it was far too late by then. He came to see me, hoped I would admit the truth, but I owed him money—a lot of money. I refused to help him, since he was better dead and disowned to me. I threatened to do the opposite, and tell Edward I'd seen him with Joanna, that he'd forced her. I heard that someone broke into Edward's London house and took all Joanna's jewels from the safe. They never caught the thief, but now I assume it was Merritt."

"Probably," Stephen said, gritting his teeth. Stewart was even more loathsome than he could have imagined. He had hoped to hear that Merritt was a wastrel, a philanderer, a depraved rake guilty of terrible crimes. Instead, it turned out he'd done the honorable thing to defend a woman. He shut his eyes. It did not make Merritt's seduction of Julia any more bearable, or even understandable.

Stewart dropped into a chair and fixed Stephen with a one-eyed glare, completely without a shred of remorse for ruining a man's life. "So Tom's a thief, eh? How the hell did he end up here, in Vienna, helping you with . . . ?" Stewart pointed at the folder in Stephen's hand. "*Why* would he help you?"

Why indeed. For Julia? He didn't want to believe that. "I told him we'd hang him if he didn't."

"The Tom Merritt I knew wouldn't care about that. Not if helping wasn't already in his best interest. Not anymore. What was his price?"

Stephen hesitated. "He wants money, of course, and Castlereagh's Order of the Garter star."

Stewart chuckled. "The star? Why? Does he want revenge on the whole bloody British aristocracy?"

"I don't know. He made having it a condition of his help."

"Then I can only imagine he wants to embarrass this embassy out of spite." Stewart regarded the folder again. "Does he know what's in there?"

Stephen nodded. "I assume so."

"And if he were to tell anyone?"

Stephen considered. Who would believe that Wellington was involved in a plot to set Napoleon free? No one would, without the documents. Without them, Talleyrand had nothing.

"You don't like Tom, do you, Ives?"

"No," he admitted.

"I won't ask why. He's the kind of man women adore, and other men despise him for it. Is that sufficient to say? I'd love to be rid of Tom too. He has a few too many interesting tales to tell, and that makes him dangerous, even a potential traitor. It's my job—and yours—as part of this embassy to ensure traitors are harshly dealt with. I don't know why you have cause to hate him, but let's just say that this"—he pointed to his broken nose—"cannot go unpunished."

Stephen clutched the folder tighter. Actually, Merritt wasn't a traitor, he was a hero. Except for the fact that he had asked for a reward. And Julia still had *feelings* for him, even after he'd used her, abandoned her. "I'll help you arrest Merritt under one condition, my lord," he said. Stewart waited without comment, his one good eye gleaming. "Leave Julia Leighton alone."

Stewart's laugh was a dark gutter innuendo. "Ah, so that's it, is it? No wonder she refused me. Are you . . . ?" He made an obscene hand gesture that made Stephen's skin crawl. He stiffened.

"No."

"It doesn't matter to me, but whether she stays or goes is up to Castlereagh. But we can be rid of Merritt if we work together. So are we friends?"

Stephen considered how Stewart treated his friends. He also considered how Julia had looked at Thomas Merritt, the way her breath had caught in her throat when he left the coach, and the fact that she'd hesitated in accepting his proposal.

"What did you have in mind?" he asked Stewart.

"**J**ulia Leighton is to be dismissed at once," Castlereagh said an hour later, once Stephen had presented the stolen documents to him and he had quietly looked them over. "I will pay her passage back to London, but nothing else. She will not receive a commendation or any other acknowledgment."

Stephen felt indignation fill him. "She has not asked for anything at all, my lord, and she took a great risk to get these letters back."

"She will be expected to sign a document promising never to disclose this incident to anyone," Castlereagh said. He got up and dropped the stolen pages on the fire, watched the flames obliterate them and poked the ashes to dust.

Stephen stood at attention. "I'll know, your lordship. I will be expected to make a full report to the Duke of Wellington when he arrives to take over the embassy. He'll wish to know, don't you think, in case it comes up again, in case Talleyrand kept copies—or originals."

He paused, waiting for Castlereagh's face to soften in defeat, but it did not.

"I also know, my lord, that you have exceeded your mandate here in Vienna."

Castlereagh's face creased into a rare smile, but it did not meet his eyes. "A good try, Major. You could take Charles Stewart's place when Wellington arrives, if I recommend you. Are you truly willing to risk your career for a woman like Julia Leighton?"

Stephen felt his throat tighten. "I intend to marry her."

Castlereagh's brows rose. "Did you know that my wife is a dear friend of the Countess of Carrindale? She is— was—Miss Leighton's mother. She has been writing to my wife, insisting that Julia not be allowed to remain here, that it is an embarrassment to her husband. My wife has been pressing me most strongly to send Julia away. She fears she will embarrass us. It turns out she was quite right. Shooting a thief in the park appears quite brave and heroic to some, but others would see her as a woman who is dangerous, overbold. And if the other tales of her— accomplishments—here in Vienna come to light, do you see how that could work against our mission here?"

Stephen did indeed. *A fallen women, stolen documents, thieves . . .*

"I can, of course, insist on her dismissal, Major. It is within my rights. I can even order soldiers to eject her from the premises if she will not go. You will do as you must, of course, but it will mean the end of your career." He paused. "Perhaps we can come to an agreement."

Stephen waited.

"There is an excellent posting available in Spain. I am offering it to you. In return, if you decide to marry Julia Leighton, you will keep her silent and obedient. No more listening, or shooting, or daring adventures, is that clear? You have an estate somewhere in England, do you not? Take your wife there, *keep* her there, out of sight."

"Yes, my lord." Stephen's heart sang. "I will tell her at once."

Chapter 48

~~⌒⌒~~

Julia hurried along the snowy street wrapped tightly in her cloak, her hood up. She ignored the street vendors, the shoppers, the carriages rolling by. When she reached Thomas Merritt's lodgings, she hurried up the stairs and knocked on the door. She wasn't sure what she would say when he opened the door, or worse, if a servant opened it. In England a lady did not call upon a man at his home, and even if she was far from England, and no longer a lady, she still obeyed the rules of correct behavior—except this one, just this once. Still, if anyone recognized her, it would be most embarrassing trying to explain herself.

She had to see him again, had to know. The kiss he'd given her in Talleyrand's library still burned on her lips. She'd spent a restless night thinking about Thomas when she should have been considering Stephen's proposal. How could she say yes, be his wife, when she could not stop thinking about another man?

She would ask him about the letter on her pillow. Another kindness, perhaps, like his return of Dorothea's watch? Then she would thank him for his assistance the previous evening, and take her leave well within the fifteen minutes allowed for polite calls. Once all that had been done, she would be able to forget him, see him as a perfectly ordinary man and not—

The door opened.

His shirt was undone at the neck, and he hadn't shaved. She could still see the bruise on his forehead, read the surprise in his eyes.

"Julia," he said as her breath caught in her throat. "Why are you here?" He stepped aside to let her in. The room was filled with the scent of his soap, his discarded clothing and books, *his bed*, visible through an open door.

"Is anything wrong?" he asked, but she threw herself into his arms and pressed her mouth to his.

His arms came around her, clasping her to him as he met her kiss and let his lips melt into hers. It felt right, perfect, she realized. She fit against him as if they'd done this a thousand times.

"Julia, what are you doing?" he asked, holding her away from him, cupping her face in his hands, stroking her cheek with his thumb. "Why are you here?" he asked again as his eyes drank her in, bored into her.

She felt tears in her eyes. "I need to know—I have to know—why I can't forget you."

He stared at her for a moment, searching her face, and she held her breath. If he laughed, told her she was mad, she would shatter, fall to pieces. But she would be able to go on, move forward with her life without forever wondering if her feelings at her betrothal ball—and now— were a mistake, a trick of the light, or too much champagne.

She straightened her spine. She was being foolish. In a moment he'd offer her a sherry to calm her nerves, suggest she sit down for a moment . . .

"I should go," she said, and moved toward the door. He caught her wrist.

"Stay," he said softly.

He kissed her, sipped at her lips, twined his fingers into her hair, loosening it. Pins fell to the floor like rain. She gripped the folds of his shirt, holding him to her. His mouth tasted of whisky, and she found she liked that as much as the taste of champagne, maybe more.

He trailed kisses over her cheeks and down her throat as he untied her cloak and let it drop away, then kissed her collarbone as he undid the buttons of her gown, let it fall to her elbows.

She slid her hands into the open collar of his shirt, caressed the warmth of his flesh, the hardness of bones and muscles, felt his heart beating under his skin.

His hands moved to cup her breast through the fine linen of her shift. She gasped. Oh yes, this is what she wanted, what she dreamed of. She tangled her hands in his hair as his mouth found her nipple through the thin garment, then moved to the other. She was caught in her gown, couldn't move, only able to *feel* what he was doing to her.

"Thomas," she sighed, arching against him.

He lifted her into his arms and carried her into the bedroom, kicking the half open door out of the way. He fell to the mattress with her, kissing her still, trying to fight his way out of his own clothing at the same time, both of them breathless.

"Why is it like this with you, and no one else?" he muttered.

She couldn't answer that, had no idea, since he was the first, the only man she had ever— She drew a sharp breath as he left her, began to prowl the bedroom, running his hand through his hair. His shirt hung open, revealing the muscles and planes of his chest.

"I'm famous for my control, for my bloody prowess in bed—ask anyone."

She leaned on her elbow, her loose hair falling over her open bodice. "There's no one else here."

He looked at her as if she were daft. "I didn't mean that. I meant that I can't stop with you. I don't want to. I haven't forgotten you either, or one single detail of that night."

"Then it isn't always like this?"

He stared at her. "Don't you know? What about David, after me, and Ives?"

She didn't reply, had no words to tell him he was the only one.

He sat on the edge of the bed, brushed a long lock of hair over her shoulder, stared at the deep vee between her breasts. "I don't know a single thing about you, except that I want you like I've never wanted any woman, and I don't know why. One rushed, clumsy tumble in the dark, a few brief moments, that's all it was, and yet—" He caressed her cheek, cupped it, ran his thumb over her lower lip. "I can't stop thinking about it."

She pressed her cheek into his palm. "Is that why you made this a condition of the bargain?"

He pulled his hand away as if she'd burned him. "Is that why you're here? It was a stupid thing to say. I didn't mean it."

She felt a flash of anger. She was tempted to say yes, but the look in his eyes stopped her. There was hurt in the depths of his eyes, longing, and something she'd never seen before in any man's eyes, and it took her breath away. "You were in my room last night. Why didn't you wait for me, demand your payment then?"

"I climbed that damned wall to prove I could. I waited, Julia. I thought you must be with—" He stopped. "You belong to someone else."

She reached up to caress the bruise on his forehead,

gently, with the tip of her finger. "I belonged to some-one else then too, that night, and it didn't stop you—us—from—"

He caught her hand, brought it to his mouth, kissed her palm. "You still don't blame me for what happened that night, do you? You should. You have every right to hate me. I had experience. I should have stopped. You should have told me you were a virgin."

She squeezed his hand. "I wanted it, wanted you. I want you now."

He leaned over to kiss her, and she lay back, slid her arms around his neck, drawing him down to her. "You . . ." He kissed her again. " . . . are the most remarkable woman I've ever met."

"Show me," she said.

He didn't need a second invitation. They undressed each other. She took his shirt. He tugged her gown over her head and tossed it aside, then untied the ribbons on her shift and peeled that away too, leaving her naked. He stared down at her, and she fought the urge to cover her breasts with her hands, suddenly shy.

"What's the matter?" she asked.

"You're beautiful, Julia Leighton, even more beautiful than I imagined. I wished, afterward, that we hadn't made love in the dark, that I'd been able to see you."

She closed her eyes and ran her hands over the hard planes of his chest. She caressed the muscles of his shoulders and arms, familiar, but new, as well, thrilling. "You are just as I remember," she murmured as she opened her eyes. "Better, now we have light, and privacy and—" But that was all they had—not time, beyond a few short hours, not tomorrow. Her heart contracted in her chest.

He held her for a moment, his chin resting on the top of her head, hers in the hollow of his neck, and she breathed him in, memorizing him for the days to come, when she would be without him again. She marveled at the feeling of his naked flesh against her breasts, the heat of his skin, the sensation of his heart beating next to her own, and raised her mouth to his. His tongue sought hers, tangled until they were both panting.

She fumbled with the buttons of his flies, her hands brushing against the hardness trapped under the fabric. She couldn't make her fingers work, not while he kissed her, stroked her, drove every sensible thought out of her head with his tongue, his hands, his body on hers. He found places she had never even known existed— wonderful, secret, delicious places—driving her beyond reason, to a place of pure sensation. He took over the task, deftly opening his breeches. She hadn't touched him that night, hadn't had the chance or the experience in their frenzied encounter. She explored him now, reveling in the new experience and in his response. He groaned as she caressed him, his erection hot against her palm.

"Julia . . ." He whispered her name, watched what she was doing to him, his jaw tight. He pressed her back into the bed, sought her mouth with his as he stroked her breasts, her back, her hips, and the curve of her buttocks. She did the same things to him, since she knew very little of how to proceed, but trusted that he did. It had worked before.

His body was magnificent. She marveled at the play and flex of his muscles, the hard, hairy surfaces that melded so perfectly with her softness. His legs tangled with hers, his body fit against her curves perfectly, as if she were made just for him and no other.

His hands parted her thighs, and she gasped as she felt his fingers dip beneath the curls to touch her flesh. He teased her, tormented her, and she nipped at his lips, his tongue, as he kissed her, arched her hips, wordlessly demanding more, but he took his time, moved slowly when she wanted speed, touched lightly when she wanted friction and pressure. His erection brushed her hip, and she closed her hand around it, felt it leap, and squeezed gently. His breath turned into grunts of suppressed desire, and the tempo of his fingers increased. He caught her cries in his mouth as the pleasure peaked, poured over her. Surely she would die of this. She cried out again as he plunged his fingers into her, working her, pleasing her until she thought she couldn't stand any more. He positioned himself above her then and drove into her, sending her soaring even higher. She dug her nails into his shoulders as her body rippled around him, drawing him in, lost to everything but the feeling of his body joined to hers, the heat, the friction, the need. Again, and again. Could she ever have enough of him?

By the time he groaned and arched into her one last time, she was spent, sated with pleasure, exhausted. He put his arms around her, holding her against his pounding heart. She felt tears in her eyes.

It had not been anything like she recalled.

It was better.

Chapter 49

It was almost dark when Thomas helped her dress, slowly tying the ribbons that he'd untied so eagerly, doing up the tiny buttons, trying to stem the desire to undo them again, just once more. Neither of them asked what they were both thinking. What now?

He doubted that the long afternoon of making love had helped anything at all.

"You were right—Stephen asked me to marry him," she said as she was donning her cloak.

He felt his heart stop for a moment. He forced his features into a calm mask. "Did you accept?" he asked, keeping his tone as bland as his expression. Would she have come here, to him, if she had? He held his breath, watched as she drew on her gloves.

"I've been avoiding him all day."

He swallowed. "You should accept. He's a good man. Reliable, honorable, noble."

"Are you trying to convince me or yourself?" she asked. She was blinking back tears.

"I can't offer you the same, Julia. Why didn't you say yes?"

"I don't know."

He caught her hands in his. "Yes, you do. Tell me."

She lowered her gaze. "Fear, perhaps, that I'll never be able to be the kind of wife he wants."

He didn't understand. She was smart, brave, clever, passionate. What more could a man want? "You would have made a perfect duchess. You'll make an excellent diplomat's wife," he said, kissing her forehead. She raised her lips to his, kissed him again, and he tasted tears. He let her go reluctantly, stepping back, looking at her. He handed her his handkerchief, and she looked at it in her hand, touched the monogram with her fingertips.

"I still have the last handkerchief you gave me. The first time you rescued me, in Hyde Park."

She was looking up at him, her hazel eyes wide and wet, her mouth still red and soft from his kisses. There was a dangerous emotion written there. He felt a hard jab of anger. Was she hoping he'd rescue her now, make the choice for her, beg her to stay with him, here, in his pauper's quarters? "Is that what this is about? I'm not a hero, Julia. Stephen Ives is the hero. Say yes, marry him, live happily ever after," he said harshly, as if his heart wasn't breaking in his chest. "Forget me."

She stared at him, her lips parting, pain clear in her eyes. He stayed where he was, though he wanted to pull her into his arms. *Stay with me* hovered on his lips, but he clamped them shut. She swelled with dignity and hurt pride, drawing herself up, straightening her spine. She flicked her hood over her head like a nun's cowl.

"Good-bye, Mr. Merritt." She left without a backward glance.

He sat in the dark by the window and watched her walk away. The room smelled of sex and violets. The smell of her body clung to his hands, his hair. "Tom," he whispered to the empty air. "My name is Tom."

Chapter 50

❧

The Prince de Ligne set his mouth in a pout as Katerina swept in. "You are looking very plain this afternoon, Princess. Hardly any jewels at all."

She kissed his wrinkled cheek and sent Thomas a smoldering look. "You shall have to make do with some hot soup, old roué. It has become far too dangerous to wear jewels of any value. I am in the process of having paste copies made of some of my favorite pieces. Kostov insists. There have been many thefts—in the park, in dark corners at even the best parties." She sent Thomas a baleful glance. "Where is your little English friend and her pistol now?"

Accepting Stephen Ives's proposal of marriage, Thomas thought, his stomach tight.

De Ligne smiled. "She was here just this morning—"

He broke into a coughing fit, and Katerina patted him on the back and held a handkerchief to his lips, looking worried.

"Tell me, is Kostov's directive about your jewels because he is worried about them or about you?" the prince asked Katerina when he'd recovered.

She sent him a sad smile. "He loves me in his way.

He said I could have one of his soldiers to guard me if I wished. I refused, of course. He would have chosen his biggest, strongest man, and there is no room for such a one here in your little birdcage."

"Good, because I would not share you, and neither would the viscount," de Ligne replied, winking at Thomas. Katerina snapped her fingers and her maid brought a tray forward, laden with soup, bread, and watered wine. The prince made a face, but the princess sat on the edge of the bed and took charge of the spoon herself.

"You must eat," she insisted, and he took a little to please her.

"So tell me, my dear, which lady was robbed of her jewels?" the prince asked.

She frowned. "One of the Tsar's bedmates. They say she was on her way home, near dawn, and she was way-laid in the park. And an Italian baroness too—she lost a necklace that had been in her family for years. Thieves are everywhere, bold as you please." She cast a glance at Thomas. "Perhaps your English miss should give shooting lessons to ladies in the park."

De Ligne chuckled. "A fine idea. Do you think it would become a fashion? Bands of elegant ladies, dressed to the nines and armed to the teeth, roaming the parks?"

Thomas folded his arms over his chest. Erich, again, no doubt, playing Robin Hood. The damned fool was going to kill someone before long.

He still owed the man a debt.

"I think I have a better idea on how to stop the thieves," he said. "How would you like to help?"

Katerina grinned. "If I can wear my jewels again, I will do anything."

Chapter 51

"**T**homas Merritt has arrived to see you, Major Lord Ives." Stephen glanced at the clock. It was nearly nine, and Merritt was right on time, obviously eager to receive his reward. Upstairs, Castlereagh and Lady Castlereagh were dressing for a ball. Stewart had arranged it all. All he himself had to do was hand over the Order of the Garter and wait for the alarm, and Stewart would do the rest. Tom Merritt would be dragged away in chains, and neither he nor Julia would ever have to see him again. Once out of sight, Julia would forget him quickly enough, wouldn't she?

"Merritt," he said, greeting the thief coolly as he was shown into the library.

"Ives," he replied, equally cool. "I trust everything went well after the other night?" Merritt had the audacity to ask.

"Your job is done, and if you are referring to Julia, she is perfectly well."

Stephen crossed to the liquor cabinet in the corner, unlocked it, and drew out a bundle wrapped in a handkerchief. He flicked it open, revealing Castlereagh's Order of the Garter star. It twinkled on the white cloth.

"I believe this is what you came for." He rewrapped it and held it out, glancing at the clock. Any moment now all hell would break loose.

Merritt didn't reach for it. In fact, he looked amused. "So we have something in common after all, it seems, Ives."

Stephen felt anger rise. "What do you mean? I have nothing in common with you!"

Thomas tilted his head. "Would you have me believe that his lordship gave this to you, with his blessing?" he asked sarcastically. "Charles Stewart's monogram is on the handkerchief."

Stephen felt his skin heat. "Just take it," he snapped, "and then I never want to set eyes on you again."

But Merritt sat down instead, made himself comfortable. "I have a different proposition to make."

Stephen glared at him. "I'm not interested." He glanced at the door. Any moment . . .

"You might be. It's sure to impress Castlereagh, and a lot of other important people. It would ensure you are commended in official reports, noticed in London. It could very well lead to promotion. You'd be a hero."

"No," he said, then considered. "Yes. What's this about?" His heart was pounding. Any moment . . .

"Catching a real thief. Have you heard the tales of the man they call Robin Hood? It might interest you to know that he was the one in the park, the day Julia shot his accomplice."

Stephen shrugged. "Everyone wants to catch him, but no one knows where he is."

"I do," Thomas said. "And I can help you catch him—with the Garter star as bait."

Stephen glanced at the door again, and closed his hand over the star. He had a choice to make—trust Charles

Stewart or Thomas Merritt. Was it worth the risk? Such an arrest would indeed earn him recognition, more than he'd get for capturing Merritt. Stewart would take credit for that. It would impress Julia too.

A shrill scream echoed through the marble halls of the palace.

Merritt looked up, his brows rising.

Stephen gabbed his arm. "Come out, you've got to get out of here now. I'll stall them. They're expecting you'll be in the sitting room upstairs, so you can still make it out—"

"You set a trap for me?" Merritt asked calmly.

Stephen felt his skin flush. "Look, you can call me out next time we meet. Go, I'll come to your lodgings tomorrow and we'll discuss this then."

Merritt hesitated. "You'll need something to convince them I escaped, won't you?" he asked, then slammed his fist into Stephen's jaw. Stephen staggered backward, seeing stars. He hoped he wouldn't look as bad as Charles Stewart did, but he supposed he deserved it.

He stayed where he was on the floor and watched as Merritt climbed through the window. Had he made the right choice? He was a man of honor, not dark plots. He wanted to be rid of Merritt as much as Stewart did, but not by treachery, betrayal. He would never be able to look at himself in the mirror again. He put a hand to his aching jaw and winced.

Thomas Merritt was a gentleman after all, and that made him *likable*. And far more dangerous.

Upstairs, Julia handed Jamie to Mrs. Hawes when Lady Castlereagh began to scream. "What on earth is happening?" the nurse asked. "Are we about to be murdered in our beds again? Marauders coming through the windows, making ladies scream, putting us all in peril of our very lives. Vienna is not a civilized place, I tell you, and I long for dear old London!"

"I'll see what's happening," Julia said. The hall was filled with people rushing to and fro.

"Lady Castlereagh says she's been robbed, that all her jewels are missing, and so is his lordship's Order of the Garter star," one of the footmen said. "Lord Stewart thinks the thief may still be in the building, miss, so please keep to your rooms until we've caught him."

Julia's heart sank. The Order of the Garter, the jeweled star that Lady Castlereagh wore as a tiara to the most formal balls and parties. The very thing that Thomas Merritt had come to steal. "Oh no," she murmured, and hurried to the window.

She saw his familiar figure striding through the snow, hurrying away from the embassy.

He had failed the first time, but he'd come back again, and this time he had what he wanted. She leaned her forehead on the cold glass, watching long after he'd disappeared from view. This time he'd come for the star, the money, and—it was too shameful to think about. His conditions had been met. She sank into a chair, her stomach aching. It wasn't true. It couldn't be. Bitterness filled her throat.

He hadn't come for her. He'd come to steal.

He was a thief indeed. This time he'd stolen her heart, and she would never ever be able to forget him.

Chapter 52

Thomas wrote a note to Erich and left it at the tavern, telling the King of Thieves that he had the goods he wanted and would exchange them for Donovan that night. Everything was in place. Stephen Ives and General Kostov would be there shortly after he arrived to arrest Erich. It was risky, and it could well get him killed, but he'd take Erich with him.

He took out the star and turned it in his palm. It glittered pompously, throwing sparks around his shabby room like Lady Castlereagh threw commands. He had no doubt Erich planned to wear it himself, pinned to his cloak as a kind of jest when he committed his increasingly daring robberies. Robin Hood's career would end tonight.

There was a substantial reward for the capture of the thief, and he had Stephen Ives's promise that he would get Donovan back to England with enough money to buy a horse farm.

And he, himself? In a few days, when this was over, he was leaving Vienna. He had no idea where he might go next. He didn't care. Without Julia, the future yawned like a bottomless pit. He would have liked to see her one more time, but that would just make it more difficult to let her go.

She'd marry Ives, a good, respectable gentleman with prospects and a fortune. He would make her happy and keep her safe. Thomas knew he couldn't even promise her a place to live. He put the star on his desk and drew on his cloak. It was nearly time to go.

Hearing footsteps pounding up the stairs, he took the pistol out of his pocket, cocked it. Had Ives double-crossed him after all? He felt a bead of sweat run down his back, and he raised the gun, aimed it, as the door burst open.

"Julia!" He lowered the gun as she rushed into the room. "Damn it, I nearly shot you. What the devil are you doing here?"

She was breathless from running, her cheeks red from cold and tears. "I came to get it back. You stole it, didn't you? I saw you leaving the embassy!"

He tucked the pistol into his coat. "Don't be a fool. Go home."

But her eyes fell on the star on the desk. He read the horror on her face, the disappointment. She thought the worst of him, but what had she expected? It was better this way. He hoped Ives appreciated this, because she'd run to Ives now, disillusioned by him at last. He turned away, picked up the star, but she closed her hand on his wrist.

"There's still time. They'll look here first, and if they find it, you'll hang," she sobbed. "Give it to me."

He let his expression harden, shook her off. "I had an agreement with Ives. The star is mine."

"What will you do with it?"

"Sell it, what else? I have to live, eat. How do you think I pay for that?"

She looked around at the threadbare lodgings, then at him, noted his cloak. "Where are you going?" she asked, choking on the words.

"I have an appointment," he said.

She shut her eyes. "With the Russian princess?"

He saw the pain in her face. There wasn't time to salve her feelings. "Yes," he said, and pushed past her, taking her arm as he did. Touching her nearly undid him. He wanted to sweep her into his arms, kiss her, promise he would love her forever, hike up her skirts and sate this unquenchable desire right here on the floor. Instead he pushed her away, out the door. "Get out, Julia," he growled, letting his pain make him cruel. "You shouldn't have come. Go back to Ives."

"Give me the star. I'll return it, put it back. No one will know," she said stubbornly.

His breath caught. She would take such a risk for him? If Lady Castlereagh caught *her*, she would be the one to hang. Her ladyship would make certain of it, and Charles Stewart would gladly assist. If she'd come tomorrow, she wouldn't have found the damned star at all. It would be over, the thief caught, the jeweled star back in its rightful place.

"I don't need you to rescue me," he snapped. He left her there in the doorway of his rooms, knowing she was crying. He kept walking, did not look back.

He went to collect Madam Anna's ruby, General Semyon, from Katerina, promising that it would come to no harm. Katerina kissed his cheeks, wished him luck, her green eyes sober.

It was still hours before the rendezvous at the tavern, and he walked through the snow, thinking, not considering where he was going. He wasn't entirely surprised to find himself outside the Minoritenplatz Palace, staring up at Julia's dark window. How many nights had he done this in London?

He forced himself to walk away. Twenty-four hours, and it would all be over. He would be dead or on his way to—somewhere else, someplace as far from Julia as he could get. Either way, he would never see her again, though she would haunt him for the rest of his life.

Chapter 53

She followed him. She should have gone home to bed, to her son, to a sensible, ordinary life, but she could not. He was on a fool's errand, intent on selling the star. Surely Stephen, or worse, Charles Stewart, would find him, and arrest him.

He visited the princess's apartments, and she stood in the snow, numb with fear and jealousy. She couldn't help it. She was in love with him. They had no future, no hope of ever seeing each other again. He was a thief, and she had a son to raise, but she could not let him hang. She would rather think of him with another woman, a score of other women, than dead.

When he left Kostova's luxurious lodgings, she watched him prowl the city, a black specter against the snow. He stopped by the Minoritenplatz Palace, stood staring at the lighted windows. She held her breath. Why? Did he plan to steal something else? They'd be watching, waiting for him this time. Stephen would shoot him on sight.

The bells in the Minoritenkirche chimed eleven, shattering the silence, making her jump. She watched him check his own watch and walk away, striding down the street. She wrapped her cloak more tightly around her icy limbs and followed.

The streets grew narrower and darker, more dangerous, and Julia touched the pistol in her pocket nervously. Dogs barked, splitting the frigid air with noise as he passed, and she shied away from the growling shadows. People too lurked in the dark, watching. She held her breath.

Was this his life, a life lived in the dark? She had no doubt he was going to sell the star now, tonight. She had to stop him. She hurried to keep up with his long strides, slipping through the shadows, staying out of sight, her heart pounding against her ribs, her hand cramping on the pistol.

He stopped at the door of a tavern. A burly man stepped out of the shadows by the door and nodded to Thomas, let him in. The guard cast a suspicious glance along the street and shut the door. What now? She drew a breath and stepped out of the shadows.

The tavern was well guarded, Thomas noted as he approached, as if the thief king were expecting trouble. His skin prickled.

The gatekeeper jerked his head as he approached the door. "He's waiting inside."

Thomas's stomach knotted. Surely the guard would shout an alarm when Ives arrived, give the game away before the deal could be completed, the arrest made. Erich would have time to shoot Donovan—and him too—and slip away with the jewels in hand. He'd have to shoot first, take the thief down quickly. He had promised a tearful Madam Anna that the general would return to her safely, be home from his adventures by morning. If something happened, even Katerina would never be able to replace the priceless gem.

It was nearly as dark inside as it was on the street. A low red fire burned in the grate like the mouth of hell, illuminating a dozen dirty faces that turned to regard him suspiciously.

"Erich?" He didn't bother to waste words on greetings.

A hard-faced barmaid pointed to a closed door behind the bar. A rim of light shone out under the crooked panels, across the unswept floor, leaving long jagged shadows.

Thomas strode toward the door, giving the impression of far more confidence than he felt. He didn't bother to knock. The thief king would be expecting him. A distant church bell chimed midnight. He was right on time.

The back room was as brilliantly lit as the tavern was dark, and Thomas squinted at the light. Lanterns hung from the scarred wooden beams of the low ceiling, and candles hugged the walls like sentries. Two men flanked the doorway.

Erich didn't bother to get up. His long thin knife was stuck in the boards of the table, and it quivered as Thomas approached. "Herr Merritt. I expected you yesterday."

"It took a little longer to get the tiara. Where's Donovan?"

"Close by. Did you bring the jewels with you?"

"When I see Donovan."

Erich jerked his head, and the two thugs grabbed Thomas and pinned him to the wall. As one held a knife to his throat, the other rifled through his pockets, took the pistol and the jewels. He laid the gems on the table in front of Erich and tucked the gun into his own belt.

The ruby's sparkle caught in the thief king's eyes as he picked up the jewel and examined it. "Very good—and the real thing, not paste or imitations. I'm impressed." He smiled, his teeth yellow in the lantern light. "Too many ladies are wearing paste jewels lately. Let him go."

He was released at once, and the guards slid back to their places. Thomas straightened his cravat and sat down in the room's only other chair, opposite Erich's seat at the table. "Your fault, I'm afraid. Thieves make people nervous, especially women."

Erich looked pleased rather than worried. "You see— this is why you are so good at this. You understand these matters. I see rich bastards flaunting the spoils of war that belong to the men who did the fighting and dying. You see better, subtler ways to take what rightfully belongs to us. You really should reconsider my offer and join us. You could name your price—within reason, of course— especially if you continue to bring me things like these." He held up the star, and the diamonds reflected a thousand pinpoints of colored light around the room. Erich laughed with guttural delight. "Magnificent!"

"What will you do with it?" Thomas asked, keeping his tone conversational as the thief continued to play with the star. Points of light freckled his yellow skin.

"I have a new uniform. A British colonel's dress tunic. I shall add the star to the breast—just here." He pointed to his heart. "Then I'll start attending the best parties myself, and enjoying the good life. What do you say to that? We could go together, charm the ladies, drink the champagne, reap the rewards . . ."

Frighten, steal, kill . . . Thomas kept his face from twisting with disgust. "I'm leaving town, I'm afraid. With Donovan."

Erich shrugged. "A pity. Then let's have a drink together to celebrate." He held up two fingers for two glasses, and one of the thugs moved toward the door.

"Let's ask Donovan to join the party, shall we?"

Thomas said. "We made a deal. Are you going back on your word?"

Erich grunted and looked at the other guard. "Bring him downstairs."

They were alone. Thomas felt his fingers twitch, and he looked at the knife stuck in the table. He could grab it, have Erich by the throat in a matter of seconds now that the guards were gone, but the thief's eyes were on him, daring him, waiting for him to do it.

Thomas sat back to wait instead, crossing his legs at the ankles as if he had all the time in the world. Where the hell was Ives? He braced himself. Any moment the door would burst open and—

The door *did* burst open, and both he and Erich leaped to their feet in surprise. But it wasn't Stephen Ives or Kostov. Thomas's limbs turned to water.

It was Julia.

As Julia followed Thomas toward the door of the tavern, she heard soft footfalls around her and realized that the shadows were filling up. A dozen men or more were watching the tavern.

"One man at the door, Captain," she heard someone whisper in English. "More inside. When—"

"Quiet!" the answer came. "Wait for the signal."

Julia's eyes burned into the darkness, trying to see. Soldiers. Her heart began to hammer again. It was a trap. Any moment they would rush toward the inn, swords drawn, pistols at the ready, and arrest Thomas Merritt. On whose orders?

Stephen had promised that no harm would come to Thomas, that he would be exonerated of his crimes, but Charles Stewart had made no such bargain. It gave her courage, and she slipped out of the shadows and moved toward the inn.

"Who's that?" a voice asked.

"Pfennig for a good time?" she asked, blushing.

"Go ply your trade elsewhere, whore."

She forced herself to laugh, though fear made her legs shake as she strolled up to the door of the inn, feeling the eyes of the watchers burning into her back. Would they hesitate, think twice if there was a woman in the tavern? Not likely. She clutched the pistol in her pocket.

A burly gatekeeper blocked the door. She smiled. "Is this not a public house? It's a cold night. Can I come in for a drink or two?" she purred. He stepped aside and she slipped in.

Julia stopped with a gasp as faces turned on her, squinted with hard suspicion. She forced herself to smile as she looked around. Thomas wasn't here, at least not in this room. She made herself take one step forward, then another, moving toward the bar, focusing on the unfriendly face of the woman behind it.

"What do you want?" the woman asked in German.

"Schnapps," she managed, her voice a thread of sound, doubting they had sherry to calm a lady's nerves, or champagne. The woman raked her with a hard glance and went to get it.

Julia saw a ramshackle staircase leading to a second floor, and a doorway at the back with light shining around the panels like rays of salvation—or damnation, more likely.

The barmaid slammed a dented pewter mug before her. No glass? She nodded her thanks as she lifted the tankard, sipped the schnapps, felt it burn a trail down her throat. Her eyes watered.

Two men emerged from the back room. One came to

the bar. "Schnapps, and some decent glasses," he growled. The other one headed up the stairs, which creaked ominously under his weight.

"Who's the toff?" the barmaid asked the man at the bar as she found three grimy glasses and wiped them on her apron.

"Just a gent with some goods for Erich. Make sure it's the good schnapps, none of the muck you serve the poor bastards out here."

Julia drew a sharp breath. Thomas was in the back room. It must be him, since toffs were rather thin on the ground in this part of town. She set her tankard down. Would they let her simply walk in? She doubted she'd make it three steps before someone stopped her.

She glanced at the front door. In a moment they'd come for him, burst in, knock down the door and drag Thomas to the nearest gallows.

"My earring!" she cried loudly. "I've dropped it, a lovely pearl." No one came to look for it. "And a diamond too," she tried again. "A real diamond! I won't go until I find it!"

There was a rush of movement, and the shadows emptied like rats leaving their nests at the scent of food. They came to look for the treasure. Even the barmaid looked eager, her attention on the crowd moving around the floor at Julia's feet.

Julia didn't hesitate. She crossed to the door and drew the pistol out of her pocket. She put her hand on the latch, felt the greasy iron give under her fingers.

Two men jumped to their feet.

Thomas was there, thank heavens, and she watched his eyes widen at the sight of her.

"Well, well, what have we here?" the other man said, recovering first.

She hadn't thought of what to say. What did highwaymen say? Stand and deliver? She aimed the pistol at his chest.

"Stand!" she said, her voice a croak, but they were already on their feet. The man laughed.

"Friend of yours, Erich?" Thomas said, looking her over as if he'd never seen her before. "I had no idea you'd invited guests. Is she here for the jewels?"

It's a trap, she told him with her eyes, but Thomas looked away, studied his nails.

"Are you, my dear?" Erich asked. "You're a bold one, I'll give you that."

Julia felt her stomach tighten, every nerve on alert as he came out from behind the table. She backed up until she ran into the wall.

"Stay where you are. I've shot men before," she said. He was tall, taller even than Thomas, and twice as wide, and dangerous, though he was smiling. Her hand was sweating on the pistol.

He laughed as if they were meeting at a dinner party and she amused him. "Have you really? So have I. Now just where did you come from, sweeting, and how did you get in here?"

The door opened, and Julia felt a scream gather in her throat. "Run," she said to Thomas, but it came out as another croak. "Run." Erich's smile instantly evaporated and he reached out and grabbed her by the throat. Thomas crashed his weight into the half-open door, knocking the returning guard into the jamb. The tray of glasses and schnapps flew, smashing on the stone floor, and the guard cursed in guttural German.

Erich twisted her arm behind her, wrenched the pistol out of her grip, and jabbed it under her chin. Thomas slammed the door, leaving the unconscious guard outside, and drew a wicked-looking dagger from the table.

"Let her go," he ordered.

She felt the big man's laugh rumble through her. "So she is with you after all. How disappointing."

He pointed the gun at Thomas instead, wrapping a meaty arm around her throat. "I don't like to be double-crossed. I think I'll shoot you and break her neck." He looked at her, craning his head around her shoulder to do so. "She's a beauty. Maybe I'll keep her for a while. Tell me, do you like pretty things, sweeting?" He grabbed the ruby pendant off the table and draped it around her neck. "There now, that's perfect. It will hang right between your lovely—"

She stomped down on his foot. He grunted in pain and the gun went off. She saw the flash light Thomas's eyes, watched him slide, his body hitting the table.

"No!" she screamed, and twisted free, dropping to the floor, trying to reach him, but Erich caught her by the chain that held the ruby and twisted it. It tightened against her throat, cutting off her air. She met Thomas's eyes as black spots appeared in her vision. He threw the knife, and it flew past her face, hit her captor in the leg, mere inches from her eyes. He screamed, and the chain loosened for a second. She drew a ragged breath.

"Run, Tom, get away, it's a trap," she cried before the thief caught her by the hair and dragged her back, screaming obscenities. She jabbed her elbow into the knife still sticking out of his flesh. He staggered then, let her go, and she sagged to her knees again.

Then the door burst open and men poured into the room. Thomas grabbed her, rolled to the floor and covered her with his body as the shooting began.

"No," she panted, struggling against him, fighting him. "Run—they've come for you!"

She looked up into Thomas Merritt's furious eyes. "What the hell are you doing here?" he demanded. "You might have gotten yourself killed! Don't tell me this was Ives's idea."

She pounded on his chest. "Listen to me! It's a trap—they'll hang you. They know you took the star. You've got to get out!"

He held her easily, his eyes warming. "You little fool. I don't know whether to kiss you or thrash you. This isn't what you think, Julia."

"Merritt!" She heard Stephen's voice. "Kostov's men have Erich." He looked down over Thomas's shoulder, his eyes widening with shock. "Julia? What the devil are you doing here? Are you all right?"

"She's fine," Thomas growled, getting up at last, then hauling her to her feet. He picked up her pistol and handed it to Stephen.

"We had a deal, Merritt!" the thief yelled, his arms pinioned behind him by a pair of English soldiers. "You cheated, bringing that hellcat here!"

Thomas regarded him. "If not her, some other lady would have eventually found you, done worse, no doubt. But she didn't come for you. She came for me."

Julia stood in front of Thomas and faced Stephen. "I won't let you arrest him. You promised he would not face charges if he assisted us. You cannot do this!"

Stephen took her arm, sat her in a chair. "What on earth are you talking about? How did you get here?" he asked. He grasped her chin, turned her face to the light. "Is that blood on your cheek?" She pulled away. It was Erich's blood, not hers, and it didn't matter.

"You're not here to arrest Thomas?" she asked, breathless.

He frowned. "Of course not. Merritt led us here to arrest Robin Hood and his men. I gave him the star to use as bait, which reminds me . . ." He picked up the star from the table and put it into his pocket. "It will be returned to the safe in Lord Castlereagh's office before morning."

"Better drop it behind the sofa, or under the desk," Thomas suggested. "Make it look like an accident rather than a miracle."

Stephen grinned at him. "An excellent idea." Julia gaped. When had they become so chummy?

A Russian officer came forward and bowed to Julia. "As charming as the pendant looks," he said, "I must relieve you of it, madam." He looked from Stephen to Thomas. "One of you gentlemen owes her a jewel to equal this, I believe."

She felt Stephen's hand on her shoulder, possessive. "Allow me to present my fiancée. Lady Julia Leighton, Your Highness. Julia, this is Prince Kostov, advisor to the Tsar, and one of his finest generals."

And Katerina's husband. Julia met Thomas's eyes. She read a touch of sadness, but it was masked so quickly she might have been mistaken.

"Then congratulations are in order," Thomas said, his eyes on Stephen's hand on her shoulder. She wanted to throw it off, run to him, but the look in his eyes stopped her. His gaze was cold as ice. Instead she shrank into Stephen's reassuring grip.

There was no time to explain. A ragged man appeared in the doorway, on crutches, his eyes hollow. "God in Heaven, I thought you'd never come for me," he said to Thomas.

"Good evening, Patrick. I see you've survived your ordeal."

He ran his eyes over Thomas's clothing. "Your cravat's tied wrong, and you need a proper shave."

Kostov produced a flask, raised it to Thomas and

grinned. "The evening has been a great success, thanks to you, Mr. Merritt. It was a brilliant plan. Did you know there is a hefty reward for the capture of these men? You'll be a rich man." He took a drink and passed the flask to Thomas.

Thomas took a sip, passed the flask back, but the Russian waved it away. "Keep it. It's silver, and the diamond is from one of Catherine the Great's dresses. It's worth a fortune. It was a gift from the Tsar, but he will give me another when he hears this tale. He admires bravery and wit. In fact, come and see me tomorrow, we'll have a feast in your honor. I'm sure the Tsar will want to meet you in person."

Before he could reply to the invitation, Patrick Donovan moaned. Julia looked up to find him staring at her in horror, pointing. "That's the woman who shot me!" he said, trying to back away. "It was her, in the park!" Thomas caught him as he stumbled.

"Shut up, Donovan. A good valet—a *smart* valet—knows his place, and when to keep his mouth shut. Let's go home." He bowed to Kostov and nodded at Stephen, then turned to her. His expression was polite, nothing more. "Farewell, Miss Leighton. I wish you every happiness."

Her heart lurched, but Stephen's hand tightened again, holding her in place. She could do nothing but watch as Thomas left the room without a backward glance. Her heart snapped inside her chest.

She would never see him again.

She was dreadfully tired as Stephen helped her into the coach and they set off for home. "I hope you don't mind that I introduced you as my fiancée," he said brightly. "I think of you that way—at least until I can call you my wife. My heart nearly stopped when I saw you there tonight, in that den of thieves. You came to get the star back, didn't you, to keep Merritt from selling it?"

She was too weary to correct him. "I saw him leaving the embassy when it was taken."

He gathered her in his arms. "You thought he'd led me into a trap, and you came to save me, didn't you? You do love me. So you will put me out of my agony and say you will marry me after all? I know you had feelings for him once. I hope they are resolved. He is not the right man for you. He is an adventurer, a wastrel. Marry me, sweetheart. I'll spend my life making you happy."

She shut her eyes. No, Thomas Merritt was not the right man for her. She could pine for him forever, her lost love, a man she barely knew and yet knew more intimately and completely than anyone else. She might be useful to Stephen, but could she ever make him happy? Would he remember the scandal, and Thomas, every time he looked at Jamie, or wonder if she might stray again? She couldn't bear it if suspicion destroyed the love he had for her, and the regard she had for him. He deserved a woman as honorable as he was, who loved him for the truly wonderful man he was. Still, it was tempting, She might never get another such offer, a chance to live an honorable life again.

"We have Castlereagh's blessing," Stephen said. "I'm to be posted to Spain when he returns to England, so we'll need to marry very soon. You and Dorothea will go to my estate in Somerset for the time being. It's not Temberlay Castle, but—"

Temberlay. Her past would always haunt her. She shut her eyes. "I'm so tired. Can we talk about it tomorrow? I'll give you my answer then. Dorothea will be wondering where I've been."

He kissed the top of her head. "Of course, darling. I hadn't thought of all you'd been through. Just promise me that you will never, ever do anything like that again."

The time for boldness and adventure was over. It was time to choose a future. "I promise," she murmured.

Chapter 54

❧

"**S**o she is to marry the dull English diplomat," Katerina said the next day, when Thomas visited to ensure that General Semyon had indeed returned to Madam Anna. The old lady was delighted that her handsome hero had enjoyed such a grand adventure, as if the ruby itself had saved the day.

"It's an excellent match, Katerina. She will be safe and—"

"Bored to tears," Katerina interjected. "A woman brave enough to shoot a man, bold enough to risk her own life to save yours under such circumstances, deserves better than a junior diplomat."

He sipped his champagne. "He'll rise. He's a smart man."

She slid her green eyes over him. "You sound as if you are trying to convince me, or yourself, perhaps. Why did you not sweep her up in your arms, take her away?"

"How very Russian that would have been!" he quipped, but her raised brows demanded an answer. "Where could I take her? I have nothing to offer her."

She sniffed. "You have love, and passion. You are the only one of my lovers that my husband actually admires, even though we never actually got around to *being* lovers."

"You're in love with your husband, Princess. You don't really want me. You came to Vienna for him, to make him jealous."

She sent him a sad smile. "You are the first to understand that. Not even Anna, or my old roué knows."

"Tell him," Thomas said. "Kostov, I mean."

"What, and miss out on the jewelry he gives me every time he is away from me, just to keep me happy?" She shrugged. "Perhaps I will, when this dreadful conference is over."

She regarded Thomas thoughtfully. "You have distracted me on purpose, I think, but I will not be put off. What will you do about Lady Julia? Even de Ligne noticed. He will say he brought you together, dine out upon the tales of your romance once he knows how it ends. He'll get more invitations for a story that ends happily."

"It does end happily, just not with me," he said, feeling the sadness of that. He could not stay in Vienna, knowing she was here too, and about to marry another man. He'd envied David Temberlay, but try as he might, he could not dislike Stephen Ives. He'd make a perfect husband, caring, considerate, and honorable. And if their life together was a trifle dull, at least it would be safe. It was hard to imagine Julia contentedly embroidering samplers, or spending her days reading improving books. She was more than that, vital, brilliant, glowing. He clenched his fist on the stem of the champagne glass and vowed silently he'd kill Stephen Ives if he ever put out that glow.

"Tell her how you feel. Let her choose," Katerina said again.

"I'm leaving Vienna as soon as Donovan's ready to travel. That should be only a few days."

"Then I shall go and shoot his other leg!"

Thomas laughed. "I gave him part of the reward money to buy a horse farm in Ireland. He'll need his legs."

"A valet with a horse farm?" she scoffed. "It would never happen in Russia! At least the beasts will be well groomed, I suppose. Do you intend to go with him to Ireland?"

"He says he wants to get married, raise a family. There's no place for me there." He set his glass down. "I must go, sweetheart."

She rose and put her arms around him, kissing him on both cheeks. "You are a fool. I shall pray for you to change your mind before it's too late."

He smiled. "I'm not the marrying kind."

Katerina sniffed. "Every man is the marrying kind if it's the right woman," she said.

Chapter 55

Every afternoon at precisely three-twenty Prince de Talleyrand left the French Embassy for his daily ride in the park. At exactly 3:28 his coach would turn down the tree-lined lane, and Talleyrand's manservant would open the windows of the vehicle so His Highness could take the air. If the weather was sunny and dry, the prince would descend from his coach and walk a short way. At 4:35 he would return to the coach and go back to Kaunitz Palace, and work.

Julia made sure she was on the path, waiting when the coach turned. The prince knocked on the roof. "Stop here." She waited until the groom had opened the door and let down the steps for the ambassador to descend. "Lady Julia, what a pleasure to see you here today. Shall we walk for a while? It is a pleasant day for winter, is it not?"

She held out the letter. "I came to return your gift, Your Highness. I cannot accept it."

His brows rose. "You have no desire to go to Louisiana? I understand it is quite lovely, and the plantation I am giving you has over ten thousand acres of prime land. Of course, I've never been there. I negotiated the agreement between the American government and Napoleon, you see, for the sale of the Louisiana Territories. There was a very generous reward for my assistance, including land which I will never see, because I am an old man, and not likely to find a reason to ever leave France again when this conference is over. I did not give it frivolously. I meant for you to have it."

Julia looked at the people strolling along the path, enjoying the rarity of a mild day. "Why, Your Highness? Your plan did not work. The documents were retrieved."

He smiled like a cat. "Oh, that. Yes indeed. I'm sorry, my dear Julia, but it was a ruse. I wished to make Castlereagh nervous, see how he would react if I pressed him just a little. Now I know. Our meeting went well. He refused to give in to blackmail by anyone, said that he had only the best interests of Europe at heart, and wanted a lasting peace."

"I don't understand," she said, wondering if he was lying. His face gave nothing away. "Doesn't everyone want peace?"

He chuckled. "You are not the politician I thought you were, or perhaps it is just that you are young and hold high ideals. No, there are many here who can be bought. I can usually tell who, and figure out what they want, but not Castlereagh. He is a closed book. I think even his own government does not know him well. That's why he's gone, and Wellington will be arriving soon. I had to put Castlereagh to the test, see what he would do, and I was curious, I admit, to see what you would do. You have been a breath of fresh air at this dreadful affair." He paused, and beckoned his coach. "And so, you will humor an old man and take the deed. I hear from Diana that you are to be married, to the young officer you were with in the park that day. Perhaps you will—"

My, how quickly news traveled! She felt her cheeks heat.

"May I say I think you have chosen badly?" he said frankly. "I thought you would choose Viscount Merritton. You appeared to be so very much in love at my salon that night."

"We are merely—acquaintances. He is leaving Vienna, I understand," she said.

"And you have chosen not to go with him. How sad."

"You don't know him!" she said sharply.

He smiled blandly. "I know everyone. He's a rascal, an adventurer, a man with a tarnished reputation, and yet, he is not. He has a deep sense of honor—the right kind of honor—the kind that does not scruple at doing something wrong for the right reasons. Does that describe him?"

She set her jaw. "Yes, perfectly."

The coach rolled to a stop beside them. He looked at his watch and smiled, and bent over her hand to kiss it. "Good-bye, Lady Julia. I hope you will make the right choice before it is too late. It is a peace conference, and perhaps you must make peace with your desires, choose your path carefully. Be bold, my dear, it is my favorite part of your remarkable nature." He folded her hand over the letter. "Keep the deed. If you marry the major, perhaps someday your son will want it. Or—well, who knows what the future holds?"

She watched as he got into the coach and drove away. Who was Talleyrand to know what was right for her? She'd make Stephen an excellent wife. She had been raised for this kind of life. She spoke four languages, knew etiquette and protocol, and she could plan a dinner for four hundred, if she had to. Boldness had no place in that kind of life.

Surely, given time, she could grow to love Stephen, make him trust her, as much as she loved—

No. She refused to even *think* his name again, ever. He was part of the past, and she had a future to plan.

Chapter 56

Julia heard the lullaby as she reached the door of the nursery. "Dorothea?" She pushed open the door to find her friend holding Jamie, humming the familiar lullaby to the baby as she waltzed around the room. Dorothea looked up and smiled at her. Jamie was fast asleep in her arms.

"Hello. I sent Mrs. Hawes downstairs for a cup of tea. I hope you don't mind."

Julia swallowed. "Was he crying?"

"Oh, no, he's a perfect angel," Dorothea said. "All smiles."

"I didn't think you . . ." Julia paused, not knowing what to say.

Dorothea's smile faded. "I know. I couldn't bear to even look at him. I didn't think I would ever be able to face seeing another child, Julia. I wasn't sure, you see, and I had to be sure." She brushed Jamie's sleeping face with a kiss. "I'm with child."

Julia's jaw dropped. "Doe . . ."

She put Jamie gently into his cot. "I hope you aren't shocked. When Peter found out, he proposed at once, but I had to know it was right." She sighed. "I love him. It's been a secret all these weeks because Stephen doesn't seem to like him. I thought perhaps if he married you . . . I've said yes, Julia."

Julia hugged her. "How wonderful!"

"It is, isn't it? I was so afraid when I realized I was pregnant. My little boy was just Jamie's age when he died. He was so perfect, but so fragile. I couldn't bear for it to happen again, to lose another child. I started to worry about Jamie. I came to look at him a dozen times a day. Mrs. Hawes watched me like a hawk. But he's strong. I know that he'll grow up healthy, and so will this child." She patted her flat stomach. "Do you think Stephen will mind?"

Julia smiled. "Of course he won't. He'll be pleased to see you so happy."

"I never thought I'd love anyone again the way I loved Matthew. When Mr. Merritt brought my watch back, and I looked into Matthew's eyes, I realized that I would always love him, but I needed Peter, someone alive to love me back."

"Peter's a wonderful man. I'm sure you'll both be very happy."

"You'll make my brother happy too. Does Mr. Merritt mind very much?"

"What?" Julia looked up.

"Jamie is the very image of Thomas Merritt, Julia, but Stephen will be Jamie's father. When I saw the two of you together, I thought that perhaps you might still—"

"Oh, no, Dorothea. There is nothing between us. Thomas doesn't even know about Jamie. He isn't the kind of man who would want—" She felt the sting of tears behind her eyes.

Dorothea made a sound of disbelief. "What man wouldn't want to know? Do you love him? You don't have to answer, of course. It's just that every time you look at Jamie, you will see his father. I know you love Stephen, but I suspect it's different with Mr. Merritt. You love Stephen because he's a good man. It's right to love him. Yet sometimes, passion just happens, and that's right too. I found that out with Peter. I had not known there could be such passion, though I loved Matthew too, very much. Is that how you feel?"

Julia shook her head. "I hold Stephen in very highest regard. By now, Thomas Merritt has probably left town. I won't be seeing him again."

"Not ever?" Dorothea asked, her face clouding.

"Never," Julia said firmly. "Now, the betrothal party is just three days off and we should make plans."

"Of course. I think I shall wear yellow . . ."

"I thought you detested yellow," Julia said, but Dorothea laughed.

"Not at all. It's Peter's favorite color in the world."

Chapter 57

Donovan was driving him crazy, and he'd only been back for a week. He talked of nothing but prime Irish horses and fine, fat Irish lasses—or was it the other way around? And why not? He was going home, had something to look forward to. Thomas envied him.

Come morning, he would help his limping valet into a hired coach and make sure he got safely to Antwerp. There, he would put him on a boat for England, alone. There was a letter of credit waiting for him at a reputable London bank, and Patrick Donovan wouldn't need him any longer—nor would he ever need to steal again, even if he was so inclined after his misadventure in Vienna.

They'd hanged Erich and ten of his not-so-merry men the day before, and everyone had breathed a sigh of relief, thinking Vienna would be a much safer place without him. But there were other desperate men, former soldiers like Erich who would do anything to survive.

"I think I'll buy a roan stallion, just for riding to the village to court the lasses," Donovan prattled on. "Or do you think a black stallion would be more impressive?"

"I think," Thomas said, "I will go for a walk." He left a bottle of schnapps by his valet's elbow, told him to rest his wounded leg, and hoped he'd be asleep by the time he got back.

It was a fine afternoon, crisp and sunny. Vienna would be beautiful in the spring, but he'd be gone by then. He had no plans past Belgium and bidding Donovan farewell. Egypt, perhaps, or even India. Or America. He could buy land, farm. But he discarded the idea. He didn't want to do it alone. He had the money to travel for a few years.

"Mr. Merritt!"

Thomas looked up to see Dorothea Hallam coming toward him, following a servant pushing a pram.

He tipped his hat. "Good afternoon, my lady. What a fine afternoon for a walk. Is this the child whose portrait I saw in your watch?"

She looked at him oddly. "No, Mr. Merritt, this is Julia's son. His name is Jamie."

He felt as if the path had subsided under his feet. "Julia's son?" Julia had a child? But David Temberlay had died . . . Stephen then? He frowned.

"Yes. He's nearly nine months old. Big for his age, isn't he?"

"Is he?" The child stared up at him with round gray eyes. To Thomas, he looked just like the child in the portrait, but then, most babies did, didn't they? But he was Julia's child, and Stephen's. Or David's. Envy hit him like a blow to the belly. He looked for signs of her in the child's plump face. There, in the lift of his brows, the delicate cheekbones. He was as beautiful as his mother.

"I've heard you're leaving town," Dorothea said. "Will you have time to visit before you go? We're having a party this evening, and there's the wedding tomorrow morning, of course, in the church across from the embassy. You would be most welcome."

Julia was getting married tomorrow? As soon as that?

He managed to smile. "I think not, my lady. I'm leaving in the morning, actually."

She frowned at that. "And what is your destination?"

"India," he said, trying it out on his tongue, but it sounded wrong. "Belgium first. Perhaps Egypt."

"I see."

Did she? She looked baffled, and he had no idea what else to say. He tipped his hat and walked away.

Julia Leighton had a son.

Chapter 58

Julia Leighton had a son.

Thomas sat in the window of his lodgings finishing the schnapps Donovan hadn't touched, since he was too busy making notes about acreages, horses, breeding stock, brood mares, and crops. Oats, or perhaps barley and potatoes, he'd decided. And fruit trees as well, since horses liked apples. He'd hire three strong stable lads, no, four, and train them himself, well, perhaps with a stable master to help out. It would be the best, most prosperous horse farm in all Ireland . . .

"Are you listening?" Donovan asked.

"The best horse farm in all England," Thomas parroted.

"Ireland!"

What had Dorothea said the boy's name was? Jamie. James, he supposed. A good name. He recalled that there had been a James Leighton, a captain of dragoons. His portrait held pride of place in Carrindale House, and he remembered seeing it the night of Julia's betrothal ball, all those months ago.

It struck him like lightning. "How long have we been gone from England?" he asked Donovan.

"Why, do you miss the place?"

"No. We left in the fall, didn't we?"

"October," Donovan said. "It was raining buckets in Paris."

"And it's February now."

"Are you feeling all right?" Donovan asked.

Thomas counted back to the day he'd first met her, trying to remember when exactly he had made love to her on the settee in her father's library. He'd left London a few weeks later— He felt the shock of the truth pass through him. He counted again.

He crossed to the mirror and stared into it. The child had gray eyes like his, and a dimple in his chin, a Merritt family trait. And dark hair, like Julia's—and his. He stared into his own bloodshot eyes as his stomach dropped into his boots. He swore softly.

He was a father.

It meant that he'd left her pregnant after their brief encounter. He paced the room, ignoring Donovan's questions.

That's why she hadn't married. That's why she was *Miss* Julia Leighton, far from home, unwed. He felt shame burn through his belly, sear away the schnapps until he was entirely sober. He'd not only taken her virginity, he'd left her pregnant and alone. Her family must have disowned her, and David Temberlay had refused to marry her.

"How the hell did she manage?" he muttered. Donovan was silent now, watching him.

Only Stephen Ives had been there to help her, bloody perfect, honorable, gracious Stephen Ives. No wonder she wanted to marry him.

He looked in the mirror again. Could he be sure? He read the certainty in his own eyes.

"I have to see her," he said. "I have to know."

"See who? Know what? You're scaring me," Donovan said. But Thomas was looking for his evening clothes in the trunk, making a mess of it. He pulled out his coat and a clean shirt, and began tearing off his old clothes.

"If she loves him, tells me to go, I will, but I have to know, damn it. I have to tell her I love her and I never meant to leave her like that."

Donovan got up, leaning on his crutch, and came to help. "Here now, you're making a rat's nest of everything." He found a waistcoat and helped Thomas into it, and tied his cravat. He held his evening coat and Thomas shrugged into it. "I've never seen you like this," Donovan said. "Not over a woman. Is it the princess? Kostov will shoot you between the eyes if you show up like this. Wait until morning."

"It will be too late then," Thomas said. "She'll be married." He looked at the clock. Nine o'clock. The betrothal ball would be starting soon. Ives would lead her out for the first dance—a waltz, no doubt. He would smile into her eyes and twirl her out onto the terrace under the stars and kiss her.

"The hell he will," Thomas said, and grabbed his cloak.

Chapter 59

Thomas entered the ballroom without waiting to be announced. Julia stood in the crowd, talking with her guests, and he pushed through the crush toward her. She was wearing ice blue tonight, with a simple necklace of pearls. She still took his breath away, just as she had when he'd first seen her from across the room at Carrindale House, and every time he'd set eyes on her since.

Life—and motherhood—had added a luster to her beauty. He felt another stab of guilt. He should have been there. He would have been had he'd known.

The orchestra struck the first notes of a waltz as he reached her. "My dance, I believe," he said firmly, brooking no argument, and she looked up in surprise, her eyes widening, her polite smile fading, but there was little she could do but set her hand in his and let him lead her out.

"What are you doing here?" she whispered, her eyes darting around the room, no doubt to see who was watching them. He hadn't seen Ives, hadn't looked for him. He was here for Julia. He couldn't take his eyes off her. He could smell her perfume, feel the heat of her body so close to his. Love, stronger than mere desire, hit him like a brick.

"Do you remember the last time we waltzed?"

She blushed deeply. "Yes, of course. Why are you doing this?"

He ignored the question. "I believe I said then that you were beautiful."

She swallowed, and he watched the pearl necklace bob in the candlelight. "Thank you."

"And yet you're more beautiful now. Motherhood agrees with you."

She stumbled and he caught her, and lifted her off her feet for a moment, carrying her through the next steps, meeting her startled eyes, inches from his own. He set her on her feet again, but she didn't move.

"You look flushed, my lady," he said now, just as he had then. "Perhaps some air?"

"It's freezing outside!"

"Still, we need to talk before you marry tomorrow, I believe. Perhaps the library?"

"Not the library," Julia said quickly. Was she remembering her father's library, or was Ives there?

She led the way to the conservatory instead, fragrant with roses and damp earth. She stood on the stone path between the pots and boxes, a pale ghost in the dim light.

"Is Jamie my son?" he asked, his throat tight as he waited for her answer. She searched his eyes, perhaps looking for the man inside, someone worthy enough. He didn't smile, or flinch, or look away. Would she see only the thief, the rake, the seducer?

"Yes," she said. "How did you find out?"

"I saw him with Dorothea in the park today. He's beautiful. He looks like you."

She smiled softly, a look of love in her eyes—maternal love. "He has your smile."

"Do you love Stephen Ives?"

She studied her gloves. "Of course. I love him the same way I loved—" She stopped. "I seem to recall you asked me that about David too. Do you always ask this question when you attend a betrothal ball?"

He shut his eyes for a moment, disappointment cold in his breast, anger too. "Then perhaps I should ask if he makes you feel the way I do? Do you see stars when *he* kisses you?"

He pulled her into his arms and kissed her. He felt her melt against him, fit herself to him, kiss him back. She tasted of champagne, and something infinitely sweeter, that he knew now was the indefinable essence of Julia herself.

He put his hand on her cheek, felt tears, and broke the kiss to look down at her. "Tell me you love him, and I'll go, Julia. It will be the hardest thing I've ever done, but I will."

"I love him the way I loved David, and my brother. I love him for his goodness, his kindness, his honor."

She loved Ives. "He'll make a good husband, a good—" He choked on the word father. He wanted to be the one to hold his son, to give him brothers and sisters, to wake up next to Julia every morning for the rest of his life.

She shook her head. "I thought I might, that I could grow to love him the way I love you, but I don't think that's possible. I could never love anyone else like that. You're part of my soul, and it would not be fair, or right, to give Stephen only part of me."

He heard the tears in her voice. "So what do we do now?" he asked her. "I am the cause of breaking yet another of your betrothals, and I strongly suspect that this fiancé will not let you go so easily."

"I am not betrothed to Stephen, Tom. I told him I couldn't marry him. I have honor too, and I could never be so cruel, not to myself or to him. He deserves better."

He felt his knees weaken. "You aren't getting married in the morning?"

"No."

"Then why the betrothal ball?"

She smiled gently. "Dorothea is marrying Peter Bowen tomorrow morning. The new ambassador arrives within the week, and they did not want it to interfere with official events to welcome him."

"Dorothea?" he asked like a ninny, his tongue suddenly knotted around his tonsils.

She looked up at him, her hands at her waist. "Will you marry me, Thomas Merritt? I have some lands, it seems, in Louisiana, and I will do my best to be a good wife—"

He set his finger against her lips and smiled at her. "I'm supposed to ask you, sweetheart." He took a breath and dropped to one knee, taking her hand in his. "Julia Leighton, will you do me the honor of being my wife?"

It sounded right. No, it sounded perfect.

"Yes," she sighed. "Oh, yes."

"Am I interrupting?" Stephen Ives stood in the doorway. "I see you arrived after all, Merritt, just as Doe predicted. I had hoped you wouldn't come. I would have proposed again, you see, and again, until Julia accepted me, but now . . ." He shrugged, remained in the shadows.

Julia crossed to him and kissed his cheek. "I wouldn't have said yes. I wouldn't make you happy."

He gazed down at her. "No, I suppose not. I have never seen you as happy as you look right now. Still, forgive me for hoping." He shook his head sadly. "First Doe, now you, Julia. Everyone is getting married, it seems. That's why I came to find you. Will you help me raise a toast to Doe and Peter?"

"Of course," Julia said, and Thomas took her hand. For

a moment Stephen stared at the link between them, his lips pinched.

"What will you do now?" Julia asked Stephen, taking his arm as well.

"There's still that posting in Spain. Or I could stay here, see if Wellington needs me when he arrives. I will leave, if you are staying in town."

"We're going to America," Thomas said, liking the sound of that. It could be the ends of the earth, as long as he was with Julia.

Stephen glanced at him. "America? A new start in a new land. You'll do well there, both of you."

They reached the ballroom, and Stephen let her go and crossed to toast the bride and groom. "I wish you every happiness, and a lifetime of love and joy," he said, raising his glass.

His words were for Dorothea and Peter, but his eyes were on Thomas and Julia.

"Do you think a lifetime will be long enough?" Thomas asked Julia. "We're getting a late start."

She smiled at him with so much love in her eyes his chest ached. To have a woman like Julia, a family—perhaps this was what honor felt like, and pride, and peace. "We shall have to make the most of it. Come and meet your son."

She led him upstairs to the nursery and placed the child in his arms. The baby looked up at him with wide eyes—his eyes—and raised a chubby hand to touch his cheek. Julia put her arms around his waist and smiled at them both.

"Louisiana," she sighed as the child cooed, caught hold of Thomas's finger and squeezed. He drew a breath, felt something open inside him.

"We'll build a home, give him brothers and sisters."

Wherever they went, he would be home, as long as he had Julia. He was whole again in her eyes, his honor restored. "I love you," he said to her, his voice choked with emotion, and she kissed him gently and laid her head on his shoulder.

Thomas Merritt, Julia Merritt, and Master James Merritt.

He liked it. It sounded perfect.

Epilogue

Waterloo, June 1815

Major Lord Stephen Ives tightened his hands on the reins. The stallion was nervous as the guns crackled and the cannon boomed. He was nervous himself, and he looked at the grim faces of the dragoons around him, all of them waiting for the order to charge across the plain to overrun the deadly French guns.

He thought of Julia, as he had every single day since she left Vienna with Thomas Merritt. She was probably in Louisiana by now. Was she happy? He could not wish her otherwise, though the familiar ache of loss filled him.

She and Thomas had stayed for Doe's wedding, and she helped his sister pack for her journey to England. Peter had wanted their child to be born in Kent, at his family home, and Doe was eager to start her new life. He missed her company.

The peace conference had been a failure. It had ended when Napoleon fulfilled Talleyrand's prediction and escaped from Elba. He'd marched on Paris, gathering an army, and declared himself Emperor once again. Wellington had no time for peace talks then.

And so they stood on yet another battlefield, this time in Belgium, churning up peaceful farmlands, leaving them red with blood once more.

Stephen stared ahead at the French bastion. The bugle would sound and they would charge. His feet twitched, eager to set his spurs to the stallion's flanks, to get on with it, to stem the pain, to cover himself in glory before— if—he was fated to die today.

"A forlorn hope, if ever there was one," the captain next to him muttered, his eyes on the muzzles of the French guns, belching fire and death across the very path they would ride.

Stephen heard the signal and drew his sword, raising it over his head. He opened his lungs to let out a battle cry as the stallion lunged forward, leaping into the fray, as eager as he was to see it done.

He felt the wind in his hair, smelled gunpowder and blood, felt the hot June sun on his skin. "Julia," he whispered, and wondered if she'd hear.

*Next month, don't miss these exciting
new love stories only from
Avon Books*

A Kiss of Blood by Pamela Palmer
Quinn Lennox vowed never to return to Vamp City, and
when rugged vampire Arturo Mazza comes for her, Quinn
can't forget the betrayal she suffered at his hands. But with
her brother's fate hanging in the balance, Quinn will have to
risk another journey to the twilight city . . . and another
chance at love with a ruthless vamp.

It Happened One Midnight by Julie Anne Long
There's nothing like a gypsy prophecy to make a man
rethink his priorities. For Jonathan Redmond, that priority
is now avoiding the one thing he can't seem to escape:
matrimony. But on one fateful midnight, he's drawn into the
world of the intoxicating Thomasina de Ballesteros and
suddenly he's rethinking everything—including the
possibility that succumbing to prophecy might just mean
surrendering to love.

Anything But Sweet by Candis Terry
Ex-Marine Reno Wilder is determined to protect the town
of Sweet, Texas, from any and *all* intruders. Especially
intruders like Charlotte Brooks and her TV makeover show.
Reno may be gorgeous and a one-man *unwelcoming*
committee to boot, but Charli isn't taking no for an answer.
When push comes to shove, she's gonna show this gruff
cowboy just how fun a little change can be . . .

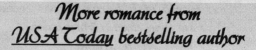

EN THINGS I LOVE ABOUT YOU

978-0-06-149189-4

the elderly Earl of Newbury dies without an heir, his
ested nephew Sebastian inherits everything. Newbury
ides that Annabel Winslow is the answer to his problems.
the thought of marrying the earl makes Annabel's skin
wl, even though the union would save her family from ruin.
haps the earl's machinations will leave him out in the cold
and spur a love match instead?

JUST LIKE HEAVEN

978-0-06-149190-0

rcus Holroyd has promised his best friend, David Smythe-
ith, that he'll look out for David's sister, Honoria. Not an
y task when Honoria sets off for Cambridge determined
marry by the end of the season. When her advances are
spurned can Marcus swoop in and steal her heart?

A NIGHT LIKE THIS

978-0-06-207290-0

niel Smythe-Smith vows to pursue the mysterious young
verness Anne Wynter, even if that means spending his days
h a ten-year-old who thinks she's a unicorn. And after years
dodging unwanted advances, the oh-so-dashing Earl of
Winstead is the first man to truly tempt Anne.

At Avon Books, we know your passion for romance—once you finish one of our novels, you find yourself wanting more.

May we tempt you with . . .

- **Excerpts** from our upcoming releases.

- Entertaining **extras**, including authors' personal photo albums and book lists.

- Behind-the-scenes **scoop** on your favorite characters and series.

- **Sweepstakes** for the chance to win free books, romantic getaways, and other fun prizes.

- Writing **tips** from our authors and editors.

- **Blog** with our authors and find out why they love to write romance.

- **Exclusive content** that's not contained within the pages of our novels.

Join us at
www.avonbooks.com

*G*ive in to your Impulses!

These unforgettable stories only take a second to buy and give you hours of reading pleasure!

Go to *www.AvonImpulse.com* and see what we have to offer.

Available wherever e-books are sold.

IMP 08

JUL 2013